I0634170

Graven Images

This is the first novel from Ray Norris, a British and Australian astrophysicist whose day-job is to research the origin and evolution of galaxies shortly after the Big Bang. He also researches Australian Aboriginal astronomy, and the astronomy of British Bronze-age stone circles and other megalithic monuments. As well as over 250 professional publications, he frequently appears on radio and TV, and performs in a stage show called "The First Astronomers". For relaxation, he walks the moors of Dartmoor and the Australian bush, and writes. But not at the same time. And, no, he's not Owen.

Graven Images

Ray Norris

Published by Emu Dreaming

Graven Images

First published December 2010 by

Emu Dreaming
PO Box 4335
North Rocks
NSW 2151
Australia

ISBN 978-0-9806570-1-2

This version published April 2011

Prologue

On the bonfire sat a papier-maché witch, with black pointed hat and broomstick, leering at the passing traffic, as she waited to be burned at the stake. That evening, she would be surrounded by children laughing at her slow death, waving their sparklers as the oil in her face crackled and spat. Or was her burning in sad remembrance of the thousands of witches hundreds of years ago who met their destiny in this cruel way? Owen saw the flowers laid around her on the funeral pyre, and understood. For those with eyes to see, witchcraft was flourishing in the shires, a simple faith openly celebrated in every village, every town, every festival.

Speeding out towards Huntingdon, Owen watched the grey November fields slip by. More bonfires. Colourful hand-painted banners draped across school entrances. Fireworks tonight outside the Parish Hall. Soup and hot potatoes to warm frozen hands as feet stomped to restore the circulation, eyes gazing upwards through the sulphurous air to a distant starburst spraying coloured incendiaries over the countryside. If only they knew.

By the time he reached the M6, he was questioning his decision. They'd killed Sarah. Luring him into some corner of a Northern field might be a very clean way of disposing of him. A service area beckoned, and he accepted the invitation gratefully.

Passing the shop in the service area, he saw they had a special on Halloween costumes. Plastic witches' hats and broomsticks. And especially for tonight, a plastic witch to burn on top of the bonfire, made in Korea, guaranteed to please, just the thing for the kids.

He queued for his coffee.

5

"Yes sir, what can I get you?"

A latte please, double shot, skimmed milk.

"Certainly sir. Going far today? Having a bit of celebration with the family?"

Going to burn anyone interesting to death tonight? Owen grunted non-committally, and the man nodded as if he understood.

Sipping his coffee, he gazed into the car park, ignoring the tattered posters falling into soggy shreds before their time. Today he might meet Sarah's killers, and the thought was greeted by unfocussed emotion rising within him. Myopically, he studied it like an interested bystander. He could pick out fear, and apprehension. Of course - after all, his months of flirting with this terrorist group were about to be consummated, as he finally penetrated their inner circle. But how? Even if he stood face to face with Sarah's killers, knew for certain who they were, what form would his vengeance take? Once, months ago, it had seemed simple. Find the killers. Report them to the police. Job done. But he needed evidence. And he needed to stay alive. The denouement wouldn't be today, and from now on the danger would increase inexorably.

Was this a stupid, foolish stunt? Who was he trying to impress? Option A: get in the car, turn round, back down the M6, and get on with your life. Option B; get killed, granting another victory to her killers. Option C: meet them, get evidence, report them to the police. And how likely was that? Molecular biologist versus trained killers. No bookie would offer odds on his life.

Even as he left the restaurant, his direction was still uncertain. North or South? The news-stands showed a headline: "Riot in London: Muslim boy killed." He glanced at the paper: Jewish thugs had beaten up a ten-year old Muslim boy out walking his dog. Beaten him to death. And it was Owen's fault, a direct consequence of the fire he'd started in the synagogue. The decision made, he turned onto the Northbound lane of the M6.

Chapter 1
30 May 2005

Nothing was further from Owen's stumbling mind than witchcraft. He felt awful. God knows how much he'd drunk. He vaguely remembered trying to pour another scotch, Sarah stopping him, helping him upstairs to bed. Hold on - that's not right - that was days ago. Another scene slid into focus. Hadn't they gone to Norfolk? Or was that a dream? Everything seemed mixed up. Forcing his eyes open, he saw the room was bathed in a diffuse blue light. He was surrounded by curtains. Not his bedroom, then. He awoke, startled. But still the fog of confusion failed to disperse. Another scene. Chasing Sarah along the beach. Then driving out of the car-park. The four-wheel-drive coming at them. He'd slammed on the brakes. Nothing happened. He'd pumped the brakes furiously. But the car failed to respond, coasting forward, inevitably, into the path of the Range Rover. Oh God...

The curtains rustled and a nurse appeared. "Owen. You're awake. How are you feeling?"

With a strange smile, and amazing blue eyes, she was one of the most beautiful creatures he had ever seen. He tried to answer, but something stuck to his mouth. He raised a hand to brush it away, but his arm didn't respond. He became aware of pipes, bandages, splints. What was wrong with him? He tried to ask, but couldn't find the muscles to move his lips.

Her smile was wonky and unnatural. "Don't worry," she said, "You've had a car accident and you're in hospital. A bit beaten up but nothing too serious."

Good. Nothing too serious.

"Just relax. You'll be OK"

Later, woken by a chisel-sharp pain in his head, he found a bell push in his hand. The nurse drew aside the curtains and stood by his bedside. That weird smile again. "How are you feeling? Can I get you anything?"

He tried to talk, but could only grunt. She placed a straw between his lips, and icy water ran into his mouth, cooling his throat. His voice returned, hoarsely. "My head. It hurts."

"That's alright; you're over the worst of it. I'll increase your analgesic."

He heard a keyboard tapping next to his bed. Seconds later a pleasant coolness ran up his arm, and the pain in his head switched off. He looked at her again. That smile - if only his head weren't so jumbled...

"Sorry. I'm ... confused. Where am I?"

"Norwich General Hospital. You've been asleep for three days, but you're on the mend now. You'll be out of here in a couple of days."

Lucidity dawned, and he remembered that Sarah had been in the car too. "And Sarah - how's Sarah?"

"Don't worry - the doctor will come and talk to you about Sarah later. Rest now."

"But is she OK?"

"She's resting now. Don't worry."

"Can I see her in the morning?"

"We'll see. Go back to sleep now."

Settling back, he dozed off.

He was woken by the sound of cheerful voices and rattling trays. He must be in a ward with other patients. A nurse appeared, briskly efficient, and drew back the curtains.

"Could you manage some breakfast?" she asked.

"Not sure. I've been - I mean - I'm still a bit muddled."

She helped him sit, his body aching and creaking, as though unused for years. A couple of tubes still ran into a bandage on his wrist.

"I'll take those out after breakfast," she said, brightly.

"Can I see my girlfriend Sarah then?"

A shadow of panic flitted across her face, instantly replaced by that weird smile.

"I'll ask the doctor when you've had breakfast." She bustled out before he could ask more questions.

A growing uneasiness gnawed at him.

They told him after breakfast. Sarah had received severe head injuries. After two days of fighting for life, her body had succumbed to the inevitable. They were very sorry. He had screamed, shouted at them, said they were lying, hadn't tried hard enough. Then broke into uncontrollable sobbing, until a nurse gave him an injection and he slept.

The funeral was held in Cambridge three days later. Friends phoned, commiserated, and offered to take him. But Owen couldn't face any of them. Instead, Sarah's friend Kim picked him up from hospital. Kim was safe, neutral, and he'd gratefully accepted her hesitant offer, in her funny Australian accent. Her darkened eyes, long black hair and black clothes seemed appropriately funereal, but he'd never seen her dressed any other way. Typical goth.

He saw the shock on Kim's face as she walked towards him. He'd seen in the mirror that his blue eyes were bloodshot and heavy-lidded, his fresh round face grey and morose, his sandy-brown hair an untidy mop. He was incapable of his usual witty and self-confident banter, and could manage only a few terse grunts, his feelings betrayed by the tears that welled at any mention of Sarah.

As he followed Kim into her waiting car, he felt cocooned in a bubble of misery disconnected from the outside world. Driving through the familiar streets of Cambridge, nothing was familiar. All his points of reference had vanished. Nothing was fixed, nothing was permanent. Everything was changing, evaporating. Other than his grief for Sarah, which filled his entire horizon.

After Kim guided him to the rear of the chapel, he stood motionless, staring at the box sitting woodenly in centre stage, surrounded by flowers. Within it lay his Sarah. Gone.

Pachelbel's Canon, which Sarah particularly detested, played softly in the background. With effort, he tore his focus from Sarah and saw her parents in the front row. Sarah's mother was dabbing her eyes with a lace handkerchief, while relatives rallied round, consoling her. Sarah's father glanced at Owen, and a few heads followed the glance. Some, recognising him, returned awkwardly to their commiserations. Owen attempted a smile and a nod to her parents. None was returned.

He walked to the front aisle and exchanged civilities. Her parents were polite but frosty. The unspoken accusation hung in the air. You think it was my fault, you uncaring, supercilious bastards.

Pachelbel's Canon faded, and the crematorium organ played a nameless church anthem. Her parents shuffled to face the front where a chaplain had appeared, trying to look holy. The front rows were occupied by family, and Owen found a seat four rows back. Of course I'm just the boyfriend. I don't belong here. Sarah and I have lived and loved together for three years, while you bastards didn't have the time of day for her, and I'm just the fucking boyfriend.

Grief welled in his throat as he fought back a wave of desperation and loneliness. The church and the people seemed distant, irrelevant, as if through the wrong end of a pair of binoculars. Sarah's father and brother were reading their tributes. Owen, who hadn't been invited to speak, barely heard them as he stared at the coffin. A hiss in his ears became a roar, a wave of nausea hit him, and he sank to the pew. The chaplain muttered words, inaudible above the rushing in Owen's ears, as the coffin slid out of sight into the flames beyond. Sarah. Gone.

A terrible connection crept into his mind - the flames - their car being burnt by that stupid Wiccan spell, the sacrificial rabbit struggling within, as it met a fiery death. Was Sarah the rabbit? But he didn't believe in that stuff. He refused to accept the connection. And yet...

Drifting in and out of lucidity, he found himself walking along a shore of consciousness. One moment the water rose up to his ankles, the next his bare toes found purchase in the crumbling sand. And as the water rose and fell, he knew he could be washed away at any moment, into that black ghastliness that was just out of sight. As he struggled to keep his balance, he became aware of the church emptying. Kim helped him to his feet and guided him to the chapel door. The fresh air and sunlight felt good as he emerged from his nightmare. And how many more nightmares lay ahead of him?

He surveyed the scene. Nameless relatives swarming around Sarah's parents, trying to think of things to say that hadn't been said a thousand times before. Others laughed and joked as they greeted distant cousins. None of it seemed to have much to do with Sarah. His Sarah. His beautiful intelligent loving Sarah. Gone.

"I can't stay here," he growled to Kim, and they started sidling away. But, betrayed by his height, Owen saw Sarah's father approaching.

"Owen. I need to talk to you. You have Sarah's belongings. You can't keep them, you know."

Jeez. What was eating him? No wonder Sarah had left home. Owen ran his hand through his hair, giving him time to think, stifling the retort.

"I'm sorry, Mr. Ashworth. I'm really not feeling very well."

"I see. Then we'll talk at the wake."

"Umm. Yes. I'll see you there." He had no intention of being there.

Kim drove Owen to his deserted house. "I really appreciate you picking me up from the hospital. And the funeral, and everything... I guess you met Sarah when you started your PhD?"

She hesitated before speaking. "Nah, we go way back. My family moved here from Sydney when I was 15. Everybody at school made fun of my accent, but Sarah just accepted me. We became best mates. But then we kinda drifted apart."

Really? Sarah had never mentioned it. She answered his puzzled glance.

"Her parents didn't like me. Always cranky with me. Didn't approve of our relationship. Said that I was leading Sarah astray."

Relationship? What sort of "relationship"?

"How do you mean, leading her astray?"

11

"We got into trouble. Totally dumb. Went through a red light, with a police car behind. They searched the car, and found... our stuff."

"Stuff? You mean drugs?"

She nodded.

"Marijuana?"

She shook her head. "If only."

"So what happened?"

"Got suspended sentences. Sarah had an almighty bust-up with her parents. Her Dad told her he never wanted to see her again. Worried about his precious reputation. All that crap. Her mother calmed things down a bit, but I don't think Sarah ever forgave her father. She was like "Dad I need your help" and all she got was this total ratbag yelling at her."

Sarah? Drugs? It didn't make sense. Sarah didn't do stuff like that. And why had Sarah never said anything about this? He knew she couldn't stand her father, but she'd never told him why. Too late to ask her now. If only the brakes hadn't failed. If only the Range Rover hadn't been driving so fast. If only they'd never had anything to do with Wicca. If only.

Kim and Owen spent the evening talking, over a bottle of wine, which she sipped while he drank heavily. He was dreading the inquest next week. They'd found alcohol in his blood, fortunately below the legal limit, so no manslaughter charge. But, charged or not, he had seen his guilt reflected in the faces of Sarah's family, and expected his share of blame at the inquest. The real blame, of course, would be on the failed brakes. The police were still examining the car.

He studied Kim's face, gothic pale with dark eyes, matching her black flowing clothes. A pretty face, despite her lip-stud, two rings in her left eyebrow, and a collection of hardware dangling from her multiply pierced ears. Amongst them was a Wiccan pentacle.

"Are you Wiccan?" he exclaimed, startled.

"Used to be. Like..." Her voice trailed off as she saw him shuffle, agitated.

"You know Sarah would probably still be alive if it hadn't been for those stupid bloody Wiccans? Casting their so-called spells on us because we dared to touch their precious stone circles?"

"You think Sarah was killed by a spell?" asked Kim in astonishment.

"No of course not. Nobody with any sense believes in that stuff. But they set fire to our car, and then that lost me my job, and then... You know Sarah was terrified of witches? I should have listened to her."

He paused. Car brakes squealed in the distance. He shook his head, ashamed of his outburst.

"Let's open another bottle," he suggested.

He drained one glass after another, while Kim barely touched hers. She told him how Sarah energised the department with her silly quips and asides, her ability to see the positive side of everything. Owen talked about their life together, how Sarah had changed him, saved him from becoming a total geek. He told Kim of their wild adventures together, and their quiet times, sharing a book, a play, a thought. Sharing inane video clips off the web until they collapsed together in helpless giggles, tears streaming down their cheeks. Plotting their ascent together through the ranks of academia, until they would occupy the two most senior chairs in the University. And the bad times. How Sarah could be so stubborn, so sure of herself. Suddenly angry, he started listing her faults. And then cried like a baby at his betrayal. He went to fetch a third bottle, tripped, and fell. Mercifully, he fell into a drunken stupor, snoring wetly on the floor.

oooOooo

He woke, his mind befuddled, barely coherent. He could hear Sarah making coffee in the kitchen. But something was not right. It wasn't Sarah... The dam burst, and the awful realisation swept over him. Sarah. Dead.

A figure entered from the kitchen. What's her name? Kim. What's she doing here?

Kneeling next to him, she put a hand to his cheek.

"Don't touch me, witch. Why don't you piss off?" She hesitated, and withdrew. He continued yelling abuse at her through the open door, until he broke into sobs.

Kim withdrew to the kitchen, to make a pot of coffee.

A few minutes later he entered the kitchen, dressed in underpants and T-shirt. Kim sat nestling the hot cup in her hands, staring into space. "I'm sorry. I'm terribly sorry," he said. "You didn't deserve that. I'm just so screwed at the moment."

Nodding, her eyes lowered, she moved to pour him a cup. He took it gratefully. She laid her hand on his arm. "No worries, Owen. I understand."

Tenderly, she embraced him, nestling his head under her chin, murmuring soothing words as he grieved, child-like.

"If only I'd realised," he moaned, "Sarah knew. I didn't understand what she was saying. I should've seen it coming."

"Poor Owen. But it was driving too fast..."

"No, not the bloody car. I should have seen Sarah's death coming. Ever since Easter..."

Chapter 2
Easter 2005

The Christian Church determines the date of Easter as the Sunday following the first full Moon after the Spring equinox. This ancient prescription is said to have its roots buried in those misty times when men and women worshipped spirits of nature, the Sun and Moon. This religion in Britain subsequently came to be known as witchcraft. Christian missionaries, realising they'd have no hope of banishing the people's pagan festivals, instead absorbed and built on them. Easter retained its name, its date, its pagan symbols of eggs and rabbits, and its celebration of a time of birth, of re-awakening.

Because the Sun and Moon each have their own cycles, the date of Easter moves from year to year - sometimes as early as March, sometimes late in April. Those who believe in such things (Owen and Sarah most definitely did not) say that these changing cycles also affect the rhythms of life on Earth, blowing winds of change, of fortune and misery.

A month before Sarah's death, the Easter winds loosened the first thread from the carefully woven fabric of their lives.

Her scream soared over the moor stretching stark and treeless around them, rolled over hills, ricocheted off wind-rounded granite tors, and returned as no more than a memory. Owen, startled from his work, jumped up in alarm. He saw Sarah crouched by one of the Bronze-Age stones, her strawberry-blonde hair tied back and held in place by a ballpoint pen forced through the knot. He ran over.

"You alright, love?"

Wordlessly, her eyes still scared and teary, she nodded in a way that said she was not alright, but would cope. He followed her gaze to a carving on the stone: a circle with a crescent either side. Like something from an archaeologist's dream, a clue to the purpose of these enigmatic stone monuments.

"Bloody hell!"

But even as he spoke, he realised that the carving was modern. Sheer bloody vandalism. With one arm around her shoulders, he reached out with the other to touch the carving, fresh white rock showing through thousand-year-old lichens. He turned to her, puzzled. "But why the scream, love? What do you reckon it is?"

"No... it's not that... There was a snake. I bent down to look at the carving." Her voice rose. "Thought there was a coil of rope next to it. Went to touch it. But it suddenly reared up and hissed at me. A viper. It was horrible."

His concern deepened.

"A viper? You sure? But... You OK?"

"I suppose so. It didn't bite me. Just hissed and then slithered away."

Warily, he scanned the long grass surrounding them. The circle of waist-high stones was about 50 metres across, each stone a pace from its neighbours. A snake could be behind any of them. Owen returned his attention to Sarah. "Probably gone now. Vipera berus, I guess. They don't often hiss, though..."

"Owen, please ... Not now..."

Her face was naked. Rarely was she not smiling, her brown eyes radiating a warmth guaranteed to make you feel good about yourself. At other times, her face revealed nothing but a subdued reserve. Despite the warmth she chose to portray to the world, the inner Sarah was an intensely private person, seldom glimpsed even by those closest to her. So he was almost as unnerved by her open fear as by the idea of a deadly snake. Wrapping himself around her soft body, he felt her shaking like a frightened rabbit, as she snuggled into him.

"I'm sorry, my love."

As he stroked the back of her head, he felt her body relax, even as his own body hardened in response. Knight in shining armour comforting damsel in distress.

16

Suddenly embarrassed by her childish display of weakness, she stood, shaking herself, disowning irrelevant primeval fears, lowering the appropriate backdrop behind her eyes. Sarah Ashworth. Ultra-cool archaeologist, setting the world on fire.

She crouched next to the carving again. "Owen, look. This is totally weird. What do you reckon?"

"Pretty cool. But it's not archaeology is it?"

"No. Probably only a few weeks old."

He nodded. "Bugger. Would have been nice if you'd made your first big discovery."

She seemed to have forgotten about her fear of the snake. Or was suppressing it. Whatever. He watched her staring at the carving, trying to figure her out. As he seemed to spend half his life doing. This wonderful, fascinating, mysterious girl. The girl who brought sunshine to a grey day. The girl with whom he planned to share his life. And one day, perhaps, he'd know what made her tick. Still focussed on the carving, she cocked her head to one side as if expecting an answer. "Who'd come all the way up here? To vandalise a stone circle in the middle of the moor?"

He took her question seriously, following her gaze. "God knows. Probably some new-age weirdo. Pretending to be a Druid or something. Like that old bloke in the shop? Totally loony. Wouldn't be surprised if he came up here at midnight with his hammer and chisel."

Turning to him, smiling, she brushed a strand of blonde hair from her face. Her hands were so small, her cheek like that of a child, her movements so feminine. God how he loved her.

"Come on, Owen," she laughed, "He was just a silly old hippy with a thing about scientists. Probably had a traumatic experience at the hands of his physics teacher. Somehow I don't see him traipsing all the way up here. More likely to be one of these new-age sects. Apparently stone circles contain vortices of psychic energy or something. Do you know, I've seen money pushed into cracks in these stone circles? Offerings to their Goddess or something. Trouble is, they damage the stones. Ought to be illegal. Probably is.

Apparently Professor Lightfoot - she's our head of department - is campaigning for access to the circles to be restricted. God knows how you'd do it. I mean, they're on common land and ... Owen?"

Owen was gazing solemnly into space as he replayed the incident at the shop. The guy had suddenly started shouting at them. It had unnerved him more than he cared to admit. "Can't help thinking about how that guy went off at us." He paused. "Seemed to think he owned these circles. Like those people you're talking about."

She nodded absent-mindedly, returning her attention to the carving. Pulling her phone from the backpack, she took a photo, locking it away in an insulating cocoon of technology, impersonal, unthreatening. After replacing the phone, she followed Owen around the circle, examining each stone for more carvings. Unsuccessful, they returned and stared at the design. A circle flanked by two crescents.

Owen frowned. "Is that spooky, or what? Never seen anything like that before."

She nodded. "Yeh - spooky as. Bloody shame though. Lovely old stones stand here undisturbed for thousands of years until some psycho..." She shook her head sadly. "Anyway, I suppose worse things happen. C'mon. Back to work."

They returned to their measurements. Stooping next to a post, she spoke into the recorder. "Height one point two seven metres, distance from number 23, one point four three metres."

As he recorded the contours of the stone with the digital SLR, Owen spotted a movement out of the corner of his eye, a few steps away. He peered at it. Nothing. Other than the long grass swaying in the wind. And their small orange tent pitched beyond, further down the hill.

"Guess we'd better keep an eye out for snakes when we're walking back."

Sarah looked up. "Sorry?"

"Snakes. We'd better be careful."

She shrugged and returned to her work, her lithe body visible even through the waterproofs. He gazed past her at the stone circle.

Since childhood he had been bewitched by the wind-blown spaces of Dartmoor, and the circles of standing stones that cluttered them. Built four thousand years earlier by a small group of men and women struggling for survival through harsh bronze-age winters. Why on earth did they do it? How did they find the time? That's how he'd met Sarah.

He'd been looking at some stone circles down near Ashburton. Came across a group of archaeologists digging a trench. She was one of them. Cute. Doing a PhD, trying to figure out what stone circles were for. So one thing led to another, and now he spent weekends and vacations helping with her project. But his passion for Dartmoor encompassed much more than circles and standing stones.

On each return, he found himself entranced by the welcoming hills, the springiness of the fragrant turf and peat. The solitude, the warm summer days when the wind whispered through the knee-high grass, lonely yet intimate. The cold clear winter days when a person may be swallowed up by the Moor as much as by his own thoughts, set free to fly over the rounded hills and craggy tors or be sucked into the greener-than-green sphagnum bogs. Where the stark ethereal beauty of the landscape played counterpoint to a sinister childhood undertone of ghosts and witches. And those autumnal days when the fog, smelling of waterlogged peat, defeating wet-weather gear, insinuated icy trickles between skin and clothing. When the world shrank to an arms-length horizon of visibility, beyond which shadows of forgotten ghosts flitted in the mist: another world, an alternative reality.

"Penny for your thoughts?"

Her question startled him, snapping him out of his reverie. "Nothing - just thinking."

She smiled tolerantly.

"You are such a romantic, Owen. So transparent. I love the way you gaze at these hills - you get so misty-eyed. What is it about you and this place, Owen?"

He considered her question. "Dunno. It's as if... as if I'm connected... As if I belong here. "

"Love you, Owen. But don't ever let the people in the department hear you say stuff like that. Like scientists aren't supposed to have feelings, right?"

Laughing, he linked arms with her. It had been a long day, and his body ached. His watch said nearly six. An hour to sunset.

"Let's go make dinner. We can finish this tomorrow."

They trudged downhill to their tent, pitched within the shelter of a stone wall, one of a cluster of roofless hut circles straggling up the gentle hill, the skeleton of a bronze-age village.

As the kettle hissed on the camp stove, they pulled off their waterproofs. Sarah took over the tea-making while he pulled out the laptop and slotted in a fresh battery from the backpack. Opening the file to enter the data, he surveyed their notes.

"Not much to show for a day's work."

Handing him a mug of tea, she smiled. "You worry too much. We spent all morning getting here. We'll be able to finish it tomorrow."

A clap of thunder echoed across the moor. The sky was clouding over, and within an hour, rain was falling. They could hear the water trickling down the flysheet, but within the darkening space of the tent, they were snug and dry.

Owen closed the laptop and leant back on his elbows. "Sarah, do you realise that we're probably sitting in the same spot as the people who built the stone circle?"

"Funny - the same thought crossed my mind. Awesome, isn't it? Wonder what they were like? I mean, biologically, they'd be the same, but mentally they'd be so like, alien."

"Dunno. Whoever built the stone circle - were they so very different from us? Trying to understand the secrets of the Universe. And prepared to spend their lives doing it. Just because we're scientists and they were ..."

"Speak for yourself, Owen. You see all of life as one great intellectual journey, don't you. Me - I'm after a comfortable life."

"Come on, don't try to tell me that the only reason you're doing your PhD is to increase your earning power?"

"Pretty much, yes."

He grinned. "Don't believe you. How's a PhD in archaeology going to get you a high-power job? Besides, what about the other day when you came home thrilled to bits by that radio-carbon date?"

"Yeh - that was pretty cool. But ultimately a means to an end."

"You know what Lennon said: Life is what happens while you're making other plans."

She shrugged. He might have been speaking Greek. But he didn't believe for one moment that she was as coldly focussed on the future as she claimed.

Lighting the stove again, Sarah poured a packet of dried risotto into the pan of water. Owen put away his notes, tapped a few keys on the laptop, and out of the tinny speakers ventured the first movement of Mozart's Clarinet Concerto. By the time the glorious second movement burst forth, the risotto was ready. Sarah poured the gooey mess onto plates while Owen filled two plastic glasses from a cheap wine box. The music soared, the risotto and wine tasted excellent, and this outpost of reconstituted sophistication stood confident and solitary amidst the crumbling ruins of ancient civilisations in the timeless moorland.

The surface tension of their bubble of existence drew them closer until they were entwined, while the random forces of rain, wind, and wilderness crackled and drummed on the tent above them. They made love drowsily, savouring the fusion of two bodies into one, before at last they fell apart and crawled into their sleeping bags.

A gust of wind rumbled across the flysheet, making Sarah stir. Owen looked at her, breathing softly beside him, her face barely visible in the dark. He loved her, achingly. But she didn't want to get married. Said it was an obsolete concept. She'd agreed to make a vow, though.

They'd done it properly. Just the two of them. Didn't need anybody else. They'd found the perfect spot, on top of

Mardon Down, and solemnly exchanged vows under a blue sky filled with lark song. Till death us do part.

He recognised that day as one of those pivots around which a life turns. A day that fused his life with Sarah's into a lifeline stretching into the unknowable future.

But now, he had to get some sleep. Rolling over, he watched patterns of sleeplessness form and dissolve, and then the whorls turned to circles, stone circles. An old crone came running out from between the stones, screeching at him, waving her finger in admonishment. But not a word was intelligible. Other men, women, children, joined her, surrounding him, chanting in a strange language. They stopped abruptly as a child stood before him, thrusting a bunch of flowers towards his face. Cautiously, he took them, not knowing what was expected. As his head spun from the pungent vapour, he fell to his knees, hearing the crowd cheer, yelling at him...

He woke to a crashing noise outside. Confused, he jumped up, and scrambled to the front of the tent, fumbling with the zip. Under the flysheet, their dirty plates lay in a heap, the pan pulled half-out from under the canvas.

Suddenly fearful, he drew back inside, painfully aware of the flimsiness of the fabric separating them from axe-wielding murderers. Looking back at Sarah, sleeping undisturbed by the noise, he wondered whether to wake her. As clouds of confusion cleared, he reasoned that it was more likely to be a fox than a psychopath. Besides, as far as he knew, psychopaths generally weren't interested in dirty pots and pans. Definitely a fox. He paused, listening. The rain had eased, and only a light patter now sounded on the flysheet, through which faint moonlight filtered. No fox sounds. Must have been scared off by the crash of the pans. He wouldn't come again.

Zipping up the tent, he climbed back into the sleeping bag.

"Goodnight, love," he whispered.

"G'night, Owen," came a groggy murmur from the shapeless sleeping bag, the untidy mop of blonde hair the only clue to its inhabitant. Heavy-lidded, he closed his eyes and drifted off.

He staggered awake from a dream. It was time to leave but he couldn't get his schoolbooks into his bag. The bus was waiting, but his books had acquired a life of their own, snapping open and shut as they slithered uncontrollably on the hallway floor. He chased them in an attempt to force them into his bag, while on the bus his friends laughed at his pathetic attempts. But consciousness summoned him with even more urgency, and as he fought upwards through successive levels of awakening, the laughter morphed into a snarling noise, accompanied by the clanking of saucepans. That bloody fox! Owen clambered out of the tent to see that the fox - God knows how - had managed to get into the backpack, and was now trying to chew its way into a Tupperware box containing bacon. At least it was only a fox. Could have been the Hound of the Baskervilles.

"Damn!" He tried to grab the box. The fox jumped playfully away, and at a safe distance continued to gnaw through the box while keeping a wary eye on him.

"You bugger!" Scrambling out, torch in hand, he chased the fox up the hill.

Pale moonlight filtered through the drizzle, bathing the scene in a strange half-light. Naked, he pursued the fox through the icy rain, a sense of absurdity creeping over him. As he chased the animal out of the cluster of huts, he realised it had become personal, primeval. Up towards the stone circle they ran, the fox pausing every so often to gnaw the box, always keeping a few paces away from him, taunting him. Then it ran far ahead, into the stone circle.

Owen refused to give up. Flashing his torch behind each stone, he circumnavigated the circle, hoping to find either fox or bacon. He sat heavily at the base of a stone. The situation was absurd and anachronistic: he was naked, reduced to primal elements, man versus fox. Unaccountably, he seized the cold monolith. Hugging it, placing his forehead against it, he wept. Reality flooded in from the stone, through his fingers, through his forehead, through every sense, and at once he understood how this great circle of circumstance had now closed, how he was part of a larger reality, as much a part of this earth as the fox or the people who built the circle, even the rock itself. The feeling of one-ness was overwhelming. He staggered back, tripped, fell clumsily, and lay still. What on earth had just happened? Gingerly, approaching the stone, he placed his hand on it. Nothing. Except - a fleeting glimpse of something remembered, out of reach. The fog rolled in. It was gone.

Trudging back to the tent, his mind worked over the experience. Weird. Totally weird. Didn't make any sense. Must have been half-asleep.

Sarah was holding her arms out to him, her voice soft with concern. "Owen - You poor thing - you're frozen - come and cuddle up - I was worried about you. You were such a long time. Catch him?"

Owen crawled over and snuggled up to her warm body. She had that drowsy female smell that transforms a man into a child.

"Um - no. He ran off with the bacon," he mumbled from the nape of her neck.

He felt her smiling, and a hand stroked his head. "Not to worry. We can live without it. What took you so long?"

He started to shake his head, but instead mumbled "Nothing, really. It was a bit strange, that's all."

He felt her pull away from him, as if to see his face in the darkness of the tent. "Really? What happened?"

Hesitating, he realised he had no idea how, or what, to start telling her. "Not now. It was nothing. A sort of dream. Tell you about it in the morning."

"Hope he doesn't come back. Sleep well, Owen." She reached up, ruffled his hair, dismissing him, and snuggled back in her bag.

As he crawled back into his sleeping bag, his mind buzzed. Probably the result of wine and fatigue. Yawning, he drifted into a restless sleep filled with strange half-dreams.

By morning, the rain had faded to a grey drizzle. After a breakfast of tea and marmalade sandwiches, they struggled into waterproofs and trudged up to the circle. Owen paced around the stones, replaying the events of the night.

Gingerly, he touched a stone, then clasped it. Nothing. Glancing up, he saw the puzzled expression on Sarah's face. He turned to her with a self-conscious grin.

"You know, I had the oddest experience up here last night."

She cocked her head to one side. "Really? What?"

"Not sure. It was as if I could touch... It was so real." A hesitation. He blundered on.

"It was like I was sort of connecting to reality. I know that sounds crazy. Like some hippy thing. But it's the nearest I can get. It was such an odd feeling."

He paused and looked at Sarah, expecting her ridicule. Instead she gazed at him wide-eyed, and replied in a subdued voice.

"Owen, I'm just having the most awful déjà vu. Well, not déjà vu exactly, but more like a premonition. Like something awful's going to happen, and this is the beginning. I...."

She stopped, stared at him blankly for a fraction of a second, then exploded into a laugh.

"Jeez Owen, you've got me going now! What is it about this place?"

"No Sarah, what were you saying? I want to hear."

Rolling her eyes, she smiled at him with affection. "Come on, Owen, that's enough of this superstitious rubbish. We're letting our imaginations run away with us. You and your hotlink to reality."

He grinned sheepishly. "Anyway, Mizz Rational Archaeologist, what do you reckon? I don't think we'll get much done in this weather."

"Yeh - this rain sucks. Probably set in for the day." She rocked back on her heels, frowning at the rain. Her face lit up with sudden inspiration. "Hey - why don't we go back to the car, drive into Exeter. We can check into a motel, go to a pub and have dinner, maybe go see a movie. Then explore the night-life of Exeter."

"Or mount a search for it."

Her smile contrasted with the wet hair plastered to her cheeks. "Or stay in the motel, enjoy warm beds and hot meals..." She eyed him mischievously. "Maybe just stay in bed all day..."

It was wasted on him. He ducked into a depression in the ground and stood holding up the Tupperware box triumphantly. "Look what I've found!" The box was unopened, but the polythene was scored by teeth-marks.

"Stupid fox!" Owen 1. Fox 0. Flipping it open, he sniffed it. "Seems OK."

"Sweet. Hey - let's have bacon sandwiches before we leave," she said, "We could use the energy for the walk back."

"Yeh - sure. But did you see where I found it?"

The shallow coffin-shaped hole in the ground was lined with stone slabs. These bronze-age burial chambers, or kistvaens, had once contained bodies and burial treasures, but now yawned empty. The grey drizzle had darkened the stones and the heather, casting a sombre pall around the grave.

Slowly, frowning, as if forced against her will, Sarah stepped down into the kistvaen, and examined the floor. "What do you reckon, Owen?"

Bunches of faded flowers, weighed down by pebbles, were scattered over the floor of the grave. Picking up a flat crescent-shaped stone, Owen saw it had symbols scratched on it.

"Weird." He picked up others, to find that each was marked with a roughly-drawn design. "This pattern's like the one carved on the stone circle. What the hell do you think they are?"

She shook her head, and said casually. "Absolutely no idea."

An edge to her voice made him look up at her. Her eyes were round, as if she'd seen a ghost. She of the rational intellect.

"You alright?" he asked.

"Yes of course," she answered, and her cheeks reddened even in the cold air. "Just wondering who put these here."

Unconvinced, he turned back to the pebbles. "Probably the same people who carved on the stone circle. Let's take these stones back. See if we can find out what they are."

Turning one in her hand, Sarah stared at it, as if trying to comprehend its significance. "I don't know. It might be really important to someone."

"You mean some sort of religious thing?"

She glanced up at him, and then laughed. "Maybe. God knows what the poor old sods round here get up to. Better leave them to it, I suppose. Let's take some photos and get out of here."

After photographing the pebbles, they replaced them on the dead flowers. Yet Owen couldn't shake off an odd feeling - like a pair of kids caught misbehaving, and let off with a warning.

oooOooo

After dismantling the tent, they started their sodden trek back to the car. Although only five kilometres by crow, the path was wet and boggy by foot, compounded by the disorienting Dartmoor mists. As a result, the journey could take close to three hours.

The ground was firm and made easy walking, but the mist thickened until their feet faded into indistinct blurs. "I love it like this," mused Owen, "So creepy - immersed in this little cocoon of reality. The whole world might have ceased to exist. But..."

Sarah stopped. "Hey - listen!"

Someone was coming towards them.

"Hello!" called Owen. The voices continued without pause. A woman seemed to be chatting to a child.

Again he called, even louder, but still they didn't hear him.

"They're going to be totally blown when they bump into us," said Sarah, with a nervous laugh.

The voices came closer until they seemed within arms length. Now they could hear the steady plodding of a horse, but still couldn't see anyone.

"Hello there," Owen called.

"Where are you?" Sarah shouted.

They were ignored. The people sounded so close, yet were invisible. The horse coughed with a rasp, seemed to stumble, and the woman made soothing noises to it. The child laughed. Unaware of Owen and Sarah, they resumed their conversation. Slowly, the voices faded into the distance, leaving the pair motionless. Owen felt the hairs bristling on the back of his neck.

"Umm... I guess they couldn't hear us," he said, glancing at Sarah.

Her face was pale. "Fog does funny things to sounds. Probably miles away." She thrust her arm around him, their waterproofs rustling together, accentuating the silence.

Ancient fears churned, at length subsiding to no more than a shiver. Affecting a cheerful briskness, Owen retreated to the map and GPS to check their bearing.

"Once more unto the breach dear friends," he pronounced heartily.

"Or close the wall up with our English dead!" she responded, automatically, unthinking. He glanced at her, startled by her words, but she peered at the ground silently, refusing to acknowledge his look as they moved off.

As they climbed, the fog thinned, and the ground became easier, with short fragrant heather punctuating cushions of sphagnum. When they reached the broken mess of rock at the top of the hill, Gidleigh Common stretched away before them - a boggy place where unfamiliar hikers could flounder for hours. Owen knew it well enough to avoid the quagmires.

The rain had made the Common treacherous. Several times they were forced to retrace their steps, trying to cross again on higher ground, only to be thwarted, their path taking them back into the bog. Finally, Owen, in the lead, found a path through a mossy clearing that seemed to skirt the mire.

"Stop!" shouted Sarah, pointing, panic in her voice.

He froze and stared at the ground around him. As he shifted, slow concentric undulations radiated away.

"Damn! How did I manage that?"

These featherbeds, notorious to Dartmoor walkers, were formed by skins of moss that grew over darkly submerged pools of water. From above, they were indistinguishable from solid ground. But the deceitful layer could split and pitch the unwary into the watery blackness below. Once below the skin, disorientation made it nearly impossible to find the way back up. Coroners' reports recorded how hikers had drowned while digging deeper into the soil at the bottom of the pool.

Owen's face drained of colour. His voice shook as he tried to appear calm. "OK - you move back first."

Terrified, she retraced her steps as if in a minefield. Being closer to the edge of the featherbed, her feet soon found solid ground. She breathed out.

Owen's face sweated in the cold air as he reversed his steps. One at a time, arms spread out in case he fell through, hesitating before each step in case it was his last. The water was seeping through the moss under his weight, rising up to embrace him, and was now ankle-deep. How long would this skin support him before casting him into the netherworld? Not a word was spoken as his feet gingerly tested the quivering ground beneath each footfall. After an age, he trod more firmly, and the deadly ripples subsided. He collapsed into her arms.

"Owen, my love, thank God! You could have been killed!"

Sinking his face in her neck, he stayed silent, and then lifted his head to stare accusingly at the featherbed. "I'd be under there now if you hadn't spotted it." There was a quaver in his voice as he turned to her, his face serious and intense. "You saved my life."

Her laugh was betrayed by the tremble in her words. "Whatever," she said, her grip fierce on his wrist, "I expect the locals exaggerate these things to scare away the tourists."

Maybe. But an image haunted him. If she had been in front... As they walked away, the image nagged him, clamouring attention, demanding to be examined, tried on for size.

Sarah under the ground. Sarah dead.

He shook the thought from his mind, aware that it lay in wait, lurking to attack him when he was least expecting. Instead, he focussed on navigating a path forward through the boggy peat.

After a frustrating hour trampling around in the mire, firmer ground rose beneath them. As they crossed the grassy perimeter of the Common, the elegant standing stones of Scorhill Circle appeared dimly in the broad valley below. Only a few minutes further to the car, their home-from-home, with food, dry clothes, security.

"Hey - there's chocolate biscuits in the car."

"Awesome," said Sarah.

"And a change of clothes. I'm totally soaked."

At last, they spotted the dry-stone wall delineating the moorland's edge. They turned the corner into the grassy car park, and stopped dead. The burnt skeleton of their car glared back at them.

oooOooo

The air hung heavy with the stench of burnt rubber and plastic. Shards of glass were scattered over the ground like sacred crystals, the silence broken only by the crunch of Owen's tread. Inside the eyeless car were piled the ashes that had once been their clothes, their books, their refuge from the wilderness.

He walked round the car, kicking it and cursing, and stared into the yawning boot. "Bloody hell. I don't believe it. Everything - maps, books... They're all gone - everything." He rifled through the ash in the boot, angry. "Christ Almighty."

Sarah stood frozen in a trance, pale-faced, shivering. "What do you think happened? A short circuit or something?"

"No way. I reckon some bloody vandal's set fire to it. What a pain. Jeez - I can't believe it. What sodding bastard would do something like this?" Scowling at the car, he fought a growing sense of disorientation, tried to ignore the feeling - it was only a car for Christ's sake. But the injustice: why would anybody do this? What had he done to deserve it?

He noticed a blackened object dangling in the space once occupied by the windscreen. He peered at it, but couldn't make out what the charred remains might once have been. Suddenly, recognition slammed into him, and he ran to the grass, retching.

Standing frozen to the ground, still wearing her backpack, Sarah watched, unnerved by his behaviour, afraid to approach. Curiosity got the better of her, and she moved towards the car, looking inwards and upwards at the charred lump. Like a bit of burnt meat - no - a small animal - a blackened bone sticking out where its leg had been. And then she saw the wire noose around its neck, the charred twigs tied to its body. Strangling a cry, she backed away from the hideous object. She exhaled, battening down the lid so nearly opened, so nearly releasing the childhood wraiths of primeval fear.

She heard the scrunch of Owen's feet on the gravel, felt his arms wrapping around her. The touch of his body was sufficient to crumble her outer defences, filling her eyes with tears. "I don't understand," she wailed, "What's going on? What's that ... thing ... doing in our car?"

"Buggered if I know. What a mess."

"You'd better call the police," she cried, her self-control on the point of breaking, her voice degenerating into sobs.

Pulling the mobile from her backpack she handed it to him.

He dialled.

"Emergency Services. How may I help you?"

"Um. I'm on the edge of Dartmoor. Near Chagford. Someone's set fire to our car."

"Just a moment please," said the operator. Owen was transferred to Devon County Police. Somebody would be with him within an hour.

A cold wind gusted from the darkening moor. Twigs dropped from the trees, and leaves twisted around the burned black hulk. Together they huddled against the empty chill that descended, enveloping them.

Chapter 3
April 2005

The emblems of power and authority adorning the police car - its chequered stripes and bold no-nonsense lettering, its throbbing V8 engine - seemed to come from a world quite different from that inhabited by dry-stone walls and bleating sheep. The inconsistency deepened as Sergeant Bradworthy climbed out, his crisp blue-serge uniform and hi-tech transceiver struggling against his broad Devon accent. He shook hands with Owen, issued a cursory nod at Sarah, and walked over to the burnt-out shell. "'Ow long was 'ee yer?"

"Two nights. We left it Wednesday afternoon."

He peered inside the car. "Aah. Oi'll get forensics dreckly. See what they can find. Don't fancy yer chances. You upset anyone round 'ere?"

"Umm. No. Not really," mumbled Owen.

The Sergeant's eyebrows invited him to elaborate.

"Well... The thing is, we went into a shop in Chagford on Wednesday - a sort of new-age hippy place with crystals and things, near the church...."

"Oh... I knows 'ee - 'Good Vibrations' - stupid bloody name."

"The guy there went stark raving mad and started shouting for no reason."

The policeman grinned. "That'll be old Alfred 'uxtable. Funny ol' gatfer. So what did yer say to upset the ol' bugger?"

Owen explained that they had been chatting about stone circles. The shopkeeper was a mine of information, until Owen mentioned that they were scientists, at which point the guy had exploded.

32

"He went totally non-linear," added Sarah, moving closer, "Told us to get out of his shop and not meddle in things that were none of our business. So we just went. It was all so like - weird."

"No, No... not weird for ol' Alfred, " chuckled Sergeant Bradworthy. "Ee be right billid at times. But if yer arsk me, can't see 'im coming up 'ere to set fire to yer car! Too far from th' pub!"

As he continued walking round the car, the wind blew a swirl of ash from the boot, banging one of the doors. A crow cawed mournfully before swooping down, its wings beating audibly as it rose. The policemen glanced at it without interest, and kicked a flattened tyre. He rubbed his fingers on the tyre-wall and sniffed them.

"That be petrol aright. Prob'ly local good-fer-norts after too much beer. But they made a proper job an' all this time... Ohhh - my lord - what the divil's that?" He peered at the burnt shape hanging from the windscreen mirror.

Owen came alongside him. "I think it's a dead rabbit. Revolting, isn't it? Why would anyone do that?"

Sarah joined in "It's so gross. Do you think it was dead before they set fire to it? I can't think why..."

Her voice faltered. The policeman was staring at them. Abruptly, he lowered his eyes and walked a few paces away. He stood, his back to them, contemplating the ground, and then turned on them angrily. "An' I s'pose yer've nort idea?"

"What?" Was this supposed to be their fault in some twisted way? "No - have you?"

The policeman shook his head, but avoided their interrogating gaze. His self-confidence and authority, already struggling, had evaporated.

"You do know something about it, don't you," persisted Owen.

Glaring back, the sergeant spoke in a low growl. "I dunno what yer people are up to but I wish you wouldn't bloody bring it 'ere. Ye bist nort but trouble. You come down here with yer..."

He stopped, cursing under his breath, kicking the ground.

Sarah shrugged at Owen. What the hell was that supposed to mean? Owen shook his head in response.

The policeman paced back to his car. "Get in th' car," he scowled, "Oi'll take ye back down to Chagford."

Sarah strode up to block his way, confronting him, while Owen looked on. "I don't understand. What's the rabbit doing there? There's something you're not telling us."

"Don't yer bliddy bate wi' me young lady - get in the car."

Seeing the baffled expressions on their faces, his voice softened. "Look - just you take m' word for it. There be some weird types round yer with funny ideas. Course, don't believe that mumbo-jumbo meself, but, like Alfred said, don't you poke yer nose into things that ain't none of yer bus'ness."

The policeman got into his car, started the engine, and sat waiting. Owen and Sarah exchanged glances, but then climbed in the back. On the way down to Chagford, Sarah tried to talk to the sergeant, but all he offered were non-committal grunts. Owen remained silent. What the hell was going on? Should he mention the symbols in the stone circle, or would that complicate things?

In the market square, they took their backpacks from the boot. The sergeant pulled out a pad of forms and rested them on the car roof as he started writing. "Right now. Let's get this over an' done. Oi'll sign off these 'ere forms, and then you two g'awn 'ome. And jest yer forget any of this 'appened."

"Hold on.." Owen began, but was stopped by a dig in the ribs from Sarah.

The policeman wrote on the forms as he continued. "Prob'ly local lads 'aving a bit o' fun. No evidence, so not much uz can do. Case closed."

"But what about forensics? You didn't even search for evidence."

Ignoring the challenge, he handed Owen a form.

" 'Ere's the police report. Yer'll need 'ee for insurance. There's a bus in haf'n hour t' Exeter. Leaves from right 'ere. You two make sure yer on it."

34

Without another word, he jumped back in the car and drove off, leaving them alone in the square with their backpacks.

Owen contemplated the uncaring passers-by, the time-tarnished shops, the inscrutable window of "Good Vibrations". Directly above, a crow on the roof mocked them. Sarah shuddered at the gravestone rasp, and threaded her arm around his waist as they made their way to the bus stop.

A timetable confirmed that the Exeter bus was indeed due in half an hour. Nearby was a small café with the curious name "The Tinner's Rabbits". After their ordeal, a cup of tea was irresistible.

Sipping his tea, Owen gazed out of the window, on which was etched a bizarre design of three rabbits in a triangle, linked by their conjoined ears. Sarah read aloud a note on the back of the menu. "Our café is named after this ancient symbol. Although dating back to pagan times, it was traditionally used as the badge of the guild of Devon stannary workers, who supplied tin for the Royal Mint."

His face froze. "Damn! We don't have any money."

"What?"

"I left my wallet in the car for safety."

"Owen! You couldn't have! How are we going to get home?" Fumbling through their pockets and backpacks, they found a five-pound note and a few coins - eight pounds thirty-five altogether. "Thank God. I guess this will get us to Exeter. We can sort something out then." They left the shop and waited at the bus stop, feeling alienated from the shoppers around them. Eventually the bus rumbled into the square.

After paying for the tickets, Owen counted the change in his hand. "Only sixty p. We'll need to organise some money as soon as we get to Exeter."

oooOooo

In a run-down two-star hotel in Exeter, an acne-challenged clerk took their details. "That's fine, sir, and if I could take an imprint of your credit card?"

"Ah, well, that's the thing," said Owen, "I'm afraid I've lost my wallet so..." he shrugged, "No credit card. But I'll phone the bank and arrange to get some money tomorrow." The clerk regarded their dishevelled clothes and grubby backpacks. "I'm sorry sir," he said, "but I do need either a credit card or a deposit before I can check you in."

"For heaven's sake. Where's the manager? Let me talk to the manager."

"Certainly, sir. One moment please." From the back room appeared a greasy dark-haired man in his forties. "Yes sir, can I help you?" The manager nodded sympathetically as they explained their predicament. "I'm afraid my young colleague is correct - we do need a credit card or deposit. But use the phone here to contact the bank. When you've arranged for some cash we'll be only too pleased to check you in." Owen picked up the phone and dialled.

"If you are reporting a lost or stolen credit card, press 1. If you wish to speak to a customer service representative, press 2. If you..." He pressed 2.

"Our office hours are 9am to 4pm Monday to Friday. Please call back during office hours and we will be delighted to help you."

He cursed, hung up, and dialled again.

"If you are reporting..."

He pressed one.

After a long message about the call being monitored to improve the quality of the service, he found himself speaking to a human being.

"Good evening. My name is Brian. How may I help you?"

Owen started explaining their situation, but was stopped short.

"No problem," purred Brian, "if I could have your full name?"

"Owen Davies."

"Date of birth?"

"First of March 1979"

"And the secret password you gave us when you opened the account?"

"Of course I don't know that - that was ten years ago - how would I know that?"

"Sir, these questions are for your protection."

"OK." Owen calmed himself. "Can you give me a clue?"

"No, not really," said Brian, "Let me ask you some questions instead." And so they went through his billing address, his home phone number, who else had secondary cards on his accounts, his credit limit (Owen guessed correctly on his second attempt), and his last transaction date.

"Right, let's sort you out Mr. Davies."

Owen briefly considered correcting him - Dr. rather than Mr. - but they needed this idiot's help.

"Now. I see you have a Visa card and a Cirrus card. Do you want both of these stopped?"

"I guess so."

"OK - bear with me....right, both those cards are stopped. Now what else can we do for you?"

"I need to be able to access the funds in my savings account."

"Certainly, sir. No problem. Go in to any branch and they will be able to establish your identity and give you a cash withdrawal. Anything else I can do for you?" Owen tried to tame his rising temper. "Um - you're missing the point. It's Friday night. The banks aren't open until Monday. I need some money now, to check into a hotel, buy food and transport. Don't you understand?"

"I'm sorry sir, but when you shout I can't hear what you're saying." Owen tried to calm himself. He breathed deeply, and saw Sarah was making "cool it" gestures to him.

"Listen. You have my money and I need it. Could you please simply make a transfer from my account to the account of the hotel, so they can accommodate us over the weekend?"

"I'm sorry, Mr. Davies, but this is the lost/stolen cards department. Transfers between accounts are handled by the branches. And they're closed at the moment," he added helpfully.

Owen's knuckles around the phone whitened as he swallowed his rising anger. "Listen. I'm stuck in the middle of Devon. My car and my wallet have been burnt. I'm asking for your help. Surely you have some sort of procedure for helping customers when they get stuck like this?"

"I'm afraid we're a bank, not a rescue service. Have you thought of contacting the police?" Owen slammed the receiver down. Everyone in the lobby was gazing intently in other directions. He stared at the phone. At the clerk and the manager, who shrugged helplessly. Fuming, he picked up his backpack, stormed out, and slumped onto a bench in the street. Sarah sat next to him. He turned to her, expecting her sympathy.

"Way to go," she said. He met her eyes, expecting her hard expression to soften, her arms to console him. Instead she glared back icily.

"I'm sorry," began Owen, "There was this complete idiot on the other end of the line. I lost my cool."

"So I heard. You couldn't swallow your pride for once and ask for his help, could you! You're so bloody full of yourself - always rubbing people up the wrong way."

Stunned by her outburst, Owen found himself bristling with hurt and indignation. "What the hell is that supposed to mean? You talk such crap sometimes. If you're going to call me names, you could at least try to think of something sensible rather than the first mindless drivel that comes into your head."

"Oh yes you think you're so bloody wonderful, don't you. So what possessed you, Mr. Wonderful, to leave your wallet in the car? That has to be the most moronic thing you've ever done. Christ Almighty! If it weren't for you we wouldn't be in this mess!" The bickering broke into a full-blooded yelling match until Sarah stormed off. Owen sat on the bench, disoriented. He peered at his surroundings, at the water splashing out of the hideous mouth of a gargoyle on the building opposite. To either side of it stretched a line of grinning stone faces, mocking his misery. They were right. He had no bloody idea what to do, no will to do it, and he'd just lost the support of the one person he could always count on. Putting his head in his hands, he stared at the rain splashing around his feet, feeling as if the rain trickling down his neck and filling his boots were somehow making a point.

He was startled by Sarah's quiet voice. "Owen - I'm sorry - can we start again?" Her hair was soaked, plastered in untidy streaks over her face. She had been crying. He suddenly wanted to protect her, get her out of this mess. "Yeh - I'm sorry too, love."

As she huddled close, they clasped hands, gazing morosely at the rain.

"Look - I've been thinking," he said, "This is stupid. We have a tent. We don't need a hotel. And we can hitch a ride back to Cambridge. We'll be home by tomorrow."

"I could do with something to eat, though," she said, doubtfully. She seemed unusually subdued, her habitual optimism worn away by the events of the day.

"Sorry. Only sixty p left. Don't think we'll get much for that. Maybe we can buy some chips or something." He squeezed her hand, and felt her respond. "Let's head down to the motorway to hitch a lift, and see what we find on the way."

They shouldered their back-packs and walked down Fore Street, arms around each others' waists. Amongst the darkened shops was a brilliantly lit window selling Indian clothes, crystals, and jewellery. In the centre was displayed a book entitled "The Magick of the Druids", a picture of Stonehenge on the front. He shuddered. "Can't believe people buy that rubbish." Turning away from the beckoning light, they continued down the dark hill. An appetising smell wafted across the street. Not appetising as in French restaurant, but appetising as in tomato sauce on soggy chips. For those hungry enough. They paused, and were drawn to its source, following their noses as the aroma wafted this way and that. The trail led to a side street, where light and steam spilled out from a shop-front along with a warm fug of humanity.

Owen hesitated. "A café. But what use is that? We don't have any money." Grabbing his arm, Sarah urged him forward. "Come on, Owen, we've got 60p. Must be enough for a cup of tea. Anything to get out of this rain."

An open door showed a large, brightly-lit room in which the ketchupy food-smell mingled with that of cigarettes and wet bodies - young, old, ragged, tidy. Motley posters covered flaking walls. At one end, behind a counter, a middle-aged man and a teenage boy ladled out food. Owen and Sarah hesitated at the doorway, and watched. Seeing them, the man nodded encouragingly. Owen responded with a hesitant smile, turned and bolted.

"What are you doing?" asked Sarah as she caught up with him.

"It's a soup kitchen for derelicts."

"Like us."

"We're not derelicts. It's not meant for people like us. It wouldn't be right."

She grabbed his hand. "C'mon Owen... I'm starving." She turned and marched towards the doorway, Owen sheepishly in tow.

The man serving food saw him pausing, and beckoned. "Come on in - don't be shy!" They entered, feeling out of place.

"Hi - I'm Stan. Can I tempt you to a bowl of soup? Made it fresh today."

"That would be wonderful but... I'm afraid we don't have any money," said Sarah, forcing a nervous grin.

The warmth of Stan's smile had some undefinable quality that made you trust him. "Then you're in the right place. Sit down. Relax. Enjoy some good food."

"Umm," started Owen nervously, "But we're not down-and-out, or anything. It's just that I've lost my wallet..."

"Really? Bit of a bugger." replied Stan, cheerfully. "Still, there's people here with more to worry about than that. Relax. Have some soup. There's fresh bread there. Jam and peanut butter over there. Help yourself." The sparsely furnished room was buzzing with chatter. Some people were wrapped in coats and scarves, while others were threadbare. An unshaven man with wild greying hair sat in the corner, his eyes half closed, muttering to nobody in particular, with occasional obscenities rising above the sea of incoherent babble. As they passed, he shouted "Bugger Off!" Pausing, Owen saw that nobody paid any attention, and moved on. Two elderly men were playing chess, and people read books as they ate. Some wouldn't have seemed out of place in a Cambridge wine bar.

Sitting at the only empty table, they tucked into the thick homemade vegetable soup, followed by jam sandwiches and tea. Their spirits began to revive.

oooOooo

Thanking Stan, they plunged back into the wet night, bustling under the shopfront awnings to miss the worst of the rain. They were drenched by the time they reached the motorway exit. Up the ramp and under a light, thumbs out, they tried to catch the attention of one of the black shapes thundering past. An hour later, they were still standing there, the rain even heavier.

Perhaps Sarah on her own would have more luck, while he stayed back in the bushes. After a few minutes a car stopped, and Owen walked forward enthusiastically.

"Hi. We were wondering if you..."

"Fuck off," replied the driver. He accelerated away, and was gone.

An hour and three similar results later, they abandoned the idea.

"No way are we going to get a lift tonight," Sarah sighed.

"This is ridiculous," said Owen, "These people are treating us like we're vagrants or something. It shouldn't be happening."

"C'mon, Owen. It's not the end of the world." She put her arms around him and snuggled her wet hair against his cheek.

He tore himself away, refusing to be placated in mid-rant. "This is stupid. The thing is, I've got a PhD. I've got a healthy bank account. Why can't the banks get their act together and set up a process to deal with this. And as for that idiot on the phone... Loads of people must lose their wallets. I can't believe they all have to go through this."

"Whatever," she said soothingly, "Don't you see, Owen? It doesn't matter. You said yourself: we have a tent. We've been camping on Dartmoor the last few days. What's different about camping here, tonight? Come on, don't let it get you down. We'll be alright."

He stared at her, ready to argue, then slumped. "I guess you're right. I'm fed up and I want to go home. It's been a long day. Let's pitch the tent."

They walked down from the exit ramp, and camped in a grassy field. An hour later they were asleep.

oooOooo

As the sky lightened, Owen's consciousness gradually encompassed the silence. No rain. Poking his head out, he saw a patch of blue sky appear between the retreating clouds. Seven o'clock, and now Sarah was awake. Packing up their tent, they retraced their steps up the motorway ramp and started hitching.

An hour later, the driver of a large delivery van stopped. Having been on the road since midnight, he was glad of their company, and lent a sympathetic ear to their predicament. His rambling chatter slowly elevated their spirits. He dropped them in London, and lent them the rail fare to Cambridge.

Later that afternoon, they walked home happily through the Saturday tourists thronging the Cambridge colleges. With an enormous sense of relief Owen turned the key in their front door, dropped his backpack, and flopped down in their lounge, physically and emotionally drained.

A rattling from the cat-flap in the kitchen announced the arrival of Natalie, who jumped onto Sarah's lap, her purring and miaowing reaching ecstatic proportions, matched only by Sarah's cooing noises as she stroked and fondled her. After a dutiful rub against Owen, who responded with a stroke and a smile, Natalie returned to the real love of her life. She lay dreamily on Sarah's lap, soaking up the attention so painfully absent for the last week, having scorned the children next door, with their noisy laughs and grabbing hands.

After a shower and change of clothes, Sarah defrosted steak from the freezer, while Owen opened a bottle. Natalie, now bloated with steak, lay watching from the sofa with purring approval, her delicate Siamese frame occasionally shaken by a seismic belch.

"Let's have a totally lazy weekend," Owen said, through a mouthful of Chardonnay, "and come Monday I'll sort out the insurance and banks." He yawned. "Wonder if we'll ever discover what happened to our car?"

"Doubt it - you heard what that policeman said." She paused. "And I for one am not going to mess with those people, whoever they are."

As she prepared the meal, he hovered behind her, glass in hand, speculating on who had set fire to their car, and whether "old Alfred" had anything to do with it.

"I wonder if that shop's on the web?"

Glass in hand, he ambled to his computer. Opening Google, he searched for "Chagford" and "Good Vibrations".

Owen set down his glass and Googled "Wicca".

"Here's their site!"

Sarah drew close behind him, put her arms around his neck, and peered over his shoulder at the web site. There were pages devoted to crystals with all sorts of magical powers, another on "Health Healing", one on jewellery, and another on Tarot cards. He clicked on a page called "Celtic Art", and found pictures of crosses and rings, Irish whistles, prints, and books. He continued browsing the site, while Sarah seemed to lose interest and carried her glass back into the kitchen. Searching more systematically, he started copying addresses into a file, and scribbling notes. He had soon penetrated the outer public pages of the site and was browsing many levels deeper, on pages apparently intended for true believers.

"Sarah! Look!" he shouted.

She returned and saw a collection of patterns on the screen. "What am I supposed to be looking at?"

"Don't you see - these are the patterns we saw on those pebbles! They're Celtic runes."

"Could be. But not the one we saw carved on the stone circle."

"OK - I'll keep searching."

As she fetched her wine from the kitchen, he continued clicking on links. "There's a pile of seriously weird stuff here."

On the screen was a page headed "Dartmoor Wicca".

"Seems to be some sort of religious cult," he said. "As far as I can tell it's all tied up with Earth spirits and things."

Turning away, she picked up the TV guide. "I've heard of Wicca. It's one of these New-Age things, isn't it?" He glanced at her curiously. A tautness in her voice betrayed her studied indifference. He turned back to the screen.

"Yeh - but there's more to it than that," he replied, "This page claims that Wicca was the original pagan religion of Britain. Same as medieval witches."

He continued clicking on links, exploring the site. Drawn back against her will, she began reading the screen over his shoulder. It told the story of a witch burned to death in 1637 in Hertfordshire, referring to her as a martyr, killed by religious intolerance.

He felt her hands gripping his shoulders. When she spoke, her voice was strained. "When I was a kid, witches were evil old hags with black cats who rode on broomsticks. Went around eating children and casting wicked spells. I had a real thing about witches - used to have nightmares about them, didn't like being left alone in case the witches got me. When I grew up I learned they were harmless old ladies who were burnt at the stake for being different. And now you're saying that they were followers of an ancient pagan religion. I'm sorry, but it's giving me the creeps."

He glanced at her curiously, starting to understand her odd behaviour over the last day or two. He turned to her, acknowledging her fear, sharing it.

"Me too. When I was a kid there was a ruined church near our house, with an overgrown graveyard. When I was in the sixth form, I read in the local paper that the police had arrested a local coven of witches. They sacrificed animals there. A few evenings later, I was with a group of friends coming out of the pub." He gazed beyond the computer to that night. "We'd had a few pints, and dared each other to walk through the church. There wasn't any roof, so it was lit inside by moonlight, the floor almost impassable with brambles. We hacked our way through, ever so bold, until we came across a black pentacle drawn on the cleared floor of the church. It had black candle stumps on its points." He paused, his face serious. He turned to her, shaking his head slowly. "Scariest thing I've ever seen."

Returning with an effort to the present, he said in a dismissive voice. "Anyway, we panicked, and bolted. Vowed never to tell a soul about that night."

Sarah's face was serious. "So you've just broken your vow."

He shivered. "We were only kids. Guess we were spooked. It didn't mean anything."

He stood, assuming a "now-I-know-better" smile, and went to pour another glass of wine. By the time he returned, Sarah had moved into the front room to make a fuss of Natalie. He continued clicking through web sites.

"Hey there's a link to stone circles here - Wow! That's him! Come here, Sarah."

With Natalie draped over one shoulder, purring loudly, Sarah looked at the screen.

Standing in the middle of a stone circle was "old Alfred" from the shop in Chagford, surrounded by about 30 people, all dressed in flowing robes. According to the caption, they were "Celebrating Beltane at Scorhill", and the Chagford coven welcomed visiting Wiccans to join their celebrations.

"That is so weird," she exclaimed, a shiver in her voice. "I can't believe we were actually talking to a real witch."

He noticed her tension again, despite her calm facade. Best to play it down. "Who says they're real? Perhaps they're just loony old people playing out their fantasies."

She nodded. "In any case, your friend Alfred seems to be some sort of leader."

oooOooo

An hour later, she served up an excellent Rogan Josh, accompanied by saffron rice, raita, and naan, together with an award-winning Australian Shiraz recommended in the Guardian a couple of weeks earlier. They were home.

Over dinner, they replayed the events of the previous few days, which no longer seemed quite so traumatic. Insurance covered everything they had lost. Apart from control of their lives, that was.

Pouring himself another glass of wine, Owen explained what he had discovered on the web. "I found this great page explaining the origins of Wicca. These people claim that both the Romans and the Christians tried to stamp out their religion, but pockets survived and are now flourishing. They don't have a god as such, but say they draw energy from nature - the Earth, Moon, trees, and so on."

"Find anything about dead rabbits hanging in burnt-out cars?" she asked casually, twirling the wine in her glass.

"I didn't look specifically for that. But I did find a bit claiming there's no such thing as 'black magic'. They said it was propaganda put out by the medieval Christian church."

"Let's see what we can find about dead rabbits in cars," she said.

He followed Sarah to the computer, and watched as she opened Google and typed "Wicca, dead rabbit, hang". None of the entries seemed relevant. She added the word "spell". Still nothing. She tried again with "magic spell, small animal". Nope.

"Try spelling 'Magick' with a k" he suggested, "A lot of the Wiccan pages seem to ..."

She clicked on the first search result: "Rianan's Wiccan Spell Page", whoever Rianan was. Scrolling down, she found the relevant piece.

"Magick Spell for Defeating Enemies"
Warning: This powerful spell should be used only when absolutely necessary, as it involves harming an innocent living creature. While this may be justified in extreme circumstances, for the greater good, it will inevitably bring three-fold harm, which may be severe, to the person who casts

46

the spell. So use this spell only if you are prepared to make a personal sacrifice for a greater cause.

Procedure: Procure a small animal such as a rabbit or cat, in good health, and preferably young. Take it outdoors at sunset and rub it with sprigs of fresh lavender and mint, which you keep till later. Raise the animal in the air towards the East and invoke the Goddess. Shortly before midnight, give it a strong dose of valerian to make it drowsy, and then hang it by its neck together with the sprigs of lavender and mint, and an item belonging to the enemy. If you can hang it inside a closed container belonging to the enemy, or include articles of their clothing, then this spell will be even more effective. Soak all of it in petrol or alcohol (pure wood alcohol is best), and then set fire to it on the stroke of midnight. Immediately afterwards, scatter the mint and lavender leaves that you used earlier to the four quarters, beginning and ending in the North. This spell is said to be very powerful, and immediately drives away or thwarts the intentions of enemies. It will sometimes cause them extreme harm.

Chapter 4
April 2005

On Monday morning, they cycled together into the University. He dumped the insurance papers on his desk in the office shared with Peter Chambers, another biochemistry postdoc. Peter wasn't in yet, lending him some privacy. After shutting the door, he prepared to explain his story to the half-wits who no doubt manned the call centre.

The phone was answered by "Victoria". She listened to his story, clarified a few details, and briskly answered his questions. As soon as they had checked his story with the police, they'd post him the cheque. And did he realise he could hire a car on his insurance? The thought of asking her out flashed across his mind for milliseconds before being dismissed with a shock of guilt. Thanking her more than necessary, he hung up.

He was startled by a voice from behind. "Bad luck, old chap - are they going to pay up?"

"Christ - Peter - what are you doing here - I didn't hear you come in."

"Sorry old boy. You sounded a bit tense. Didn't want to disturb you."

"Bloody hell - were you listening to the entire conversation?"

Peter shrugged. "Couldn't help it. It's a frightfully small office you know. So you had a bit of a tizwoz?"

"Not really. Sort of thing you hear about all the time. Some vandals set fire to our car."

"Rotten luck! You must be devastated. Any leads on the perpetrator?" Typical Peter. Always probing. Looking for a snippet that he might later use to his advantage.

"No - of course not. Probably vandals." And Owen knew from the triumphant smirk on Peter's face that his words had carried some hint, some tremor, that there was more to it than that.

Owen turned back to his desk. "Sorry. Got to get on." A few seconds later, he heard Peter's swivel chair creak. He'd have to leave early and phone the bank from home.

He checked his email. Amongst Viagra advertisements, and generous offers to share Nigerian fortunes, shone an email from Journal of Molecular Biology. It was the referee's report on his paper, the main result from his PhD thesis. Starting with a few simple proteins on the early Earth, his thesis had shown how the first cell structures might have evolved, eventually leading to life as we know it. He wasn't the first person to tread this path, but his steps had been a little firmer, his pace a little longer, than those who had passed this way before. All of whom had hit the same problem: living cells seemed to have appeared almost as soon as the Earth had cooled after its genesis, but the standard model of cell formation was far too slow for that. Something was wrong with the model.

But then Owen had had an idea - one of those moments of inspiration that distinguished great scientists from the merely competent. Perhaps the carbon-rich molecules that arrived on the newly-born Earth were already encoded with protein sequences. If he was right, he might be the first to understand how life formed on Earth.

The idea was exhilarating. Intoxicating. As a child, he had read about the great scientists of history, giants among men, who had prised open the secrets of the Universe. His dream was that, one day, he might join their ranks. Now, reduced to an email attachment, was his first tentative addition to the growing edifice of human knowledge. Once launched into the international scientific literature, it would be scrutinised by some of the finest minds alive. If he was right, this paper would make his name. In the highly-charged competitive world of molecular biology, a postdoc had a window of perhaps three years after PhD in which to make a splash. Fail to do so, and he would end up doing computer support for some midlands IT company. But if the splash was big enough, he'd be offered a coveted tenured position, to spend his life struggling to understand the very origins of life. And even being paid to do it.

After a deep breath, he double-clicked on the referee's report, and scanned through it. The referee was excited by Owen's idea (Awesome!), made a few trivial comments about format (yes - good point - I'll fix that), then delivered one piercing question about the methodology. What? Systematic errors? What's the daft bugger on about? Oh - I see - so if... Christ!

A void opened up around him. His face whitened and his breathing laboured. The referee was right - he had neglected systematic errors. Bloody hell. Surely they couldn't get big enough to matter? But it had to be checked. It would take months to pull out the data and rerun the simulation to look for systematics. Christ Almighty.

"Problem?"

Owen gritted his teeth. "What? No - I've got the referee's report on my paper. Needs a bit more work."

"You sound a touch edgy, old chap - you sure you're all right?"

"Yes, thankyou Peter. Fine."

Owen's self-confidence had evaporated. He started working out which of his data files to pull out of archive, but his mind refused to cooperate. Fleeing from the pain and embarrassment of his carelessness, it wandered back to the events of the last few days and that ghastly web page. He shuddered.

Of course, he didn't believe in that nonsense, the so-called spell. No, that wasn't the problem at all. The problem was that someone out there did believe this stuff and was out to get him. How far did these people go? Were they still on his case? Would they be able to track them down in Cambridge, or only if they returned to Devon? Opening up Google, he found the Wiccan web page with the picture of Alfred in Scorhill Circle. He started following links again.

"I didn't know you were a devotee of Wicca."

Owen spun his head to find Peter standing close behind him, reading the screen over his shoulder.

"For chrissake, Peter, what the hell do you think you're doing, creeping up on me like that? Do you realise what an intrusion of privacy that is?"

"Terribly sorry, dear chap. Didn't realise you were so sensitive about it. But your religious beliefs are your own affair - as I've always said - each to his own."

Turning to face him, Owen spat back, "Look. Wicca is not my religion. I don't have a religion, as you well know. I don't have "beliefs" either. Now leave me alone, can't you?"

"Of course. Mortified to have ruffled your feathers. But you might find it easier to come out rather than hiding these things away, you know."

"Christ almighty! Shut up and go away." Turning back to his desk, he heard Peter leave the office.

Too wound up to work on his paper, he decided to slip out unobserved. He stuffed his papers and laptop into his backpack and crept out of his office.

"Ah. Owen - I was just coming to see you. Have you got a minute, or are you on your way somewhere?"

His heart sank. The Head of Department, Professor Sir Ashley Pusch, bustled towards him.

"Oh -er - hello Ashley - umm - no - on my way to talk to someone over at Applied Maths, actually. It can wait."

"Excellent. Can we talk in your office?" Damn. Something confidential. A problem? Owen returned to his office and Ashley closed the door behind them.

"About the new lectureship. You will of course apply?"

"I was thinking about it." He was desperate for it. It would give him tenure - the freedom to choose his own research, to work on an ambitious project that might take years to reach a conclusion, instead of having to produce papers like clockwork to justify his next grant application.

"Yes - a young man like you. Job for life and all that. Good salary too." Owen hadn't noticed the salary. Presumably a decent living wage, whatever it was.

"You realise this appointment will be an important one for the department. We have to be sure that the successful candidate is well-aligned with our future direction. Someone to whom we can entrust the future. So papers and citations won't be enough. We need to have someone who can, shall we say, embrace the wider issues. Like the relationship of this department to ... certain others. It will need someone prepared to put in the hard graft to achieve that. Are you that person, Owen?"

Where the hell was this leading? Best to be assertive. "Yes, I am, Ashley." But this wasn't sufficient. Pusch was staring at him intently, as if checking that the message had been received. Owen nodded slowly, acknowledging the implications, and said "Yes I see what you mean." He hadn't the foggiest clue what the old coot was on about.

"Excellent. I'm glad we see eye-to-eye. I'll be having lunch with the Vice-Chancellor tomorrow. Of course, it will be an open competitive selection process. But as you and I know, these things have to be worked out carefully. Taking all factors into account. The VC and I are keen that this works out correctly, from a strategic point of view."

Owen wasn't sure whether or not a thankyou was appropriate at this point. Best not to risk it.

"Yes I can see that. Great!"

Bugger. Wrong response. Ashley opened the door, still peering at Owen.

"I'm so glad we had this little chat."

"Yes, thankyou - I really appreciate it." He gave Ashley a knowing smile, held eye-contact for a moment longer than necessary.

Bullseye! Ashley smiled and nodded as he left.

After a safe interval Owen left his office and cycled home. Odd. Sarah's bike leaned next to the front door. Turning the key in the lock, he called out, "Hi Love!"

No response. She was lying on the couch, teary-eyed, stroking Natalie who was draped across her chest.

He rushed over and put his arm around Sarah. "What's the matter?"

"This."

A crumpled piece of paper, with a letterhead: "University of Cambridge, Department of Archaeology".

He scanned it.

"Dear Ms. Ashworth...review your progress ...failed to meet milestones... unsatisfactory ... review your PhD candidature ... requested to meet a departmental advisory panel...Yours Sincerely, Karen Lightfoot, Head of Department"

"What the hell? Didn't Phil tell you last week how well you were doing?"

"Huh. He's just my supervisor. What would he know? He was like `Don't worry. They do this all the time'. But you know what it means don't you?"

He did. He'd seen the other side of the fence, while helping supervise a graduate student who simply wasn't up to it. The student had been "reviewed", then told to write up a thesis for a Master's degree instead of a Doctorate, thus evicting the hapless young man from academia. The letter was pretty damning.

"But I don't understand!" wailed Sarah, causing Natalie to jump off in alarm. "It's so screwed. I am doing so well. I came top in the year in the coursework. And I've already got a first-author paper submitted. How many first-year PhD students can say that? It's ridiculous. And I got awesome comments on my colloquium last month. Like not just friends, but faculty too. Even that visiting professor, asking for a copy of my lit review so he could give it to his students. Everybody says I'm way ahead of the other PhD students in my year. And my project's pretty well on schedule, and everything!"

She turned to him, shaking her balled fists in frustration. "It makes no sense at all! It's totally stupid!"

He checked the words on the paper again, and laid it aside. It was pretty damning. The paper signified that, in the opinion of a senior member of the department, she didn't have what it took. Regardless of the outcome of the review, or of what she achieved, or whether she actually got her PhD, her chances of getting a post-doctoral fellowship were now small. Her references, both formal and informal, would always be a shade less than enthusiastic. In this competitive field, anything less than unequivocal support from her department was tantamount to rejection.

"Listen, love - don't worry about it - as Phil said, this is probably a formality."

She glared at him. "Don't patronise me. I wasn't born yesterday."

"I'm only trying to help!" he flung back, stung by her accusation.

"Whatever. Go away if that's the best you can do."

Wordless, he stormed into the kitchen, and stared out of the window. Probably hadn't been the right thing to say. This was a real crisis for her - no point him adding to her problems by taking offence.

Returning, he saw her face was carefully arranged, her outburst tidied away. As he sat down, she allowed him to hug her. Her composure broke again. Grabbing the paper, she screwed it into a ball and flung it at the window.

"God knows where this came from," she exploded, "Apart from the people at the colloquium, the only person who really knows how I'm doing is Phil. He might be a crap supervisor but he wouldn't do this."

Pulling her close to him, he stroked her head, feeling her anger subside. Hesitating, he broached one of the two explanations simmering in his mind. "Sarah, do you think... could this have anything to do with that stupid Wicca stuff?"

Doubtfully, she raised her head. "It did cross my mind."

"Not the so-called magic, I mean..."

"Of course not," she snapped, a little too hurriedly.

"...but the fact that someone may be trying to harm us."

Shifting in her seat, she spoke in a low whisper, as if ashamed to voice her thoughts. "Do you really think so, Owen? I did wonder, but it's too soon. It was only three days ago when we found our car burnt out."

"But six days ago when we argued with that guy in the shop."

"True." She broke into an unconvincing laugh. "But Owen - can you see a bunch of fanatical Devon yokels having any influence in a Cambridge Archaeology Department?"

54

"I suppose you're right. There must be a simpler explanation. Have you upset anyone in your department?"

She shook her head, but he could see her mind was elsewhere. Beneath her cool facade hid a little girl, still frightened of witches and spells. He wanted to protect and coddle her, but she resisted, locked up in her mind, too private even for him.

"What about your head of department? What does she think of you?"

She wrenched her mind back to the present. "Professor Lighfoot? She wanted me to work on her stupid stone circle project. Can't be too bad if the head of department wants you as her student, can it?"

"So why didn't you work with her?"

"She wanted me to work on pollen counts, trying to work out what time of the year the circles were built. Duh... as if. Totally boring. I wanted to follow my own ideas on rituals in stone circles, and Phil was happy to supervise me on that. It seemed to piss her off a bit. But not enough to do this, surely?"

"You sure?"

"Well...She did go on at me for weeks about it, trying to get me to change my mind. Told me I had made a bad choice. But a professor's not going to fail a student for not working with her, is she?"

Probably not. There had to be a more prosaic explanation for the letter. Who in her department might have triggered it? He thought back to the time when he had met her supervisor and colleagues at a garden party at the Back of Trinity, on the long green lawn sloping down to the river. One of those glorious warm summer evenings when you had to practice the art, so well-taught in Cambridge, of balancing a Chardonnay and canapé in one hand while shaking hands with the other. Nobody that evening seemed especially memorable, or antagonistic, and they had spent much of the time talking to her friend Kim.

oooOooo

Sarah passed the rest of the afternoon vacillating between shades of anger, indignation, and self-pity, with an undercurrent of some emotion that Owen couldn't identify. He resigned himself to spending the evening as her sounding board and sympathetic ear, and had to admit to relief when she decided to go to bed early with a headache.

Too emotionally exhausted to work, he occupied the rest of the evening browsing web pages about Wicca. Curious. Beneath the adolescent fantasies and hippy weirdos ran an undercurrent of something like a serious religion. But no sign of structure. No high priests. No organised church.

The US Wiccans had an organisation called "Pagan Pride", and had even persuaded the military to recognise Wicca as a legitimate religion for its soldiers, who were thus provided with Wiccan chaplains. Only in America. But they claimed it to be the fastest-growing religion in the US.

Back to the British sites. Nothing more than a loose association of individuals and small groups following a mixed bag of vaguely related beliefs about Earth spirits. The more he read, the less he felt threatened. Just a motley crowd of people with an incoherent belief system based, so they claimed, on that of pre-Christian witches.

Spells didn't appear to be very important. They were certainly there, but seemed to be a peripheral part of the religion. Instead, most of the stuff on the web was preoccupied with ceremonies and rituals for self-enlightenment.

They didn't even seem to have anything like a Bible. But there were a couple of obscure references to something called "The Book of One". This legendary book appeared to be a written account of the core of their religion. But was it real? Or just wishful thinking? They said it was centuries old, perhaps even millennia. Assuming, of course, that it existed at all. There seemed to be an unnamed group of fanatics who had dedicated their lives to finding it. Amazing what people will believe.

oooOooo

The next morning he stayed at home. After a series of phone calls, a new set of credit cards and ATM cards were in the post, and a new driving licence was being issued. He cycled to the car rental place on Hills Road, and hired a small hatchback for two weeks, courtesy of his insurance company. With the seat folded down, his bike just fitted in the back.

For the next two weeks, both he and Sarah were preoccupied with work - he on the corrections to his paper, she on finalising hers for submission to the journal. They worked solidly through the weekend, oblivious to a Royal wedding that flung the media into hysteria. On the Tuesday before the review board meeting, she emailed her paper to the journal, leaving a little over two days to prepare for the review board. Each night she worked in the Department until the early hours of the morning, and then set the alarm for seven.

On Thursday afternoon she phoned him at his office, announcing in a shaky voice, "I'm so bloody stressed. Let's go away for the weekend. As soon as the review finishes tomorrow."

He considered it. His paper was almost there, so he'd been planning to work over the weekend. On the other hand, it would be good to get away, and no doubt she needed it. "OK, love, where?"

"Somewhere where there aren't any professors of archaeology. An open space with clean air where we can walk all day. Dartmoor would be good. But I think we should stay away from there for a bit."

He agreed. "How about Wales? Or the Lake District?"

"Too crowded. How about that cliff-walk around the North coast of Cornwall?"

"Great idea. Let's do it. I'll ask the kids next door to feed Natalie."

He remembered a web page he had seen. "There's a museum of witchcraft in Tintagel, right on the cliff-walk. We could drop in there and find out a bit more about this stuff. Without getting involved, of course."

Chapter 5
April 2005

The Review took place the next morning behind the locked doors of the Departmental meeting room. He waited outside, ready to console or celebrate as required. Eventually she emerged, white faced.

"How did it go?"

She shook her head. "Don't ask."

"Sarah, my love - I'm so sorry." He wrapped himself around her, and felt her squeezing against him, draining the tension that had accumulated within her. She pulled away from him.

"It could have been worse, I suppose. They haven't actually cancelled my PhD candidature, but they've put me on probation. Gave me a totally full-on grilling." Her anger flared. "And Phil didn't support me - like they had got to him. Couldn't even look me in the eye. God knows what was going on in there, but I don't think it had much to do with me. I was merely a pawn in someone's stinking departmental political manoeuvres."

His arm around her shoulders, Owen guided her towards the car. She seemed to be coping by making out it was someone else's fault. Maybe it was. He remembered Ashley Pusch once crushing a competitor by publicly denouncing the work of his student. The student lost his PhD candidature and Ashley won the position he coveted. The student, a promising young geneticist with a good first, abandoned his aspirations and left academia, disillusioned and rudderless, to work for a real-estate company. One more casualty in the trail of destruction left by Ashley and his ilk, as they clambered over each other in pursuit of prestigious positions and academic honours.

"Did you manage to hold your ground? Tell them about your referees' reports?"

She nodded. "I think I gave as good as could be expected, given that I wasn't actually privy to what was behind it all. It was so Kafka. Bastards."

"But you're still doing your PhD?"

"I suppose so. Come on. Let's get out of this place. I need to breathe fresh air, run as far away as I can from those pompous dorks."

The rental car was already packed, and minutes later they were heading out of Cambridge. They stopped only once, to refuel themselves and the car, at a shabby motorway service area outside Bristol, and later that afternoon pulled into the car park of an old pub. After checking in at the bar, they strolled through the town of Tintagel in the early evening sun, their limbs recovering from six hours of driving. The street was lined with New Age shops selling Celtic jewellery, crystals, and purported souvenirs of King Arthur. They sat on a crumbling stone wall facing Tintagel Castle, watching the waves crashing far below, feeling the salty up-draught exorcising the stench of motorways and PhD reviews.

He took a deep breath. "Don't you wish you could live in a place like this?"

She smiled and swung her feet. "I guess that's why King Arthur built the castle here."

"If he existed. Probably a figment of propaganda put about by some post-Roman warlord. All those tales of Camelot, Excalibur, Guinevere seem to be based on a hotch-potch of unrelated myths and legends."

A wave crashed into the cliffs below, ejecting a shower of gulls high into the sky, screeching at the intrusion. The gulls swooped and wheeled in the air currents, eventually descending to their accustomed paths skimming the waves. A tourist bus sounded its horn in the distance, summoning the day trippers back to their fish and chips motels.

An undernourished tabby kitten appeared and jumped up next to Sarah. She seemed to attract cats out of thin air, and it was now revelling in her attention as she chucked it under the chin. Its purr throbbed deeply in her hands, filling her with a sense of contentment, evaporating her stress. Her focus drifted from the purr to the fresh salt air, the distant sea horizon, and Owen, her bedrock, beside her. Around her towered ancient stones which had seen great civilisations come and go, casting the drama over her PhD into a distant perspective, an insignificant departmental squabble. And yet. Something dark, older than these stones, hovered menacingly just beyond the edge of her psyche. Something she couldn't quite put her finger on.

"Owen, why is there a witchcraft museum in King Arthur's birthplace? What's the connection?"

His brow furrowed. "When Arthur dies, he is taken by boat to the mystic island of Avalon by the sorceress Morgana, who's probably the same person as the Wiccan mother-goddess. The Arthurian stories seem to be based on Wiccan mythology."

She smirked. "You suddenly know a lot about this stuff."

He smiled sheepishly back. "Oh - just poking around on the web."

Her soft brown eyes laughed at him, but underneath were shades of tender concern. "Hmm. You shouldn't believe everything you read. How much time have you been spending on the web, anyway?"

"Too much, I guess."

She suddenly became serious and stopped stroking the kitten. "You know I said I wanted to keep away from all this Wiccan stuff?"

"Yes," he said slowly, wondering where this was leading, "We don't need to go to the witchcraft museum if you're getting cold feet about it."

"No - it's not that. Actually it's the opposite. I'd like to go. I think it would be pretty good to get to the bottom of this. You know, our car being burnt and everything. And all that childhood scary stuff? I've got to get over it. Like I want some answers."

Owen smiled. This was more like his Sarah. He grabbed her hand and pecked her on the cheek. "You're on. We'll do it."

"Come on," she laughed, "Let's go back and get some dinner. I'm starving."

As they jumped off the wall, sending the kitten scurrying away, she slid her hand into the back pocket of his jeans and squeezed. He responded likewise, and they walked back into Tintagel like any two young lovers, arm in arm, a smirk playing on their faces telling the world that they were complete, with no need for anyone else.

Entering the main room, they paused to let their eyes adjust to the dark interior. The room was suffused with that comfortable musty old pub smell engendered by centuries of spilt beer and shared blood. Thick oak beams lined the ceiling, so low in places that Owen had to duck. Along the ancient wooden bar were ranged old-fashioned pumps of Real Ale, along with the usual selection of gassy Australian fizz. A cheerful, florid-faced man behind the bar swiped Owen's credit card and poured them a pint of "Doom Bar" and a half of "Scrumpy Jack". From the menu on the wall they both selected the cottage pie with local vegetables, and sat at a table in the corner.

At one end of the bar huddled a group of middle-aged men in shabby working clothes discussing politics in a thick Cornish dialect. At the other was a solitary sleaze-bag with a braying laugh and a London accent who called everyone "matey" and was carrying on a loud one-sided conversation with the barman.

Seeing a customer enter, the barman gratefully seized the opportunity to escape. "Is that so, sir? If you'll excuse me while I serve this gentleman."

The newcomer's loud neo-gothic clothes failed to conceal his shyness and discomfort. His arms were tattooed with strange symbols, and he stuttered as he ordered.

To Owen's surprise, Sarah stood and went to the bar. "Can I have a packet of crisps, please?"

Owen's straining ears failed to detect a single word of her conversation with the Goth, who responded brightly, and their discussion became animated. What on Earth had possessed her to pick up this loser? What could they possibly have in common? She brought him back to the table.

"Owen, this is Nigel. Just telling him about our Wiccan group at Cambridge."

Owen's flash of astonishment was immediately replaced by a forced smile of welcome, and a glance at Sarah to confirm receipt of her message.

"Oh yes. Right. Glad to meet you Nigel."

They shook hands awkwardly.

"Nigel's waiting for a friend, so I thought he might as well hang out with us."

"Er - yeh - excellent. So are you from round here, Nigel?"

But Nigel clammed up again in Owen's presence. When Sarah made furtive sweeping movements with her eyes, Owen stared at her and then, understanding, downed his beer. "Think I'll get another. Can I get either of you anything?"

"I think we should celebrate meeting a fellow-Wiccan. How about a wee dram of that malt whisky for Nigel and me. Make it a double." Startled by her odd request, Owen registered her almost imperceptible nod, and swallowed his exclamation.

He waited for the beer and whisky at the bar.

"Looks like your girlfriend has taken a shine to Dracula there, Matey".

Owen responded with a withering stare which, too subtle for its target, elicited no more than a wink. Carrying the drinks to the table, he saw Sarah and Nigel had drawn closer together, and her face told Owen to stay away.

"Umm. I have to get something from my room. Will you excuse me a minute?"

He sat on the bed in his room. Ten minutes should do it. How had she known this guy was a Wiccan? And how come she was blowing hot and cold? One minute avoiding the subject of witchcraft, the next chatting up some neo-pagan geek? He lay on his back counting the minutes, worrying about Sarah.

He returned to the bar as the meals were being served. Nigel and Sarah were deep in animated conversation, but stopped as Owen joined them.

Nigel turned nervously to Owen. "Er... I better go and see where my f-f-friend's got to."

"It was awesome talking to you. I hope we meet again," said Sarah. And then to the astonishment of both Nigel and Owen, she kissed Nigel on the cheek. His face flushed scarlet as he backed away, knocking over a stool.

As she waved goodbye to him, he waved back hesitantly, closing the door behind him.

"What the hell was all that about?"

"Didn't you see his tattoos?" she asked, in an excited sotto voce.

"I saw he had some. That's what Goths do."

Her eyes were bright, her face flushed. "Owen - one was a pentacle, meaning he was a Wiccan, or at least a wannabe Wiccan. But what really got me was that he had that symbol we saw carved on the stone circle on Dartmoor. Remember? The circle with a crescent either side of it."

"And?"

"Apparently it's called `the Lunar Triple Goddess'."

She paused, awaiting his reaction, unable to understand why he wasn't as spun up as she was.

"Go on."

"It represents the waxing, waning, and full moon, and also the three ages of a human."

"So why did he have it on his arm?"

"It was his mother's symbol. She was Wiccan too. And her mother, and her grandmother, and her great-grandmother, and so on."

Owen thought back to the web pages. "But... this Wicca stuff started in the fifties. You're saying his great-grandmother and so on were doing Wicca before then?"

"I think it depends what you mean by Wicca. They called themselves witches." She said the last word in a low voice, as if accompanied by a roll of drums, and her face carried a sort of horrified fascination as she said it.

"You're kidding."

She lowered her voice. "He told me that in Cornwall the pagan religion never really died out - it just went into hiding. Occasionally someone would get caught out and be burnt as a witch, but on the whole they were left alone. They were able to come out when Wicca became popular a few decades ago. He said that round here there are as many Wiccans as Christians, but most of the older folk still keep their religion to themselves because of prejudice. Younger people feel more able to come out."

Owen was intrigued. "What about the pentacle?"

"He said the pentacle was to identify him to other Wiccans. Apparently most of them have one tattooed on their arms. When he asked why I didn't, I told him that persecution is a problem in Cambridge. Which he seemed to buy. Probably never been outside Cornwall."

"Didn't he suspect anything? How come he was so open with you?"

She cocked her head and winked flirtatiously at him. "There are some advantages to being female, you know. Especially with a gawky boy who's probably never had much luck with girls."

As they ate their meal she explained the meanings of the other symbols on Nigel's arm - a wheel, a cauldron, and an assortment of runic letters.

oooOooo

Helped by several pints of the wonderful ale and a hard days driving, Owen was asleep as soon as he lay down.

He found himself back on Dartmoor with Sarah, measuring a stone. He noticed a young girl standing in the centre of the circle, smiling at him, her blonde hair rippling in the breeze, her clear blue eyes almost too large for her face. Entranced, he put aside the tape measure and walked towards her, but, running around him, she skipped off, laughing. As he reached the centre she circled him, close, teasing his clumsy attempts to grab at the flimsy skirt that brushed his hands. Sarah was calling from afar, summoning him back to work.

He called back "Just a minute, love, I'll be right with you."

The girl slowed, turned to him. Her face, lit by the morning sun, radiated innocence, while her knowing gaze penetrated deep within him, knew him, summoned him, offered herself to him. He ached for her, and yet she remained out of reach. She stopped moving, and approached him, swaying seductively. Surely she was too young, too unworldly, to move like that?

"You poor boy," her voice sang. "You poor, silly, innocent, boy. You've no idea, have you?" She kissed him on the forehead. In her hands were two sprays of a pungent herb, which she placed in his hair. He melted, his arms clutching her tiny waist, not wanting to move his eyes from her breasts, his hands not daring touch.

Sarah was yelling at him from far away. Just a minute, love...

Come home with me. Taking him by the hand, her face promising everything, she led him to the kistvaen. They stepped down into it, and she lay on her back on the floor of the grave. Surrounded by cold granite slabs, he lowered himself on hands and knees above her. Sarah's cries had become faint, as from a distant world, "Owen, no, help me, the witches ... please don't leave me."

He knelt over the girl, a fragrance of wild spring flowers, and kissed her inviting lips.

A grinding sound from above, a darkening sky, and the slab of granite slid over the top of the kistvaen, covering him. In the shocking blackness he panicked, scrambling. The girl was gone. Nothing below him but cold rock, a few pebbles and dead flowers. He arched his back to lift the stone lid, but it wouldn't budge. He rolled over, placing his feet and hands squarely on the slab above, pushing until his arms ached. Something moved, very slightly. He pushed again, harder, straining every sinew. With a crack the slab beneath him gave way and he was falling into the pitch-black abyss below. His hands flailed but there was nothing but empty darkness into which he fell, ever accelerating, ever screaming, ashes to ashes, dust to dust.

He sat up, shivering, drenched with sweat. Sarah was still asleep.

oooOooo

The next morning they asked the way to the witchcraft museum.

"I wouldn't waste your time going there," replied the publican, an edge to his voice, "Bunch of weirdos." Owen, curious, gently started probing. But the publican curtly gave them directions, and went back to his job.

Walking down to the harbour, they found an ancient whitewashed building, like an old barn but with black-framed windows set in thick stone walls. Outside hung a black wrought-iron frame bearing a white sign with black gothic lettering: "Tintagel Museum of Witchcraft".

Sarah paused, and pulled Owen towards her. "Remember, Owen. Not a word about stone circles. Or the car. Or that spell. We're just a couple of tourists. Right?"

"Yes of course," he replied, irritated, "we've already been through all that." Why was she making such a big deal of it? It was only a museum, for chrissake.

They entered to the clang of an old-fashioned bell, and waited obediently at a sign saying, "Entrance £5. Children £3. The museum may not be suitable for young children. If in doubt, please enquire."

A man wearing jeans and a thick sweater, topped by a bushy grey beard, bustled in. He looked sixty but had the bearing of a younger man. His rheumy blue eyes seemed to tunnel down inside you and laugh at what they found there.

"Can I help you?" Something appeared to be amusing him. Owen found he vaguely disliked the man for no good reason, except that he was probably one of these Wiccan nutcases.

"Umm... Two tickets to the museum, please," answered Owen, digging to find his wallet.

"Yes of course. That will be ten pounds." What the hell was so funny? "Thankyou. Take your time going round the museum, and then I'll be here to answer your questions." How did he know they had questions?

They entered through a red velvet curtain, and found themselves in a small room lined with glass cabinets, containing all the paraphernalia of mediaeval witchcraft. There were church parish records describing the seizure and burning of witches. Bits of animal floated in glass jars. The largest contained a baby pig with two heads, evidently considered to be sacred in some obscure way.

A large black cauldron sat in the corner, surrounded by rusty knives, wooden spoons, and glass jars containing unrecognisable substances. An old book was open on the table next to the cauldron. The handwritten text was indecipherable, and accompanied by strange illustrations of pentacles and other symbols. Owen grinned. Cute. Almost convincing. He studied the captions, and learnt that the book and tools had been recovered from old houses. The book was dated to the sixteenth century.

It dawned on him slowly. This was the real thing.

They continued their tour. There were accounts of men and women through the ages who had lived and died for their religion, condemned by Romans and then Christians to be outcasts on the edge of society. Vilified, hunted down, and burnt. There were memorials to witches who had died for their faith, and lurid accounts of midnight festivals, naked in the moonlight. There were even sixteenth-century sex-toys. He imagined the medieval Church's reaction to those.

They moved to the next section. It told how witches were hunted until their religion was almost extinct. It included an 1803 newspaper report of a priest who had died in a house fire in Lancashire, the night before he was due to testify in court against a witch. His dog was found hanging by its neck from a window of the burnt-out house. The court dismissed the charges against the witch through lack of evidence, and the newspaper suggested that the priest's death was suicide, although the local constable claimed it was an "accident". Owen paled as he read it. The exhibit included a portrait of an old woman, said to be the witch in the trial. She stared out of the display at him, smiling across two centuries, triumphant.

"Have you read this?" he whispered, shocked, to Sarah, standing behind him.

A voice replied, deep and rasping, as if from the grave. "Yes. Not a good idea to upset these people, is it?"

Owen spun round in horror, to see that Sarah was at the next display on the opposite side of the room, and that the shape behind him was an elderly tourist wearing a checked jacket and carrying an umbrella.

"Sorry, I thought you were talking to me," the man faltered in his gravelly voice.

"Umm... No. No, I'm sorry. I thought you were my girlfriend."

"No I'm not...," he smiled weakly.

Each of them, flustered and embarrassed, returned to read the display. The man, watching him warily out of the corner of his eye, skimmed through the remaining displays and disappeared out of the gallery.

"Sarah. Come over here - look at this! So spooky."

Following his eyes, she put her arm around his waist. "I know. I saw it earlier." She hesitated, wide-eyed. "Did you think it was a bit like... y'know?"

"Our car?"

Her answering shrug was more of a question than a statement. She waited, grim faced, for his reaction. He decided that there was only one possible response.

"Nah." He replied, "Totally different. Probably just a coincidence."

"Mmm. Probably. That's what I thought." The shutters had gone up, and her face was a perfect replica of casual indifference.

He glanced at her, concerned. Her facade may have been carefully rebuilt with weapons-grade armour plating, but he could still see the chinks in it. Maybe he shouldn't have brought her here.

As Sarah hovered behind him, reading over his shoulder, her hands around his waist, he continued reading how witchcraft was thought to have died out, but was revived in the 1930's by Gerald Gardner, a man now revered as the father of Wicca, who claimed to have drawn his knowledge from ancient witchcraft sources.

"Bloody hell!" exclaimed Owen, "Did you know witchcraft was illegal in Britain until 1951? It says here that the last witch in Britain was prosecuted in 1944!"

They emerged from the last gallery through another curtain into the entrance room of the museum. He felt sobered, chastised. Still didn't believe this stuff, of course, any more than he believed in a Christian or Muslim God, but he was starting to respect these people who had clung at such cost to their beliefs. Sarah's fluctuating reactions, on the other hand, worried him.

"Did you find what you were after?" asked the old man.

Startled, Owen stared at him, wordless.

"Yes thankyou. Very interesting," prattled Sarah.

The museum owner looked at Owen. "What would you like to ask me?"

"I'm not sure", he replied, cautiously. Something about this man unnerved him. "We were curious to find out about Wicca."

"Wonderful. Tell me what you'd like to know."

Owen hesitated. "Well, for a start, how much does modern Wicca actually have to do with traditional witchcraft? I've heard that Gardner made up a lot of the stuff."

The man smiled. "Maybe. He was a wonderful man, even if he wasn't always honest about his sources. But modern Wicca isn't based on what Gardner alone said, you know. There are covens around here over a thousand years old." He shook his head. "Even Gardner didn't know about them. Nowadays some feel able to come out and proclaim their religion, try to set the Faith back on the true path."

"Doesn't that cause friction within Wicca?" Sarah asked, her face unreadable even to Owen.

The old man studied her face before replying. "Of course, my dear. Like any religion, Wicca has its factions and sects. Extreme Gardnerites who won't have anything to do with traditional witchcraft. Hereditary witches who won't have anything to do with Gardner's Wicca. That sort of thing."

"And where do you stand on that?" she asked.

He paused, taken aback by her directness. "You know, young lady, I'd say that the museum and I represent mainstream Wicca. We follow Gardner's teachings, but we're always keen to absorb and learn from the traditional witchcraft covens."

Owen peered at him curiously. "So you're like a priest?"

"Well - I suppose so - you could say that. Wicca is my faith. In my own humble way, I help it grow and flourish. Look, if you're interested, why don't you join me for coffee and I can explain. I've some old books that will interest you."

"We can't stay long - we're planning to walk along the cliff-path today," interjected Sarah.

Owen stared at her, torn between protecting her and finding out about Wicca. Curiosity won. "I'd be really interested."

The quirky smile had returned to the man's face. "I could do with a break anyway, and there aren't any other visitors. Let's grab a coffee."

He put a sign on the door saying "Back in ten minutes." and locked it after them.

He introduced himself as Aleister, and led them towards a cluster of whitewashed cottages.

"All these witch-burnings in the middle ages..." started Owen.

"Yes?"

"So the witches were a small minority cult, persecuted by everyone around them? "

"I don't think so. Not really. Many still believed in the old faith. Do you know, probably half the village still secretly observed bits of the old religion. The ruling classes didn't even suspect that all this was going on. The only people who got burnt were those who flaunted it."

Sarah watched Owen, who had once told her that the only way you really understood something was when you have a good argument about it. Expose all the fallacies, all the shoddy thinking. Leaving behind nothing but pure reason and hard fact. Maybe he should have been a lawyer. She saw he had that look on his face.

"I find that hard to believe," challenged Owen, true to form.

"Have you been to Exeter cathedral?" asked Aleister, unexpectedly.

"Yes - it's a beautiful old church," replied Owen, uncertain of where this was going. Sarah could see his mind spinning, trying to anticipate Aleister's next move.

"Did you know that amongst the cathedral carvings are over fifty statues of the pagan spirits and their God and Goddess?"

"Really?"

"And under the Dean's misericord is carved a "Green Man" - a pagan fertility spirit. Go and have a look next time you're there. It's no secret."

Owen had fallen silent, assessing and assimilating this information. Sarah, who had been trailing behind, interposed herself between them, giving her Owen time to think while she joined his side.

"But why was it tolerated by the church, when they were burning witches?" she demanded.

"If you want to replace the old religion by the new, my dear, you can't just tell people to deny their cherished beliefs. They'd never convert if they had to give up their festivals. Instead, Christianity tried to absorb the old pagan religion. It was still tolerated when the cathedral was built - the witch-burnings didn't start till much later."

Despite objecting to being called "my dear", Sarah saw that the old man knew his stuff. She glanced at Owen, still deep in thought. All three fell silent.

On the other side of the road, an old man sat on the seawall, fishing. As they passed, he turned, saw Aleister, and spat messily on the ground. Aleister seemed not to notice. Sarah and Owen exchanged glances, said nothing.

"Can I ask you something that's bugging me?" started Owen as Aleister opened the gate to his cottage.

"Fire away, dear boy."

"Why were you laughing at us when we first came in?"

He smiled. "I'm sorry. I didn't mean to give that impression. But it was obvious that you were on a mission, determined to learn about witchcraft. A bit different from most of my visitors - seaside tourists hoping to be shocked."

"Why was it obvious?"

"Being a Wiccan isn't only about magick. It's about being in tune with your surroundings, being sensitive to small changes in the world, in plants, animals, and people. Wiccans are acute observers of humans. I saw you walking down the hill to the museum, and there was purpose in your stride. Your eyes lit up when you saw the sign, as if this was going to answer a burning question for you. And then you paused before coming in, heads together, agreeing on what you would say. And when you entered I could see you weren't Wiccans..."

"How?" interrupted Sarah

"Ah. We have ways." He winked.

"And you invite all your visitors over for coffee?" There was a doubting edge to her voice.

He turned to face her. "No. I don't. But I love to talk about the Faith to people who are genuinely interested. If you're uncomfortable, my dear, then please don't feel I'm pressuring you."

"No you're not," interjected Owen, "Please, I'd love to hear more about it."

Aleister raised his eyebrows at Sarah.

"Yeh... whatever." Her wide-eyed glance at Owen contrasted with her casual shrug.

Aleister fiddled with the solid locks at the door, while Owen gazed at the beautiful old cottage, freshly whitewashed, the window frames lovingly restored and painted, its prettiness marred only by a sheet of plywood covering a window.

"Got a brick through the window last night," explained Aleister. "You wouldn't believe it, would you? People still frightened of witchcraft. In this day and age!"

Sarah looked at the ground.

Leading them into the house, he motioned them to sit at the kitchen table, while he busied himself with the coffee. The room was clean but modest, with furniture and a carpet that had seen better days. One side of the room was lined with shelves supporting a huge and motley collection of books.

72

Most seemed to be about witchcraft, while others covered environmental issues, folklore, history, even geology. On the lowest shelf were ancient books with unreadable titles on their leather-bound spines.

"Do you own the museum?" asked Owen.

"Legally, yes, though I prefer to think of myself as the custodian. It was passed on to me, you see. One day I will pass it on to my successor."

"How did you get involved?"

Aleister hesitated. "I was Gardner's protégé. I grew up in Fordingbridge. He lived nearby, you know. Lots of people round there took part in traditional witchcraft ceremonies. My parents included. I was more interested in rock music and motorbikes, and witchcraft was boring and old-fashioned - old people's stuff. Until one evening Gerald Gardner came to dinner with my parents, and I was hooked. I realised afterwards it was no accident - we'd been destined to meet."

Seeing the scepticism on their faces, he smiled. "Whether or not you believe in Wicca, Gardner was a charismatic man, who talked about changing the world, re-aligning it to the ancient Wiccan beliefs."

"You became his student?" asked Sarah.

"Not at first. I was after a job at the time, and Gardner offered me one. Later he moved to Hertfordshire, then to the Isle of Man. I followed him, first as his assistant, and then as his disciple. I came to worship him."

The phone rang.

"Excuse me." He picked it up. "Good morning. Aleister here."...

"Wednesday evening? Yes I think I'm free. They'll want a candle-lit tour, I suppose."...

"That's wonderful. Will they have an interpreter?"...

"Terrific. I think that's fine with me, but my diary's in the museum so I'll phone you back after I've checked."...

"Good. Talk to you later then."

He hung up, and swivelled back to them. "Coach load of Japanese tourists. Pays the bills. Where were we?"

"You were telling us about Gardner."

"Oh yes. After he died, we discovered that many of Gardner's "ancient secrets" were plain fiction. He had such hubris, that man. Which doesn't diminish what he was trying to do. Not one iota. I've spent my life following his path, although perhaps sticking to the truth a little more closely. I've tried to learn from the ancient covens, to return Wicca to the original roots of witchcraft."

He stood up, moved to the bookshelf, and ran his hand over the ancient spines before selecting one. Placing it on the table, he opened it at an illegible page of faded handwriting. "This is a Grimoire from the fifteenth century. It seems to have been written by several different witches. Judging by the dialect and the herbs, I think it's from round here."

"What language is it in?"

"Old English, with bits of Latin."

"So what does this page say?"

"This is a binding spell to keep someone away from you."

As Owen gently took the opened book from Aleister, he shuddered. A real spell-book used by fifteenth-century witches? "You're kidding! Eye of newt and all that stuff?"

Aleister grinned. "Yes - all that stuff."

"It must be worth a fortune," breathed Owen, showing it to Sarah, who shuddered for an eyeblink before asking casually, "What about black magic spells?" Aleister shifted uncomfortably. "There may be one or two. But nobody would use them nowadays, my dear. Modern Wiccans don't have any truck with that stuff."

Leaning towards him, she asked, "Really? Nobody would use harmful spells?"

He avoided her inquisitorial stare. "Well, I can't say 'nobody'. Any community, any religion, has its fanatic fringe."

They lapsed into silence, and Sarah sat in one of the old armchairs, nodding thoughtfully.

"So what brought you two here?" asked Aleister suddenly.

Owen looked at the old man. He clearly knew more than he was telling. Was he somehow involved in the attack

74

on their car? Doubtful. Didn't seem the type. Too innocent, too trusting not to be trusted himself.

"We're interested in stone circles..."

Sarah glared at him. "Owen, no..."

He shrugged apologetically at her and continued. "...and found a symbol carved on one. We think it's Wiccan. The Triple Goddess?"

Sarah arms and legs folded decisively, her jaw set firm.

Pretending not to notice her movement, Owen continued. "So what's Wicca got to do with stone circles?"

Aleister studied Sarah's face before returning his attention to Owen, meeting his questioning eyes. Drumming his fingers, he stood abruptly and crossed to the bookshelf, searching. His fingers pulled out a faded red cloth-bound book and placed it on the table. After hunting down his glasses, he started reading.

"At the Reikin, the Goddess kisses the Earth, rewarding the good, and punishing the bad, measure for measure. Where her lips touch the ground, the rocks themselves rise up to greet her, forming a sacred circle so pure that, whilst a Reikin will traverse it, a lifetime may be measured along its perimeter, no more, no less."

He put the book down and peered at Owen over the top of his glasses. "Mean anything to you?"

"So it's saying that the Goddess created the stone circles?"

"Isn't it beautiful? Came across it the other day."

"Where's it from?"

"It's a passage from an old witchcraft book. I don't know whether it's important or not, but I'd love to know what a Reikin is. Anyway, now you know how stone circles were created." His eyes were laughing at them again.

Owen decided to trust him. "The thing is, someone hung an animal in our car and set fire to it. We think they were Wiccans."

Receiving a furious kick from Sarah, he turned to remonstrate with her, justifying himself. As they argued in low voices, Aleister stood and walked to the window, staring out. When he turned to them, his face was hard-set, his mocking expression evaporated. "That's bad. That's really bad. What did you do to upset them?"

Sarah stood and made for the door. "I think we should go. Thankyou for the..."

"No!" hissed Owen. "I'm sorry, Sarah, but this is important, and we should listen to what Aleister can tell us."

He faced Aleister again, while Sarah hovered in the doorway, uncertain. "We didn't mean to do anything, but they may have been upset because we were studying the stone circles on Dartmoor. You see, we're trying to understand how..."

"Christ Almighty!" yelled Sarah as she stormed out, slamming the door behind her.

"Is she alright?" asked Aleister.

"She'll get over it. We'd agreed not to talk about this. But then you seemed so helpful and knowledgeable..."

Aleister interrupted. "You've got a big problem, dear boy. Not her, I mean. The spell. It's a nasty one, hardly ever used nowadays..."

"Yes we found a bit about it on the web."

"...and it means that someone intends to stop you at all costs. At any cost. Whatever you were doing, you must have trodden on their toes. Rather painfully, by the looks of it."

"What can we do?"

"Not much, I'm afraid. I could give you a spell to protect you, but I don't know how much use it will be. But what I do know is that their spell will probably lose its toxicity after a while unless it's renewed. You may well be better off just keeping out of the way and hope they lose interest."

Owen cleared his throat. "I hope you don't mind me saying, but I don't actually believe in spells. I'm more concerned that there's someone who wants to harm me - us. What really worries me is that they may do something worse than casting spells. I was wondering if you could help us find the people so we can report them to the police."

"I'm sorry, but I can't."

"But why?" pleaded Owen.

Aleister sat down again, and spoke quietly. "You don't know what you're up against, dear boy." He paused and looked intently into Owen's eyes. "You've no idea, have you?"

Chapter 6
April 2005

Leaving the museum, Owen found Sarah sitting on the sea-wall, stroking a cat that had evidently adopted her, ecstatically rubbing its cheek against her hand, lapping up the unaccustomed attention. As Owen sat next to her, the cat jumped off the wall and sat a few paces away, regarding him with suspicion. Owen took Sarah's hand tenderly, but she withdrew it and turned her expressionless face to him.

"I can't trust you, can I? We agreed..." she said. Her shutters were in place and he couldn't tell whether she was hurt or merely furious. Best play it softly.

He sighed. "Okay, okay. I'm sorry. You're right. But we didn't expect to find someone like that, did we? It's obvious he doesn't have anything to do with whoever set fire to our car."

"Whatever. You should still have asked me first. We agreed we wouldn't get involved. Jeez."

He surveyed his feet. "I'm sorry."

She shook her head, resigned to his habit of apologising without conviction. Both knew he'd do exactly the same thing again.

"I'm sorry I took you in there," he continued, "I should have understood..."

"Understood what?"

"Umm... that you have a real phobia about witches. I'm sorry - I never realised."

She softened. "It's nothing. Just one of those childhood fears that never quite goes away, even when you think it's dead and buried. Silly really. I'll get over it."

He nodded and put his arm around her, feeling that it went deeper than she'd admit.

"Anyway, what did he have to say for himself?" she asked, more softly.

Owen heaved a theatrical sigh. "He went on and on about 'confronting powerful forces'. That guy's worse than my school chaplain. Anyway, it seems we may have run across one of the darker sects within Wicca. His advice was to steer clear of them."

"Would he... could he... pass them a message that we'll stop researching stone circles if they leave us alone?"

"Apparently not. My guess is he's a bit scared of them. Didn't want to get involved."

Sarah nodded. "Maybe that would be good advice for us too. Perhaps we should let it go."

oooOooo

The topic was buried. Not only for that weekend, but for successive eighty-hour weeks in which Owen became deeply embedded in re-analysing his data. Thoughts of Wicca were not so much dismissed as squeezed out by the pressure of his waking life, seeping back to haunt him only in the monochrome hours before dawn, the realm of childhood demons and suppressed adult fears. By daylight, the ghosts were exorcised by a condescending amusement that anybody might take that stupid Wiccan spell seriously.

One evening at a party, he was helping prop up the beer-barrel in the kitchen, along with half a dozen other semi-coherent males. The conversation, such as it was, meandered drunkenly to religion. Owen told the story of their car, the spell, and the witchcraft museum. His friends were agog as he told them about the strange old man who believed in Earth-spirits and Goddesses, about the people who would walk all the way to the middle of the Moor to scratch symbols on stones, about their claim that they could trace their religion back a thousand years. Reactions ranged from hoots of laughter to open-mouthed astonishment.

"Owen, I need to talk to you." Sarah suddenly appeared at his elbow, her face furious.

Ignoring the jeers and laughter, Owen followed her through the back door, into the cool of the garden.

"What's wrong, love?"

"Owen, we agreed not to tell anyone about it", she scolded.

"C'mon, Sarah. All that's in the past. Nothing's going to happen. Trust me."

"No, Owen. You don't seem to get it - these people are real, and they're dangerous."

"Sarah - listen to yourself. Do you seriously think some group of crazy ageing hippies are going to know or care what we discuss at a party?"

He hardly heard her retort. Even through his alcohol-bolstered infallibility, he realised he'd misread the expression on her face. It was fear. Not anger, but real fear. He became concerned, and her tirade fizzled out as he put his arms around her.

"Sarah, what's the matter? What are you afraid of?"

Her shoulders sagged, and she snuggled into him.

"Don't know. It's a feeling I have... Owen, these people worry me. I don't know what it is, but... Anyway, please can we keep away from them, and don't talk or even think about them. I just don't want to give them any excuse."

oooOooo

Sarah prepared another paper for a journal, determined to show the incompetents in her department that she was one of the leading archaeologists of her generation. Owen busied himself with simulating the impact of errors on his cell model.

Then there was the lectureship. He decided to ask Sir Ashley Pusch for advice on how to frame his application. Pusch was in the departmental secretary's office, dictating a letter over her shoulder while she typed.

"Good morning Owen. How goes it?"

What was it about the man that always set him on edge? "Fine, thankyou, Ashley. I was wondering if I might have a chat in the next few days about the lectureship?"

"Why don't you come in right now? Hold my calls, Helen. Owen and I need to have some quality time together."

"Really? Thankyou, Ashley. That would be so cool. I really appreciate it."

The lavish office was in stark contrast to the rest of the impoverished department. Owen sat awkwardly in one of the over-stuffed leather armchairs between the gigantic rainforest plants, as Ashley paced the room, thumbs in lapels, pontificating. He spoke as if it were all a done deal. Apparently, the powers-that-be had already decided that Owen was the man for the job.

As Ashley prattled on, bragging of his familiarity with people and matters at stratospheric heights, Owen couldn't forget that this man held his fate in his hand. He tried to remind himself that beneath the puffed-up ego and power-play lay a total idiot. Well, OK, maybe not an idiot, but a man who hid his lack of creative intelligence beneath an amazing skill at manipulating people and events.

Owen remembered a morning in his undergraduate days. He had been awoken as usual by the BBC news on the alarm radio in his tiny room in college. As he drowsily struggled to achieve consciousness, an item summoned his startled attention. Two Cambridge scientists, Dr. Jacklyn and Prof. Pusch, had won the Nobel Prize in chemistry. Owen sat bolt upright. Jacklyn he could understand - the unassuming man had almost single-handedly engineered a rethink of industrial fermentation, altering the course of the discipline in every continent, triggering the growth of billion-dollar companies in Europe and the US. But Pusch? The man was a bumbling nincompoop who had achieved his eminence through the brilliance of Jacklyn and the hard work of his students and postdocs.

Lying in bed, listening to the news story, he realised that Pusch was due to give a lecture that morning. Would Pusch actually turn up for the lecture, or would he be too busy strutting in front of the media?

At the appointed hour, to his credit, Pusch strode beaming into the lecture theatre. Naturally, all the students jumped to their feet and gave a thunderous round of applause. Pusch's grin could stretch no wider as he acknowledged the honour and tribute that were so rightly his. He then gave a long-winded speech: his Nobel Prize was not so much a personal award as an accolade to the entire team. While saying these words, he somehow managed to convey the impression that it was really he alone who deserved it, and he was being immensely gracious and modest in attributing it to a team effort. Owen was forced to concede that Pusch, despite his considerable limitations in chemistry, was a grand master at saying one thing while helping the listener hear something else.

Pusch finished his speech and, beaming, asked for questions. Sitting dead centre in the front row was Peter Chambers, who now shared Owen's office. He climbed to his feet, and said that, on behalf of his fellow students, he would like to congratulate Professor Pusch. Fair enough. Not only that, but he was sure that all his colleagues would agree that it was the visionary drive and intellectual leadership of Pusch, and Pusch alone, that had kept the department at its current top-ranking place in the world. Peter continued on in this vein, his praises increasingly purple and bereft of reality, to the extent that a few students started to snigger. But the irony was lost on Pusch, who had no doubt that every word was the bible truth, and what a perceptive young man to recognise it.

"Thankyou, you're too kind, er...um..."

"Peter Chambers," suggested Peter, helpfully.

"Ah yes, Chambers, of course. Well, thank you, Chambers. And I have to say what a pleasure it is to be here with such a group of brilliant, eager young minds such as yourself. I remember sitting more or less where you are now, as a young undergraduate, listening to a talk by Francis Crick, wondering if I could ever fill his shoes. And here we are. So who knows where you will be in a few years time?"

Christ Almighty. Was there no limit to the man's conceit? To compare himself to Crick? But the comparison between Chambers and Pusch perhaps wasn't so far-fetched.

Owen pulled himself back to the present with difficulty. Pusch was recounting a conversation he'd had over lunch with the Vice-Chancellor of Oxford, in which the VC had asked his advice on setting a new strategic direction for the University.

"So you see, Owen. We might both be going places in the near future."

"Yes, thank you, Ashley, I really appreciate your advice. But there must be other good candidates for this job too. Peter Chambers, for example. Probably others from outside."

"Chambers? A good man, but doesn't have your publication record. I don't think he's quite ready. Off the record, of course."

"Yes of course."

"So, no promises, but I think you'll like the outcome."

"That is so cool. Thankyou so much Ashley."

"My pleasure. And if you need any more advice, you know my door is always open."

He left, feeling pleased at Pusch's confidence in him, but well aware of the man's track record of mis-reading events.

oooOooo

Over dinner that evening, he related the conversation to Sarah.

"Owen, that's awesome. But don't count your chickens."

"Course not. The thing is, though, Ashley's chairing the selection panel, so..." He shrugged.

"He's still only got one vote. He may not be able to bully the other members of the selection committee. But then again, if it's a fair fight, you'll be way ahead of the other... What are you grinning at?"

"You. Always so cautious. Sarah, we're nearly there! And only a few weeks ago, we were worried about that stupid witchcraft stuff, worried about your PhD, worried where my next postdoc was going to come from. Don't you see, everything's falling into place. This is how life is meant to be!"

He leaned back, a satisfied smirk on his face.

"I wish you wouldn't talk like that, Owen," she frowned. "You're inviting trouble."

He grinned. "C'mon, I can't believe you're superstitious? You of all people?"

Was her face reddening? She bent down, flustered, to pick up Natalie who was rubbing against her legs. "No, of course not. It's just that...I don't know. For one thing, I can't get that stupid spell out of my mind. Do you think they're still after us?"

This was so weird. So unlike her. What was up with her? She was the last person to take any of that stuff seriously. But she had been behaving strangely. Last night she'd woken bolt upright in the middle of the night, as if she'd seen a premonition. Said it had been a nightmare.

He leaned forward and took her hand.

"Sarah, my love. Don't get screwed up about that. It's ancient history. Nothing to do with us now. Dead and buried. Mark my words."

oooOooo

Two days before the application deadline, Peter Chambers came in and shut the door. "Owen, my dear chap. I have to talk to you in confidence."

Swivelling towards him, Owen saw his face was uncharacteristically serious. "Yes?"

"I wanted you to be the first to know that I've withdrawn my application for the lectureship."

"What?" He was certain that Peter wanted it above all else.

"I've taken a look at your publications and citations, and I realise that in a head-on competition, there's no way I can beat you. So the glittering prize is yours, with my best wishes."

"Peter, I have to say I'm a bit shaken. Publications aren't everything, and you know how appointment committees can sometimes make strange decisions." And then, blushing, added lamely, "Not that appointing you would be a strange decision, of course. You'd be a natural choice."

84

Peter grinned at Owen's discomfort and lack of finesse. "No, my mind's made up. It should give you an easy ride in. Good luck, old friend. And maybe one day you'll return the favour."

Peter put his hand briefly on Owen's shoulder as he turned and left. Owen was amazed. Had he really mis-judged Peter so badly? He knew that he would beat him on the formal selection criteria, but he'd expected him to try some underhand ploy to even the odds. Maybe Peter wasn't such a bad sort. And he was at least realistic. One day, once Owen had tenure, he would repay Peter.

oooOooo

A week after the deadline, he returned home to find Sarah at the computer, while Natalie sat in her accustomed spot next to the screen.

Sarah was grinning. "Have you seen this, Owen?"

He looked over her shoulder as he tickled Natalie under the chin, and saw the infamous web page www.cambridgerumours.net.uk, which listed who was applying for what job and who was on the shortlist. It was often correct. He wondered what would drive a person to leak this highly confidential information. On the other hand, he was only human, and now it was open in front of him, he couldn't resist reading it.

Apparently the candidates had been short-listed. Fast work - as if they already knew who they wanted. According to the website, there were only three people besides him on the shortlist: one from Manchester, one from Princeton, and a French girl working at Scripps. He'd met the Princeton guy at a conference and, although a little older, he seemed bright and full of ideas. Here was serious competition.

He recognised the other two only from their publications. Owen and Sarah Googled the other candidates together. All about his age, and all with creditable if not outstanding publication records. His heart raced as he realised that, if the rumour page was correct, he'd be the clear favourite.

Returning to the rumour page, they found a list of the selection committee members. The usual suspects, of course - Pusch and other senior staff from the department, admin people from the University. Then, to Owen's surprise, Peter Chambers was listed as the `student and equal opportunity representative'. Fair enough. Peter would be good at that. Odd he hadn't mentioned it.

oooOooo

The day of the interview came. Each of the four candidates had given a seminar the previous day, with members of the selection committee in the audience. Owen's had gone smoothly, and he was well-prepared for the tough questions which followed. He'd heard that the other three candidates had also given good seminars, although one had stumbled badly after being drawn outside his field. There but for the grace of God, he thought. Today was reserved for the interviews themselves.

Before Owen entered the room, the committee discussed the candidates. The newly-appointed professor of physics argued that it would be good to get a female in the department, to help redress the abysmal gender imbalance. After a few minutes discussion, they agreed that they should simply choose the best candidate, regardless of gender, sexual orientation, religion or race. The committee reached a consensus that Owen was clearly the strongest candidate.

"But suppose a candidate openly adhered to some fanatical religious sect? I suppose we could take that into account?" asked Peter. "Completely hypothetically, of course."

Ashley considered the proposition, forming his fingers into a steeple as he stared at the ceiling. "Interesting question. We couldn't possibly discount them on their religious affiliation per se. But I suppose that if someone joined some fanatic cult, you'd have to question their ability to conduct research impartially." They all murmured agreement at this correct solution.

"Anyway," Pusch continued, "Fascinating though these questions are, it's time to return to the real world. Any further discussion on Owen before we call him in?"

The interview started well with questions about his work, the paper he'd just submitted, and his plans for continuing the research. They touched briefly on his teaching experience, and the role he played in helping undergraduates. They worked their way through the selection criteria without a hitch, until they came to interdisciplinary research. Later, nobody could quite remember who amongst the selection panel had suggested this unusual but harmless criterion.

"Owen, a healthy University grows by creating linkages between disciplines. Do you have any links with other disciplines?"

Owen considered the question, nodding, weighed his answer, and spoke. "I would be dishonest if I claimed to work in any area than biology. But I'm passionate about biology and I think you'll agree that my record speaks for itself there."

"I think you're doing yourself a disservice," said Peter.

"I'm sorry?" said Owen.

"Your work on stone circles."

"Oh. That." Owen started explaining his project, which evidently fascinated some members of the panel. Noticing their interest, he warmed to the subject, outlining the current archaeological paradigm, and explained how he was testing it in his spare time by making accurate measurements of bronze-age stone circles.

Peter interrupted. "And it also supports the tenets of your religion, Wicca, doesn't it?"

Flustered, Owen was uncertain where this was heading. "What? No. Sorry, I think you've misunderstood something." His voice firmed, tinged with suspicion. "Wicca isn't my religion. I don't have a religion. I don't have anything to do with Wicca."

"Owen, you can be honest here," said Peter soothingly. "This committee takes no account of people's religion. It sticks firmly to principles of equal opportunity."

Owen's face was livid as he started to remonstrate with Peter.

"What's Wicca?" interrupted the Dean of Science.

Peter explained graciously. "It's a religion based on medieval witchcraft, that summons the forces of the occult to do one's bidding. Wiccans believe they can cast spells and do magic, like witches and wizards."

"It's not that at all," Owen exploded, losing control. "You have so got the wrong end of the stick!"

"I see," smiled Peter pleasantly. "So you do know about Wicca after all. I thought you just said you didn't. OK, please put me right then." His tone was ingratiating. "What exactly is it?"

Pusch interrupted. "Look I don't think we need to discuss this. Whatever peculiar religion Owen adheres to is his business. Not the business of this committee."

The members of the committee agreed. Pusch thanked him for his time, and Owen left the room, fuming.

After he door closed, Pusch spoke to the committee. "What a pity. Such a promising young man. But I really don't think we can have someone in the department studying the foundations of biology, when he actually believes he can change it all by casting a spell."

They all agreed. Such a shame.

Towards the end of the next interview, it came out, quite by chance, that the young man had been involved in some hushed-up scandal about falsification of data. By the end of the interview process, the committee had found significant and unexpected problems with all four candidates.

At the end of the day, the committee met once again, tired and discouraged.

"I've never seen anything like it!" fumed Pusch. "Where are all the bright young scientists of this generation? I cannot believe there was not a single good applicant. Especially Owen Davies. What a dark horse. To think he's been engaged in this secret witchcraft business all this time without letting on to anyone in the department. I have to say, speaking personally, I feel abused by his deceit."

The committee murmured its sympathies.

Ashley continued. "It's a disappointing outcome, but I think we can congratulate ourselves that at least we did a thorough job. Didn't make the mistake of appointing an unsuitable candidate." He slapped his hands on the table. "But now we must start the search process all over again."

"Do we have to re-advertise?" queried the Dean.

"I think we must. Unless we can find someone who applied but didn't make it onto the short list. But we've been through that process, and the only reason the other people aren't on the short list is because they aren't appointable."

"Except for one," interrupted the Dean.

"I beg your pardon?"

"Young Peter here withdrew voluntarily."

The panel members turned to Peter, who looked modestly at the floor. "I couldn't possibly," he protested, "I really think due process should be followed, and the position re-advertised."

"Very commendable," replied Ashley, "but why go through the motions again, wasting time and effort? We know what the outcome will be. It's obvious that if he hadn't withdrawn, Peter would have made the short list." He sighed. "Given the performance of the other candidates here today, he would clearly have been selected."

Peter shook his head "I don't think it would be right."

Impressed by his integrity, the other members of the committee pressed him to re-apply.

Ashley made the point that finally clinched it. "There is another thing. It would be embarrassing for the Department to re-advertise. As if we were unable to attract people of the right calibre. Peter, please agree, if only for the sake of the Department."

Reluctantly, for the greater good, Peter consented to allow his name to go forward, and the members of the committee agreed to meet the next morning to interview him. Thus due process would be satisfied, with all five short-listed candidates having been given an identical interview. The following day, the interview went smoothly. No hidden surprises this time.

That evening, Owen returned home to find Sarah opening a bottle of Scotch. Good stuff too - Lagavulin. Must have bought it that day. She poured a generous tumbler-full and handed to him. But her smile was forced, and he knew he was about to hear bad news.

"What's the occasion?" he asked, smiling back nervously, with a growing premonition that he already knew the answer. She led him wordlessly to the computer, her arm around him, already consoling him. On the screen was the rumour page. Peter had the job. There was another tidbit of information. Apparently one of the candidates had been disqualified after claiming in the interview to be a Satanist, with occult powers. Presumably the stress had caused him to crack, poor chap.

Owen sat, stunned, at the dining table. It should have been no surprise, but to see it in black and white was too much. He groaned and slumped, his face in his hands.

Sarah spoke first. "It's only the rumour page, Owen. It could be wrong."

"No - it's not bloody wrong. That bastard Peter. He's stage-managed the whole thing. I couldn't understand why they had that stupid selection criterion about inter-disciplinary research. He put that in to set me up. I guess he pulled a trick like that with each of the other candidates. And then manipulated the selection committee. How can he live with himself?" He stood and paced the room. "And why does have to rub it in with that stupid story about the Satanist?"

"Maybe someone else leaked it to the rumour page."

He pondered. Maybe. Even so, it couldn't change the fact that the devious bastard had orchestrated the whole thing. Demolished Owen's career to give himself a leg-up.

"I was wondering, Owen..."

"What?"

"That spell... you don't suppose..."

"No I don't frigging suppose! Here I am trying to cope with the treachery of that snake, and you start rabbiting on about stupid spells. Forget it, Sarah. This is the real world. Witches don't bloody exist!"

oooOooo

The story of the Satanist spread quickly within the University. Naturally, it was picked up by the local media, who just as naturally lost interest when they found it was no more than an unsubstantiated rumour on an anonymous web page.

Owen's scientific colleagues were less discerning. Ashley refused to discuss it with him, saying it was "water under the bridge". Owen tried to make another appointment, but Ashley was permanently "busy". His colleagues in the department would quietly ask Owen about the Satanism, yet were unconvinced when he denied all knowledge. After all, he'd been the obvious candidate for the job, but didn't get it. So he had to have some skeleton in his closet, didn't he? No smoke without fire.

Hardest of all were the condolences from his fellow postdocs. When they went to the pub for lunch, Owen, unusually, declined, saying he had to work on a paper. He immersed himself in his office, the door shut. He couldn't stand the thought of swilling beer with them, listening to their stupid jokes, while his insides churned silently with anger and injustice.

When Peter strode in, beaming, Owen spun round and stared at him. He had already decided that he could only lose by arguing, and that his best course of action was to put on a brave face, avoid looking like a bad loser. So he stood and extended his hand. "Congratulations."

Peter took his hand and shook it. "Thankyou so much, old boy. Listen, I know how hard it is for you. But all's fair in love, war, and job applications, right?"

Owen's resolve cracked. "You bastard. You set me up! How can you live with yourself?"

Peter drew back, offended. Owen was astonished to see genuine surprise and hurt on his face. Peter regained his composure in a split second.

"Hold on, old chap. I think you've got the wrong end of the stick. I out-manoeuvred you, that's all. Didn't break any rules. Told no lies, committed no crimes. I won. End of story."

"You didn't break any rules? What about the simple rules of human decency?"

Peter's face was impassive. "You're so naive, Owen. In the real world, people do whatever it takes to achieve their goals. The Universities are in decline. Standards are dropping. This job isn't only about teaching and research. It's about fighting for the department, against all odds, against adversaries who will be fighting tooth and nail. You just blundered into the interview with no more preparation than polishing up your research goals. Like a novice playing chess, taking whatever pieces lie within reach. That's not what this job needs."

He sat, easing his feet up to the desk, "I researched the likely candidates, figured out their strategy, and chose my own accordingly. You never gave a thought to strategy."

Tapping his hands on the desk, he regarded Owen's silent stare. "Owen old chap, to put it bluntly, you really aren't the right man for the job."

It was Owen's turn to be shocked. He'd assumed that Peter would at least be ashamed of his skulduggery. But here he was actually justifying his actions. Owen's mind spun, confusion churning within, attacking the very foundation of his world view. He glared silently at Peter, unable to respond.

Peter stood and touched Owen's arm sympathetically, speaking quietly. "I'm sorry, Owen. You probably think I'm a total bastard. But it will be a bastard like me who saves this department, not some idealist like you with his head in the clouds."

Owen glared at him, unable to think of any reply that could adequately express his disgust at Peter's words.

Peter, misunderstanding his silence, placed his hand on Owen's shoulder, "Sorry, Owen."

Sorry? Sympathy? He had always felt superior to Peter, both intellectually and morally. He had tolerated him, maybe even patronised him. And now, suddenly, he had become aware of an alternative view of the world. One in which he was the underdog, with Peter lording it over him.

He felt his eyes prickling. A rushing noise threatened to drown Peter's words. He turned, and fled outside, jumping in his car, gunning the engine, screeching out of the car park, before the humiliation and rage became overwhelming.

Chapter 7
28 May 2005

"My head's killing me," growled Owen.

"Not surprised," replied Sarah, rolling over to look at him. "You were totally wasted last night. Almost a whole bottle of Glenlivet."

Rubbing his eyes triggered a bolt of pain across his forehead. Why on Earth had he drunk so much? Oh God. That. He moaned, shaking his head, trying not to think. How can you not think about something you don't want to think about?

Abandoning him to his demons, Sarah crept downstairs, followed by Natalie miaowing for breakfast. Not much she could do - better to let him sleep it off.

An hour later, as she made her second and last cappuccino, Owen staggered into the kitchen. After handing him a glass of water, Sarah watched him as the machine heated. She saw his bitterness, his vulnerability. Poor Owen - if only there were something she could do... Instead, she made him a double espresso, and carried it outside for him. He stumbled after her to the white wrought-iron table on the patio where the remains of her breakfast were being finished by a crow. At their approach, it flew off, its wings beating audibly, and sat on the roof of the house opposite, awaiting her departure.

"I feel bloody awful," he announced, and then raised his face, challenging her. "That snake Peter. I could kill him. Not just the job, I mean, but now everyone thinks I'm some sort of new-age weirdo weaving spells under the full moon. Jeez. I walked straight into it, didn't I?"

"You need fresh air and exercise," she diagnosed. He groaned again.

She laid her hand on his knee. "Owen, there's more to life than faculties and committees. It's a beautiful morning. Enjoy it. This is what life is about, not those short-sighted bureaucrats in the University."

"That's pretty strange coming from you," he growled.

She decided against taking offence. Not after what he had been through. Moving her chair closer, she put her arms around him. He responded, allowing her to mother him.

"Come on, Owen. Have a shower while I pack a picnic, and we'll go find some fresh air to blow away those stupid people and their stupid job."

Grumbling assent, he disappeared upstairs. As she went to make sandwiches, she switched on the TV. Some gothic woman in black flowing robes was enthusing about the growth of neo-paganism. Sarah turned off the TV with a shiver. Never again.

Three hours later, they were walking barefoot along a Norfolk beach. Splashing along the water's edge, they threw crumbs to the gulls screeching above. At one end of the beach was the squat tower of an ancient Saxon church. Once miles from the sea, it now clung desperately to its graveyard, before that too was swept into the advancing waves. Owen chased Sarah towards it as he splashed water at her with his hand. Springing nimbly over the stile into the churchyard, she teased him as he clambered over the rickety posts in clumsy pursuit.

She skipped over the gravestones in the sunshine, scorning the putrefaction, failed dreams, lost lovers, unfinished plans, lying six feet below that fragile membrane of life on which her feet danced carelessly.

"Did you hear about the two worms that made love in dead Earnest?" she shouted.

Laughing, he yelled back, "I bet they were just dying to get there." For years afterwards, this unthinking exchange would haunt him. Mock death as much as you like but it always gets the last laugh.

"Let's go to the pub and get a beer," shouted Owen.

She smiled tolerantly. So predictable. And so much for the picnic.

Much later, Owen found his memory was almost blank from that moment until the slow-motion memory of coasting helplessly into the path of the Range-Rover, his foot pumping up and down on the useless brake pedal. The only other surviving memory was that of Sarah's blood-curdling scream, the scream of someone watching their own approaching death, knowing they are powerless to avoid it.

oooOooo

The day after Sarah's funeral, Owen isolated himself in his empty house, sometimes sleeping, sometimes restless, mainly drunk, his mood swinging erratically from tearful misery to all-consuming anger. He downloaded Manson tracks from the web, playing them at full volume until his ears rang, anything to drown the echo of Sarah's screams. Or were they his? As day turned to night he fell into the tangled sheets, his mind erased by Manson and scotch.

He awoke the next morning knowing he had to come to terms with her death. Death. Such an uncompromising word, so simple. And yet such a shiver to it. Death. Death. Death.

They had offered him counselling. Maybe he should have accepted. But what good would it do? It wouldn't bring her back, would it? But he couldn't stay like this. He showered - the first for three days - aware that the phone was ringing. It had been ringing for ever. Maybe he should answer it.

"Hello?" he croaked.

"Owen. Didn't see you at the wake," accused the voice of Sarah's father. Owen was silent, his hand gripping the phone tensely, knowing he had to say something.

"Sorry, Mr. Ashworth. I was... unwell," he replied, with difficulty.

"You should think about others, Owen. Sarah's mother was very upset you hadn't come to see her."

Owen swallowed the angry retort forming in his throat, and instead said meekly, "I'm sorry Mr. Ashworth."

"Anyway - you can make amends. Sarah's ashes are still at the crematorium. If you can run them down here, then

96

it will give us a chance to talk. Discuss what to do about her belongings."

Christ almighty. As if it was some minor errand: "Run them down here". Next thing, he'll be talking about "A pleasant drive in the country". Doesn't he realise he's talking about his dead daughter. No, not his daughter. He'd disowned her, right? It was Owen's Sarah they were discussing. Ashes to ashes. Dust to dust.

Might as well get it over and done with. Gritting his teeth, Owen replied "OK - yes - I suppose so. Maybe this afternoon?"

"I've phoned the crematorium and they're expecting you. See you for lunch?"

"Lunch?" God this was going to be painful. "Yes - er - thankyou."

"Good. See you later then."

oooOooo

Sarah was in a wooden box barely larger than a paperback, with a lock and a tiny key. On the lid a small brass plaque announced, simply, "Sarah Jane Ashworth". No date, no indication of who she was, all that she had done in her life, all that they would do together, of the wonderful future stretched out ahead. As if in a nightmare, he carried her out from the crematorium and placed her on the passenger's seat. Seatbelt? Bit late now. As was Sarah.

The last time he had sat in a car next to Sarah had been the day of her death. Now, where she should have been sitting, was a box containing her ashes. And it was all your fault, murmured a voice in his head. No - it wasn't - the brakes failed, he screamed back silently. He collapsed in tears, his head buried in his arms on the steering wheel. His shoulders heaved as he allowed the tears to stream, distantly becoming aware of a voice, his voice, roaring with misery and black despair.

He was awoken by a persistent tapping on the window.

"Are you alright?"

Looking up to see the face and dog-collar of the chaplain, he wound down the window.

"I'm fine," he replied shakily, his face wet with tears, his eyes puffy and bloodshot.

"If I can help... Would you like to come in and talk, have a cup of tea?"

"No, really, I'll be fine. Thankyou."

 oooOooo

Driving towards the motorway, he passed a small copse alive with flowers. Life goes on. But how could his ever move on? Laboriously, he pulled himself out of the slough, trying to focus on the moment, and joined the purposeful stream of the motorway. The morning Sun beat down from a crisp blue sky, not quite yet summer, but too warm for springtime. A kestrel hovered above the edge of the motorway, awaiting some mouse to be scared out of hiding by the roar of traffic.

He started chatting to her, realising the absurdity.

"There's a kestrel over there, Sarah."

His grief had been replaced by a matter-of-fact acceptance. Just giving Sarah a lift down to her parents' place for the weekend. He wondered what she looked like in the casket. Bits of bone sticking out? Or nothing more than white ash? Pulling on to the hard shoulder, he picked up the box. He turned the key in the lock, but then dropped it back on the seat, jumped out of the car and spilled his guts onto the road, overwhelmed by the obscenity of what he had been about to do.

He locked the box again, and drove on, his eyes repeatedly drawn to it, mesmerised. A lump rose in his throat as he kept glancing at the lifeless container, unable to understand how it could contain Sarah. A loud blast jolted him awake, accusing him of straying into the next lane. Once more he pulled onto the hard shoulder, his head on the steering wheel, allowing the tears to flow, relieving the pressure.

"Sarah, why did you leave me? Why did you give up so easily?"

Recognising the betrayal of his words, he collapsed into another bout of hopeless sobbing, alone in a loveless world.

A knock on the window. He wound it down and became aware of the flashing blue light in his rear mirror.

"Are you alright, sir?"

"Yes - I pulled over because I wasn't feeling well. I'm OK now."

Suspicious eyes peered at him, and took in the rest of the car. A breathalyser appeared. "Could you blow into here please, sir?"

Owen blew as instructed, and the policeman seemed disappointed with the result.

"Would you mind if I checked the boot, sir?"

Whatever. He pressed the button and heard the boot click open, his bags being moved about, then the boot shut.

"Thankyou sir. Can I ask what's in that box on the passenger's seat?"

Owen stared dumbly at him. How could he ask such a thing?

Suppressing his rising anger at the stupid oaf's question, he answered through clenched teeth. "The ashes of my girlfriend. She was cremated on Friday."

"I'm sorry to hear that sir. Could I have a look inside please?"

Roaring, Owen slammed open the car door, almost knocking the startled man into the road, and jumped out of the car. "No you frigging may not, Mr frigging oh-so-polite interfering busybody policeman."

He jabbed his finger into the chest of the retreating constable. "What gives you the right to pry into people's lives, intrude on their privacy, peep into their caskets? Does it make you feel good? Mr Frigging Superior Pig?"

"Calm down sir, we're only doing our job."

A second policeman was running from their car, unbuttoning his pocket. He came up behind Owen, pinned his arms behind him, forced him onto the front of the car, and snapped the handcuffs shut.

Held down on the bonnet, Owen was yelling incoherently.

"Calm down!" the policemen shouted at him.

Trembling with suppressed rage, Owen was bundled into the back of the police car, struggling impotently, unable to hear the policemen's directions above the roar of surf returning to his ears, the incoming tide of nausea about to envelop him.

oooOooo

The door to the police cell clanged open, and the young constable returned Owen's belt and shoelaces. Forensics had confirmed that the box contained human ash, and the assault charges had been dropped "on compassionate grounds". Still shaken from the shock of the arrest, from being locked in a police cell, he followed the young police woman to the front desk, where he was handed the box containing Sarah. He took it tenderly from the rough hands of the policeman, knowing it had been opened, violated. After signing a form thrust in front of him, he followed the police woman to a small car park at the back of the building, and climbed into his car, breathing deeply, trying to regain control. Too late now to continue to the Ashworth's. Pulling his mobile from the glove-box, he spun them a story about the car breaking down. As he made his apologies and hung up, he could hear the scepticism in her father's bark.

It was after midnight when he opened the front door and carried Sarah inside, back home. The house was dark, empty, lifeless. Not even Natalie to greet him as she was still in the cattery where they'd taken her on the way to Norfolk. The flashing display on the phone announced that there were fifteen messages. They could wait. Walking from room to room, he switched on every light, but was unable to make the house come alive. The scotch failed to quench his thirst. Sitting heavily on the sofa, he stared at the wooden box. He would do anything to hear her voice again.

On an impulse, he went to the phone and dialled her mobile.

"Hi. Sarah here. Sorry, I can't come to the phone right now. Please leave a message." Beep.

"Sarah!" Hoarse, fighting tears, he crashed the handset down. Her voice was comforting, even though he knew, must accept, that she was gone. He picked up the phone again, pressed redial, and listened to the message. Beep.

"Sarah, I know you can't hear me, but I wanted to say how much I loved you, how I miss you, how I... Oh God!"

The receiver crashed down again. He dissolved, sobbing, on the sofa, and lay there, observing himself with a curious disinterest as the self-pity turned to self-contempt. Pull yourself together man. Yet it had been good to speak to her. Therapeutic. Maybe. Redial.

"Sarah, I'm lost. It all seems so pointless. I don't even know why I'm talking to you when you're dead. Gone. At the hospital they said this is part of the "grieving process". That I need to get "closure". Words. All these words. I suppose they make sense. But... I don't know. I don't know if I can handle it." He hung up abruptly and gazed at the box.

"I'm going to bed now. Good-night, love."

Helped by the whisky and sleeping tablets, he fell asleep.

He found himself in the Archaeology Department, having come to collect her belongings. He had been dreading the pity on the faces of her friends, the halting words of condolence, the avoidance from those who found young death too embarrassing, too taboo.

Approaching her office, he heard her voice. Must be his imagination. Reaching the door, he saw her at her desk, chatting to a colleague. He backed off, stunned, disoriented, mouth dry, his mind in turmoil.

"Owen, what's the matter? You look as if you've seen a ghost."

He fumbled his words, his voice strangled. "Sarah, my love, it can't be you. You're..."

Her face showed blank incomprehension. She didn't know. Nobody had told her. Her friend bustled out with apologies, remembering something else he had to do. Owen shut the door and sat down in shock.

"Sarah... You're not here. You're dead."

"What? I can't be. I'm here. It's me."

As her eyes filled with tears, she watched him, horrified. Understanding dawned, and was eclipsed. "No. This can't be... I've too much to do. It's not fair. Not now..."

Her face was ashen, terrified, as she was pulled away, screaming.

"Owen, please, help me..."

He awoke drenched in sweat, adrenalin spurring his body to action, to save her. Jumping out of bed, he ran from room to room, switching on lights. He poured a scotch, which bit his tongue, burnt his throat, opening the door to a cold reality, ushering the nightmare away into darkness. It was replaced by an emptiness, a wasteland with no purpose.

He turned on the TV and flicked through the channels. Sam was playing it again, while the other Sam wrinkled her nose to fend off her mother. The English army had just won the war, and all was quiet on the western front. Cute young things scampered, scantily-clad, up the beach, while a grunge band mistook aggression for wisdom.

Sighing, he switched off the pulp fiction, poured another scotch, and swallowed more sleeping tablets. Walking slowly round the house, swallowing the liquor, he turned off the lights and retreated to his damp bed.

The sun was high in the sky when he awoke. He lay drowsily, acknowledging that he had to come to terms with his new life, whatever it might be. He remembered his ambitions of a few weeks earlier - his sense of purpose, of dedicating his life to higher goals. Now he was rudderless, subject to random waves and unpredictable tides. Laboriously, he climbed out of bed, showered, and had breakfast.

A hand-delivered note lay inside the front door. It was from Phil from the Archaeology Department. So sorry to hear ... Condolences... Share your grief...will be missed by all her friends in the department... would you like to pick up her things?

It was early afternoon when he met Phil at the Department. Following him through the corridor, he was faintly aware of people ahead suddenly walking the other way, to avoid having to face him, express an awkward condolence, as if it was somehow their fault. An office door opened to his right, and a middle-aged man bustled out, almost colliding with him. He stared, shocked, at Owen. " I... I'm most terribly sorry..", and, turning scarlet, rushed away. Owen had no idea who he was, but apparently the entire department knew who Owen was.

Unlike the dream, Sarah was not sitting in her office. But her tangible absence occupied her room even more solidly than the ghost of her spirit. Her bag slung over the back of her chair. A jar of Smarties next to her workstation. A tacky Devon Pixie fridge-magnet on the side of her monitor, one she'd insisted buying in Chagford. He opened the top drawer of her desk. Chewed pencils, discarded biros grieving for their long-lost tops. A phone-book with names and numbers of people he didn't know. He was an intruder, rifling through this other life of hers, a life separate from the one shared with him. Hesitantly, he opened the filing cabinet, full of papers from her research, another world only glimpsed. A row of books stood on the shelf. Next to "European Societies in the Bronze Age" was a tatty copy of Roget's Thesaurus he'd found in David's Bookshop. The recognition shook him: never again would they browse through second-hand bookshops together, a regular Saturday-morning activity ending with coffee at an outside restaurant, comparing finds in the mid-morning sun. An uncomplicated, innocent pursuit that each week brought them even closer together. Distantly, he heard a hesitant cough, and became aware of tears on his cheeks.

Phil was standing in the doorway, wishing he could be somewhere else. "Maybe I should leave you to it, then?"

"No - I'm sorry." He wiped his eyes. "I think it might be better if someone sorted out her research stuff first. All these textbooks and things ... I've got no use for them. Why don't you give those to the other students. Or anyone else who wants them. And maybe you could put her personal stuff in a box, which I could pick up and sort out at home." He paused. "Then I'll be out of your hair."

Phil tried not to show relief. "Yes, that might be the best thing. What about her laptop? It belongs to the

103

department, but there may be personal stuff there that you want."

Owen stared at it - did he really want to go though all her personal correspondence?

"Could you give me a backup on a DVD? Then I can sort through it at my leisure."

A tall grey-haired lady with brown-rimmed glasses appeared behind Phil, and held out her hand to Owen.

"You must be Owen. I'm Karen Lightfoot. So sorry to hear about your loss. We will all miss Sarah," she said without warmth. Owen muttered his thanks.

"Owen's just come to collect Sarah's things," explained Phil.

"Ah. Yes of course. Oh - er - there is just one thing, Owen. Terrible time to raise it, but the bureaucrats go mad if we don't."

Owen looked at her blankly.

"Intellectual Property," she explained, "Sarah's research belongs to the department."

Phil stared at her, amazed that she would raise this at such a time, unwilling to disagree with her. "Yes of course... um... would you like me to go through it with Owen?"

"That won't be necessary. Bring everything to my office and I'll work through it. Then you can give Owen whatever rightfully belonged to Sarah. Sorry, Owen. But I'm afraid we have to go along with the red tape." She pivoted on her heel and disappeared without a further word.

Phil shrugged apologetically at Owen. "Sorry. She's a cold fish. But I suppose she's right."

Owen stared at him. A cold bitch more like. But why would a professor worry about intellectual property in a first-year student's work? How can supposedly intelligent people show such mindless adherence to bureaucracy? He left the department numbly, Phil still mumbling condolences and reassurances.

Driving home, Owen felt drained by the experience, by the act of dismantling a person's life, distributing its shards to the survivors. Then closing up the hole where she had stood, as if she had never existed. Only the signifiers remained - an obituary in the newspaper, letters she had written, the void that remained within him, gnawing hungrily, threatening to consume him. No. He would keep her memory alive, find a way to make her immortal.

But first, the practicalities. Entering his front door, he saw the light on the phone flashing insistently. More messages. He'd start by going through those.

The first was from the bank. Delete.

The next was from the police, letting him know, in a casual voice, that they had been unable to find anything wrong with the brakes. Damn!

Punching the cancel button, he headed out into the fresh air. Head in hands, he sat at the table where he and Sarah had eaten their last breakfast together. He watched a robin pecking on the ground, unafraid of him, uncaring. He groaned. Impossible. He distinctly remembered pushing the brake pedal. It offered no resistance, went all the way down, while the car kept going. The Range Rover hurtling towards them, just a few feet away, no time to stop. Sarah screaming in mortal fear. But the pedal had definitely gone to the floor, with no effect. They must have made a mistake, mixed his car up with another. He'd phone them and sort this out right away.

"I'm sorry sir, but there's no mistake. And the car - it was a rental car, wasn't it sir? - was serviced only three weeks ago, including a brake test. I have the test report here. But I should emphasise that we cannot rule out a brake failure, as the wheel was destroyed in the collision. All we're saying, sir, is that we can find no evidence of a brake failure, and so it seems unlikely..."

He explained how distinctly he remembered pressing down on the brake pedal, with no result.

"Are you sure it was the brake pedal, sir? After all, you had had a bit to drink, and..."

Owen slammed the receiver down. Slumped in an armchair, feeling very lost and alone, he gazed at the box.

"Sarah?" The sound of his own voice startled him. He continued, experimentally.

"They said there's nothing wrong with the brakes. That maybe I was pressing the accelerator. But they're idiots. I wasn't drunk. And it was the brake pedal. And it went right down to the floor."

He paused. Did it? Did it really? Maybe it was the accelerator pedal. He'd had a bit to drink. And when he ran the replay, was it really a replay? Or had he touched up the memory afterwards - a sort of mental Photoshop?

"No, damn it. I know it was the brake pedal. They're going to blame me for your death. But Sarah, it was the brakes. Maybe somebody fiddled with them, the previous renter, or someone else..."

The words hung in the air, echoing in the silent room, as Owen stared into the maelstrom of his mind, random thoughts churning alongside moments of clear insight. One such pool clarified as he watched it, formed itself into a cogent thought, startling in its lucidity.

"Damn! Those bloody Wiccans. It was them! You were right, Sarah, I should've listened to you. They set fire to our car. Just as easy to tamper with the brakes. Damn! They murdered you. Sarah. Murder! Bloody hell - why didn't I tell this to the police before?"

He paced up and down, thinking it through. It made sense. They had set fire to his car, cast one of their so-called spells that would bring "extreme harm" to Sarah and him. And then cut the brake lines to make sure the spell worked. Those crazy bloody people. Not even that - cold-blooded murderers. Nutcases. Psychopaths. And they'd killed Sarah.

Over the next two days, he tried to interest the police in his story. They were sympathetic, placated him with maybes, gave him the name of a good counsellor. They followed up his story with Devon County Police, who confirmed that vandals had indeed set fire to his car, but considered it unlikely to be connected to an alcohol-influenced accident in a rental car.

oooOooo

After the inquest, with its predictable "Death by Misadventure" and the equally predictable daggers of blame hurled in his direction, his mind was a mess of guilt, revenge, and an overwhelming frustration that nobody listened to his story. The next day he phoned the sergeant who had presented the evidence at the inquest.

"I was wondering if you could tell me where the car is, if I could have a look at the brake lines? I know the brakes failed. I want to know why."

"I don't think you understand your situation, Mr. Davies. First, you heard the verdict. Misadventure. Case closed. Second, IF the case were to be opened, which is what you seem to be suggesting, and a very big if, then you'd be a person of interest to us. So..."

"Sorry? Person of interest?"

"A potential suspect, Mr Davies. There is no way we'd allow you access to potential evidence. Who knows how you might tamper with it? Let sleeping dogs lie, Mr..."

He slammed the phone down. Bastards. Stupid bastards. Couldn't even get his name right.

The week continued in isolation, apart from Natalie, whom he'd finally collected from the cattery. She roamed the house, searching for Sarah, miaowing piteously. In the evenings he would curl up with her, pouring out his heart, his loneliness. Together they grieved for Sarah.

There was a phone message from Sarah's Dad, demanding to know when he would get Sarah's ashes, her belongings. Why should the bastard have custody of her ashes, when he didn't support her in life? Over his dead body. No way. Owen took the box containing Sarah and steeled himself for the shock. He turned the key and opened it. Ashes. As advertised. Nothing but a few ashes in a polythene bag. No bones. No Sarah. No revelation. No spiritual moment. Just ashes. Owen stared at them, trying to cope with his sense of anti-climax. They seemed to have nothing whatsoever to do with that laughing girl who'd transformed his existence, given him her love, her body, and her life.

All the same, there was no way that bastard was going to get them. He took out the bag of ashes, and looked for a suitable container. On the shelf was an earthenware urn from Athens - a silly tourist urn decorated with nymphs and satyrs. It would do for now. He carefully placed Sarah's ashes inside.

Out in the garden, he gathered some branches, and set fire to them, with difficulty and a great deal of newspaper, on the barbecue. Once the fire had died down and cooled, he scooped the resulting ashes into a polythene bag, careful to avoid any bits of twig or charcoal. Indistinguishable from the real thing. He placed the bag of ash in the box which had previously contained Sarah.

He spent the morning going through the house, collecting any of Sarah's ephemera on which her family might reasonably have some claim. Her clothes, some ornaments, some family jewellery, keeping anything of significance for himself. After filling his car, and with the box on the seat next to him, he drove down to her parents' place.

Increasingly apprehensive, he pulled into the drive and rang the doorbell. He'd never been here before without Sarah. Would her father be there? Would he demand to sort through the rest of her stuff? Would he realise the ashes had been switched?

The house remained silent, the door unopened. He should have rung first. So what to do? He couldn't leave Sarah on the doorstep like a laundry delivery, even if it wasn't really Sarah. But on the other hand he didn't want to drive all the way back to Cambridge and have to repeat the trip another day. Plus the fact that he was enormously relieved not to have to face her father. He decided to pile the stuff next to the front to door with an apologetic note, and escape before they returned. He'd phone in the evening to make sure they'd got the stuff, that they hadn't gone away for a month's holiday. A cowardly solution, he acknowledged, but no more than they deserved. He hurriedly emptied the car of its boxes and bags, scribbled a grovelling apology on a piece of paper, and left it under the box of ashes which he placed on the doorstep. He'd apologise again on the phone, and absorb her father's undoubted wrath by remote control.

As he drove away, he felt as if a door had been closed, as if he'd severed his connection to her family. Other than a brief phone call, there'd be no reason to meet them, ever again. All that remained of the real Sarah was in his care, and in his mind, to be cherished for ever.

oooOooo

He arrived home to find a message from Kim on the phone. Something about finding Sarah's birthday-present on a table in the library with a sign saying "Help Yourself". So that's how Phil had disposed of Sarah's books.

Owen phoned Kim back and apologised. All this bloody apologising. As if it were his fault.

"You could have asked me, first, you know." she said in an aggrieved voice. "That book was a pressie from me. For her twenty-first. I might have liked it back. Something to remember her by. I was bloody ropable when I saw it."

"I'm sorry, I didn't think..."

"No you don't, do you, You men are all the same. Sarah was all yours wasn't she? Never occurred to you that other people miss her as much as you do..." She paused, while Owen remained silent, hurt, unable to respond.

Kim spoke again. "Sorry. Shouldn't have said that. I know how close you were. But I do miss her, Owen. She was important to me..."

"Look, would you like to come over? In case there's anything else of yours, or anything you'd like to have? A memento? And we could talk... "

"Thanks Owen, I'd like that. I'll be right over. But I won't stay."

oooOooo

Owen opened the door, and immediately felt the sexual tension as she pushed past him into the house. She was brittle and edgy, but feigning a casualness that neither of them felt. She walked straight into the kitchen, avoiding any possibility of a welcoming kiss. So that was it. He decided to do the decent thing and put her at ease.

"Kim, I'm really sorry..."

She nodded unconvincingly. Still hadn't forgiven him, then.

"I haven't moved any of her stuff, Except for the things I took down to her parents. Help yourself. Like a coffee?"

She nodded again, and started walking round, scanning the bookshelves. Her eyes rested briefly on the unglazed replica Roman pot which he'd bought at the Fitzwilliam Museum, and then moved on. He couldn't tell her that Sarah's ashes lay within it. The Grecian urn had been too tacky.

"Sarah's clothes are all upstairs in the wardrobe - if there's anything you'd like..."

She turned, her eyes tearful.

"No, Owen. Sorry but this all feels wrong. I can't take anything. I don't know what I expected, but I just thought... Oh - Natalie!"

Natalie had entered through the cat flap and was rubbing around Kim's ankles, purring. Odd. The only time Kim had been in this house was the night of the funeral, and Natalie had been in kennels then. So how...?

Kim was sitting on the couch, fussing with Natalie who was loving every minute.

"I didn't know you knew Natalie." he said, trying to avoid it sounding like an accusation.

"She was my pressie to Sarah. Before you two met."

Ah. That Relationship again. Sarah had never told him where Natalie came from, and he'd never asked. He'd assumed she had been a childhood present from her parents. Anyway, that was the past. No point going there.

"Kim, would you like to take Natalie home with you? I'm out of the house so often I don't think she gets the attention she needs. And... "

Kim smiled through her tears. "Owen, I'd love that. Thank you so much." She stood and kissed him, squeezing Natalie, still purring, between them.

They bustled around, collecting cat food, the cat-carrier, Natalie's favourite blanket. Five minutes later, Kim and Natalie had departed, leaving Owen alone in the house.

Over the following days and nights, he began to miss the little cat. He was now totally alone in the house. But he couldn't face the outside world, couldn't face the sympathy, the absence of Sarah. Friends phoned to invite him to the pub, or for dinner. They said that life must go on, that he should talk it all out over a pint or two. So he stopped answering the phone or reading his email, but instead spent his days in long solitary walks through the Cambridgeshire fens, drowning his nights in private alcohol-sodden rampages through his memories of Sarah.

He became obsessive about her ashes, trying one container after another. The replica Roman pot was too contrived. A jewellery box too pedestrian. She needed something natural, not fashioned by some stranger's hand. He tried a cowrie shell. No way. Nothing was right. And why was he wasting so much time trying to find a container anyway? It wouldn't bring her back. So what was he trying to achieve?

He went to bed asking himself that question. What was he trying to achieve? What was the point in any of it now that Sarah had gone? He woke to find the torrent of confused thoughts had crystallised into one pure idea.

He no longer cared about the opinions of others. The need to prove his innocence had evaporated. It had been replaced by a private contract with Sarah. There was one more thing he could do for her: find those bloody Wiccans who had killed her. He would bring them to justice, make sure they paid dearly for their crime.

He searched the web feverishly for clues before realising the futility of this approach. Instead, he took a pad of paper into the garden, attacking the problem as he would in biology. After sketching out possible strategies, a plan started taking shape. He'd become familiar with Wicca, infiltrate the movement, until he was accepted as a Wiccan and could move freely through their community. Then he'd find out why he and Sarah had aroused such hostility, who would gain from her death, and bring them to justice.

A potential obstacle was that someone within Wicca had already marked him as a foe, and would be suspicious if they discovered him. He briefly considered adopting a false identity, severing contact with family, friends, and work, before concluding this was unrealistic. Instead, why not build on the rumours that Peter had spread about his Wiccan beliefs, making sure that those rumours were propagated as widely as possible? Driven irrational by grief and distress, he would turn to religion, and his chosen religion would be Wicca.

And what about Kim? Was she involved? Bit of a coincidence that she turned up wearing Wiccan jewellery on the day of Sarah's funeral. But half the girls in the department seemed to be ornamented like that. Maybe it meant nothing. However, safest to avoid her.

So where to start? He spent a morning in Heffers, emerging with a pile of books. He scoured the web, broadening his knowledge of paganism, and found a group called "Cambridge Wicca". They met on the first Wednesday of each month, and newcomers were welcome. He clicked on the link, and sent an email, using his real name, saying he was a solitary practitioner keen to join the local Wiccan community. A day later, a reply arrived, inviting him to their next meeting in a house off Cherry Hinton Road.

The quest had started.

oooOooo

A visitor punting along the Backs on a dreamy afternoon may not notice that there are two Cambridges. The inhabitants of one discuss spacetime or Wittgenstein in an improbable upper-class bray known throughout the world as a "Cambridge accent". The residents of the other talk of bus services and agricultural prices in flat voices redolent of a leafless fen awaiting its winter sowing of peas, the tone falling away at the end of each sentence, imparting a curious sadness to the conversation. But the two Cambridges depend on each other like partners in a stable but loveless marriage. The University provides income to the town, and the town provides the University with shops, pubs, porters and bedders.

Unwittingly, Owen had strayed through the silk curtain of distrust that divides town from gown. He stood alone, ill at ease, nursing his untasted cup of instant coffee while the Wiccans around him exchanged mundane news and gossip, waiting for the meeting to start. A few wore ostentatiously Wiccan garb, with black cloaks and silver pentacles, but the majority were dressed casually, often adorned with unobtrusive Celtic jewellery. Some men were even dressed in suits and ties, looking like prosperous businessmen who had dropped in on their way home from work.

The room, like the house, was decorated in unexciting suburban colours. Armchairs had evidently been moved out of the room for this meeting, and in their place were rows of rented plastic chairs, with a dining table at the front, like an altar. Large for a suburban living room, it was still far too small for a gathering of thirty people.

He tried to make his way to the front to take his seat, but the chattering throng didn't even notice his futile efforts.

"Um... excuse me."

"I'm sorry, could I just...?"

He was half-way to the front, planning the next leg of his route, when a silver-haired man in a pin-stripe suit entered from the back, radiating self-importance. As the man strolled to the front, the room parted around him like butter around a hot wire, closing behind, the conversation never pausing.

With no discernible signal, the conversation lulled and the Wiccans dispersed to their seats. Owen found himself in the third row, between two large middle-aged ladies wearing hairy coats, handbags on their laps. Realising he still had the coffee cup in his hand, he tried to put it under his seat, and succeeded in spilling it onto the polished wooden floor. Heads turned in his direction, frowns of disapproval and tutting noises, and a dishcloth was passed from the back for him to mop it up. Red faced, fumbling, awkward, he mopped the spillage while the room stayed silent, watching him, waiting for the meeting to start.

He passed the hateful sopping cloth to a lady standing impatiently at the end of the row. Taking it between thumb and forefinger, she extracted it to the back of the room.

"If we may get started," said the silver haired man, frowning at Owen, whose blush deepened as he muttered his apology.

Ignoring him, the man stood.

"Brothers and Sisters, merry meet," he intoned dramatically.

"Merry meet," the congregation mumbled back.

Owen forgot the dishcloth, and moved to the edge of his seat. He was about to see a real Wiccan meeting. A sheaf of papers was handed out for distribution, but he was disappointed to find it was simply an agenda. The first part of the evening was to be "business", followed by a talk on Zoroastrianism.

First on the agenda was "news". Individuals stood up and reported on the activities of their covens, or on festivals and rituals which were to take place. Then followed a report from the finance officer. There was discussion on whether to make a donation to "Pagan Pride", and on whether to subsidise the costs of those members travelling to represent Cambridge Wicca at the Glastonbury Festival. They talked about fee increases from their internet service provider, and whether they should move their web page and chat group. The business session ended with a report from the membership officer. He asked visitors and new members to stand and introduce themselves. Owen was the third to stand.

"Hi. I'm Owen Davies, and I'm a novice practitioner of Wicca. You may have heard my name because of recent rumours..."

The blank faces confirmed his mistake - these people had not the slightest interest in academic appointments, let alone rumour web sites.

"Well, I failed to get a University job because of my beliefs - some of the media reported that I was a Satanist."

Faces turned to him with interest. An older man spoke up. "Yeh -happened to me too. Bastards say they don't

114

discriminate but they do. Wouldn't happen if you were Muslim or Buddhist. But Wicca - forget it!"

"I've just been fired from my job!" shouted a girl. Bitterly, she recounted how she had been dismissed from an Age Care Centre after confiding to an old man that she was Wiccan. The residents objected to the witch in their God-fearing midst.

Owen sat down to sympathetic smiles. He'd passed his first test.

A tea-break punctuated the meeting. As he joined the queue at the kitchen door, a voice behind him said, "Bad luck about not getting that job. Happens all the time, you know."

The speaker was in his twenties. "Hello. I'm Steve."

Owen shook his hand. "Hi Steve. Yeh - I was so pissed off. But there are more important things in life. What about you - do your colleagues know you're a Wiccan?"

"I'm not a Wiccan - I follow Mithras. I've only come here tonight because of the talk on Zoroastrianism. But yes, the people at my place put up with me. The best IT people are often pretty weird."

Trying not to show that he didn't have the foggiest idea what Zoroastrianism or Mithraism were, Owen nodded sagely.

Steve continued. "So there are quite a few IT people here. Hey! Annie! Come and meet Owen."

An attractive girl with dark hair and gothic make-up joined them and shook his hand.

"Annie's my girlfriend and she's a witch."

"Hi Annie. So have you been a ... a witch for long?"

She seemed amused. "About five years. How about you? How long have you been a ... a Wiccan?"

He looked at her sharply and saw her amusement. No use pretending. He smiled, acknowledging the dig. "Just getting to know my way around. So do you belong to a coven?"

"I'm a priestess - I run my own coven. There are eight of us. So far." She smiled, challenging him.

"So... umm...how would I go about joining a coven?"

Her face became serious. "It's not that easy. Membership of a coven is a totally full-on relationship. Start

115

by getting involved in the local witch community, let the spirits guide you, grow your knowledge and wisdom, and ...." She shrugged.

Abruptly, her eyes lowered as the silver-haired man appeared beside them. Without returning Owen's smile, he gravely took the proffered hand in his nicotine-stained fingers.

"Good Evening, Owen. Welcome to our little group."

"Hi. It's good of you to invite me. I'm sorry. I didn't catch your name."

"My name is Camus." He gave the impression that Owen should have known this.

"It's good to meet you, um, Mr. Camus."

"Not Mr. Camus. Just Camus."

Camus turned and moved away, followed by a retinue of acolytes. Pulling out a packet of cigarettes, he went outside. Pompous little man.

Owen, still smiling awkwardly, turned to Annie, aware that he had somehow committed a faux pas, but not knowing what, or how.

"So he's the high priest? Or something?"

Annie wasn't smiling. "No. He's Camus. Look him up on the web. And next time show more respect."

The sound of a hand-bell summoned them back to their seats, where Camus introduced the guest speaker, a leader within the Zoroastrian movement. His talk, delivered in a strong Eastern European accent, was more like a documentary on the History Channel than a spiritual talk to a religious group. Owen drove home alone, his feelings of futility jostling for attention with the fear of having wandered into a lion's den.

He switched on his computer, and searched for "Camus, Cambridge, Wicca". The link came up immediately. Camus had started as a disciple of the celebrated Alex Saunders, and then started his own movement to bring Wicca closer to witchcraft. Owen discovered a page that spoke of "Camusian Wicca", the brain-child of the "distinguished English Wiccan thinker and visionary, Camus". The author of the page chose

116

not to give his name, but the pompous language suggested that Camus had written it himself.

He found other pages about "Camusian Wicca". It had been quite a thriving cult in the nineties, focussing on the need to discover the true roots of witchcraft. The ultimate goal of Camusian Wicca was to find the legendary "Book of One".

Chapter 8

Owen's sleep was a confused sequence of dreams in gothic noir, the cast hand-picked from his personal childhood demons. Bubonic hags poked at him with bony fingers, undead arms pushed aside their gravestones to smother him, tattered rags dripping foul retching fluids. He fled upwards, sheltering on a ledge high above the nave of a cathedral, King Kong playing Notre Dame. The vaulted roof was an arms-length above him, while far, far below a congregation swarmed, distant dots celebrating the death of their god. Giant crows, black and menacing in their ugliness, pecked him viciously, attracted by his fear-widened eyes. He clamped one hand over his face as he failed to beat them off with the other. Their beaks continued to stab the backs of his hands, while his fingers were relentlessly pried apart, revealing a horrifying close-up of a beak. He huddled over, protecting his eyes, balanced on a narrowing ledge, and still the crows flapped around him, denying him rational thought, imprisoning him in raw fear. He had stopped moving, but the ledge continued to narrow. He found himself against a wall with no ledge, perched impossibly high above the distant floor. Scrabbling to obtain a purchase, instead he fell, screaming. Surprised faces of the congregation stared fish-like, and then cleared a space so he could hit the cold stone floor without impediment. It rushed up to meet him, horrifyingly close. Cut.

He awoke sweating, shivering. Four in the morning, with little chance of sleep. He stumbled down through the lifeless house, the crows still rasping in his ears, to make coffee. Next to the coffee machine were Sarah's ashes, now housed in a hollowed log he'd bought from a garden centre. Totally stupid. He'd have to find something else.

Automatically, he staggered over to the computer, and idly surfed the web as he sipped his espresso. The Guardian's headlines crowed about London's successful bid to host the 2012 Olympic Games. Who cares?

He watched dumbly as his fingers googled "Wicca stone circles". Page after page of new-age drivel filled his screen, explaining how stone circles would focus your energy, lend you wisdom, and sharpen your razor blades.

What about the "Book of One" ? Nothing apart from a link to the page he had stumbled across the previous evening, and countless links to the "Book of One Thousand and One Nights". And then he found a Google link to a Yahoo chat page containing the line, "Do you honestly think you can beat the Wakened to the Book of One?". But when he clicked on the link, the page was missing - deleted. He googled "Wakened" but drew a blank. So who were the "Wakened" and why might they find the Book of One? Or was this merely some metaphysical mumbo-jumbo that had nothing to do with reality?

He needed expert help. But from whom? While the pagans last night had been friendly, he didn't know them well enough. Then there was Aleister, at the museum in Tintagel. He hadn't wanted to be involved, but Owen felt he could trust him. Worth a try, anyway.

Five in the morning. Too early to call. But if he drove down to Cornwall now he could be there by lunchtime.

His sleepless night took its toll on the long drive. He pulled into a service area for coffee, and found it buzzing with the news of bombs in London that morning. Terrible.

Eventually reaching Tintagel, he decided against going straight to the witchcraft museum. He needed to unwind and collect his thoughts, so he headed into a pub, ordering a pint of beer and a cottage pie. The TV in the corner relayed the unfolding news of the London tube bombings. Dozens, perhaps even hundreds, had been killed. But no clue to the identity of the terrorists. He tried to ignore it. Horrifying though it was, it had nothing to do with him.

An hour later, relaxed by two pints of beer, he ambled down to the witchcraft museum. The door was locked. No reply. He tried Aleister's cottage. No luck there either. Bloody hell - the time and petrol he'd just wasted. Returning to the museum, he found a phone number taped to the window. As he dialled it, he could hear the phone ringing inside. A machine invited him to leave a message.

"Aleister - this is Owen. Sarah and I visited you a few months ago about ... a problem with our car, and you were so helpful? Remember? I could really use your advice, because..."

"Hello?"

"Oh. Aleister?"

"Sorry - I forgot to switch off the answering machine. How are you?"

"Actually, I'm right outside the museum. Could I come in?"

"Just a moment."

A few seconds later Aleister's face appeared behind the glass door.

Ushering him into the museum, Aleister muttered about the terrible goings-on in London, and started rambling about evil portents on the day of the New Moon. Owen stopped him short with the news of Sarah's death, and his suspicions. After exclamations of shock and sympathy, Aleister hesitated before speaking.

"My poor dear boy. But don't you think you're letting your imagination run away with you?"

"What? You told me yourself about these people and that dangerous spell."

"Yes, but the spell's dangerous in a general sort of way. I don't think it could kill someone. Not like that. And... um... anyway, I don't think anyone's going to resort to murder."

Owen sensed the hesitation - the old man didn't seem convinced by his own words. "Aleister, can I ask you something? I get the impression that all the Wiccan stuff on the web is superficial. That there's a deeper level of knowledge that never appears. Is that right?"

Aleister seemed to be choosing his words carefully. "Have you come across the term 'Fluffy Bunny'?"

Owen's face was blank. Aleister explained. "It describes people who use paganism to impress their friends, shock their

120

parents, or make a fashion statement. Usually teenagers. They truly believe they're the real thing, but rarely have more than a shadow of understanding."

"OK - I remember now. I came across the web page of a fourteen-year old girl explaining earnestly and self-importantly, how the Fluffy Bunnies were so, like, phoney. So different from lifelong true believers such as herself. Not a hint of irony."

"Exactly. Most of the stuff on the web is written by fluffies. There are indeed a few genuine Wiccan web sites, like our own, but those only go so far. The web is not a good place for intimate experiences. And the last thousand years have taught us to keep our religion secret. My dear boy, I want to help you as much as I can. But there are some things that only Wiccans can know."

"Like the Book of One?"

Aleister was satisfyingly thrown by this question. Recovering his balance, he smiled. "Well, well. I see you've been doing your research. How did you hear of that?"

"The web. Maybe it's leakier than you realise."

"What else have you found out?"

"The Wakened?"

Aleister, visibly stunned, said nothing, but his deadly serious expression eclipsed Owen's smirk. "What do you know about the Wakened?"

Owen shook his head. Best to keep some cards to himself. "If you could tell me a little more of what you know, then I could tell you more of what I know."

Aleister gazed at the ceiling, then sat, deep in thought for several minutes, silencing Owen with a dismissive flick of his hands when he tried to interrupt. He suddenly stood and crossed to the window, his back to Owen, and spoke. "Look, I think maybe we're facing the same enemies, and perhaps we could work together. But whatever passes between us must be kept absolutely secret."

"I don't understand..."

Aleister frowned. "Don't rush into this. Listen. There are some horrible people out there. Maybe Sarah's killers. If we work together, there must be absolute trust, and perhaps the absolute sacrifice. Do you understand? This could be very dangerous."

Owen nodded thoughtfully.

Aleister continued. "Now, my dear boy, why don't you leave me here, and come back at six o'clock. Think carefully about what I've said, and decide whether you want to get involved. I'll do the same. So we each have four hours to think about it. If we agree to join forces, there'll be no turning back."

Owen started to speak but Aleister put his finger to his lips and wordlessly waved him out.

As Owen left the museum he felt dazed. It sounded like a load of esoteric rubbish. He started walking up to the cliff path. The same path that he and Sarah had walked so very long ago. Or was it only a few weeks? Since her death and the inquest, he had been determined to find her killers, at any cost. Now Aleister had sown the seeds of doubt in his mind.

How much was he prepared to abandon? He was a successful up-and-coming biologist. Failing to get tenure had certainly been a setback, but nothing he couldn't ride over. And what of all that he had to offer science - the discoveries he'd make, the people he'd inspire, the students he'd teach? Above all, using his life to make a difference, to push out the horizon of knowledge? Was he now to throw this future away for a half-baked adventure with a group of crazy mystics? Which, by the way, included Aleister, not to put too fine a point on it.

All these good, sensible arguments warned him to walk away from the precipice, not to engage in this ridiculous and possibly fatal adventure. Even if you didn't believe in this witchcraft rubbish, there were clearly some very nasty people out there who did. People who would kill to achieve their sinister goals. As they'd killed Sarah.

As he trod the rocky path, immersed in these arguments, a large bird hurtled from the ground next to him, the black thrash of its wings brushing his face, startling him, causing him to trip. He landed on a steep grassy slope descending treacherously to the edge of the cliff. The crashing waves far below roared in his ears, as he started to roll helplessly towards the precipice. His hands found a clump of grass, but its roots were barely attached to the hard rock, and he continued falling towards the edge. Now panicking, thrashing, his hands found a small bush, more firmly rooted, able to halt his descent.

He lay there for a moment, his legs kicking into empty space, then laboriously pulled himself back up to the path. He lay panting, the shock of his near-fatal plunge overtaking him. He felt his limbs trembling, his heart thumping. The crow had flown to a tree further up the slope, where it watched him mutely, an intruder to its domain.

Gazing dumbly out to sea, listening to the waves crashing below, he was flooded by a tide of connectedness, of being in touch with reality, that same feeling he'd experienced at the stone circle on Dartmoor so very long ago. Complex questions dissolved into black-and-white, and the path ahead became clear.

oooOooo

At six o'clock, Owen knocked briskly on the museum door, his decision firm, his smile anticipating Aleister's reaction to his good news. Aleister opened the door without looking him in the eye.

"Aleister, I've decided. Let's do it."

"I'm terribly sorry, dear boy, but I'm not so sure it's such a good idea," started Aleister, hesitantly.

"What on Earth do you mean? Why not?"

Aleister turned wordlessly and Owen followed, shutting the door behind him. Aleister's face was troubled, pensive.

Owen failed to hide his irritation. "What do you mean it's not such a good idea? What's changed from when you thought it was a good idea?"

Aleister motioned him to sit, and sat in a facing armchair, still avoiding eye-contact. "You see, my dear boy, I've taken vows which I cannot possibly break. An outsider simply cannot be privy to the secrets which are the core of Wicca. I cannot betray Wicca."

Owen realised that his powers of persuasion would have no effect. He tried to batten down his feelings of being led on a wild goose chase, of seeing the solution slipping away from him. Instead, he tried to think rationally, logically, treat it as a challenge to be overcome. "OK. I see your problem. How can we solve it?"

"We can't. I can't." remonstrated Aleister, "They are sacred vows and there's no way I'll break them."

"You said you can't tell these secrets to an outsider. How do I cease being an outsider?"

Aleister stared at him as he thought through the implications. "I don't think you understand. You can't just say some words, go through the motions, pay lip service. You'd need to be a true believer before you could be initiated."

"And how would I become a true believer?"

"You'd have to believe," retorted Aleister, exasperated by these futile questions.

"And what would it take to convince you that I believed?"

Aleister rolled his eyes. "I'd want to see you live the life, be guided by spiritual energy, demonstrate the faith of a true Wiccan. This isn't something that can be acted out, Owen."

"OK. So who says I'm acting? Aleister, since Sarah's death I've started doubting everything I believed in. I've seen too many things, too many coincidences, too many symbols, which make me wonder if there really is more to this witchcraft stuff. Look, I'm a scientist. My life goal is to understand how the Universe works. And, as a scientist, of course I'm sceptical of superstition, of blind faith, of anything which cannot be tested and examined. But suppose there really are these other forces acting upon the world?"

Seeing the sceptical expression on Aleister's face, he drew closer, focussing his passion on the old man, trying to help him understand.

"Don't you see, Aleister? As a scientist, I'd be crazy to dismiss them out of hand. I'd look pretty silly on judgement day if I were to stand before the God and Goddess, claiming that I had dedicated my life to understanding the mysteries underlying the Universe, and all the time I had been ignoring the evidence staring me in the face. So, yes, I've started taking these neo-pagan religions seriously, and, yes, having done all this research I'm starting to understand - even admire - their philosophy. So. Yes. Count me as a believer."

Aleister had been watching him with increasing astonishment throughout this monologue, expecting the performance to be broken at any moment by a wink or a smirk. But Owen finished, his face serious and determined.

"I don't know whether to believe you," Aleister pleaded, as if this were a proposition that they might debate.

Instead, Owen turned to face Aleister full-on, his legs apart, his arms by his side, and said, "I think I've just demonstrated that I can help you. So if you choose to believe me, you get my help without breaking your vows. Or you can choose to disbelieve me, in which case you're on your own. Your choice."

Aleister stared into Owen's eyes, searching, moving from eye to the other. Apparently unsuccessful, he broke eye contact and shook his head in doubt and confusion. "I need to think about it. I need to get guidance from the God and Goddess."

"How do you do that?"

"I have ways. And I'll sleep on it. And, ultimately, I'll know because the right decision will feel right."

"OK fine. You do that. I'll check into a pub and we'll get together in the morning. To hear your decision."

"No need for that, dear boy. You can sleep here."

Owen's surprise at the offer blew apart the stern persona he'd been assuming. "Really? Well, I suppose... OK, that would be really good of you." He paused. "You live here on your own?"

"There were two of us until a month ago. Which is why I'm still a bit... frazzled."

"Oh - I'm so sorry. Did she..."

"He. Left me. Yes."

Owen paused. "Ah. I see. Sorry - didn't mean to intrude. Anyway, all I need is a couch or something."

"Yes, sure, use the couch here, and I have some blankets upstairs, unless..."

Hearing him hesitate, Owen glanced at him sharply. "The couch will be good," he said decisively.

A ghost of a smile flitted across Aleister's face. "OK - that's fine then."

They lapsed into silence.

"I suppose I should get dinner going then," suggested Aleister, unenthusiastically.

"Why don't we have dinner at the pub? My shout. Least I can do since you're putting me up for the night."

"Excellent. And Owen, there's something else. I'm curious."

"Yes?"

"When I last saw you, even this morning, you seemed hesitant, tentative. Suddenly you seem assertive, pushy even. You've changed."

"Yes, Aleister, I have."

oooOooo

Owen woke the next morning knowing that he had played a high-risk card. Both had avoided discussing it further in the pub, instead talking about the London bombings. There had been sly glances in the pub, and once he thought he heard a low mutter "...new bloody boyfriend...". But otherwise the evening had been pleasant and uneventful.

Seven in the morning, and no sign of Aleister. Owen decided to explore the kitchen. No espresso machine. While the kettle boiled, he scanned Aleister's bookshelf. He desperately wanted to pore through the spell-books and grimoires, but felt that Aleister might see it as prying. Instead he found a tatty Penguin paperback. Julius Caesar: De Bello Gallico. That would be safe enough. He sat down with his coffee to read it.

He was stunned. It was not a book about Caesar, it was a book by Caesar, written in 55 BC. Caesar's words, translated into English, spoke to him across an unimaginable space of two thousand years. He turned to a page that Aleister had marked with a coloured tag.

126

"The Druids officiate at the worship of the gods, regulate public and private sacrifices, and give rulings on all religious questions. Large numbers of young men flock to them for instruction, and they are held in great honour by the people... The Druids are exempt from military service and do not pay taxes like other citizens."

"What's the book?"

Owen spun round to see the old man, in a tattered dressing gown and crumbling slippers.

"Sorry - I hope you don't mind. It's Caesar's De Bello Gallico. Isn't it awesome?"

Aleister smiled gently. "Yes it is, as you say, awesome. Actually, I find it makes my spine tingle. Two thousand years old, and it could have been written yesterday."

Aleister had put his reading glasses on, and was looking over Owen's shoulder. He pointed down the page. "Have you read that bit there?"

Owen read it aloud.

"The Druids believe that their religion forbids them to commit their teachings to writing, although for most other purposes, such as public and private accounts, they use the Greek alphabet."

Aleister had a dreamy expression on his face. "Don't you find that truly astonishing? But I'm afraid we don't know a lot more about the Druids. Almost nothing written by them. That's pretty much the best we have. Like another coffee?"

Aleister continued as he made it. "Did you know Caesar tried to invade Britain twice? Each time the natives beat him off. He doesn't mention that in his book. Instead, you get the impression he simply decided it would be nice to go back to Italy. After that, the Romans left Britain alone as a bad job for nearly a century."

"So why did they change their mind?"

"The Emperor Claudius tried to make a name for himself by invading us. I think he expected an easy victory, but instead it dragged on for years. Seems like the Romans were rather surprised to find the British had well-trained armies, with ingenious leaders. Quite different from the rabble they expected. Anyway, the Roman Army gradually

127

forced the British into the West. Behind the battle lines, the barbarians were only too happy to..."

"So what became of the Druids?"

"You young people. Always in a rush. Relax. I'm getting to that. Toast?"

Owen nodded, and Aleister shambled to the toaster. Increasingly impatient and exasperated, Owen watched him fumbling with the bread. It was all Owen could do to stop himself walking over, pushing Aleister out of the way, shoving the bread into the toaster, and telling him to get on with the bloody story. Instead, he drummed his fingers on the table, until Aleister finally managed to insert the bread into the toaster, push it down, and amble back to the table.

"The Romans were usually tolerant of other religions. But the Druids were different. The Romans worried that the Druids had the hearts of the people, and might lead a rebellion. So they decided to erase them."

The toaster popped, and Owen sprang to retrieve the toast, but then had to watch powerlessly as Aleister carefully applied butter and marmalade.

The old man continued through a mouthful of toast, spraying crumbs over the table. A glob of marmalade lodged in his greying beard. "The Romans went to extraordinary lengths to destroy them, and lost almost as many men as the Druids did. People in Rome demanded inquiries, that sort of thing. Finally, the Druids were defeated in a massive battle on the Isle of Man."

"But you can't kill off a major religion simply by killing its leaders."

Aleister waved his knife at him, dropping a glob of marmalade on Caesar's words. "Exactly. Pockets of believers maintained it in secret for centuries. By the time Christianity arrived, these believers were called wike, meaning wise people, and this eventually evolved to the modern words 'witch' and 'Wicca'."

"So Druidism and witchcraft were the same religion?"

Aleister paused, and looked pleadingly at the toaster. Owen obliged by springing up, and inserting two more slices of bread.

Aleister continued. "Not really. Druidism seems to have been, you know, more of a formal, structured, religion. Like the established churches now. Witchcraft was a loose rural version. A people's religion. Druidism seemed to have emphasised the Sun, and its leaders were mainly male. Witchcraft is more focussed on the Moon, and many of its leaders are women..."

He paused, and turned to Owen. "Talking of which, I've been thinking about our conversation last night."

"Yes?"

Aleister's face was serious. "I can feel your energy. It feels right. Together we can succeed."

Surprise bloody surprise. "I'm so glad, Aleister. I'm so glad the spirits have ... guided you in the right direction."

Aleister glanced warily at him, trying to gauge his sincerity.

Owen stood and proffered his hand. Aleister took it, shook it slowly, and looked directly at him. "But one thing."

"Yes Aleister?"

"I do require your trust, Owen. Absolute trust. And I offer you the same. Please, don't ever, ever, lie to me."

Owen made to remonstrate but saw the intensity in the old man's face. Swallowing his words, he said gravely, "Aleister, I offer you my complete trust and loyalty, if you will do me the honour of giving me yours."

Aleister's eyes moistened as he took Owen's hands in both of his, and said in a voice shaky with emotion, "Of course, Owen. Welcome, brother."

oooOooo

Over the next few days, Aleister gave him a crash course in Wicca. Tentative at first, sharing information with difficulty, Aleister gradually became more comfortable with Owen. Owen chatted with Aleister's frequent visitors, was allowed to sit in on serious and well-organised meetings, and was surprised to find a religion largely populated by intelligent and articulate men and women, rather than the motley assembly of cranks he'd expected.

He found the tenets and values of Wicca were as sensible as any other religion, and began to appreciate the great skill and persistence of medieval propaganda, with its witches on broomsticks, and bubbling cauldrons of vile concoctions. Wiccan morality was not so different from Christianity, with a central tenet of "An' it harm none, do what ye will". Its "Threefold Rule" said that any good or harm done to another person will be returned threefold. Aleister refused to be drawn on "The Book of One" and the "Wakened", saying each time, "Not yet, Owen, not till you're ready."

After a week, Aleister invited him to witness a celebration of the full moon. Owen was nervous of the heavy eroticism that was no doubt part of the ceremony, and so welcomed Aleister's suggestion that he should watch rather than participate. On the other hand, he would be denied the necessity of ravishing some beautiful teenage goddess. Never mind. That could wait.

The following Thursday, the day of the full Moon, he woke to find the old man in a despondent mood.

"Something terrible's going to happen today," Aleister said, staring into his coffee.

"How do you know?"

"The London bombings were on the day of the New Moon. That always causes problems. Today is the Full Moon, when the evil done that day returns with vengeance."

The day dragged on, with Aleister listening morosely to the News every hour. Then, late afternoon, came the report of four more attempted bomb attacks in London. But this time the police had been successful in thwarting the terrorists. Aleister seemed pleased both that his prediction had been correct, and that the evil had been contained.

That evening, Owen met the twelve members of the coven as they arrived for a glass of wine. He was disappointed to find all were middle-aged, and his teenage goddess was conspicuously absent. A casual intimacy was evident between them, and he started to understand Aleister's assertion that membership of a coven was a very close relationship.

Aleister's coaching enabled him to pass in casual conversation as a visiting Wiccan, and at ten o'clock the group

130

bundled into four cars and drove to the cliffs. The weather was mild, and, dressed in jeans and T-shirts, they followed their torchlight up the path to the headland. The full moon was now high in the sky, casting dark shadows. A CD player was switched on, and something sounding like Enya on a bad day filled the air. Pots of assorted herbs and minerals were placed in a ring round the appointed spot, the ground ceremoniously swept, and a small fire, sweet-smelling with herbs, was lit in the centre. The coven started disrobing, and Owen retreated, nervously and awkwardly, to sit on a rock a short distance away.

His tension found expression in a suppressed giggle, as thirteen nude middle-aged men and women, with pot bellies, flaccid penises, and droopy breasts, cavorted within the circle, singing tunelessly to the CD player. Twigs were lit, substances thrown to the winds, words were spoken, and all he could see were a bunch of ridiculous old people making fools of themselves. By now he was having difficulty from not laughing out loud. These were the people he had feared?

A hand touched his shoulder and he turned, startled. No-one. Must have imagined it. A slight wind had sprung from nowhere, blowing leaves in small eddies around him. The hair on the back of his neck stiffened as he watched the spinning vortex of leaves gyrate slowly to the dancers and back towards him. The old people were now dancing together in flawless synchrony, and he no longer saw their tired old bodies, but watched instead the beauty of their movements, the spirit uniting them, focussing their energy together and upwards, up to their Goddess. The whorl of leaves spun to the centre of the circle and flew up above them. They seemed to see it too, and raised their arms in worship as it funnelled up to the sky. He realised that he was seeing the dancers from above, as if he were carried by the vortex now spiralling up towards the moon. In awe or terror, he knew not which, he was overcome by the sheer beauty of the experience, and collapsed, sobbing.

He was wakened by a hand on his back. Aleister was gently shaking him. "Are you alright Owen?"

131

Shivering, as if in shock, he looked fearfully around. All the people and cars were gone, except for Aleister's battered old Land-Rover. "Uh... Sorry. I fell asleep. Don't know what came over me."

"You weren't asleep, Owen. And the Goddess came over you."

Chapter 9

He felt bloody awful. It wasn't so much the headache as the sense of having made a fool of himself, fuelled by fatigue and a couple of glasses of wine. He remembered gushing in the car about the strange experience, and Aleister nodding wisely and ... Jeez ... Had he really done that?

Staggering into the kitchen to make coffee, he found Aleister already there.

"My dear boy, good morning. How are you feeling?"

"Horrible. I drank more than I realised."

"More likely the effect of meeting the Goddess for the first time. She does that to you, you know. People often feel strange afterwards." He looked expectantly at Owen, who said nothing, instead pouring himself a mug from the coffee pot.

Ignoring the concerned gaze, Owen sank into a chair, closed his eyes, and enjoyed the bitterness of the coffee, his mind still trying to make sense of last night's events. It was important that Aleister should accept that he was a true believer, but on the other hand he didn't want to go into raptures about meeting the Goddess. Besides, he suspected Aleister might be less gullible than he appeared.

Aleister came over and rested a hand on his arm. "How do you feel now about last night? We were all very concerned for you."

"Dunno. I feel disoriented. I'm still not sure whether something really important happened or whether it was just the effect of alcohol and tiredness."

Looking up, he saw Aleister smiling his approval. Apparently the truth was, after all, the best approach. "In that case, I think we should move on to the next step in your education. Let me tell you about the Book of One."

Owen was instantly alert. He hadn't expected this to happen so quickly.

"You remember the other day we were taking about the Roman invasion, how the Druids were beaten back into the West Country?"

Owen nodded.

"Well, the Druids seem to have been based around Stonehenge. As the Romans advanced, they were beaten back into Devon. According to legend, they realised that their religion might be lost, so they took their most sacred treasures, and hid them in a secret place somewhere near Exeter."

"And I'm guessing that the Book of One was amongst those treasures?"

"I think so. It was the most sacred possession of the Druids, after all. It was said to contain all their wisdom, all the sacred rituals, spells, knowledge of Druidism." Lowering his voice, he spoke portentously. "It contains the genesis of witchcraft."

"So where is it now?"

The old man's watery eyes had become alive, lit by a fire smouldering within. "If only we knew. Legend says there's a coded trail which tells you its hiding place. All sorts of people have tried searching for that trail, but they've all failed. So far. "

"What language is it written in?"

Aleister shook his head, smiling. "If only I knew. Latin? Greek? Runic? Remember what Caesar said? Nothing sacred could be violated by writing it down?" He paused. "But in extremis, seeing their religion about to vanish, I suppose they committed it to the profanity of paper. Your guess is as good as mine what language they used."

"So how do the Wakened fit in?"

"Just think, dear boy." Aleister was waving the knife at him again to make his point. "Imagine a Christian religion without a bible, relying on vague half-remembered bits of folklore, legend, and rumour. And then suddenly finding a bible."

134

Owen nodded, back on familiar territory. "Of course. Finding the Book of One would give Wicca legitimacy, authority."

"As usual, Owen, you've hit the nail on the head. If only we could find the Book of One, then perhaps Wicca could be restored as one of the great religions of the world."

Owen was astounded by the passion igniting the old man's face, and, for the first time, understood the dream that propelled him. This wasn't about propping up a minority cult. It was about righting a two-thousand-year-old wrong, restoring a religion whose adherents would number in millions, and giving meaning to those thousands of martyrs who had died for their faith. He gazed silently at Aleister, awed by the ambition smouldering within the old man. But was it an achievable dream, or simply a fantasy? Standing, he moved silently to the window, watching the gulls wheeling above the cliffs. He turned and faced Aleister.

"But you don't actually know whether the Book exists."

Shaking his head sadly, Aleister agreed. "You could be right. The legends could be wishful thinking. Or the Book may have been destroyed. But imagine if we found it! It's worth having a go, even if the chances are slim."

"Fair enough. But why keep it secret? Wouldn't you improve your chances if you had more people searching?"

"Maybe. But what would happen if it fell into the wrong hands? An awful lot of people still cling to the medieval Christian propaganda that witchcraft is evil. If the public knew this Book existed, we'd be racing against hordes of creationist bible-bashers, backed by millions of pounds, determined to find it before us, so they could burn it."

Owen nodded thoughtfully. "I see. And the "Wakened" are a group trying to find it?"

"Well, yes, but there's a bit more to it than that. How much do you know about the Wakened?"

Owen hesitated before replying, deciding to stick to the truth. "Almost nothing, actually. I only know them as a name, and that they might find the Book of One."

Aleister leant towards him. "There are lots of groups searching for it. The Wakened are extremists. The sort of people who give Wicca a bad name. They'd say the end justifies the means."

"Like killing Sarah...?"

As Owen said the words, his eyes watered, and his throat tightened, strangling the question before it finished. He felt betrayed by his body's reaction at the mention of her name, reducing him to a helpless victim of physiology. Aleister was shifting in his seat, as if to lean over and comfort him. Forestalling the movement, Owen asked abruptly, "Aleister, how much of this stuff do you actually know, and how much is conjecture?"

Aleister gave him a hurt look, but Owen smiled back encouragingly.

"My dear boy, you don't mince your words, do you? I suppose it's a fair question. Everything I told you about the Romans and Druids is well-documented fact. But the burial of the Treasures, and the Book of One, is based on...um...other sources."

"Other sources?"

"Owen, I'm not sure..."

He hesitated before continuing, speaking slowly. "You need to realise there are some very sacred, very secret documents. Even fully initiated Wiccans don't get to see them unless they are one of the... "

"Please, Aleister. Are we in this together or not? What was all that guff you spun me about sharing everything we knew?"

Aleister frowned at the ground. "Yes. You're right of course. I'm sorry, Owen, this is so hard..." He stood and walked to the window, staring out. Then he turned. "Stay here. I need to make a phone call."

Owen heard him dial a number on the phone in the hallway.

"Tony? Aleister here. Are you free this morning?"...

"Well I have a young friend here who I'd like you to meet. He's..."...

"No, nothing like that, I'm afraid. Strictly business."

Owen's face flushed scarlet. Why did older people always assume that others were as deaf as they were? The

136

door closed, and Aleister's voice was reduced to a mumble. Bit late for that.

He sipped his coffee as he heard Aleister's voice raised, as if arguing, but the words were still indistinct. Then they seemed to reach agreement, and Aleister's voice levelled. The door opened.

"Yes. About ten? Wonderful. See you later."

He put down the phone and came back in the room. "Tony lives in Launceston. He's writing a book on the history of Wicca. You'll like him. Lovely man. We're working together to find the Book of One. He has an ancient script which you should see, so let's go and pay him a visit."

"Actually I was thinking I ought to go back to Cambridge today. People are starting to ask where I've got to."

Aleister didn't try to hide his disappointment. "I thought you were going to stay here and work with me on this?"

"I am. But I do have a job too you know. Besides," he added as an afterthought, "I might see what I can find out from the Cambridge Wiccans."

Aleister looked doubtful. "When will you be back?"

"In a few days. I'll be back by the end of the week. Promise."

It struck him that these words would not be ones he'd normally use. But somehow his relationship with Aleister was different. Or perhaps the loneliness he'd felt since Sarah's death had left him vulnerable to any sign of affection, from whoever. The thought left him feeling uncomfortable.

Aleister retrieved the situation. "I know. I've got an idea. Look, Launceston is on your way back to Cambridge. Why don't we take both cars over to his place, and you can head off from there."

oooOooo

The road to Launceston led over the moors. As they crawled in convoy through the dense fog, Owen couldn't help imagining shapes - ghouls and witches swirling in the mist.

He shook his head to clear the images, and gradually the morning sun started to burn the fog away. Another image started to form in the thinning mist: a giant, waving its arms, running towards him. As he blinked his eyes, the image became firmer, and then resolved into one of the massive wind generators now populating the Cornish hills. He smiled at his own quixotic susceptibility - his dalliance with Wicca was affecting his brain.

The crumbling old cottage he'd imagined, with roses around the door, was nowhere to be seen in the modern housing estate on the outskirts of Launceston. Tony was about Aleister's age, but thin-lipped, close-shaven, and dressed in a fading beige cardigan and nondescript trousers His hair was as neat and thin as Aleister's was bushy and unkempt. They seemed opposite in so many ways that Owen wondered briefly if they had been lovers. But they embraced briefly like old friends, not lovers. Or even ex-lovers. Besides Owen couldn't imagine... He dismissed the unsettling thought from his mind, as Aleister introduced him to Tony. The inside of his house was tidy, even sterile, the opposite of Aleister's ramshackle home.

After the obligatory pleasantries, Tony disappeared into the next room. Furniture creaked as it was moved and replaced, and he reappeared carrying a box file. Setting it on the table between them, he opened it reverently. Inside was a slab, which he carefully lifted out. It consisted of two sheets of glass, sandwiching a tatty yellow parchment, brittle and blotchy, like a bit of old lampshade. On it were faint marks, barely discernible as writing, and at the top was a faded coloured crest.

"What's written on it?"

"This." Tony handed him a sheet of text. "I translated it with the help of a colleague at the University."

Owen read the text aloud.

"My Lord,
After I had arranged delivery of the gold, we travelled for four days to Wessex. At Exeter, an envoy met us and guided us for a further two days through rough and wild terrain, full

138

of uncouth people. We reached our destination late at night, and under a full moon saw robed figures standing in a stone circle above us on the hill. We were not permitted to approach the circle, but instead waited a few rods away. One of the wise men came to meet us. He was dressed in strange robes, yet spoke like a nobleman. We were not permitted to see the Book of One. Instead, we were instructed to remain there, while our request was carried to the circle. I could see him and his brethren walking round the circle, deep in consultation, although I was unable to see the book itself. He returned, asked for more details, and carried my reply back to the circle. Then two of the hooded figures came down to me, saying that they would perform the spell at a time and place of my choosing.

Sire, the bearer of this message is one of those two. He is fully briefed and paid, and ready to cast the spell that will defeat the Normans, as soon as you give your word.

I remain, your humble servant,
Rufus Harengus"

Owen looked up. "That's so awesome! But how do you know it's genuine?"

Tony's face became smug. "We have a radio carbon date on the parchment -1066, give or take a few years. And we had an expert check the script, and it's either genuine or an incredibly good forgery. But nobody realised its significance until now, so a forgery's not very likely."

Owen nodded silently, and thought: unless of course you forged it.

"No I didn't."

"What?"

"I could tell what you were thinking by the look on your face. But no I didn't make this up."

Owen nodded again, inwardly kicking himself. Easy to forget how these people could pick up subtle body language. Better be more careful. "How many people know about this?"

Tony had that irritating smug expression again. "Quite a few. The translation has been passed round the Wiccan groups who are searching for the Book of One, but, we hope, nobody outside Wicca. As for the location of this document, only a handful of people know its whereabouts. We want to keep it that way - have you any idea what some people would do to get their hands on this?"

Owen considered. "Yes I can imagine. If it's genuine, it tells you there really was a Book of One. Even so, it doesn't tell you if the Book still exists, or where it is."

"It tells you it still existed a thousand years after the Roman invasion, and that it was kept near a stone circle," retorted Tony.

"True. But why the connection with stone circles?" replied Owen, unperturbed.

Impatiently, Tony explained to him, as if to an idiot. "Obviously if the Druids wanted to leave clues to the Book's location, they'd have to leave them in something that would endure. Which means either stone circles or burial mounds. But where? That's what we want to find out."

"And the Wakened are another group trying to do the same thing, right?"

Tony hesitated before replying. "Yes and no. Aleister and I are in constant communication with other pagan groups, sharing information and ideas. But the Wakened pretty much keep to themselves - they seem very secretive and we suspect their motives are not so pure."

"Like?"

"I don't know. Maybe they hope to make themselves rich or powerful. But they do claim to be working for the good of Wicca, and they do sometimes help other Wiccan groups. So we think they're heading roughly in the same direction but with a sinister twist. And we don't know what that twist is."

Aleister interrupted. "I told you that there are dangerous people around, Owen. We believe the Wakened do things that mainstream Wiccans would not condone."

The penny dropped. "Like murder?"

Aleister and Tony exchanged glances. "Maybe," replied Aleister, "We don't know. And we think they have people in positions of authority, all over the place. They seem to have enormous power. You wouldn't want to cross them."

Nodding, Owen tried to articulate a half-formed idea which had been growing in a corner of his mind. "Odd you mention that. After the accident, when I told the police how the brakes had failed, they didn't seem to want to know. As if they were being told by someone high up..."

Aleister ran a hand over his creased face. "Could be. You never know with that crowd. They act like they're running things, but I don't know if they can even control their own people. Thugs, some of them. One of these days they'll do something stupid that will discredit the whole of paganism - push the cause back a thousand years.

Owen absorbed this information. "So that's the problem you referred to - how to stop the Wakened damaging the whole of the neo-pagan movement?"

"Exactly."

"And you think the Wakened may have killed Sarah?"

Owen tried to say this in a matter-of-fact way, but he felt his eyes watering, and there was that choking sensation again. A vision suddenly appeared, unbidden and unwelcome, of Sarah sitting next to him, her arm around his shoulder, comforting him. He dismissed the thought, but felt tears on his cheeks. He became aware of the embarrassed silence, of his unanswered question, and saw the two older men exchange glances. Wiping his eyes and affecting a no-nonsense expression, he repeated the question.

"You think the Wakened may have killed Sarah?"

"Possibly," replied Aleister.

"Why?"

Aleister remained silent, but Tony broke in. "You've just heard how stone circles are connected with the Book of One. My guess is that your research on stone circles threatened the Wakened in some way. Maybe you were getting in the way of their search for clues. Or perhaps you were about to uncover their tracks. Who knows?"

Chapter 10

Pulled along like a bobbing cork in the relentless current of motorway traffic, Owen's mind drifted without inspiration over the problem of infiltrating the Wakened. He pulled out his phone and dialled Aleister's number. The recording machine answered. As the message droned on, he was glad Aleister wasn't there. It meant he could leave a message explaining exactly what was on his mind without being interrupted, being forced to simplify.

"Hi Aleister. Owen here. I was wondering if you had any..."

He was interrupted by a click. Damn! Why did Aleister have to leave the machine on even when he was there?

"Owen. I'm so glad you called."

"Oh. Aleister. Hi. I just wanted to say..."

"How did you like Tony? Isn't he a lovely chap?"

"Umm. Yes. Interesting person."

"Didn't take to him then?" Aleister's voice betrayed the smile behind his words.

Owen gave a non-committal grunt. "Aleister, I need to talk to you about where we go from here. I don't think we'll get much further until we find out more about the Wakened. Any ideas?"

"Well, I think I've told you everything I know, dear boy. I'm stumped. I was hoping you might be able to do rather better than a tired old man stuck in a rural backwater. Like you said, that's what you do."

He was taken aback by the rebuke - the first criticism he'd ever heard pass Aleister's lips. Move on. "Do you think it would be possible to infiltrate them?"

"Hard. Very hard. I'm not even sure who's a member, although I have my suspicions. They're terribly secretive. Curious lot. But you might do better in Cambridge than I can down here. It seems the sort of place where…"

Owen became aware of a siren, and a flashing blue light in his mirror. The speedometer showed a few miles per hour over the limit. Surely they wouldn't pull him over for that?

"Sorry Aleister, have to go. Call you back later."

Pulling onto the hard shoulder, he wound down the window.

"Good morning sir. Are you aware that it's an offence to use a hand-held mobile phone while driving?"

"What? Since when? Everybody does it."

"Since two years ago. Can I see your driving licence please sir? Thankyou. Stay where you are for a moment."

He watched in his mirror. Damn! The policeman walked back to his car and climbed in. The blue light was still flashing, and cars slowed as they passed. White faces pressed against the windows, curious to see the victim, wondering what he had done. There but for the grace of God. Then he saw in his mirror the two policemen discussing something funny, grinning. No doubt their computer had brought up some delicious nugget about the last time he had been stopped on the motorway. No escaping from big brother. A joke was made in the police car and they both laughed. Bastards. The policeman came back, smirking, and handed him his licence and a slip of paper, which told him that he had the choice of paying a thirty pound fine or appearing in court. After passing it to him the policeman stepped back smartly, his hands in front of his face, as if frightened of being attacked. He grinned back at his colleague for approval at his bit of play-acting. Owen glared at him, and the grin dimmed only a fraction.

"Have a good day sir."

Yeh. Like you've just improved it.

Winding up his window, he drove off. In his mirror he could see the two policemen watching him, exchanging jokes at his expense.

oooOooo

It seemed a lifetime since he'd set foot in the department. Peter had moved out of their shared office, which now seemed sparse and bare. He logged in, immediately intimidated by the five hundred emails in his intray, each demanding a reply. Skimming through them, he saw his paper had finally been accepted by the Journal of Molecular Biology. It had meant so much when .... But things were different then. Now, he wasn't sure whether he even cared. Glancing at the other emails, he saw meetings, colloquia. Please could you referee this paper... Would you be able to take on that tutorial... He couldn't face them. Not yet.

Sitting back, he looked round his office, once home to his professional life, the birthplace of some of his best ideas. He had developed affection for the battered chairs, the stained whiteboard, the frivolous gossip at morning coffee with grey-cardiganed academics wearing leather patches on their elbows. But now he felt alienated by a gulf of injustice and bitterness from his work, the department, his colleagues, and his erstwhile passion for science.

Pulling out his calculations of cell growth rates, he peered at the hand-written notes, reliving the excitement. He could even see his handwriting falling apart at points in the calculation where his mind moved faster than his hand could write. If only he could recapture that passion now. But that was a different time, a time of innocence, of optimism. Life had been simple, straight-forward.

Putting the notes down, he walked to the window, staring out over the car park surrounding the Cavendish. How could he gain entry to the Wakened? He returned to the screen and went to the Cambridge Wicca site. Their next meeting was two weeks away. Might as well drop in. Back to Google, he searched for other ways to meet Wiccans, perhaps finding a path through to the Wakened. At the bottom of the page, he saw it. Cambridge University Neo-Pagan Society. Damn - should've seen it before. Clicking on the link, he found they met weekly, in a room off Trumpington Street. Next meeting Thursday night.

144

oooOooo

Entering the Lion's Yard Car Park, he cursed the exorbitant fee designed to encourage people to use public transport. As if. He made his way to Trumpington Street and found the room. Inside were about twenty people, mostly students, with a few older people - presumably academics and postdocs. Nobody he recognised, which was unusual in the confined hothouse of University society. Many of the students were Goths, wearing elaborate make-up and flowing robes. On the other hand, none would have raised an eyebrow in the streets of Cambridge, in which generations of students had asserted their individuality in loud and unusual ways.

He felt at ease in this society, whose members were largely people he could relate to, even if they did have very different beliefs and backgrounds. Open wine bottles stood on a table, surrounded by plastic glasses. Owen helped himself to a glass of Sauvignon Blanc, and nodded to a middle-aged man pouring a drink on the other side of the table.

"First time I've been here."

"In that case, welcome. New to Paganism?"

"Not really. I've been Wiccan for a while, and have celebrated rituals with other groups, but didn't know the University Society existed," replied Owen, truthfully but misleadingly.

"You must come and meet Jane. She runs the Society." The man smirked mischievously.

They pushed through the crush to an attractive purple-clad lady in her late forties, although she obviously thought she was in her twenties, holding court to a swarm of wide-eyed undergraduates. Freshers probably. Her long blonde hair was tinged with grey.

"Excuse me, Jane. This is Owen. He's Wiccan. This is his first visit to our Society."

"Owen. How delightful to meet you." She held out her hand, palm down.

He'd never kissed a hand before, but managed an adequate Clark Gable impersonation.

145

"You're gorgeous. Come and stand next to me." The boys moved aside to let him pass. If looks could kill. "And where are you from, Owen?"

"I'm at Trinity. I'm a postdoc in biology."

"Oh. Good. Not many scientists here..." she paused, peered at him, trying to remember something she had read.

"You're not the young man in the papers? Didn't get tenure because he was Wiccan?"

"I'm afraid so. The very same."

"Well I never..." She studied his face. "So you're quite a celebrity. I must introduce you to some people."

"Thankyou. That would be great. And are you at the University, Jane?"

Apparently this was hilarious. "Sorry, darling, you've no idea who I am, have you? You're so cute. Yes, dear, I'm a professor for my sins. I run the English faculty. They put me there to shut me up. Didn't work though, did it?" She laughed uproariously, while her eyes continued appraising him.

"Come over here and meet our speaker, James."

Seizing his hand, she surged through the throng, purple folds billowing like sails, dragging him in her wake. The flotilla of young men dispersed uncertainly.

Her target was a thin gawky man talking earnestly to a student in his early twenties. Jane barged between them without an apology.

"James. You must meet Owen. He's famous round here. The University refused him tenure because of his beliefs."

The two men shook hands awkwardly while Jane bustled off to organise someone else. As she left, she winked, and sailed off into the tide of chatter.

"She's quite a character, isn't she?" remarked James, and then noticed the hapless young man who had been eclipsed by her entrance.

"Uh - terribly sorry, this is Michael."

"Hi Michael. I'm Owen. Sorry for breaking into your conversation like that."

Michael shook hands.

"Not at all. She's completely unstoppable."

146

A handbell sounded, and above it Jane's strident voice asked "boys and girls" to take their seats. He sat in the front row, and as the chairs filled, others seated themselves on the floor in front. Jane plumped down next to him and squeezed his knee encouragingly. She then stood to introduce James, and for the next hour Owen was captivated by his account of the rise of the pagan religions and their struggle for legitimacy.

When questions were invited, Owen shot up his hand. "What do you think would be the impact of discovering an ancient book which might establish the genesis of Wicca?"

Apparently flustered by the question, James mumbled a bland reply while eyeing Owen warily, as if being tested. Owen felt Jane tapping him on the arm, and turned to see her looking at him curiously.

"Interesting question," she whispered, "You're not as innocent as you look are you?"

oooOooo

After the lecture, as the tables were laid with wine and nibbles, he quickly found himself pinned into a corner by Jane. This might be his big break. Best play it softly.

"So, sweetheart, tell me why you asked that question."

"It so pisses me off that the original religion of Britain seems condemned to remain a minority cult. We're supposed to live in an age of enlightenment. If I'd been a Buddhist I'd have no problem getting tenure. But because I'm Wiccan..." He shrugged.

She stroked his arm. "You poor darling. Not many here would disagree with you. But what were you asking about the book?"

So close to the bone. So quickly. Carefully does it.

"If only we had something that would show the world we're a serious religion, with real traditions. The Christians have their Bible, the Muslims their Koran. If only...". He shook his head in despair, watching her.

"You're so right, Darling." She stroked her hand up and down his forearm, soothingly, encouraging him to open up. "And where do you think you might find such a book?"

He knew damned well what she was fishing for, but he wasn't going to give it to her on a plate. "Who knows? But I'd do anything to help find it."

"So you believe it exists?"

"I've heard stories..."

"Yes?"

Careful now. "Well, it's not really the sort of thing you talk about in public, is it?"

She beamed her approval, which he acknowledged with an embarrassed smile.

Pulling out a diary and a pen, she became businesslike. "We must talk." She wrote down his email address, and snapped her handbag shut. "Good. We should get together one evening."

oooOooo

The email arrived Tuesday morning.

"Owen Darling Are you free for dinner Wednesday evening? There are a couple of people who'd like to meet you. Jane."

He emailed her back saying he'd love to, and a few minutes later received her address and a time. The signature said that her full title was Professor Jane Pemberton, MA, PhD. There was a link to a departmental web page, where Jane's face, elegant and motherly, beamed at him, welcoming him to the department. There were links to pages listing the courses, advice to new students, a section on careers in English literature, but nothing telling him any more about her as a person.

Returning to his email, he saw one from Aleister. Would he be able to come down again at the weekend? There were more documents. Damn. He didn't feel up to the drive to Cornwall, but on the other hand he felt guilty about neglecting Aleister, who might actually have useful information.

148

"Hi Aleister Yes that would be great. See you at your place for coffee on Saturday morning? Cheers Owen."

oooOooo

The next evening he found a parking spot outside Jane's house in Newnham Road. It was a beautiful old red-brick house, its walls crumbling under a thick covering of ivy. The well-tended front garden was dominated by a massive yew, whose resident crows soared up, orbiting above the house, rasping harshly as they inspected the intruder. Clutching a bottle of wine wrapped in tissue, he rang the brass doorbell.

The door was opened by a large perfumed creation in purple sequins, all hugs and kisses and Darling's. Cowering under the onslaught, he was shepherded into an oak-panelled room where an open fire, incongruent on the mild summer's eve, roared in an Inglenook fireplace. Standing in front of it were two men, who turned to greet him. He was astonished to see that one of them was Camus.

"Darlings, this is Owen. Owen this is Camus..."

"Er...we've met. Good to meet you again...er...Camus"

"Likewise, I'm sure." Camus looked him over as if to say "...and what dragged you in here?" This trick was presumably intended to intimidate people, but to Owen's analytical eye it merely diminished the man. What personal inadequacy drove him to resort to such devices?

"...and this is George."

"Glad to meet you, George."

George was a bumbling, Pickwickian little man, an eager-to-please smile on his face, and a nervous laugh. But behind his sparkling eyes seemed a more serious, intelligent, persona.

"George - get poor Owen a drink - he must be parched."

"Of course. Come and choose your poison."

Grateful for the chance to get his bearings, Owen followed him to the drinks cabinet, where a row of expensive bottles was displayed. He chose a Laphroaig.

"Ice? Water? Anything?"

"No thanks - just straight."

"Of course. Good." George poured a large cut-glass tumbler, full to the brim with the pungent liquid.

Owen closed his eyes, feeling the smoky richness biting into his mouth, dissolving the tension in his throat, triggering memories of moorlands. Wild. Unkempt. Sarah.

Back to the moment.

"Are you a neo-pagan too, George?"

"Mm. I've been a witch for quite a few years now. In Professor Pemberton's coven."

"Ah - I see." He nodded, trying to think of a question to keep the conversation going. The little man smiled, blinked, asked nothing, expected nothing.

"And what do you do for a living, George?"

"Nothing very exciting. I just keep the department ticking over."

"Oh - so you're...?"

"The departmental Executive Officer, if you want a title. I manage the day-to-day minutiae of the department, leaving Professor Pemberton free to do what she's good at." He smirked, making it clear what she was not good at.

Owen nodded, acknowledging the mild confidence. "She's a bit of a character isn't she? Larger than life."

"And we all love her for it," replied George. Owen followed him back to the fireplace, where Jane and Camus were earnestly talking in low voices.

He saw that Jane too was drinking whisky. "That's an impressive selection of malts, Jane."

For the next few minutes, the four of them shared trivia on whisky. Camus won points by mentioning obscure single malts that nobody else had heard of. Owen held his own, regaling them with an anecdote of his visit with Sarah to distilleries in the Hebrides.

"Where is Sarah this evening, Owen?" asked Jane, brightly.

He felt a lump rise in his throat, unexpectedly. "Um, she died. A few months ago."

150

Her face dropped, perhaps a fraction early? "Poor Owen. I'm so sorry. Illness? Or...?"

"Car accident. I was driving."

As he said the words, another unbidden memory crowded into his mind. He could feel the curve of her waist as they walked arm in arm through the distillery. Never again would he feel her body pressing against his. As tears welled, and his voice became hoarse, he felt betrayed by his body's response to Jane's tactless questions. Did she already know? Then why did she ask? To see his reaction? To see who he blamed?

"It was just one of those things," he choked, "I'd rather not talk about it if you don't mind".

"Of course not," purred Jane. She seemed pleased with herself. Bitch. "George, why don't you top up poor Owen's drink?"

He was surprised to see his glass half-empty. As George topped it up to the brim, he noticed that the other three were barely sipping their drinks, which were pale and watery against the rich amber of his. The penny dropped. His barriers were to be lowered by alcohol. He needed to keep his head clear while carefully feeding them his cover story.

"I'm sorry, would you mind if I went outside for a moment? I need some fresh air."

Once in the garden, Camus pulled a packet of cigarettes from his pocket, and, without offering them round, took the opportunity to light up. Owen didn't know one brand from another, but the cigarettes looked expensive, with a gold band and a peculiar syrupy smell. As Camus took the first drag, his body was convulsed by a fit of coughing.

"Are you alright? Would you like a glass of water?" asked Jane solicitously. Camus indicated with a wave of his glass that the whisky was quite sufficient, thank you.

While their attention was distracted, Owen surreptitiously spilt a finger of whisky onto the lawn, and then tilted the glass so that it appeared as full as before. As they chatted, he sipped without swallowing, gradually straightening the glass so that it appeared to be emptying. He repeated this process, until he had emptied half the glass without drinking any. He began to affect a slight slur in his speech.

Camus became uncharacteristically friendly, as if trying to put him at ease. They discussed trivia, until the conversation meandered on to Wicca.

"I've had an interest in Wicca for years," lied Owen, "but after Sarah's death I felt I could come out. I didn't know it would lose me tenure at the University." He grinned wryly, and plunged into their cross-examination. The holes in his learning, which were quickly uncovered, were exactly where they should be for someone who had been an active practitioner for only a few months.

"And did Sarah share your beliefs?"

Why did the bastards keep on mentioning Sarah? "No she was sceptical, and so we didn't discuss it much."

The welling tears were genuine, but he played them up, became emotional, accused the other driver of speeding. He complained of feeling faint and needed to sit. They took him inside.

"Let me top you up," offered George, helpfully.

"I'd better not, thankyou," replied Owen, covering his glass with his hand. It would be harder to dispose of the whisky inside.

From then on he sipped slowly, playing the part of a man who's drunk rather too much, without actually becoming incoherent.

A uniformed maid entered and spoke deferentially to Jane. Owen couldn't imagine Jane in apron and oven gloves, and had already guessed that she would use caterers. Jane announced dinner was ready, and they took their places at the elegantly arranged table, sparkling with crystal and silver.

The four of them held hands around the table as Jane chanted in a melodramatic voice,

"Oh Gracious Goddess, Source of life, We beg you grant us wit and wine, May friendship join us in your love, So mote it be."

As the maid served a delicate salad fringed with lobster and oysters, George poured an expensively crisp white Burgundy into crystal glasses, and the conversation degenerated into small-talk. Owen's mid-range Chardonnay was nowhere to be seen. He complemented Jane extravagantly on the dinner, the table, the house, her taste and style. Her face lit up, genuinely pleased at the tribute. Camus scowled, because for him to complement Jane now would be to play second fiddle to Owen. Apparently innocent of this power-play, George smiled benignly.

The conversation lulled.

"When did you first become interested in Wicca?" asked Jane suddenly.

He hesitated - he'd already told them that. Was she trying to catch him out, or had she forgotten? Out of the corner of his eye, he saw George and Camus watching him intently.

He spun a tale of his work on stone circles, and his attempts to understand their meaning. He related his experience that night when he had chased the fox, how he had felt in touch with reality. They quizzed him intensely about this, testing whether this was a personal experience or simply a borrowed anecdote.

Jane asked him about his question at the meeting.

He repeated his show of indignation. "I see documentaries on TV about the millions of Jews killed in the Holocaust, but millions of witches were burnt alive, and nobody sheds a tear for them. It makes me so angry. I'd do anything to put Wicca back in its rightful place as the first religion of Britain."

"Anything?" asked Camus.

"Anything!" he replied with the certainty distilled from half a bottle of scotch, crashing his fist on the table, knocking over a glass. As Jane called in the girl to clear it up, he apologised, appearing flustered and embarrassed. Things couldn't be going better.

"But you mentioned a book," persisted Jane.

He fiddled with his napkin. "Maybe not now..." Amused smirks darted across their faces.

153

"Please, Owen. Consider yourself amongst friends here," soothed Jane, "Friends who can keep secrets."

"Sorry, no. I'm really enjoying your friendship and your company, but I don't think we should be discussing that here."

They poured him more wine, let the conversation ramble, and then returned to the question. He resisted. Better to demonstrate that he could keep a secret even when drunk.

She tried another tack. "Suppose, hypothetically, that such a book existed. I imagine lots of people would be searching for it."

"Of course," he replied, "It would be the break we needed to get Wicca re-established."

"And, hypothetically, would you search for it?"

"Of course."

Camus broke in angrily, as Jane rolled her eyes. "And why do you think you'd have more chance than the hundreds of other people searching for it, some of whom are experts in ancient languages and history."

George's happy face had the countenance of a spectator at Wimbledon. He looked at Owen expectantly.

"Pffff. That expertise is useful for understanding the book when you find it, and maybe even interpreting clues, but it's not going to find the book. You need someone who can solve problems, unravel complexity, stick to what's indicated by the evidence without being led astray by wishful thinking. And, frankly, I'm very good at what I do." He grinned, embarrassed at his forthrightness.

"So you're going to find the book on your own?" asked Camus, a sceptical leer on his face.

"No of course not. I need to work with those people you mentioned with expertise in history and ancient languages. But I haven't met them yet."

The challenge lay on the table, as he scanned their faces, seeing if they would pick it up. Not yet, apparently.

"So there is a book," retorted Camus, as if he'd scored a point.

"Let's cut the crap, shall we?" replied Owen, "We're obviously all talking about the Book of One." He glanced around the table, at their impassive faces.

"And you'd like to help us find it, right?" asked Camus.

"No, I think you'd like me to help you find it, but I'm not yet convinced that I'm ready to share what I know with you."

"You arrogant little prick," shouted Camus, "I've had enough of this play-acting. Who the hell do you think are?"

"Ssssh", calmed Jane, as Camus stood up and walked to the window. "Don't bully the poor boy. I'm sure he means well. Owen, with all due respect, I don't think you've any idea what you're getting into. There are hundreds of us hunting for this book, and we have an enormous amount of expertise between us. If you'd like to work with us, then it may be possible. We'd have to see. But don't underestimate those who have gone before you."

"No, you're right. I'm sorry. It was the alcohol talking. Camus, I apologise."

Jane looked at Camus, a concerned expression flitting across her face. Camus nodded almost imperceptibly.

"Alright. Alright." he growled, "I need a smoke," and left the room, pulling the cigarette packet from his pocket.

The ensuing silence was broken abruptly as George started a rambling discourse on a whisky distillery he'd once visited.

Owen turned to Jane, and thanked her for the excellent meal and a wonderful evening. He stood and shook hands with George, who seemed happily oblivious of the undercurrents. As he did so, Camus returned noisily, ignoring them, and drained his glass of wine with a scowl.

Jane followed Owen to the hallway. To his astonishment, she embraced him passionately, kissing him on the mouth. He disentangled himself, stammered his thanks as he backed away.

"You're so cute!" were her last smiling words as she closed the door on him.

The wine and whisky dictated that he should abandon his car, so he started the long walk home through the dark streets, still shaken by the embrace at her door. She would be older than his mother, and he couldn't imagine anything more unlikely than an affair between them. Was her passion genuine, or simply a ploy to destabilise him, make him more vulnerable to interrogation?

He replayed the evening's conversation. Clearly they had been vetting him. And if he passed? Were they the Wakened? It seemed likely, and yet it had been too easy. Had he been manipulated into the meeting with Jane? No, it had been his idea to go. Camus seemed a sinister character, and yet Owen had the sense that underneath the superficial veneer of unpleasantness lay very little. He had expected more depth from a group with such murky overtones.

He felt pleased with the way he had handled his drink, making himself appear more drunk than he really was. But what about his distress at the mention of Sarah's name? Was that acting or was it real?

It hit him, suddenly and hard. His love for her, his grief at her loss, his faithfulness to her memory, had become no more than props in a petty game. He had betrayed her. Dimly, through streaming tears, he realised he was almost home, and made a dash for the privacy of his front door. Once inside, the dam burst.

He shouted to her, uncaring as to whether neighbours would hear. "Sarah, my love, I'm so sorry. I don't know how I could have used you that way. I'm so terribly, terribly, sorry. Sarah, my love, how can you ever forgive me?"

Wallowing on the couch, his face buried in the cushion, he blubbered like a baby. Slowly, a curious feeling of dissociation crept up on him, so although his tears were still in full flood, another, out-of-body version of him floated above the couch, looking down at the snivelling wreck immersed in self-pity, and observed it with grim satisfaction. Who was he trying to impress with these histrionics? Who would be moved by his self-pity? The answer came coldly. Nobody. Somebody. Just me. This isn't about Sarah, you pathetic little creep, this is about you. You're enjoying this aren't you?

He jumped up, shouting, "No! You're lying. I loved her! All this is for her!"

156

And then he heard Sarah's voice. "I know it is Owen. You don't have to justify it. You're doing what's right, and I love you for it. Always will. Always."

Stunned, pale-faced, his hair rising on the back of his neck, he sat stiffly on the couch and listened to the silence. He stared at the crystal vase that now contained her ashes. Nothing. Where had that voice come from?

"Sarah?"

Straining, he heard nothing but the rushing in his ears. A car door slammed down the street, people calling, a car horn, and then the car drove off.

Silence.

Chapter 11

The next morning, waking with both a hangover and a growing sense of apprehension, he walked to Jane's house to pick up his car. Turning the corner, he saw it awaiting him, apparently untouched. And yet. Something not quite right. The way it stood, alone, avoided by the other parked cars? Or the mess of fallen leaves on its roof, decaying, composting, already trying to assimilate the manufactured steel, torn from the Earth, back into the natural order. Ashes to ashes. Phf! His imagination was running away. And yet. Something about this place.

Reaching the car, he brushed off a twig that had become entangled with the aerial, and saw that it was not simply entangled, but was tied on with strands of grass. Along with fading wildflowers. Cowslip? Primrose? The twig was mistletoe. Other flowers had been inserted into gaps in the doors, in the boot. Circling the car, a heavy dread descended on him, a certainty that this was some evil Wiccan spell. He cast around as if for clues, but the road was silent in the early morning sun, other than the incessant rasp of the crows in Jane's garden. And then he saw a shape move, darkly, behind a net curtain.

There had been no attempt to hide the spell, if that's what it was. Either he was meant to notice it, or else it didn't matter. Either way, not much he could do about it now. Unless. Maybe more than just a few flowers? The doors were locked, the bonnet closed. Nothing amiss under the car, no brake fluid dripping. Standing back, he pressed the remote control. No explosion, no roaring flames. He opened the bonnet. An engine, nothing more. Nervously, climbing into the drivers seat, he looked at the ignition key. Was his imagination over-wrought? But they had killed Sarah, and set fire to his other car. It would be stupid to try starting the engine. He sat paralysed, watching his hand insert the key. He held his breath, perhaps his last, as the key slowly turned in the lock. The car started. Sliding it into gear he drove down the street cautiously, checking the operation of the brakes. Away from Jane's house, he stopped. Again he peered under the car, around it, in the boot. Nothing but fading wild flowers. Nothing but some stupid Wiccan spell.

"Ridiculous superstition!" he said aloud, and the voice renewed his confidence. "Pathetic crazy bitch. It will take more than one of her idiotic spells to stop me."

Reaching work, he started his daily chore of checking his email. He'd won the Belgian lottery, and only had to send them a few pounds to claim his prize. Yeh, right. As he deleted the mail, a security alert popped up. The Belgian email had tried to install a spyware program on his computer. Strange. He'd never been attacked like that before. Perhaps no more than a coincidence, but ... If it hadn't been for his Norton anti-virus software, someone would now have access to everything that he read, wrote, or viewed. Must be more careful. He quarantined the offending email, and started working through the genuine ones.

The phone rang. Would he like to join the other staff and postdocs down the pub at lunchtime, celebrate Peter's birthday?

He gritted his teeth. "Um - not sure - I'm a bit tied up right now. Where did you say?"

"Rose and Crown. Twelve thirty."

"OK. Maybe I'll see you there"

Or maybe not. He hung up. He couldn't face that crowd. Especially Peter, who had taken to lording it over the other postdocs since his appointment. The rat had been given the task of "Project Coordinator" for the postdocs, and had seized the role with enthusiasm, milking it of every opportunity to patronise his erstwhile contemporaries, telling them how to run their projects. As if he'd know. He'd even taken to giving them advice on how to advance their careers, reach for the glittering prizes.

Owen stood and paced the room angrily, fuming impotently at his inability to serve Peter his just deserts. He left the building, marching rapidly around the car park until his adrenalin dissipated in the fresh air.

He returned to the email. Amongst all the routine chit-chat of academic life was an email from Jane, saying she hoped he hadn't been upset by Camus's rudeness, and would he like to come to a party on Saturday, at her house. Damn. Obviously he should, but it would mean letting down Aleister. He started composing an email to Aleister, and then thought better of it. He'd phone him later, from his mobile.

Logging into the Unix system, he was informed that he had logged in three hours earlier, at a time when he had been fast asleep. Then he found his internet bank account had been accessed the previous day. No money taken, but somebody had managed to poke around in his account.

He came home that night to find the chair in his bedroom had been moved a couple of inches. Imperceptible, unless you were used to it being in exactly the same place, day in, day out. Returning downstairs, taking the post from his letterbox, he noticed the back of an envelope wasn't stuck down properly.

None of these intrusions was hard evidence. Maybe he had accidentally knocked the chair, maybe a system administrator had been checking his Unix account, maybe the envelope was badly sealed. But the ensemble of circumstantial evidence pointed unambiguously to one fact: he was under surveillance. He had a good idea who could be doing it. And relished it. He had been careful to hide his tracks, and was confident that all they found would support his story. Furthermore, now he could lay bait.

He spent the evening cleaning the disk on his computer, wiping anything that might cause suspicion. Switching off his security software, he checked his email again. This time, he opened all the junk mail, clicking on links advertising Viagra at discount prices, enquiring about mysterious amounts of money being offered from Nigeria. By the evening, his computer was running noticeably more slowly, and seemed to be sending volumes of information over his broadband connection even when he wasn't accessing the internet. Checking the task manager, he saw three new tasks running in the background whose names he didn't recognise. He didn't check them out, because that very action would betray his expertise to the spyware. Instead, he wanted the Wakened to continue thinking he was merely another dumb user, blissfully unaware of the spyware they had loaded.

The next morning he used cash to buy a cheap pre-paid mobile phone, registering it under a false name and address. A secure, anonymous, phone which wouldn't be monitored by the Wakened. Or anyone else, for that matter. He used it to call Aleister, explaining that he was hot on the trail, so wouldn't come down to Cornwall that weekend. Aleister was disappointed and concerned.

"But Owen, dear boy, these may be dangerous people. Sooner or later they'll figure out that you're seeing me... I mean ...working with me."

"I've worked out a cover story for that. I'll email you to ask you some questions about the museum. Reply to me as you would to a query from someone you don't know. Then we can subsequently talk at that level without arousing suspicion. But in the meantime, don't phone or email me except on this number."

Aleister agreed, and then Owen asked the question that had been troubling him. "One other thing. When I returned to my car, it had wild flowers pushed into the cracks, and a sprig of mistletoe tied to the aerial. Aleister? What's so funny?"

"Sorry. It sounds to me like a love spell. Someone wants you to fall in love with them!"

Damn! He slammed down the phone. That stupid crazy bitch.

That evening, he sent an email.

"Dear Aleister Thankyou very much for your email the other day. I would be very grateful if you could tell me if any records exist in your museum of witches using stone circles before the fourteenth century. With many thanks Owen Davies."

The bait laid, he retired to bed, feeling at last he was regaining control of his life. More than that, he was now on the track to exposing Sarah's murderers. His feelings towards the Wakened were curious - Vindication? Anger? Fear? Another feeling. One he couldn't recognise. As he drifted off, he was jolted awake. It was staring him in the face. Vengeance. Curious, he'd never thought of vengeance as an emotion, but there it was now, occupying his mind and body, its raw power confusing him with its unfamiliar overtones.

He explored how it felt, as one walks up and down the room in a new pair of shoes. But as he examined it, tried it on for size, it became evasive, camouflaged behind other feelings, until he could no longer perceive it as a separate entity. But he could feel its heavy presence burning through his mind as it lurked, simmering in the background, awaiting its chance.

Drifting off to sleep once more with his unfamiliar bedfellow, he reflected on the strangeness of analysing his feelings in this way. He, the quintessential logical scientist, having spent his life denying the power of his emotions, let alone analysing them, was now being driven in foreign and unpredictable directions by feelings he didn't understand. What had changed? Sarah's death, of course. He remembered reading how falling in love, real love, triggered a re-wiring of the brain, moulding your world, your perceptions, around that of your lover. Sever that love, and you perform an instant lobotomy. And then months, years, of rebuilding, re-adjustment. That's what was happening now. That's why he was having this very thought. Now. But even as he recited this analysis, a faint, irrational voice penetrated dimly through his logic.

"Owen, don't forget me."

"Sarah?" He sat bolt upright, his hair once again rising on his neck. The voice had come from downstairs. He listened. Silence. Switching on the light, he went downstairs to the empty rooms where Sarah had once been. On the shelf was the silver bowl in which her ashes now slept. Nothing. Just imagination. Back to bed.

"Goodnight, my love," he murmured as he drifted off once again.

oooOooo

The weekend arrived, and Owen realised he had no idea what sort of party he had been invited to. Informal? Dinner? Cocktails? Would her hands be all over him, or was it another step towards his initiation into the Wakened? Or both? He decided to dress cautiously - as if her mythical invitation card had been emblazoned with the problem-solving words "smart casual". But he would carry a tie in case. Maybe stay in his car for a few minutes, watch other guests arrive, and slip the tie on if necessary. And if it were a black tie affair - well, she would have said, wouldn't she? Besides, he didn't have time to rent a dinner jacket. Or was it called a tuxedo nowadays?

There were no spaces outside Jane's house, and so he parked round the corner. Fat chance of seeing the other guests. As he walked back to her house, a taxi delivered an elderly man in a dinner jacket, complete with cummerbund, and his wife in a sumptuous evening dress. Jane, resplendent in a vast billowing pink ball-gown, top-heavy with jewellery, appeared at the front door to greet them, and, as she ushered them in, spotted Owen retreating into next-door's shrubbery.

"Owen, darling!" she shrieked, in a voice that triggered a swirl of black crows to rise in alarm. He resisted the urge to turn and flee, instead greeting her with his bravest smile, while peering over her shoulder at the over-dressed throng within. Her arm round his waist, she kissed him in a way that would appear to other guests to be merely sociable, but with a simmering passion that terrified him. He disengaged himself awkwardly.

"I'm sorry, I didn't realise it was black tie. Maybe I should run home and change." He looked at her reproachfully. She should have said. Grinning, she seemed to enjoy his discomfort, as if the omission had been deliberate.

"Nonsense, darling. You're beautiful. Come and meet everybody."

Dismayed, he saw that most men were dressed in full formal regalia, and he alone was tieless. But to retrieve his tie from his pocket would seem pitiful, merely elevating him to the ranks of the under-dressed. Better to brazen it out, flaunt his individuality, pretend that he felt relaxed. At least he wasn't wearing jeans and trainers.

After equipping him with a glass of champagne, she introduced him to two middle-aged men talking nearby. William was a tall, gaunt man, with receding black hair, hook nose, and disapproving prim lips, who blatantly looked him up and down to show him what a pitiful worm he was to come dressed in the Wrong Clothes. Must be a friend of Camus. But the man's studied insult only bolstered Owen's resolve to assert that he had chosen not to come dressed as a stuffed penguin. The other man smiled, appearing not to notice his eccentric garb, and greeted him warmly. Owen politely but unenthusiastically joined their conversation about genetically modified crops, while scanning the other guests.

In a corner stood Camus and George, in earnest conversation with three men. There were others from the Cambridge Wicca group, some of whom acknowledged him with a nod and a smile. He saw the guy he had chatted with, before the lecture - what was his name - David? David saw him and raised his glass in acknowledgement as he continued his conversation with a beautiful young girl. God she was cute. Who was she? He'd seen her somewhere before... Making his excuses, he sauntered over.

"Hello, David. Owen. Remember we met at the Wiccan meeting?"

"Er... Michael, actually. Good to meet you again. This is Geneviève." He pronounced it the French way.

Owen fumbled his apologies for misremembering Michael's name, and then stumbled over Geneviève's name as he shook hands with her.

"Call me Jenny," she laughed. Her elfin face was framed by long blonde hair tumbling over flawless creamy-white shoulders. He thought at first she might have been some magazine starlet, but now he was close, he could see her beauty was quite different from the glossy perfection of magazine covers. She wore hardly any make-up, and where the light struck her cheek there was a softness, a natural unblemished fuzziness, to the line. But her enchantment originated above all from her laughing blue eyes, which were

164

a little too large, perhaps even a little too far apart. Their focus was deep within him, as if penetrating superficial appearances, recognising the soul of dreams and ideas hidden inside. She made him feel they had a special affinity, that he was the most important person in her world. As he shook her hand he was entranced by the fragility of her child-like wrist. Where had he seen her?

The three of them joked about the stuffed shirts around them, as he recounted how Jane had neglected to mention the evening's dress code. It now seemed so unimportant, comical even, and whether it was the champagne, or this bewitching girl, he found himself relaxing, enjoying her warmth, her wide-eyed innocence, her uncompromising openness. Trays of champagne came and went, and they were becoming a little tipsy. As Michael evaporated, she led him by the hand into the coolness of the garden outside. They sat on a love seat under a huge old oak.

They discussed their respective entries into Wicca. Jenny had been Wiccan for years, and proclaimed that making love was the ultimate expression of divine worship.

"I believe in worshipping every night," she murmured, barely audibly. He stared back. Had she really said that? And those eyes. Where had he seen them before, teasing him in the same way?

"Er - awesome - yes. Look, my car's just around the corner. Why don't we go back to my place?"

Laughing, she put a finger to his lips. "Patience!" was all she said.

She became serious again, explaining the importance of coupling spirituality with the physical act of love, that two people could only enjoin once they understood each other completely, knew each other's motivations and yearnings. So what were his beliefs? What drove him?

He moved closer as he told her about Sarah, how after her accidental death he had looked for a deeper meaning, and had found it in Wicca. She drew back.

"But there's something else - an anger inside you, something you've not told me, something secret and precious. What is it Owen?"

165

Shrugging, he told her of his anger at himself for losing Sarah through his drinking, and at the other driver for going too fast. Still she persisted.

"Poor Owen. But there's something else, something simmering deep inside you. You need to release it. Until you do, it will divide us." Her hand caressed him as she spoke. He desperately wanted release, and longed to tell her about his anger at the bastards who had murdered Sarah. But even now, when both his sobbing heart and his throbbing hormones urged him to tell this sweet, caring girl, his reason cautioned him otherwise.

"Dearest Owen. It must be terrible for you."

He swung the focus. "What about you, Jenny? You seem so open and innocent, but there's a much more complex person inside you, isn't there. What do you keep hidden? What's the passion that keeps your flame burning?"

Lowering her eyes, she became silent for a moment. "You're right - you are so perceptive."

She paused, and then drew an audible breath, as if signalling a decision. "Can you keep a secret?"

"Of course."

"My mother died three years ago. They said it was a heart attack. It wasn't."

"I'm so sorry. What was it?"

"Owen, most Wiccans are beautiful, spiritual people - some of the loveliest people on our planet."

"Yes, of course."

"But in our midst is a small group of dark-hearted individuals with a lust for power, who would do anything to achieve their wicked ends."

He said nothing, but frowned questioningly.

"My mother was a wise and magical woman, and many Wiccans from all over the country were guided by her words. She spoke out against this group, and was murdered, poisoned, for it. Owen, I have never told this to anyone before, but I have vowed to find her killers and bring them to justice."

"Have you any idea who they are?"

166

"Yes - but..." She paused. "I'm sorry. I've told you too much. I am already risking my own life, and I don't want to risk yours too."

"But Jenny, let me help you, I..." He was on the point of saying it, but even now, his intellect warned him. He paused, balanced on the edge of decision. She had opened up to him, entrusted her secret, why shouldn't he reciprocate?

"Yes Owen?"

As she looked up at him, childlike, innocent, desperately needing his help, he kissed her, stroked her hair, and said nothing.

"Owen, would you really help me? Maybe I could help you with your secret too?"

"Jenny, I'll do anything to help you. But the thing is, I have no secret."

Putting her arms around him, she nestled her head against his neck. "Thankyou so much. But I'm not sure you're being..."

"Ssh.. don't worry about it. Let's go somewhere private."

She shook her head, and raised it. "Owen, I think the people who killed my mother belong to a group called the 'Wakened'. But I only know the name. I'd do anything, anything, to find out more about them. Have you heard of them?" Her hand caressed him again as she spoke.

He turned and kissed her passionately on the lips, then raised his face, and said, "No, sorry, never heard of them. Let's go to my place."

"I'm sorry, Owen. Not tonight. Not while there's this thing lying unresolved between us. I cannot worship with you until we have a completely open, trusting relationship. There's something you're not telling me, and I know it's very hard for you. Maybe you don't need to tell me everything. Just one word will do." She kissed him, still massaging him with her hand.

His body screamed at him. Go on, you fool. Bloody tell her something. A hint. A word. Say you may have heard of the Wakened. You don't have to betray anything.

He kissed her again, and said "Sorry. I really don't have anything to tell."

Pulling away, she stood, and said, "I'm sorry too, Owen." And walked away.

He sat alone in the dark, seething with frustration. Surely he could have told her, could have trusted her. But she had been persistent, and it was all a bit too much of a coincidence that she was trying to avenge her mother, killed by the Wakened. In the end, he decided his instincts had been correct. Maybe he could try again. But he didn't have her email address or phone number, or even her last name. Perhaps he didn't even have her real first name. He gave a sigh of opportunity lost. Maybe he would meet her again in some Wiccan circle.

As his consciousness returned to the present, he became aware of the noise of the party around him, as he sat alone in the darkness under a tree. A man brayed loudly at some stupid joke, followed by a shriek of laughter that could only be Jane. The ugly rasp of crows in the tree counterpointed the trivial noises of the party that had disturbed them, and suddenly Owen was alarmed by the swish of wings close to his face. He was hit by an overwhelming feeling of being in the wrong place, out of his depth, threatened by unseen creatures swimming deep below him. He had to leave, quickly. A path led around the side of the house, avoiding the party. He stumbled along it, pitched into blackness, and sensed breathing on his neck. But he couldn't turn to look, because by then he would have lost it, capitulated to his imagination. Instead, he ploughed on grimly, denying panic, denying the feeling of doom riding on his shoulders, his hasty walk breaking into a stumbling run. By the time he hit the sharp edge of the wheelbarrow he was in full flight. Garden spades and forks tumbled on to him, the bruising rain of wood and metal followed by shouts from the garden.

"Who's there? Are you alright?"

But the road was in sight, and he picked himself up, hurting and bleeding, and ran towards his car.

He sat in it, ashamed of his flight, ashamed of these primeval fears intruding into his rational psyche. Ever since the accident ....

oooOooo

2am, lying awake in bed. He'd tried everything - counting backwards, meditating, deep breathing, but each time the image of Geneviève insisted on taking centre stage. His emotions tumbled uncontrollably, mortified by the sense of lost opportunity, tempered by a feeling that he'd somehow beaten off an attack. But where had he seen her before?

In the dream. It was her, standing in the stone circle, teasing him, persuading him to enter the grave. He sat bolt upright, sweating, and switched on the light. Clambering out of bed, he drank a glass of water thirstily, pacing the floor, waiting for reason to flood in. It was ridiculous. A resemblance, no more. Imagination and a pretty face had done the rest.

oooOooo

Over the next few days, he became certain that his email was being monitored, his files scrutinised. Strange clicks were heard on the phone. The small splinter of wood positioned inside the front door was one day moved, although nothing else seemed disturbed. He phoned Aleister on his secret mobile, explaining he was under close surveillance, and shouldn't see him for a few weeks.

At work, he started running the cell growth simulations, but his heart wasn't in it, and he found himself staring out of the window, wondering if the Wakened would call him, or worse.

The following Tuesday, he received a phone call from George. Could they meet for lunch. With Jane? A laugh. No. Jane won't be there.

Entering the pub from the bright sunshine, he paused a moment to let his vision adjust. George wasn't in the main bar, so he explored the maze of bars and snugs surrounding it. He found him sitting at a table against the far wall of a small side-room. Next to him was another man. And Geneviève.

In the two seconds that it took him to walk from the door to their table, Owen's feelings passed through astonishment, bewilderment, and disorientation, to the gnawing realisation that Geneviève had been part of his initiation test, that she had not meant any of what she had said. Nothing was as it seemed.

George rose as he approached, and held out his hand, which Owen shook numbly, while looking at Geneviève. To his surprise, the deceiver stood and rewarded him with a warm smile and a chaste peck on his cheek. He couldn't help staring at her, but then realised George was talking.

"...and I gather you already know Jenny."

She smiled at him, a smile that thawed the ice in his heart, her eyes boring into him as they had that evening, still singling him out, still asserting, that, come what may, there was a special bond between them. How could someone who radiated such simple, innocent love have a heart so duplicitous? Desperately trying to recover his balance, Owen shook hands with the man, a few years older, who sat the other side of George.

"I'm sorry, I didn't catch your name."

"Sebastian. Glad to meet you Owen. Merry meet."

Owen fumbled with the menus, isolating himself while he grasped at composure.

Jenny grabbed his hand. "Come and help me look at the specials on the blackboard."

He followed her meekly, and once out of earshot she said, "I'm so sorry, Owen. But much of what I said the other night was true. And even if I deceived you, it was for the best reasons. I'd really like you to join our team, and I had to prove to George that you were reliable. Please forgive me."

He said nothing, his thoughts whirling aimlessly without settling. If only he could believe her, they could become close again, and then... But if she had been lying that evening, she might well be lying now. Without thinking, he found himself kissing her on the forehead, and immediately

170

regretted it. Wordlessly, she took his hand and led him back to the table.

After ordering meals and drinks, George got down to business. He nodded to Sebastian, who closed the door, separating them from the lunchtime crowd in the main bar outside. George seemed a different person from that night at Jane's, his Pickwickian bumbling replaced by a casual down-to-earth directness. After asking Sebastian to place a chair against the door, he turned to face Owen.

"First, I must stress that, whatever the outcome of this meeting, every word must remain completely confidential. I can't emphasise too much the serious consequences of revealing to anyone what I'm about to tell you. If you're not comfortable with this, then we'll shake hands and go our separate ways. So do you want to continue this conversation?"

Owen agreed.

"Good. Let me explain what this is all about. You're no fool, and so I'm going to put my cards on the table. No doubt you have already guessed that we are members of a group dedicated to re-establishing Wicca once more as a major religion. We are moving on several fronts, one of which is to re-discover the Book of One, and I believe you'd like to help us with that."

There was a knock on the door, and they paused while Sebastian moved the chair to allow the waiter to carry in the tray of drinks. Owen took a long draught of the ale, feeling its comforting mellow bitterness drain his tension, at the same time telling himself not to drink too much if he was to be interrogated. He asked for a mineral water. As the waiter left, and the chair was replaced, George continued.

"We feel that you could be a useful member of our group, and our research has confirmed that impression."

"Research?"

George paused, looked at him, and nodded slowly, leaving no doubt just how thorough that research had been.

"There are areas in which you have impressive skills and knowledge, whose value you don't yet appreciate. Equally, you don't yet appreciate how little you know, and frankly, your knowledge of witchcraft seems a bit thin. If you

171

join our group, meld your skills with ours, I think we can help you realise your full potential. I believe that, together, we are close to finding the Book of One."

At last. It had come. After months of scheming and planning, he had infiltrated them. Brushing those jubilant thoughts aside, trying not to appear over-excited, he started to stammer his thanks, but George held up his hand.

"However. There remain a few unanswered questions, which we would like to ask you, if you agree."

They spent the next hour gently grilling him on his beliefs, his work on stone circles, Sarah's death, and his relationship with Aleister. Although the tone of the questions was amiable, he felt like a criminal being interrogated by a pair of skilled but superficially friendly detectives, the bad cop being kept for later. He was horrified to discover how much they knew about him, as if they had opened him like a book, read every chapter, and written footnotes and indices.

"So how did you feel when the police wanted to open Sarah's casket?"

"What?"

He remembered his fury at that idiot policeman, his distress that Sarah had been violated. But the point of the question was to tell him how far their tentacles spread. He hadn't told anybody about that episode. So they had contacts within the police.

As they continued to throw questions at him, they seemed less interested in his answers than in his reactions. Sebastian said little, scribbling from time to time in a small note book. Owen guessed that he had a background in psychology.

They started asking strange, unfocussed questions, apparently sensing that hidden in the labyrinth of his answers was a secret compartment not yet penetrated. They were walking round his mind, knocking on the panelling, pressing on bookshelves, hoping to find the concealed entrance, some musty tunnel to a hidden chamber containing Owen's darkest secrets. But he had known this time would come, and had bricked over the entrance. He hoped.

The momentum slowed, their avenues exhausted, and still his brickwork was intact. They seemed pleased. George and Jenny exchanged glances and asked if he'd mind if they spoke in private. Remaining in the deserted room, he sipped his beer, his energy drained by the intense questioning, but daring to hope that he had convinced them of his sincerity. His fake sincerity.

They returned, beaming. "Owen, I'm glad to say that we think you'd be a wonderful member of our group, and we'd like you to consider joining us."

"That's wonderful. Thankyou. Yes I'd..."

But George held up his hand. "Before you agree, I need to tell you a little more about us, and then I want you to go away and think about it carefully before you make a decision."

He felt foolish. "Oh, yes, of course."

"We are a select group, totally committed to our goal. We will do anything, anything, to achieve it. Re-discovering the Book of One would be an enormous step forward for all of Wicca, but our group has other goals too."

"Really? Like what?"

George paused, and took a swig of beer as he weighed his answer. "I can't tell you yet, but you need to be aware that there is more to our group than finding the Book of One. All our members have a definite contribution to make in their respective spheres. And we carry no passengers."

He pronounced the last words deliberately, as a general might say, "and we take no prisoners."

Staring into his beer again, George seemed to be searching for the right words, while the others sipped their drinks, watching his face. "I believe that you have plenty to offer us, Owen, and I am convinced that, if you join us, you will become a leading and valued member of our group. But we also ask a lot from our members, and so you have to decide very carefully if you are willing to make the commitment we ask of you."

He began to feel concerned at the gravity of the words. "What commitment is that?"

"First, if you decide to join us, we will require you to make a solemn oath of secrecy. You need to know that the penalty for breaking the oath is severe."

"How severe?"

George turned on him, quickly, dangerously, as if he had just given a wrong answer. "Why do you ask? Are you planning to break the oath even before you've made it?"

"No. I just... Just wondered, that's all," he replied, limply.

George looked calmly at him, needling him with the weapon of silence. At last he spoke, with no trace of his habitual smile.

"Terminally severe."

Owen knew he shouldn't have been surprised, but he was shaken to hear it spoken out loud. He thought of Sarah lying in her box at the funeral. That severe. He found the lump rising in his throat once more.

But was it really news? He was sailing into uncharted and dangerous, possibly fatal, waters. He had already made the decision, both intellectually and emotionally, to risk his life, avenge Sarah's death, commit the ultimate consummation of his love. Another reaction was the grim satisfaction that he had at last infiltrated a group prepared to kill for the sake of Wicca.

"OK. That's no problem."

"Good. Second, we need your total commitment. If you join us, we demand that you place our quest above everything else you do - your job, your career, your friends, your social life. Are you prepared to make that degree of commitment? Because if not, you should say so now. In which case we shake hands, part as friends, with no hard feelings, and you'll never hear from us again."

Owen was cautious not to appear over-eager. He also recognised George's tactics: such daunting obstacles might be a barrier for the merely enthusiastic, but would be a magnet for a true believer.

"OK. I think I can make that commitment, but I'll need a few days to think about it."

"Good. Now have you any questions for us?"

"Umm... Are you the Wakened?"

George smiled, lightening the tension. "Glad to see you've been doing your homework. I'm happy to answer generalities now, but not specifics. Not until you agree to join us."

"How many people are in your group?"

"Difficult to say. There are a handful of us in Cambridge."

"And Jane is a member of your group?"

George snorted. "What do you think? After all I've told you about the level of commitment and secrecy we require?"

Stung by the rebuke, he felt foolish and defensive. "Well, I didn't know if Jane's manner was just a front. Like yours," Owen retorted.

The answering smile was patronising, but also acknowledged the point. "She helps us, but isn't herself a member. It wouldn't really be her forte. I'd call her a friend of the organisation. An elder stateswoman, who is kind enough to play a part when asked. Anything else?"

"What do you mean, play a part? All that... infatuation. Was that a part?"

George smiled. "I couldn't possibly comment on her feelings for you. I think that should be something between you two, and nobody else."

Owen wasn't going to get any useful answers. "OK. No more questions. I'll go away and think about it." He drained the beer in front of him, and stood.

But George motioned for him to be seated.

"Sorry, one more thing."

"Yes?"

"Before you make this grave decision, and before we decide whether to welcome you into our group, I think we should seek guidance."

"Oh. Yes. Of course."

Jenny reached into her pocket, and pulled out a small ziplock bag of herbs. Marijuana? She produced a small brass bowl, emptied the bag into it, and lit a match. The tinder-dry mixture caught immediately, and instead of marijuana, the small room filled with the heady fragrance of incense, sage,

175

basil, cinnamon. They held hands around the pungent flames, and closed their eyes.

Jenny chanted in a strange, high-pitched voice,

"We have the will and have harnessed the power of the spirit,
The God and Goddess will receive our dreams and know our
hearts to be pure.
If it be their will as it is ours, so mote it be."

George and Sebastian responded, "So mote it be."
"... it be." added Owen.
After a pause, she continued

"Flame of love, of holy power,
Pray help us find the path to truth,
And guide us in this solemn hour.
Grant us now your sacred sight,
That we may see each others hearts,
And lead us to your blessèd light.
So mote it be."

"So mote it be"
Silence.
Cautiously, Owen opened his eyes, to see the other three staring at him. Suddenly, overwhelmingly, he was seized by an irrational impulse to turn and flee. But he was caught, held in their gaze like a rabbit in headlights, unable to move. A tide of horror welled up within, threatening to engulf him. His mind thrashed wildly, blindly searching for escape from its inquisitors.

Then, from a hidden corner of his mind, came an even stronger voice, soft, clear, distinct. It was Sarah's. "Owen, my love, be strong. For me. For our love."

The tide of panic turned, and receded, to be replaced by a feeling of balance, of peace, the sunlight after the storm. Whether the spell was real magic, which was obviously absurd, or superstitious mumbo-jumbo designed to intimidate, it was no match for the strength of his feeling for

Sarah. He looked up calmly, confidently, into each of the inquisitorial eyes.

The grave faces collapsed into warm, welcoming, smiles. They stood, and Jenny reached over and kissed him. Sebastian shuffled round and gave him a hug. Beaming, George reached over and gave him a two-handed handshake.

"The Goddess favours you, Owen. I do hope you decide to join us." Hmm. Quite. But which goddess?

That night, Owen slept poorly, questioning through long hours the wisdom of his decision to join the Wakened. A few weeks ago, it had seemed clear that he would go to any length to avenge Sarah, to express his love in the only way left to him. But in the grey hours of the false dawn, decisions made by the heart must be arraigned before the cold unblinking stare of mortality.

He could still change his mind. Why take this risky path leading either to his own death, or that of Sarah's killers? Better to work out a lower-risk way of bringing them to justice. Take his time, plan it out, not rush into the first opportunity that arises. As dawn broke he went downstairs to phone George, to say "no thanks".

Passing Sarah's ashes, he lifted them down, cradling them in his arms as he sat on the sofa. For an hour he slowly rocked back and forth, holding the ashes to his chest, his cheeks moistened with tears. Abruptly he stood, went to the phone, and dialled. A machine answered.

"Hi George. Owen here. The answer is yes. I'm with you. Blessed be." He put the phone down before he could change his mind.

Chapter 12

The call wasn't returned until mid-morning.

"So glad you decided to join us. We need to take you through a short initiation ceremony - are you free Monday night?"

He was given an address, and instructed to arrive at 11 p.m., no earlier, no later.

The weekend dragged on interminably, enlivened by neither work nor pleasure. But Monday evening arrived, and he set out 30 minutes before the instructed time. It was a large secluded house near the Gog Magog Hills, hidden from Babraham Road by a row of trees and dense foliage. The entrance was marked by an electric security gate set between two imposing gateposts. He climbed out of the car to give his name at the intercom panel, but the gate opened as he approached it. Must be a surveillance camera somewhere. He cautiously entered the leafy drive, beyond which a dozen cars were parked untidily. From the back of the house flickered the glow of a bonfire, and he could hear people chanting. As he manoeuvred his car into a narrow space between two others, he was startled by a sharp knock on the window.

"Hurry up!" Jenny mouthed, smiling. Behind her he could see the bonfire clearly, sparks soaring like fireflies into the crow-black void above. Silhouetted against the fire were black figures, dancing to the measured pace of their rhythmic chant. She kissed him chastely as he climbed out, and led him inside the house, reflections of the bonfire and dancers following them, one window at a time. Standing in the dining room were George and Sebastian, both of whom greeted him warmly, and Camus, who did not.

George poured whisky into three crystal tumblers, and a sherry into a small glass which he handed to Jenny.

"To Owen, and to his long and fruitful association with the Wakened." They chinked their glasses together. It was the first time he'd heard that name confirmed by one of its members. Shouldn't there have been a roll of drums?

George winked at him and said, in a stage whisper, "You don't need to spill your whisky this evening."

Acknowledging this revelation with a bashful grin, he registered that Camus seemed as baffled as the other two by the cryptic remark.

"Don't underestimate him", said George, as if in explanation. Camus scowled, as if he understood what they were talking about. Jenny's face slid from bewilderment to hurt, as if Owen were concealing something from her. As if.

"Right now, down to business," said George, rubbing his hands theatrically. "Don't mind the crowd out there, by the way. It's the weekly celebration of our coven. I'm afraid you can't join them quite yet, but they'll witness your oath."

"Oh. Yes. Right."

George handed him a sheet of paper. "Read it carefully and thoroughly. Take your time, don't rush. It's pretty straight-forward. Ask me if you'd like anything explained."

The document was thick, handmade parchment, scribed in a beautiful old-fashioned copperplate.

"I, Owen Lloyd Davies, hereby solemnly declare to the God and the Goddess, and to my peers, priests, and all members of the Wakened, that I will henceforth dedicate my life to the Art of the Wakened. I solemnly vow that I will not reveal the existence of the Wakened, or the identity of its members, or any aspects of its Art, to any person who has not been so initiated. I make these sacred vows willingly, knowingly, and with Perfect Love and Perfect Trust, and I acknowledge the right of the Wakened to exact any penalty from me, including the forfeit of my life, if I should break them. I sign this vow with my own blood, of my own free will, under no duress or persuasion."

He looked George in the face with a grave, thoughtful expression.

"Yes. I'm willing to sign it."

"Give me your left hand." As expected of him, as if this was the point of no return, he hesitated. But that point had been a long time ago. George produced a razor blade from his pocket, and swiftly cut the end of a finger. Owen had no time to flinch, and barely felt the sting, despite the copious flow. Jenny handed a thimble to George, who filled it with blood, and then dipped an old-fashioned quill into it, while she placed a Band-Aid on the cut. The whole process had taken perhaps twenty seconds, in complete silence. Owen took the quill. He signed, and looked up, expectantly. They were smiling, and George shook his hand, warmly, but seriously, as he took the paper.

"Now we need to go outside, to complete the Ritual of Oath. Don't do anything except when Camus tells you. And put this on." As he puzzled once more over the relationship between George and Camus, he was handed a black academic gown, which failed to conceal his scruffy shirt and jeans. The others also donned gowns, and they trooped outside. The dancers, who he now saw were of both sexes and all ages, had finished and were seated on logs around the bonfire, talking in whispers. They stood as the party approached. Some were arrayed in elaborate robes and decorations, while others simply wore black academic gowns over their clothes. Owen didn't recognise any of their faces, each of which glanced surreptitiously at this new member of the Wakened, their eyes meeting briefly before returning, coyly, to the flames. George passed him the paper, and stood him next to the fire. The others joined hands, forming a circle, and slowly danced around him, singing an entreaty to the God and Goddess to join them, to hear these sacred vows. Owen gazed soberly at the paper signed in blood, and felt panic stir within him. Was it the heat, the heady chanting, or the disorienting movement of bodies in the flickering firelight? He tore his mind away from these images, focussing on the reason he was here: to avenge Sarah. Concentrating on this goal, he regained his composure, and nervously waited to act his part. The dancers drew to a close, and became still. The fire crackled in the silence.

180

"We breathe in your golden healing light, and we breathe out our bane. So mote it be."

"So mote it be." Camus moved from the circle, and stood opposite.

"Owen Davies, are you prepared to make your Vow before this sacred Coven?"

"Yes, I am."

"Then do so." Camus gestured at the document, and, seeing him hesitate, whispered, "Read it!" His clear voice broke the hushed evening. "I, Owen Lloyd Davies, hereby solemnly declare to the God and the Goddess, and to my peers, priests ...". He finished the oath, and Camus motioned him to place the document on the fire. As the flames gratefully embraced it, Jenny stepped forward and threw the thimble of blood onto the flickering tongues. Camus raised his arms to the sky and called in a high monotone,

"We beseech the God and Goddess to receive Owen's vow, and by his blood know his heart to be pure. If it be Their will as it is ours, so mote it be."

"So mote it be." Silence. Owen raised his gaze from the burning document to find them all watching him, expectantly. He looked questioningly at Camus and George, but they remained silent, watching his face. Understanding dawned as panic rose within him, as he felt the inquisitorial stares beating down on him, testing the strength and purity of his vow, searching for deceit. Closing his eyes, he tried to regain balance, conscious of the growing roar in his ears, feeling the pressure of the coven around him. He clung to a memory of Sarah telling him how she dealt with a panic attack by breaking the cycle. He fell to his knees, felt embers burning through his jeans, searing his flesh. Drawing strength from the pain, he opened his eyes, wildly unfocussed on the infinite darkness above, and his scream shocked the roar into silence, "My Goddess, help me." His head fell forward, singeing his hair. Now he could feel the stillness around him, could hear only the crackle of the fire. The tide of panic ebbed, and he felt his strength returning. Camus spoke, as if from afar, but his voice had changed, somehow becoming softer, less aggressive. "Owen. The Goddess has responded to your call.

Rise, and join us." Awakening as if from a dream, he acknowledged the concerned and approving glances of the coven now clustered around him. He climbed to his feet, shaken by the intensity of emotion, but unable to name it, barely registering the pain in his knees. George moved forward, handing out branches drawn from a bundle under his arm, each bearing green leaves. Owen found himself guided into the circle, and they slowly danced round the fire once more, each person waving the stems above the fire in their right hand, while clasping their neighbour's forearm with their left. As they danced, they chanted:

"Together, tonight, we harness our power, and the power of the spirit, to make an unbreakable bond, binding Owen to the Wakened, and strengthening the bond between us. We harness that power to witness and enforce his vows..."

As they repeated the chant, the leaves singed, blackened, and fell into the flames. Finally, they cast their branches into the fire, watching in silence until the last twig was consumed, emitting a fragrant vapour of apple.

"So mote it be", chanted Camus.

"So mote it be."

Crowding round Owen, they hugged and kissed him, wishing him the blessings of the God and Goddess. Relaxed now, and dissolving their tension in meaningless chatter like guests at the end of a wedding, they filed into the house, now fragrant with the cinnamon aroma of a large silver bowl of mulled wine.

An hour later, a little drunk, and little the wiser, he drove home, trying to ignore his tortured knees. Far sooner than expected, he was now a member of the Wakened. But he was nagged by a troubling doubt. With the possible exception of Camus, these people didn't seem like Sarah's killers.

oooOooo

George had arranged to meet him at the English Department the next day. Owen eventually found a door inscribed "Dr. George Ables, Executive Officer". A secretary announced his arrival, and George came out to meet him, shaking hands. He had once more assumed his Pickwickian persona, leaving Owen to wonder how many people knew of the razor-sharp intellect obscured by this bumbling mask.

He glanced at the title on the door as George closed it behind them. "I see you have a PhD."

"Yes. I started as a research fellow in this Department, but my real passion was for witchcraft, not English. So, I didn't publish very much, and never managed to get tenure." He grinned. "So let that be a warning to you."

Motioning Owen to sit at the desk, he continued.

"Anyway, when the opportunity arose to stay in the Department in an administrative capacity, I jumped at the chance. I still dabble in English Literature, attend colloquia, that sort of thing, but there's no pressure on me to publish. Which suits me fine. My real research can never be public. And I get good support from Jane."

There was a knock on the door, and the secretary carried in a tray of coffee and biscuits. George seamlessly moved the conversation. "How are your knees?"

"Fine. I think the Goddess protected me." He declined to mention the restless night fuelled by pain-killers, and George looked at him sceptically. They continued to mutter trivia until the secretary had left, closing the door behind her.

"Right, Owen, let's get down to business. First thing, don't expect me to tell you everything about the Wakened straight away. I'll tell you a little now, and then, with time, you'll gradually learn more."

He stirred sugar into his black coffee. "We are a very secret and compartmentalised society, and no-one, not even me, knows everything about it. At first you'll only meet a few people, learn a little about our movement, and as you build your relationship, you'll find more is shared with you. But right now, I'd like you to engage in the quest for the Book of One, as quickly as possible. We need to win this race, and I think you'll be valuable in helping us do so."

Noticing a caution behind the words, Owen felt that he was still being tested, evaluated.

"The first thing you need to know about is our web site. This is our reference library, where all members can deposit their findings, and see the progress of others."

Owen was astounded. "You have a web site? But what about all this secrecy?"

Turning to his computer, George typed an address. A soft-core pornography site appeared on the screen.

"Each image," explained George, "has text encrypted within it. You install a small program on your laptop, type in a personal encryption key, and the site changes to this." He typed a few characters on his keyboard, and the screen changed to a low-tech page of text, containing a brief introduction followed by a contents page

Owen smiled. "Nice. I guess you encode information in the difference between images? How good's your encryption?"

"128-bit public-key RSA. You can leave information here, decide who you want to see it, and only those individuals will have access. Nobody, not I, the guy who set this up for us, or anyone else in the Wakened, MI5, CIA, whoever, even with their supercomputers, can crack it, even if they knew about it. Which they don't."

"OK. Can I see everything that Wakened does?"

"No. Our group here in Cambridge rejoices under the name of "Chapter 47", and we focus on discovering the location of the Book of One. You'll find that Chapter 47 is the only page you can access at present. You'll eventually meet other Chapters too, and they may let you have access to their pages. But none of them perform rituals or ceremonies - we leave that to the covens. This organisation is strictly business."

"Sounds good. How do I put information on it?"

"It has a wiki interface, so you can post anything you want. If you want to post whole pages, feel free to do so. If you want to contact others, you should leave messages on their personal pages - it's far more secure than phones or email. And please check for messages on your page at least every couple of days."

"You don't use commercial privacy software?"

George snorted. "Most of the "privacy software" sold on the internet is a honey-trap for criminals and terrorists. At least, those who are stupid enough to use it. If anyone wants to protect his privacy that much, governments around the world would like to know what he has to hide."

Owen nodded. As he'd guessed. "So how do I start working on the Book of One?"

"Perhaps we should start by pooling our knowledge. Tell me what you know about it."

He smiled. Best to come clean. "Not very much actually, except that it probably exists, and that it may contain the foundation of witchcraft."

"Fair enough. Let me give you a puzzle to work on, and we'll go from there. Have you heard of the North Mymms Manuscript?"

Owen shook his head.

"In 1859, during renovations of a small church in Hertfordshire, workmen digging under the crypt discovered burnt cooking vessels, pots, and bones, and fragments of parchment. It appears that they were the remains of a witch and her possessions from the tenth century."

"Tenth century? That's incredible!" He frowned. "But weren't witches usually burnt and buried outside consecrated ground?"

"Not in the tenth century. Witchcraft was tolerated in varying degrees by the Christians until the fifteenth century. And they probably thought her spells would be neutralised by putting her remains under the church. Anyway, a few fragments of paper survived the fire, and came into my possession. Amongst them was this."

He handed Owen a print out.

"This is a translation. We think it was written a few years after the Roman invasion by a Latin-speaking Druid. Probably around 60 AD. It's one of only three written pieces surviving from the Druids. The witch probably kept it as a sacred ancient text."

Wordless, wide-eyed, Owen took the paper and read it.

"As the Reikin approached, we expected the Romans to receive their just reward from the Goddess. Initiates travelled to the sacred site of Callunus to witness the Reikin, but they never returned. We know not what happened to them, but suspect they were caught and destroyed by Romans. And the Goddess did not punish the Romans. Instead they destroyed our armies, and slaughtered our people. Why does the Goddess not bring retribution down upon them? What have we done to deserve this cruel treatment?"

Owen looked up. "I've heard of the Reikin, but I don't know what it is. Do you?"

"Where did you hear of the Reikin?"

"Someone mentioned it to me in passing," said Owen casually.

With a dangerous quietness in his voice, George said, "Including this, we know of only four documents mentioning the Reikin. And none are public. So where did you hear of it?"

Owen considered his options. He needed to keep some cards to his chest.

"George, you told me that I will initially have access to only a little of the Wakened material, and, as my relationship with the Wakened grows, I'll learn more. I have no problem with that. But you need to appreciate that it must work in both directions. I look forward to the day when there is Perfect Trust, when I can share every scintilla of information I have with you and other Wakened members, and vice versa. But, as you've told me, that day has not yet arrived. So let's build this relationship one brick at a time."

Listening to his words, George became thoughtful. Owen paused, waiting for an angry retort. Instead, George smiled.

"Good. That's the answer I would have given in your shoes. I think we'll get on very well."

Owen nodded. Everything George said was calculated for its effect, like a chess move. He wasn't sure where this one was heading.

"I'll tell you about the Reikin, Owen. It appears to have been a major Druid festival, but we don't know what time of year it took place, nor what it signified, although we do have information that the Book of One is somehow connected to it. We also have no idea where Callunus is. You said you're good at solving riddles. Solve that."

George leaned back, evidently satisfied with his delivery. Check.

Gathering the last shreds of his ebbing self-confidence, Owen returned the stare. Obviously this was yet another initiation test. Did they already know the answer? Or was it insoluble?

He remembered back to one school vacation, when a maths teacher had set the class a problem involving prime numbers. Determined to solve it, he fretted and worried all through his holidays. The last week approached, and still no solution. Back at school, he could barely meet the eyes of his classmates. He was better at maths than any of them, and yet he'd failed to solve a simple piece of homework. He avoided any discussion of it, until the first maths lesson.

"Anybody solve it?" boomed the maths master.

From the murmurs, it was clear that most of the class had forgotten all about the problem, hadn't even tried. Peering round the class, Owen saw that Litchfield, whom he regarded as his challenger, was glumly looking at his desk.

"Nobody? Davies? Litchfield?" goaded the teacher, mischievously.

Owen felt himself turning scarlet. It was the first time he'd failed a maths homework problem.

"Don't blush, Davies. Most unbecoming. Besides, you're in good company."

The teacher went on to tell them about Fermat's Last Theorem, which no human had been able to prove, except possibly Fermat himself, although even that was doubted.

Owen felt cheated, deceived. His summer holiday had been ruined by a wild goose chase set up by a thoughtless teacher. And yet. Later, the teacher had discussed his failed attempts with him, and seemed impressed. He lent him a book telling the story of how other mathematicians had tried to climb that mountain and had failed. Owen was gratified to find that he was closer than some to a solution. Sometimes a challenging climb can be more rewarding than the view from the summit. The episode had been one of the most valuable lessons of his schooldays.

So what about the test George had just set him? Was it merely that, or had he been asked to make his first contribution to the quest for the Book of One? And how dangerous was the climb?

Chapter 13

Arriving home, his mind spun with disconnected fragments of information. Assembling these into a coherent puzzle would be hard. Solving it would be even harder.

He needed to visualise the information. Finding an old poster, he stuck its face to the wall, and started writing notes on its blank back, connecting them with circles and arrows, jotting down half-formed ideas.

First, there was that bit that Aleister had read to him, when Sarah was alive. Something about the Goddess kissing the Earth at the Reikin to form a stone circle. He'd have to ask Aleister for the exact words.

Second, there was the passage that Aleister and Tony had shown him. As late as 1066 AD, there were still people who knew where to find the Book of One, and they went to a stone circle to consult it, two days west of Exeter. Probably on Dartmoor somewhere.

Third, there was the passage that George had just given him, from the "North Mymms manuscript", implying that the Druids expected the Romans to be punished at the Reikin.

Finally, George had told him that the Reikin seemed to be a major Druid festival. So what could that be? Their largest temple, Stonehenge, was built around the direction to the rising sun on midsummer day. Was the Reikin something to do with that? Was there anything that suggested what time of year the Reikin took place? He recited the passages, with no success. Other than referring to the rout of the Britons around 60AD, they told him nothing.

His sleep that night was restless and confused, the fragments of information spinning a tortured path through his drowsing thoughts, refusing to be assembled into any pattern. He found himself on a full moonlit night, standing on the broad plain below Stonehenge, watching the Druids as they walked back and forth amongst the great monoliths, practicing strange unseen rituals. He crept closer, to see what they were up to. With a shock, he recognised Camus amongst them, and wondered if George knew what Camus was up to. He turned to Jenny beside him, and wondered why she was laughing. Then he realised that he wasn't wearing any trousers. Or underpants.

She started laughing, horribly, and as he unsuccessfully fumbled to cover his nakedness, he tried to shut her up, lest they be discovered. Too late. He saw George and Camus approaching, dressed in Druid robes, mocking him. Jenny seized his hands behind him and tied them, his shame and nakedness exposed for all to see.

Their laughs had turned to hoarse-throated rumbles that seemed to rise out of the ground on which they stood. They led him, trembling, into the circle, forcing him to lie on the dead-cold slaughter stone, facing up towards the black sky. Above him stood Jane, the Wiccan symbols on her knife glinting in the moonlight. She kissed him on the lips, a long, revolting, wet kiss. He could hear Sarah screaming in the background. The bastards had her too. He redoubled his struggles - he had to save her. As Jane laughed at his ineffectual thrashing and twisting, she put the knife to his throat. He yelled that he was only trying to help, that he could find the Book of One, but as he screamed and writhed, he felt the cold steel press on his throat. Searing pain flooded his body, and he heard, rather than felt, the scream turn to a gurgle as his wind-pipe was severed. Still wide-eyed with horror, he felt the knife press against his spine, followed by an audible crack as his head separated from his body. Through tortured eyes, he watched Jane's leering face retreating against the full moon, as his severed head tumbled to the ground.

Waking in a tangle of sodden bedclothes, he saw it was midnight. Switching on the light to exorcise the dream, fragments still floated past him, threatening to pounce from dark corners of the room. He sat on the edge of the bed, rubbing his eyes, trying to purge the image of Jane's head framed against the full moon. For some reason it refused to be banished.

With a shock, he understood its significance. The Moon! Stupid stupid stupid! The Reikin wasn't about the Sun, it was about the Moon. What had he been thinking? Of course - the Goddess! She's the Moon, not the Sun. A two year old could have figured that out. And the Goddess kissing the Earth? That's when the Moon is low in the sky, touching the Horizon.

He imagined the Druids watching the full Moon, in that moment as it left the Earth before rising into the sky. Didn't seem quite right. A rising Moon hardly "kissed" the earth. Same with the setting Moon. "Kissing" implied that it touched the Earth lightly without rising or setting. But how could that be? There had to be more. Climbing back into bed, he fell into a restless half-sleep, the ideas whirring in his mind.

He was woken by the phone. Ten o'clock. He staggered down to answer it.

"Owen, is that you? Peter here."

Why would that snake be phoning him at home? "Hello Peter."

"You know we had a meeting of postdocs at nine this morning?"

"Did we? Sorry. Must have missed the email."

"Owen, old boy, the department's been exceedingly tolerant of you since Sarah's death, but there are limits you know. The department is paying you a salary, and it's not unreasonable to expect you to put in an appearance once in a while..."

"And why is it any of your business?"

Peter's voice changed, suddenly becoming authoritative. "I'll tell you why. In case you've forgotten, I'm the postdoc coordinator, so I'm your line manager. It's my job to chase you when you're malingering..."

"Malingering? Don't be so ridiculous. I happen to be working on something here which you're probably too stupid to understand...". Damn. He shouldn't have said that.

After a pause, the voice on the other end came back dangerously reasonable.

"Owen, you're in enough trouble already. Don't make it worse for yourself. I expect to see you here in 15 minutes."

The phone went dead. Owen knew he had gone too far. Bugger. So vague mutterings about his absence from work had escalated into this.

As if he cared. Somehow it didn't seem to matter. Peter could get stuffed. As could Sir bloody Ashley pompous Pusch. On the other hand, he needed a job. Was that all it was now? A job? What had happened to his life quest to expand human knowledge? Words. Just words. They didn't mean much now.

He'd go in this afternoon. Apologise. Ask for sympathy. Yuk. Sympathy. But that would probably go down well. He'd say that Sarah's death had driven him off the rails. That he was seeing a doctor. They'd buy that.

As he made coffee, the idea of a Moon kissing the Earth still spun in his head, and it had attached itself to a name, a faint memory. He tried to focus on it, draw it out. Got it. Sarah had once told him about some ancient Greek writer - Didorus? Wrote something about the Moon visiting Britain. He rushed to his computer, paced up and down while it took forever to boot, and googled Didorus. "Did you mean Diodorus?" it asked him, nauseatingly smug. Whatever. He clicked on a link and found the quote from Diodorus of Sicily, writing about Britain in the century before Christ:

"... They also say that the moon, as viewed from this island, appears to be but a little distance from the earth and to have upon it prominences, like those of the earth, which are visible to the eye. The account is also given that the god visits the island every nineteen years..."

Of course. Why hadn't he thought of it before? Every nineteen years the Moon gets so low in the sky that it barely rises above the horizon - so it seems as if it's kissing the Earth! That's what Diodorus meant when he said the God, or Goddess, visits the island every 19 years. Remembering the astronomical name of this event - the "lunar standstill" - he looked it up in Wikipedia. OK - every 18.6 years then. Close enough. So the Reikin, or the lunar standstill, is the festival every 18.6 years when the Moon barely gets above the horizon, and seems to be "kissing the Earth". Why had everyone assumed the Reikin was an annual festival?

He remembered Sarah telling him about an old theory by a retired professor of Engineering, Alexander Thom, that stone circles marked the years of the lunar standstill. The realisation hit Owen with a thump. Perhaps Thom had been right: perhaps these circles had been built to mark the Reikin!

Sarah had been dismissive of Thom's work, but had an old copy of his book. Owen pulled out the slender green volume. Thumbing through it, he spent an hour flitting between the book and the web, laboriously assembling fragments of information into a coherent picture. Afternoon approached as he surveyed his work. Stonehenge was built not only to point at the Sun, but also at the Moon. But the most important lunar observatory seemed to be Callanish, in the Outer Hebrides, where every 18.6 years, the Moon at transit only briefly appears above the horizon, dramatically framed by two rows of standing stones. Leaning back, he confronted the idea that had been growing in the back of his mind. Callanish was Callanus.

He drew arrows on the poster, circling the clues as they fell into place, and then read George's passage again.

"As the Reikin approached, we expected the Romans to receive their just reward from the Goddess."

So the Reikin was a time when bad deeds were punished and good deeds rewarded.

"Initiates travelled to the sacred site of Callanus to witness the Reikin..."

which meant that they headed up North to Callanish,

"...but they never returned. We know not what happened to them, but suspect they were caught and destroyed by Romans."

Sounds likely. The Romans were terrified that the Druids had the minds of the people, and were determined to destroy this rebellious power.

"And the Goddess did not punish the Romans. Instead they destroyed our armies, and slaughtered our people. Why does the Goddess not bring retribution down upon them? What have we done to deserve this cruel treatment?"

So the Britons expected the Goddess to destroy the Romans at the time of the Reikin, at the time of the lunar standstill. But she didn't. Owen tried to imagine how they must have felt, deserted by their Goddess in the face of even more powerful Roman gods. Thus would end the Druid religion.

It was a nice theory. But only that. Owen knew it wouldn't be taken seriously until it could be tested.

So did this theory tell him anything that could be checked in history books? Could he find evidence of people travelling to Callanish at the time of the Roman invasion? Unlikely. Then he had it. If his theory was correct, there would have to be a lunar standstill around that time. Rushing back to his computer, he found tables of lunar motion. It was far more complicated than he expected, and his screen filled with tables and calculations, as he worked out the dates of the standstill.

Once more he was in his element, immersed in the thrill of the intellectual chase.

As the sun set, he had the answer. There was a lunar standstill in 52 AD, right in the middle of the Roman invasion. It worked. His excitement was mellowed by the realisation that it had been too easy. Clearly this had merely been a test by George, who already knew the answer.

He picked up the phone. The recorded message answered.

"Hi George. Owen here. I've solved the riddle you set me, and I know what the Reikin is. Could you phone me later if ...?"

194

"Good evening Owen. What do you mean you've solved it? You mean you've some theory as to what the Reikin is? I'm sorry to disappoint you, but I'm afraid it's unlikely to be a new one."

"No. I know what the Reikin is."

"I see. What is it?"

"It's the lunar major standstill."

Silence. Then "Maybe we should discuss this in my office. See you there in an hour?"

As he put the phone down, the realisation dawned that George hadn't known the answer, that this had been a real challenge, not a test. It didn't give him much confidence in the so-called powerful minds in the Wakened that had already been working on this problem.

He arrived to find George sprawled on an armchair in his office, smiling and relaxed, a tray of coffee waiting on the table.

"Fire away", he said, an edge to his voice betraying the tension within.

Owen sat on the chair opposite, leaning forward as if tutoring a student. He realised that he was starting to read through George's postures. "Do you know about the lunar standstill cycle?"

George rubbed his chin casually. "Something about the maximum declination of the Moon isn't it?"

Owen smirked as George stumbled over the word "declination", which apparently didn't come naturally to his lips. George had obviously looked it up in Wikipedia after Owen's phone call, but had been defeated by the terminology.

Owen explained. "You know how the summer Sun is high in the sky, and the winter Sun low in the sky?"

"Yes, of course."

Owen shifted forward on his seat. "Well the Moon does the same thing, except it does it in one month. Every month, as it waxes and wanes, it swings furiously about in the sky. One night, it will rise in the North-East, soar up to the zenith, and then descend to the North-West. Just two weeks later, it barely climbs above the horizon before setting again."

"Of course. I remember now. I don't suppose many people know that."

Owen smirked. George had obviously never heard of it. "No, not nowadays. It would have been obvious in the days before street-lights. Anyway, it gets even more complicated." Owen started moving his arm in the air to illustrate his point. "Some years it swishes about dramatically like that and other years it hardly changes during the month. The year when it moves around most is called a major standstill, and it happens once every 18.6 years. That's the Reikin."

George said nothing as he stirred his coffee, and then abruptly asked. "How do you know?"

"I think Callanus is obviously Callanish, on the Island of Lewis in the Hebrides. It's a bronze-age stone circle connected to the Moon. It's at a special latitude where the Moon just skims the horizon at the Reikin."

George nodded. "I see. Go on."

Owen proceeded to list his arguments, ending with his calculation of the standstill during the Roman invasion.

"Interesting hypothesis. Anything to back it up?"

He was stunned. After realising that George didn't already have the answer, he had expected him to be overwhelmed by this revelation.

"I don't think you understand. We know the lunar standstill was important to the Druids. This all fits in perfectly."

Leaning back, George smiled patronisingly. "Owen, don't get me wrong. This is a very nice idea, one which we didn't have before. I'm impressed that you've devised it so quickly. It might one day even turn out to be the right answer, but I think it will take a lot more supporting evidence before we discard competing ideas, some of which have also fitted together nicely."

"Like?"

"Sorry, but they're in confidence. I'll keep those confidences, just as I will protect your idea until you've had a chance to find supporting evidence. Meanwhile, I'll search our archives for anything which might test your theory."

Owen left, deflated. Why couldn't George see the significance of what he had discovered?

He drove back to his house to fetch the pre-paid phone. Then he drove out of Cambridge, along Grantchester Road, until he reached a secluded spot. There he dialled Aleister's number. It was the first time he had spoken freely to him for weeks, and so he wasted valuable minutes summarising how he had managed to penetrate the Wakened, explaining the riddle he had solved.

"That's incredible, Owen. We've been trying to figure out the Reikin for years. And you just come along..."

"Yes Aleister, but I need to know..."

"Dear boy - do you realise how important this is? This is a major step..."

"Yes I do realise, Aleister. That's how..."

"But I really think..."

"Aleister, please can you tell me the words of that passage you read to me at Tony's?"

"That's what I was trying to say, Owen. It all fits together. This is amazing."

"Aleister?"

"Oh right. Wait a tick."

He heard Aleister crashing about in the distance, and he pictured him pulling books out of shelves ("I know it's up here somewhere.") and dropping them, trying other bookshelves. There were sounds of him running heavily up the stairs, and then the clump of him racing down again. He came back to the phone, breathless.

"Got it, Owen." Panting.

"Good - read it out"

"Ok." A pause. He could hear Aleister trying to slow his breathing.

"Just a minute. Have to find my glasses."

There was a thud as the phone was put down, the sound of Aleister shuffling and muttering in the distance, and then the phone was picked up again.

Aleister cleared his throat, and read the words slowly, pausing frequently for breath.

"At the Reikin, the Goddess kisses the Earth, rewarding the good, and, punishing the bad, measure for measure. Where her lips touch the ground, the rocks themselves rise up to greet her, forming a sacred circle so pure that, whilst a Reikin will traverse it, a lifetime may be measured along its perimeter, no more, no less."

"So the first line says that the Goddess doles out rewards and punishment at the time of the Reikin. That fits in with the other script, which said that she would punish the Romans then. Or not, as it turned out. What do you think 'measure for measure' means?"

Aleister paused before replying. "I suppose it means that the reward she gives you depends on how much good you have done. If you do good, you get that much good returned to you. And vice versa."

"Sounds reasonable. No surprises there. Read the second line again."

"Where her lips touch the ground, the rocks themselves rise up to greet her,"

"Yes I remembered that bit," interrupted Owen, "so the stone circles mark the places where the Moon seems to touch the horizon. Go on."

"...forming a sacred circle so pure that, whilst a Reikin will traverse it, a lifetime may be measured along its perimeter, no more, no less."

"Any idea what that means?"

Aleister's voice sounded doubtful. "No. Perhaps it's a metaphor?"

"But it's phrased in such exact words, as if it's describing something precise. As if it takes 18.6 years to go across the diameter of the circle. But that doesn't make any sense. Read it again so I can write it down."

oooOooo

Owen's apology to Peter the following day fell on receptive ears. Owen's air of superiority had always irked Peter, and so this unaccustomed humility, this confession of depression and medical treatment, pushed all the right buttons. Owen promised to keep regular work hours again, and Peter deleted his memo to Sir Ashley. But Owen knew that his next annual review would be damning unless he pulled some rabbit out of a hat. The black cloud of IT support loomed on the horizon.

Over the next few weeks he kept his promise, and his laptop was open on his desk from early in the morning each day, visible through his open door even if he wasn't present. Of course, nobody monitored where he actually was, giving ample opportunity to meet the rest of Chapter 47 of the Wakened: academics, students, IT specialists, a schoolteacher, and a dentist. They were gentle, intelligent people linked only by their passion for uncovering the Book of One. A friendly antiquary in Wigan would find a scrap of parchment in his antique shop. A hereditary witch from Surrey would "come out", making available the grimoire used by her grandmother. All these would be forwarded to the team, who would comb them for clues. Their secure web site contained a library of these texts, with powerful tools for searching and correlating them.

Owen found himself leading the group's discussions, solving problems, and was often the first to research a newly-discovered document. He explained to them his theory about the Reikin. None had seen the connection to the Moon, and all except George were enthusiastic. But nobody could understand how it might fit the precise words in Aleister's passage.

Their web library told him that in the first few centuries AD, many people knew of the existence of the Book of One, and a few even claimed to have seen it, but he could find no clues to its location. The best description was in a letter from a Roman commander, writing home in the early days of the war:

"The Book has many chapters. All Druids have read and have memorised several, but it takes a lifetime to read them all, and only the most exalted priests have done so. Once a year, on midsummer's day, the whole book is sung at their temple in Wessex."

The Wessex temple was presumably Stonehenge, but Owen was puzzled by the fact that the piece seemed to refer to a book that existed before the Roman invasion. The other odd thing was that it took a lifetime to read the Book. How so, if the entire Book could be sung in one day? This didn't make any sense. And this excited him. When things don't make sense, then you know your assumptions are wrong. And questioning them may give answers. To do that, he needed to break into a different frame of mind. He needed to get out of the house, go somewhere.

He considered inviting Jenny, but there was no point - she'd be busy. Since the initiation ceremony, she'd continued to flirt with him, and yet it somehow never went further than that. She treated him like a younger brother, even though he was seven years her senior. That knowing, playful look, seeing right inside him, both terrifying and attracting him. But even that had faded, as if she were drawing away. He'd given up asking her out. He was on his own. Again.

He left his house with no certain destination, knowing only that walking would clear his head. With surprise, he found himself standing at the door of the pub in Grantchester. A pint wouldn't hurt. He entered, enjoying the warm fug and laughter, pleased to find nobody he knew. After ordering a pint, he settled into an anonymous corner, reciting the passage silently, searching for meaning.

Three pints later, he was no nearer a solution, and his brain had ceased to function. He staggered home and crawled into bed, his head spinning, his stomach churning.

Restlessly, he lay watching the swirling patterns in his eyes, wondering how he would get to sleep, when Sarah's voice, clear and mundane, shocking in its clarity and reality, broke the silence. "Owen, have you forgotten me?"

He sat up, startled, and of course there was nothing, nobody. Other than too much beer. Settling down, again he heard her voice. Determined to ignore this alcohol-fuelled dream, he turned away from her.

Her voice sounded hurt now. "Why are you running away?"

Why do our own brains torment us so? What evolutionary pressure causes our brain to think of the one thing we don't want to hear, and torture us with it? "It's not you, Sarah. I'm sorry, but you're dead. Gone. This is a nightmare, not the Sarah I loved."

"So why are you talking to me?"

Humph. Good point. He decided to wake up, end this nonsense, but found himself falling deeper into sleep, trapped within the dream. He was in a cave now, falling, and Sarah's voice was echoing from the walls.

"Please don't run away from me, my love."

He was screaming in his sleep now. "No, go away. It's not you. This is a dream."

"Of course it's a dream my love. How else am I to talk to you?"

Now he was crying, running from wall to wall of the cave, groping for a way upwards, out of the nightmare. "Please, I don't understand. Let me wake up."

She too was sobbing. "Please, Owen. We loved each other so much. I still love you, and it's so cold and lonely being dead. All I want is your love, Owen, to keep me warm. And I think I'm losing you. And without you, I'm nothing. Nothing."

She said it with an emptiness, a hollowness, of dusty graves and eyeless skulls. It was a word filled with the empty dreadfulness of vacuum. Nothing.

His heart bursting, he spun to face her, but her voice was all that remained.

"Sarah, my love. I don't know if this is you talking, or just my stupid brain, but of course I love you. Why else have I thrown everything away to get mixed up with the Wakened? To find your killers. To avenge you."

"I don't think so, Owen. I think you have forgotten why you set out on this journey. You spend every waking moment chasing this Book of One. You dream of solving the puzzle, of finding the Book. It has you trapped, Owen, and taken you from me. Please love me again."

The voice evaporated, the cave was gone, and he was lying in bed, shivering. He got up and switched on the light. He'd never drink that much again. Downstairs, he sat at the kitchen table, nursing his hot milk, replaying the nightmare. Obviously the words came from his alcohol-raddled brain. And yet, there was a sense in which she was still alive, but only in his brain. That was all that was left of her. As long as he loved her. And he recognised the glimmer of truth in what she had said. The pursuit of the Book had become an end in itself, a wonderful, epic, Hero's Quest, in which he pitted his wits against obstinate facts and half-truths, slaying the demons of muddled thinking with his awesome sword of razor-sharp intellect...

He'd lost the plot. And yet the route he was following was exactly right. It was only the destination that was wrong. He resolved never again to lose sight of where he was heading, and said to the empty room,

"I love you, Sarah. And I always will. Goodnight, my love."

There was no answer, but when he lay in bed, the spinning had stopped, and his body lay still, at peace he hadn't felt for weeks. He slept soundly.

Chapter 14

As weeks passed, he began to perceive the vast breadth and extent of the Wakened. There were two other Wakened Chapters, in London and Wales, working on the Book of One. And George's reports from the monthly meetings of the "Wakened Council" spoke of other chapters, dimly perceived, busy with God knows what. But still no sign that any part of it was capable of murder. He was also nagged by a persistent doubt: if the Wakened had killed Sarah, then wouldn't they be suspicious of him, and not allow him into this trusted position? Was he barking up the wrong tree? Or was the Wakened's strict code of secrecy protecting him?

In early September, during the coffee-break at the Neo-Pagan society, Jane drew him aside. Standing too close, forcing her expensive perfume on him, she stroked his arm as she spoke, further increasing his discomfort. "Owen darling, there's something important I have to ask you."

He fought his instinct to retreat from her smothering presence and wandering hands. "Yes, of course, Jane. What can I do for you?"

Giggling like a young girl, she traced a circle with her finger on his arm. "My coven is one short, and I'd like to invite you to join us."

He'd guessed this was coming, and his response was ready. "That's really kind of you, Jane - I feel so honoured that you should ask. But, um, to tell you the truth, I don't think... Well, I don't think I'm ready for it."

About half the Wiccans he had met were "solitary practitioners". Not, of course, counting the fluffies. So this reaction would be normal and understandable. There were two other reasons he didn't want to join: one was his nervousness about the intimacy of these rituals, especially if Jane were there. The other was a growing respect for the Wiccan movement, which largely consisted of ordinary, intelligent people following the faith of their ancestors. He'd already abused their trust, and acting out a sacred rite would definitely lie beyond the bounds of decent human behaviour. He denied the existence of a fourth motive: that the power manifested that night on the Cornwall cliff might threaten his belief in a rational world. Deniability was far more comfortable.

Jane accepted his rejection with bad grace and a pout. Leaving the meeting shortly afterwards, he returned to his empty house, glancing at the pile of books and papers surrounding his computer before finding the whisky bottle.

That night he had erotic dreams of Sarah, and awoke with a debilitating headache and a sense of defiling her memory. While showering, he faced the uncomfortable truth that his quest to uncover the Book of One had ground to a halt. He resolved, for Sarah's sake, to restart it with renewed vigour. Over breakfast, skimming through his notes, he made a list of what he knew, what he surmised, and what refused to make sense.

Aleister's text continued to nag:

"At the Reikin, the Goddess kisses the Earth, rewarding the good, and punishing the bad, measure for measure. Where her lips touch the ground, the rocks themselves rise up to greet her, forming a sacred circle so pure that, whilst a Reikin will traverse it, a lifetime may be measured along its perimeter, no more, no less."

Why such carefully-chosen words? It seemed to be saying that it took a Reikin -18.6 years - to cross the diameter of the circle. What the hell did that mean? He memorised the passage, and spent every spare minute over the following days looking for connections, but none came. One morning, an unconnected fact seemed to have attached itself to the passage. The circumference of a circle is pi times the diameter, so if it took a Reikin, 18.6 years, to cross the circle, then it would be about 58 years to go round the perimeter, which is roughly a lifetime, at least in Druid times. While that made some sense, it would be equally true of any circle.

Why the stress on "so pure", and "no more, no less", and why would it take a Reikin to traverse it?

By the time he'd reached his office he was convinced it was saying that the natural human life span is exactly pi times a Reikin. That seemed plausible, like a Druid version of the biblical "three score and ten". But why pi? Did the Druids even know about pi? And why a "circle so pure" ?

All afternoon, while ostensibly preparing a seminar, his mind wandered around stone circles, trying to understand the significance of those extra words. Reaching home that evening, he gazed at his bookshelves, now groaning under the weight of tomes on Wicca, medieval witchcraft, and mythology. Amongst them must lie the answer. He scanned the spines, as if the very titles must give a clue. But they remained silent.

Perhaps the rites of modern witchcraft might suggest a way forward. According to the passage, the Druids believed that reward or punishment was meted out in exact proportion to the merit or harm of their deeds. It contrasted starkly with the central tenet of Wiccan faith: the threefold rule, that both the good and the evil that one creates in the world will be returned threefold.

Or was it so different? The Druids received a measure of reward or punishment at each Reikin. So, in a lifetime of three Reikins, an individual might accumulate roughly three times the good or evil created from any single act. It dawned on him that perhaps he had stumbled on something immensely significant: a Druidic origin for the Wiccan threefold rule.

But it still didn't quite fit. "About three" was a long way from the precise words used in the passage. He needed to take a break: give time for his mind to rest, mull it over in the background.

He searched the house for a novel to accompany his dinner, now simmering on the stove. Something light, brain-candy. The two books by Thom still sat where he had left them after checking on megalithic lunar observatories. Two book dense with dubious theories. Might be amusing to read them cover to cover. Then the penny dropped.

Thom had suggested, to the amusement of Sarah and the entire archaeological community, that some circles were not exactly circular, but flattened carefully by an arcane geometrical construction. These special circles appeared to the untrained eye to be circular. But if measured carefully, their perimeter was precisely three times their diameter at the largest point. No more, no less. Circles so pure.

All the pieces fitted together. He ran through the lines again.

"At the Reikin, the Goddess kisses the Earth, rewarding the good, and, punishing the bad, measure for measure. Where her lips touch the ground, the rocks themselves rise out of the ground to greet her, forming a sacred circle so pure that, whilst a Reikin will traverse it, a lifetime may be measured along its perimeter, no more, no less."

It seemed to be saying that these special circles were constructed such that the perimeter divided by the diameter was exactly this magic number three. Which also marked how many Reikins were in a lifetime, and how much good or evil a person would be rewarded. Incredibly, stone circles, built around 2000 BC, seemed to symbolise what became known as the Wiccan threefold rule.

All the pieces had fallen into place, and the implications were staggering. Should he call George? He was wary now. He wanted to try it out on someone else first. Aleister?

Picking up the cell-phone, he drove to a lane where he couldn't be bugged. He outlined his ideas to Aleister, expecting to have cold water poured on them. He laid out his reasoning, step by step.

"You understand, Aleister? The circumference of the stone circle symbolises the natural lifetime of a human. But that's exactly three times a Reikin of 18.6 years, which is symbolised by the diameter. So if punishment is dished out at each Reikin, then people may receive three times the harm they cause in one Reikin. Hence the Wiccan threefold rule."

He stopped as he realised he'd been talking for ten minutes without a word from Aleister.

"Aleister, what do you think?"

Silence.

"Are you still there?"

A frail voice made unintelligible noises in the phone. Owen became concerned.

"Aleister - are you alright?"

The old man was crying, mumbling.

"I'm so sorry, my dear boy. Umm. You've no idea. I've been waiting for this moment for half my life. It's absolutely... I mean, I never thought I'd live to see the day. There's something... Um. Something I haven't told you."

Bloody hell... Last time he was down there, Aleister didn't look so good. Did he have some terminal illness? "Aleister, I'm terribly sorry - what is it?"

"Owen, you see, ... There was a prophecy, that one, day, around the millennium, an unbeliever would lead Wicca out of the wilderness. Do you see, Owen? I think you're it. I really do. I always thought you might be, but now I feel... Well, I'm certain of it."

For Chrissake, what was the old coot going on about? Some stupid Wiccan prophecy? He could hear Aleister smiling, talking himself from one emotional extreme to the other. He could do without this. Better humour the old man.

"Aleister, That's amazing. Don't know whether I'm ready to be a Messiah, though... Look, I'd love to hear all about it next time I'm down there. But right now...what do you think of my idea?"

"My dear boy - it's wonderful. It makes sense. It's so... It's so obvious - why couldn't we see it when it was right in front of our eyes? It's exactly what I hoped..."

"Great - that's exactly what I needed to know. Aleister, I'm afraid I have to go right now, but I'm looking forward to chatting with you about the other stuff... Thanks Aleister. Take care."

He hung up. Why those last words? It wasn't a phrase he'd normally use. It's just that... He'd grown fond of the old man and was worried about his mental stability.

Anyway, more important things. Getting into his car, he started driving back, but the phone rang. It was Aleister again.

"Sorry, there's something else you should know."

Oh God, here we go. "Yes, Aleister?" A little more sharply than intended.

"Are you cross with me, Owen?"

Damn. Not now. "No Aleister, I'm not cross. You've no idea how much I appreciate your help. I'm a bit tense, that's all. I'm sorry if I seem a bit short with you."

"I understand, dear boy. Don't concern yourself. Just a foolish old man being over-sensitive. Well, take care. I'll see you soon."

"Aleister - you say said there was something else I should know."

"Ah. Yes. Sorry. There was a bit more information I forgot to give you. It's the Reikin. The other one, I mean. The Wrekin? In Shropshire?"

"The hill - a volcanic plug, isn't it?"

"Er - yes - something like that. But did you know local legends connect it with the Moon? Perhaps it was a Southern Callanish. That far South, the Moon won't get down to the ground, so you'd need a prominent hill as a marker."

Hmm. Maybe. "That's awesome. But there's no stone circle there, right?"

"Well, not now. But there was once. Did you know the Wrekin was one of the last strongholds held by the Britons in the Roman wars? The Romans razed everything on the hill after they'd won. Nothing left now. But we should search for evidence that it was used to mark the Reikin. That would be a clincher for your theory."

"Excellent - thanks Aleister. That's wonderful. I'll try to see where it fits in. Thanks for all your help. See you soon." He hung up. It all seemed pretty circumstantial. But then - who knows?

He phoned George and met him that evening in the pub.

As soon as they had settled into a corner with their pints, Owen read him Aleister's passage. "Two things. First, at every Reikin, good and bad are returned, measure for measure. My guess is that in Druid times the maximum life expectancy might be around 56 years, so a Druid would see three Reikins in his lifetime. You see what that means? All the good or evil he performed would be returned threefold in his lifetime. Hence the three-fold law in witchcraft."

George placed his beer on the table and stared at him, his face an impenetrable mask, which then softened ever so slightly. He nodded slowly. "Fascinating. Never heard that one before. Interesting bit of speculation. But perhaps no more than that."

"I said two things. That was one of them."

"Go on."

Owen looked at him seriously. "The other fragment says that the Goddess creates a sacred circle so pure that, whilst a Reikin will traverse it, a lifetime may be measured along its perimeter, no more, no less. I think I know what that means."

"Get to the point."

"Well, you know that the perimeter of a circle is pi times the diameter?"

George nodded impatiently. "Of course - that's a bit more than three, isn't it?"

"Yes - about 3.14. Suppose you built a circle whose perimeter was exactly three times the diameter?"

A moment of confusion registered on George's face. "But that's not possible, is it?"

"No? Alexander Thom showed that some stone circles are flattened in a special way to make their perimeter exactly three times the major diameter. They're the stone circles referred to in this fragment. And they're the ones aligned to the lunar major standstill - the Reikin."

"Says who?"

Owen smiled back at him, smugly. "It's all in the academic literature, if you know where to look."

George stared at him, poker-faced, wordless. At last he spoke, smiling without warmth. "Very good. I congratulate you."

"You're not going to tell me you already knew this?"

Grinning apologetically, George opened his palms flat as if caught out. "I think we were getting there. But you've scooped us. You're good, Owen. Very good. I think you're becoming a valuable member of our group."

Jeez. Would nothing ruffle this guy's feathers? "Becoming a valuable member of our group". Owen knew he was going to say something he'd regret if he continued this conversation any longer. He took a swig of beer, finishing it. "Sorry George. Just remembered something. Gotta go."

George continued obliviously. "OK. I need to discuss this with some others. Then I think you should meet them."

Owen nodded, noticing George's movements becoming tenser, jerkier, at odds with his feigned lack of enthusiasm about this momentous discovery. Dimly at first, he began to recognise a phenomenon all too common in academic circles. George was working out how to share the credit for his protégé's discovery.

George stood to leave. "One other thing. Could you email me what you've told me? Put in references, that sort of thing? Just so we can check?"

Owen nodded as he left. Bastard.

That night he prepared a document describing his ideas in detail. Instead of emailing it to George, he distributed it to all members of Chapter 47 simultaneously by posting it on their secure web page.

At their next meeting, George seemed unperturbed at being out-manoeuvred in this way, appearing amiable and even promoting Owen's success. Having failed to share the credit for the discovery, he seemed to be positioning himself as Owen's mentor. As the meeting drew to a close, George invited him to lunch the next day. They agreed to meet at The Anchor.

Owen was halfway through his first pint when George arrived. They both ordered the vegetarian cottage pie, and then George got to the point. "Owen, I've come to ask a favour of you. There's a Wakened Council meeting next week, which I can't make - I'm in Germany on University business. Would you be able to attend in my place?"

The significance of this was not lost on Owen. Before asking, George would have cleared it with other members of the Council, and would not have done so until certain that Owen's participation would reflect well on him. The request indicated a degree of trust that Owen had thought might take years. At last he would be privy to the full panoply of activities within the Wakened.

"I'll brief you, of course, before I go. Your job will be to present our monthly report, represent our Chapter, all that sort of thing."

He accepted immediately, whilst struggling not to appear over-enthusiastic, not to give any indication that this level of infiltration was something he had been desperate to achieve.

oooOooo

As the fields flew past the window of the Heathrow Express, he re-read George's uninformative briefing notes. Doubtless George could have made this meeting if necessary, but evidently Owen was to meet the members of the council for another purpose - to be scrutinised, tested? When he had hinted at this, George had retreated, accused him of melodrama. And yet it seemed so unlikely that Owen, a newcomer, would be asked to represent the group.

Following instructions, including the directive not to carry any briefcase or umbrella, he arrived at the British Airways "conference room 3". He understood now why they had chosen to hold the meeting here, where airport security would have picked up any recorder or camera on his body. His tail, of whose unseen presence he was certain, would have seen him take anything from an accomplice.

Standing next to the coffee-pot at the side of the room were two men in expensively-cut business suits, and a girl dressed in tight jeans and a baggy angora top. Probably cost a fortune. They turned to face him, and the elder of the men stepped forward, hand extended and a warm smile on his face. "Good to meet you Owen. I'm Bill. Let me introduce you to Anne and Jonathan."

All three were welcoming. No sinister glances, but no surnames, no explanations. Friendly, anonymous, secure.

Casually, making polite small talk, they quizzed him on his beliefs, his motivation, and his quest to uncover the Book of One. George had explained that nothing was secret to this select group, and so Owen told them of the leads he was following, his success, and his puzzles. Little of this needed to be faked, as over the last few weeks he had been swept up once more in the quest, which had become just as challenging as any biology problem. You didn't need to be a believer to be obsessed by the hunt, perhaps to stand one day amongst the discoverers of those ancient texts which together told the tale of how humanity grew and blossomed: the Bible, Koran, Vedas, hieroglyphs, Dead Sea Scrolls, the Rosetta Stone.

Others came in, introduced themselves as names without contexts. And then Camus entered. He nodded, unsurprised, at Owen. Why had George not told him Camus would be there?

Bill called the meeting to order, and they carried their coffees to the table. As the agenda was written on the whiteboard, it could have been any board or faculty meeting, except for the absence of papers on the table in front of them. Bill formally welcomed Owen, reminded him of the grave responsibility he was carrying. By attending this meeting he was becoming privy to some of the most closely guarded secrets of the Wakened. Nothing said in this room could be repeated unless explicitly authorised. Owen doubted whether he would in fact be privy to the most closely guarded secrets. He suspected this meeting may have been set up to vet him before allowing him entry to the inner core. Evidently they considered he might be useful. If he passed the test.

The meeting droned on with impenetrable subtexts and unexplained acronyms. Owen decided it was simply a routine council meeting, and their scrutiny of him was merely one of its many functions. Perhaps a promising new member was introduced at each meeting.

There were reports on the activities of each Chapter, which seemed to be numbered randomly. Most of the discussion was arcane stuff concerned with the formulation of particular ceremonies, but Owen's flagging attention was galvanised by Camus's report on the activities of Chapter 12. Their project continued to develop, but there had been setbacks, with a few leading members arrested in a recent incident. Nothing to worry about, but, briefest glance at Owen, matters were being taken care of. He expected the charges to be dropped. The report carried no more than a suggestion of illegal activity, but Owen was alert. How to gain access to this group? How to overcome the waves of hostility from Camus? What motivated Camus, what would gain his acceptance? Flattery? Too obvious. He watched carefully as Camus spoke, saw the bottled anger, the brooding fury of injustice unrighted, and realised that these might be used to breach Camus's defences, perhaps even earn his trust.

As Camus sputtered to a conclusion, Bill spoke. "You know we can't possibly support illegal activities?"

Camus smirked dismissively. "Relax. Nothing will happen. Nothing you need worry about."

Bill started to say something, but, avoiding Owen's curious gaze, swallowed his words. A few polite questions. More reports - international relationships, funding, media influence.

Then Owen's turn. He spoke with fervour about their discoveries about the Book of One. He told them how the stone circles were connected to the Moon, and perhaps even linked the Wiccan three-fold rule to two-thousand year old Druid beliefs. How it was now clear that the Book of One was somehow connected to stone circles. The council members listened agog to this passionate young man who had made more progress in a few months than Chapter 47 had made in years. But then he drifted off his prepared talk to protest how other groups were trying to find it for immoral purposes. More loudly than necessary, he stressed how important it was for the Wakened to find it before them, so that it might be used as a means of righting wrong, rather than being suppressed by fascist fundamentalists. He was raising his voice, and noted an imperceptible nod of agreement from Camus before Bill called him to order. Owen apologised for becoming emotional, saw the amused, tolerant smiles from

213

other members. Such passion from youth. As it should be. A young man with strong ideals, needs to learn restraint. As they had once. He returned to his prepared talk, and finished to patronising smiles of approval. He'd passed. He glanced at Camus. Not exactly a smile, but the man's hard eyes had softened at the corners, his mouth not quite so firmly set.

A knock on the door, and the meeting paused as a trolley with fresh coffee, orange juice, and sandwiches was rolled in. Bill declared a break for lunch.

Owen explained to Camus over an artichoke and avocado sandwich wrap. "Sorry I got angry, but I'm so pissed off... Do you think things are ever going to change?"

Camus nodded without warmth. "I hope you're not under the impression that you're the only one trying to do something about it?"

Still the reproof, still the point-scoring, but perhaps a hint of acceptance? He looked directly into Camus's eyes to establish rapport, but was met by a cold stare yielding nothing.

"Camus, I now realise how little I know. I'm so embarrassed... I know I was unbelievably arrogant at Jane's that night. I just didn't understand."

"Hmm. A step in the right direction, I suppose. Still a long way to go."

Owen swallowed his pride. "Of course. I'm so glad to be able to help find the Book. But it could take years. Decades even. I wish there was something I could do that was a bit more direct, something that would help raise Wicca's status right now."

The stare had softened. Camus was looking at him quizzically. "Maybe there is. We'll see."

Owen probed further, but Camus ended the conversation abruptly, and left the room, pulling his cigarettes from his pocket.

The following Friday came the phone call.

"Owen. Camus here. If you want to join our Chapter 12 campaign, there's a sortie tonight. Interested?"

"Um... Yes. What do I have to do?"

He gave him an address. "Be there at seven sharp." The phone went dead.

The address was a terraced house in East Cambridge. As he waited for the door to open, he noticed the cracked window, the peeling paint, the overgrown garden. The door opened roughly and a thin girl in her early twenties appeared, dressed in faded denim jeans and a Marilyn Manson T-shirt. She brushed a strand of mousy hair from her face.

"Hi. You must be Owen. I'm Erika. Come on in."

He followed her down the hallway of tattered posters for ancient gigs by long-forgotten bands, the air heavy with the sweet scent of marijuana. In a dingy room with bare floorboards, four people, all about his own age, sat around a rickety wooden table sharing a bong. As he started to introduce himself, he found himself gaping at Kim's pale face, her black-lined gothic eyes staring back at him, alarmed, shocked, dismayed. A millisecond later, her mask was in place.

"Owen. I didn't know you were joining us. How cool is that? After all this time?"

He hadn't seen her since she had taken Natalie. What was she doing here? How much had he told her that night of Sarah's funeral? Would she blow his cover? Had she already blown it?

They embraced briefly, both flustered, exchanging news and explanations, while his mind reeled at that momentary glimpse into her mind. And what had his face told her at that moment? He had no idea.

She offered him the bong. "Want some?"

"Er ... no thanks".

"Sure? It will make you relax. Have a munchy then."

On the table was an open packet of chocolate biscuits, and he took one, glad of something to do with his hands. They introduced themselves in turn.

Erika spoke. "Camus said you haven't done a sortie before. Excited?"

He confessed that he had no idea what a sortie was, that Camus had told him nothing about what "Chapter 12" involved.

They looked at him strangely, and then Erika said "Sorry - just remembered I've got to make a phone call." She disappeared to the other end of the house, shutting the door behind her.

In her absence, the conversation became stilted and awkward. After an eternity, she returned.

"Seems like there's been a stuff-up. You were supposed to have been briefed. But Camus says you've been vetted so if you still want to join us you're welcome. I can fill you in as we go."

"Maybe you could give me an idea of what's involved? I really don't have the foggiest."

"Well you know of our struggle against the oppressive religions... No? Right. I'll start at the beginning. You know that the Wakened is trying to re-establish Wicca? Good." She smiled. "It would be a real worry if you didn't. Anyway, some groups are doing that by boosting Wicca's image, gaining acceptance in various places. We're taking a different approach - chipping away at the smug image portrayed by the other major religions. Our main targets are the Christians, Muslims, and Jews. Especially the fundamentalists - they're the worst. We leave Buddhists and minor religions alone - we don't have an argument with them."

"So how do you damage their image?"

"All sorts of ways. You know that vicar in Birmingham who was jailed last week for child pornography?"

"Yes... but I don't see..."

"That was Ben's project"

Ben broke in. "Have you any idea how easy it is to get someone's credit card number, enrol them in a Russian paedophile site, leave a few CDs on top of a kitchen cupboard? Make an anonymous phone call to the police? And bang. Another dent in the self-righteous image of the Church of England."

"The vicar was totally innocent?"

"He became a martyr for his faith. Bit sad for him, but nothing against the pain suffered by the thousands of witches burnt at the stake, dying for their faith. He's my seventh."

216

"Come off it, Ben," said Erika, "You didn't do all that single-handed."

"OK, one or two buddies helped me. Just helping swing the pendulum the other way."

Owen said nothing, horrified, appalled, trying not to let it show. "So what's the sortie tonight?"

"Only a bit of graffiti. We'll dress up as Muslims and spray paint a synagogue. In London. Make sure we're seen, and then phone the papers. Are you in?"

"Yes of course. Sounds like fun. Great to be able to do something for a change, rather than talk about it."

Chapter 15

After blackening his hair with boot polish, and rubbing tanning lotion over his face, neck and arms, Owen was handed a white cloth with a fine black check - the unmistakable symbol of solidarity with Palestine. Ben showed him how to fasten the kaffiyeh round his neck. With his denim jeans, T-shirt, and trainers, he would have been indistinguishable from any of the young Muslim men attending a pro-Palestinian rally. The girls also darkened their skin and hair, and wore similar clothes to his, differing only in the hijab, which they wore over the head, leaving their faces uncovered.

After emptying their pockets of wallets and purses, and removing their jewellery, they inspected each other's outfits. They must carry nothing that might identify them. Each was then issued with weapons, consisting of a Tesco carrier-bag containing a selection of spray-paint cans. Pathetically and ludicrously, the charged atmosphere was that of a group of dangerous terrorists, rather than a group of wannabe activists about to spray a bit of graffiti. Increasingly Owen felt that this was not a group who would commit murder. On the other hand, if Ben's story was true, was it not tantamount to murder to condemn harmless old men to years in prison where they would be attacked and abused by hardened criminals?

The old van banged and rattled as they trundled down the slow lane of the M11, its exhaust complaining noisily, filling the inside of the van with suffocating fumes. Opening windows made it even worse, and so they sat on the hard floor in the back, feeling increasingly nauseated. After they'd stopped to let Erika throw up on the side of the road, the smell of her vomit added to the exhaust fumes. By the time they were banging their way through the darkened streets of London, they were all feeling sick and asthmatic, and the whole escapade seemed pathetic and doomed.

They pulled up in a faceless street in East London, the two columns of grubby terraced houses rendered expressionless by drawn curtains. Climbing out of the van, they stretched and coughed, gulping in lungfuls of the cool night air, trying to resuscitate the esprit de corps of a few hours earlier.

After walking half a mile or more, they arrived at a sixties red-brick hall, decorated with a large Star of David. Ignoring the front door, they followed Ben, who had assumed the position of leader, to a sandy-coloured side-gate. They pulled on surgical gloves, to avoid leaving fingerprints. To Owen, it seemed an overkill - would the police really bother to check for fingerprints after a bit of graffiti? Ben tapped some numbers into the keypad next to the gate, and there was the click of a lock opening.

"How did you know..." whispered Owen.

Ben turned to him, a frown on his face, and a finger to his lips, shushing him to silence, trying to conceal the unmistakeable glow of pride, revelling in Owen's astonishment. But he mistook the expression on Owen's face: it was not so much astonishment as a gnawing realisation that this sortie involved rather more than a bit of graffiti.

Beyond the side door was a narrow alleyway leading to a locked door. Ben pulled out a set of tools and inexpertly fumbled with them for a few minutes before the lock grudgingly clicked and they were inside. He immediately typed a four-digit code into the burglar-alarm next to the door. The flashing light stopped.

They moved swiftly from the vestibule into the synagogue. The deserted interior was dark save for the glow of candles burning at the front, next to a wooden structure which he recognised as the Ark. On either side were galleries, and in the centre was a raised platform with a lectern.

Despite being an atheist, Owen was awed by places of worship. It was not so much the presence of a greater power as the lingering reverberation of passionate belief. He felt overwhelmed and intimidated by the strength of human feeling that had been expressed within these walls. Now he felt sickened by the desecration they were about to commit, the number of people who would be shocked, grief-stricken, by their outrageous abuse of this holy place.

He sought reassurance by reminding himself of his ultimate reason for being here: to avenge Sarah's death. Can't make an omelette without breaking eggs. Besides, it was only graffiti. Take a few days to wash off, and then all would be well again. But he knew these lame excuses were no more than that. He felt sickened, and desperately tried to think of a way out of the impossible situation in which he found himself trapped.

Unwillingly, he followed the others through the synagogue. Somehow nobody had started painting, and he realised that the others were almost as reluctant as he was. It was Ben who started. He strode up to the end of the nave, to the Ark, and on it sprayed, in red letters made stark by the candle, "Filthy Zionist pigs go home!" Then they all started. Owen stood in the centre of the synagogue, helplessly watching their spray cans deface the holy walls. Nauseated, he saw Ben write "Bring back the final solution!" His paralysis was broken by a shout, forcing him to decide: either join in, or abandon his hunt for Sarah's killers. Abandon Sarah? In a frenzied bout of nervous hysteria fuelled by shame, panic, and self-loathing, his obscene messages started to cover the sacred walls: "Freedom for Palestine!" on one wall, followed by "Zionist Murderers! Leave the Occupied Territories!" on the other.

As he climbed up next to the Ark, he accidentally knocked over the candles. They fell harmlessly, and so he continued his painting - he'd pick them up in a minute. Then he smelt burning, and saw that the cloth underneath the candles had caught fire. He jumped down to stamp out the flames, but Ben reached them first. And then, inexplicably, Ben sprayed the flames with his aerosol can. The paint spray became a blowtorch, the flickering cloth became an inferno, and he dropped the burning jet of flame. It rolled on the floor, still roaring deadly fire like a slow Catharine wheel.

220

It rocked to a halt facing the dry varnished wooden benches, which took seconds to become engulfed in flame. The others were screaming, shouting, while Owen watched, numb and helpless, as the flames licked at the galleries above. He came to his senses, searched wildly for a fire extinguisher, and then realised he was alone - the others had panicked and bolted. And to his eternal shame and humiliation, he followed.

Stumbling out through the door into the cold evening air, he found himself alone. No sign of the others. Which way to the car? Blindly he ran through the streets, tearing off his kaffiyeh, and in minutes was hopelessly lost. Stranded in London without a penny to his name, having committed a crime. And not merely a bit of graffiti, either. Criminal damage.

He heard a siren, then more. Someone must have seen the fire. Or maybe there had been a fire alarm. He desperately hoped so. Had they been seen? Now he was running aimlessly, unthinking, panicking, a small boy wanting to be back home. He tried to picture his other self, the scourge of Sarah's killers. The problem solver. The hero. Vengeance is his.

Pausing uncertainly, he looked around. He was in a dark, anonymous street. Probably safe for the moment. Breathing deeply, he tried to calm the anxiety and panic surging within, threatening to drown him. He needed to change his appearance, find a place he could wash off the black from his hair and face. The glow of shops in the distance beckoned, and he started walking towards them, forcing himself to take steady, methodical steps.

Headlights appeared from a side street, and turned like searchlights. As they swept towards him, he saw they belonged to a police car, crawling along, searching for suspects. He dived into a front garden, knocking over a row of potted shrubs. There was a crash as a ceramic pot lazily rolled off its stand and shattered on the ground. Still the police car slowly cruised past, its occupants scanning the streets. Ducking as the car passed, he became aware of a dog barking in the house, lights being switched on, and the door opening. The Doberman lunged viciously towards him, snarling. As he jumped away, it grabbed his wrist, biting hard, sending waves of pain up his arm. Instinctively he pulled away, causing the dog to grip harder. He heard someone in the house yell "Call the police!". Owen gave the dog a savage kick and broke away. Panicking again, he ran down the side-street from which the police car had emerged. His wrist was bleeding copiously, and he tried wrapping the torn shirt around it as he ran. He needed to find water to wash his arm, to get rid of the condemning blackness on his face and hair, become a human being again. Running, stumbling, he searched wildly for a water fountain, a public toilet, a stream, anything, when he saw the most beautiful sight coming towards him. The van.

They bundled him in and roared through the streets. Nobody spoke a word, other than to tell him to keep down. Just a van with a single driver, heading towards the motorway. They passed police cars, and fire engines, screaming back the way they had come.

"What d'you do that for?" hissed Kim.

"It was an accident," he protested. "Anyway, it was Ben who sprayed the paint on it. I was trying to stamp..."

"No I didn't," scowled Ben, "don't try to shift the blame on to me, you pathetic little prick."

Owen realised that nobody else had seen what had happened, and he looked at Ben, searching for a knowing glance, a conspiratorial wink. But there was only anger in Ben's face, as if Ben really believed what he had said. Owen sat back, dazed, confused. It had all happened so fast. Now he wasn't sure. It had been Ben who sprayed paint on the fire, hadn't it?

"I'm about to throw up," he yelled.

They pulled over. "Be quick about it," spat Erika, opening the door. He vomited messily onto the kerb, and climbed back in the van, aware of the eyes following him like gun-turrets.

They held their fire until they reached the anonymity of the motorway, when they sat up and started yelling at him, releasing the pent-up tide of fear and hostility that had been brewing ever since they had left the synagogue.

"What the hell did you do that for?" shouted Erika. "What have those people ever done to you?"

"But you were all attacking the synagogue. It got a bit out of hand, that's all." He looked at their hostile faces. "It was an accident," he added, but it sounded as lame as ever. Overtones of Sarah's death, the accusation that that had been his fault too. Maybe they were right - maybe he wasn't as good as he thought he was, maybe he was just screwing around ... Had Ben really sprayed the aerosol into the flames, or was that his over-heated imagination?

"There's a world of difference between spraying a bit of graffiti and burning down a synagogue," screamed Kim, and he saw her face was teary, frightened. His shame and confusion deepened, and finding a tub of wipes, he focussed on the task of removing the dark make-up from his skin. Closing his eyes, he sat hunched, head in hands.

He was woken by the doors opening. Climbing out, he saw that they were not back in Cambridge, but in some parking area he didn't recognise, surrounded by warehouses and car repair workshops. Nobody met his questioning gaze or spoke to him.

"Where are we?"

Ben was cold, impersonal, functional. "Just outside Cambridge. I'm dumping the van here until the heat's off. You stay here until we're gone. I don't ever want to meet you again." He turned and moved off without another word, following the others who had already left.

Owen felt the cool wind on his face, and saw the glow of lights on the horizon. Probably Cambridge. He sat on the ground, listening to the scrunch of their feet disappearing into the darkness. After a further ten minutes, he started walking.

The first glimmer of dawn was edging up the eastern horizon as he arrived home, keyless. Breaking a window at the back, he climbed in. As he poured a scotch, he found the panic, shame, and self-loathing was subsiding, to be replaced by a fear of being caught. He turned on the TV, flicked to a cable news channel, and was confronted by a sickening sight. Images of the blazing building, now roofless, surrounded by firemen desperately trying to save the adjacent houses. He watched the "special coverage of the terrorist attack in London". Horror welled within him, bringing guilt and remorse to the surface like flotsam on a rising tide.

Outside, dawn arrived, and still he sat in front of the TV, both fascinated and tormented by the devastation he had unleashed. Seven o'clock. *The top story this morning is a horrifying Muslim terrorist attack on a synagogue in East London. No casualties have so far been reported, but damage is estimated at millions of pounds.*

The inevitable talking heads started sprouting, their eyes boring into his guilt-racked face.

The local rabbi, his tears streaming, "Who would do such a thing?"

Pan to a grim policeman. "There are unconfirmed reports of a group of youths of middle-eastern appearance. We will catch these arsonists, whoever they are."

And flash to some politician. "This terrorism will not be tolerated. Britain remains a compassionate, multi-cultural society, and we will not tolerate these extremists bringing their wars to our country."

oooOooo

He was woken by the phone. Standing up shakily from the couch, still dressed, he staggered over. George's tone was brusque, businesslike, neither condemning nor supportive. "We need to talk. Back lounge of the Lion, one o'clock?"

Owen agreed, and hung up. At least George hadn't yelled at him. But that wouldn't have been his style. What should he tell George? The sob story about it all being an accident? Bit pathetic, really. That Ben, not he, had started it? The others would call him a liar. Would he be universally condemned for this? Or would Sarah's killers support him? Might this in fact help him gain entry to new depths of the Wakened?

224

And then the real problem hit him. Was he going to get caught by the police? Other than the surgical gloves (thank God for those!) they had taken no special precautions. They had probably left bits of DNA all over the synagogue. And his kaffiyeh, carelessly torn off and thrown into a front-yard, rich with traces of his hair, his DNA. Would they find under the black dye that he was an Anglo-Saxon with brown hair? Yes, if they found it. If someone didn't think it was an old tea-towel.

What about security cameras? At least one will have recorded the number-plate of their van.

If he was caught, he knew it would be a prison sentence, and a long one. It would be his worst nightmare - being told what to do every minute of your life by some unthinking fascist bastard with the IQ of a worm, subjected to the unspeakable acts that went on between prisoners. Especially a young good-looking man like him. And his background - different in so many ways from them, an object of curiosity, not comradeship in adverse circumstances. An object. To be used.

He decided he would take his own life rather than go to prison. And then he reprimanded himself for his melodrama. Don't be a victim. Take control. Perhaps he could turn himself in, help them catch the others. It would reduce his sentence. But what others? A group of students with no previous convictions given fifty-pound fines for graffiti? Not exactly supergrass material. What about Ben's scheme for framing innocent vicars with charges of child pornography? Was there any evidence? Did it actually happen, or was it merely a boastful fantasy?

And if he did escape detection, what about living with the crime he had committed? How could he atone for that?

Anyway, he could deal with all that if and when the time came. Right now he had to deal with George.

oooOooo

Entering the pub, he made his way through the Saturday lunchtime crowd to the back room, and was surprised to see both George and Camus waiting for him. He still didn't understand Camus's role in the Wakened. George motioned him to a seat and a pint of beer, and told him that sandwiches had already been ordered. Uncomfortable and apprehensive, he sat and waited for the barrage of recriminations. Instead, George made small talk. Which was difficult, given Camus's surly reticence, and Owen's inability to think beyond the evils of the night.

The sandwiches came, the door was closed, and George moved straight to the point.

"I have to say we're disappointed in you, Owen. I wouldn't have thought you capable of such wanton destruction, such little thought for the consequences. Do you realise that you've put the Wakened at risk? We now have a massive anti-terrorist operation trying to find you and your friends. If they're successful, it could mean the end of the Wakened. An enormous blow to the cause of Wicca." He paused.

Owen swallowed, still unsure of his decision. "I'm sorry. I didn't mean to, but it was just... I didn't go in there planning to do anything like that, but then, in the heat of the moment, I suddenly saw this chance to escalate our action into something that would hurt both the Jews and the Muslims. I'm sorry. It was impulsive, and foolish."

"Good. I'm glad you're sorry. So should you be," replied George coolly.

Camus spoke slowly, looking at George, as if challenging him. "On the other hand, it has to be said, that if you do go undetected, this may be one of the biggest blows yet struck for the cause. There are already rumours of gangs of Jewish boys going round east London, attacking anybody resembling an Arab."

George interrupted. "We are all on the same side, pursuing the same goal. But the Wakened does it within the confines of the law. We can't risk breaking the law - the backlash could be enormous. The Council had a teleconference this morning. Some members have demanded your punishment, your expulsion from the Wakened."

"While others praised your initiative," interrupted Camus, glaring at George, "Forgiving your impulsive action as being the mark of youthful idealism."

"There is a clear dividing line between ..." retorted George, and then stopped. After taking a deep breath, he continued in careful tones, each word weighed before its delivery. "Camus and I disagree about some things. But we both agree that you should be reprimanded but not expelled. You're too valuable to the cause to be kicked out because of your moment of stupidity. The council have agreed to this provided you make a full apology to them, show true remorse, understand the folly of your actions, and perform penance to the Goddess."

He looked at Camus, who said nothing, although a suggestion of a smile crept into the corners of his lips.

Owen took a gulp of beer, as George continued, his mouth now full of ham and avocado sandwich. A crumb landed in Owen's beer, which he put down on the table, no longer thirsty.

"However, you will be expelled from Chapter 12 - your actions were rather too extreme for them."

George paused while he washed down his sandwich with a swig of beer. "Your activities in Chapter 47 will not be affected at all. I don't think this is relevant to that. However, most importantly, it's Camus's job now to ensure that you and your friends aren't caught. I think it should be possible - we have friends in all the right places. They have ways of losing a bit of evidence, mix up a couple of DNA samples. I want you to work closely with Camus, tell him everything you know, everything you can remember."

George finished his sandwich, gulped down his last drops of beer, and stood. "I have to go now - I'll leave you to talk to Camus. But you might want this." He handed Owen a plastic bag containing his wallet, watch, phone, and keys. "And make no mistake about it. You are in trouble, and there are those in the Wakened who are quite distressed by your actions. But the Wakened looks after its own, and you are one of us. So we'll try to fix the problem you have created, perhaps even turn it to our advantage, and we will move on. As should you."

He reached out his hand, and shook Owen's. As he opened the door to leave, he turned and nodded with a smile. "Blessed be."

Owen sat again, and faced Camus. He was not going to enjoy this. "Umm, would you mind if I ordered a coffee? Would you like one?"

The barman was pulling a beer. "Bloody Arabs, bringing their wars with them. Send them all back, I say. That'll be three pounds fifty sir. Thankyou." He turned to Owen "Yes sir. And what can I do you for?"

"Two black coffees please."

"Right sir. It'll take a couple of minutes. You're in the back room? I'll bring them in."

Returning to the room, it seemed to Owen that Camus had dropped the unpleasant sneer and even appeared supportive. It seemed that Owen had crossed a bridge, perhaps even burnt it, and he and Camus were now on the same side. While Camus took copious notes, Owen tried to remember every detail of what had happened, realising that if Camus were to help him, he had to be as accurate as possible, mention everything that might turn up as evidence to the police.

"As I jumped onto the table, I kicked the candles over, and then I saw what a wonderful opportunity this could be. I sprayed the candles with paint, and of course the can became an instant flame-thrower. I couldn't help dropping it, and it rolled across the floor, still spraying out fire."

"Surely as soon as you released the button it shut off."

"I don't know. I guess the button must have stuck down. Maybe the heat."

Camus raised an eyebrow. "Sounds unlikely. Sure you didn't keep it forced down?"

"No really. This whole thing was an impulse. I didn't plan it."

Camus stared at him, wordless, judging him, and then scrawled an indecipherable note on his pad. There was a knock on the door, and the barman entered with coffee.

Camus sat silent, looking at Owen, who fidgeted nervously until the barman left.

Camus continued "And what did the others do?"

"I'm not sure. It was all such a blur. I hadn't expected the paint to keep on spraying. I think Ben came over and I thought he sprayed his can on to it too, but in the van he said he hadn't. So I'm not sure exactly what happened after that. Suddenly they'd all gone."

He described his nightmarish run through the streets, his encounter with the police car and with the dog. His walk back to his house that morning. Only a few hours earlier. It seemed like a lifetime ago.

oooOooo

For the next few days, Owen lived in fear of the knock on the door, the police cars screeching outside his house, the tap on the shoulder as he left work. He'd wake up in a cold sweat at four in the morning, convinced he could hear the anti-terrorist squad surrounding the house. But as days turned into weeks, the fire seemed to fade from the news, and police reassurances that they were following leads slowly evaporated. Apparently the van had been stolen a week earlier in Kent, and it had now been found, burnt out, in a Welsh quarry. Any fingerprints or DNA in the synagogue had been wiped clean by the fire. The only evidence found by the police was spray paint cans, which were being analysed.

Camus had instructed him to keep a low profile, and especially not to keep checking news stories about the synagogue fire on the web, as these would be monitored, and any unusual level of interest would be checked out. He had also told him to lead a normal life, not to show any change of behaviour. Above all, he was not to contact any of the other members of Chapter 12. Owen also decided not to tell Aleister anything about it, partly because there was no need to involve him, but partly because he knew it would diminish him in Aleister's eyes, and for some reason that seemed important. So he had to bear the weight of his secret alone, in its entirety.

At the Wiccan meeting that week, he was surprised to see no knowing glances in his direction, no winks or furtive whispered comments in dark corners. Apparently the Wakened security had been water-tight, and nobody had any reason to connect the synagogue fire with the Wakened, or with Cambridge. Just a group of Muslim youths who had faded into the background. The chance of being linked to the arson seemed to grow slimmer with each passing week. All he had to cope with now was his guilt.

There was another problem. Being part of Chapter 12 had meant he was a step closer to Sarah's killers. And now he had blown it. Up a ladder and down a snake, and back to square one. The Book of One. Probably never get invited to the Council again either.

His work on the Book had fallen by the wayside, and he resolved to pick it up again. A few weeks ago, he'd asked Aleister if he could find any more scraps of information about the Book. Aleister had so far drawn a blank. But Owen hadn't told him about his growing conviction that the path forward might lie in the study of Stone Circles.

"Hi Aleister. Owen here."

"Dear boy. How lovely to hear from you. I was thinking I ought to give you a ring, see how you're getting on."

"Not so well, I'm afraid. I seem to have hit a brick wall."

"I'm so sorry to hear that. Is there anything I can do to help?"

"Actually, there is. I was wondering if you could search through your library and find anything about stone circles in your Wiccan literature."

A pause from the other end. "That's a big job, Owen. I'm not sure I can ... on the other hand. Maybe if I did a bit of sorting out, could you come down here to go through it with me?"

He thought about it. Why not. It would be good to get away from Cambridge. "OK. How about I come down this weekend?"

"Splendid! It will be wonderful to see you again. Can you get down here Friday evening and I'll make something special for dinner?"

"That would be great Aleister. About seven? OK - see you then. "

oooOooo

After an enormous tofu stir-fry, Aleister took him through to the study, where piles of books were arranged on the floor, sorted into categories. Although there were many references to stone circles, none seemed to convey any useful information, except for a passing reference in a tatty nineteenth-century Grimoire to "reading the stones", without any explanation of what it meant.

Aleister handed him a small nineteenth-century monograph called "The History of the Druids", written and privately published by one "Sir William Hammond". Some country squire with pretensions to literacy, no doubt. Owen idly thumbed through it. He recognised excerpts from De Bello Gallico, from Diodorus, Mitchell, Aubrey, and others. It seemed as if Hammond, whoever he was, had at least done his research, which was unusual for (Owen checked the front of the book) 1882. He read it more carefully, and found himself reading a passage claiming to be an eye-witness account of a Druid priest in the early days of the Roman occupation.

"Aleister, listen to this."

"A novice priest came to our village to converse with the elders. He was young, but already had the power, and could silence any of us with a look. But he rarely chose to do so, instead telling stories to the children, and explaining mysteries to the adults. Every family vied for the honour of feeding and housing him. Each night during his stay, he went with the elders to the stone circle, and we children would hide in the bushes, watching him spend all night walking the circle, caressing the stones, learning their song. After many

231

days, when he could recite our song as well as the elders, he moved on to the next village."

Aleister gazed at him over the top of his reading glasses, bleary-eyed and doubtful. "Who wrote that?"

"The guy who wrote this book says it was taken from a thirteenth-century document called "De Historiae Druidibus", which claimed to be based on letters written by a Roman scholar."

As Owen recounted its pedigree, it seemed unlikely. It was probably a fake, or a fantasy, and yet it tied in with the clues that he had already heard. If a Druid learnt a song at each village, it could certainly take many years to learn the whole repertoire.

Aleister was staring at him silently.

Owen met his gaze. "It's probably a fake, isn't it?"

Aleister shrugged.

oooOooo

During the tea-break at the monthly Wiccan meeting, Camus motioned with his head for Owen to follow him. Outside, Camus laboriously lit his cigarette, and fussily stowed the packet and lighter back in their pocket. He took a long drag, and blew the smoke away from Owen. At last he spoke. "It seems like you're in the clear. All their leads are hopelessly in the wrong direction. The only way they'll find you now is if someone leaks. Have you mentioned it to anyone else?"

"No, of course not."

"Good. Apart from the council members, who are completely reliable, there are only six people in the world who know about this - you and your five partners in crime. I was worried about one of them, but I've told them that if you get caught, they will all be charged with arson, and so you can all expect to stay in prison until you're grey. So I think you can regard it as closed."

Closed? It didn't seem like that. He had the rest of his life to cope with it.

232

"Thanks Camus. I really appreciate what you've done for us. For me."

"Good. One other thing. I have a friend who would like to speak to you. I have told him that you have been involved in some excellent work with Chapter 12. That's all he knows. Make sure it stays that way. Not even a hint of what you've done. The fewer who know the better."

"So who is he?"

"His name's Siegfried. That's all you need to know. He'll explain."

Chapter 16

The email seemed harmless enough.

"Hi Owen C. suggested I should contact you about some work we could do together. I'm based in London, but I'm happy to drive up to meet you - how about somewhere between London and Cambridge? When is a good day for you? Cheers Siegfried."

Although Owen suspected that little connected with Camus was as innocent as it seemed, there was no way he would miss this opportunity to dig deeper into his murky circle of friends. But suppose they had blown his cover? Suppose they were going to deal with him the way they had dealt with Sarah? No matter. Life or death, he was determined to keep going until they stopped him. He emailed back, suggesting a pub, but Siegfried wanted somewhere more anonymous.

Owen pulled into the car park at the M11 Service Area at Birchanger Green a few minutes early. His mobile rang.

"Hi. Siegfried here. Where are you?"

"In the car park."

"OK - sound your horn."

He did so.

"Hang on a minute... Flash your lights. Right, got you. Drive out of the car park onto the roundabout, and take the first turning."

Leaving the car park, a red car followed him. He waved to the mirror, but there was no response.

As he turned off the roundabout, the red car kept going towards the motorway. Not him then. And no other car behind.

A few minutes later, his mobile rang again. "OK. Take the next on your left. When you reach the top of the hill, stop and wait for me." The phone went dead without waiting for a reply.

The turning led on to a muddy track between two fields. What was he getting into? After slithering up the hill, he stopped at a wooden five-bar gate leading into the field, and warily climbed out of the car. The only tyre-tracks in the mud were his own.

No other car was visible. Anywhere. Around him stretched the seductive curves of the ploughed hill. Above him larks celebrated faintly. A solitary tree stood leafless in the crisp November chill, a lonely brooding sentinel. He waited for the quiet to be broken by Siegfried's car, but none came. Instead, a crow left its perch on the black tree, and flew towards Owen, its wings thumping in the still air. As he watched it approach like some harbinger of doom, he could not escape the growing feeling that this had been a stupid, reckless thing to do. To agree to meet Sarah's killers, in a dead-end track with no witness, no hope of escape. He shivered, and decided to turn his car to face downhill, ready for a quick escape. Not so quick if the track was blocked. The barbed-wire fences were too high to jump, but if necessary he could dive under the bottom wire in a roll, and then run, weaving, as he ran for cover behind the tree.

The track was barely wide enough, but eventually his car was facing downhill, facing whoever was coming for him.

The crow sat on the gate-post, patiently watching, like a spectator arrived early for the match.

He heard it before he saw it, and then the Range Rover was clambering up the hill towards him, no room for his car to squeeze past, impossible to see how many people were inside through the darkly tinted windscreen. He wished he had waited the other side of the fence, rather than having to dive under it. The Range Rover was alongside, blocking his exit, the door opening. He tensed.

"Hi Owen, Sorry to keep you waiting. Merry meet."

Owen smiled, trying to appear relaxed, but visibly exhaling, releasing the coiled spring within. "Merry meet, Siegfried." They shook hands.

"Sorry about the cloak and dagger stuff. Had to make sure neither of us was followed."

Siegfried was older than him, but thin, craggy, athletic, with black hair and hard brown eyes. He seemed confident, poised, relaxed. "Camus tells me you've done some great work for the Wakened."

He shrugged. "I guess so. Um... what do you do?"

"Oh, you know. This and that. In the city." Siegfried breathed in deeply. "Wonderful air up here, isn't it. Absolutely marvellous to get out of the smoke. I envy you living in Cambridge."

"This and that?"

"Stocks. Shares. That sort of thing."

Siegfried turned his back and walked over to the gate. Leaning on it, admiring the view, his breath produced clouds of steam in the chilled morning air.

The crow flapped off into the distance.

Owen stood beside him and adjusted his arms on the gate to appear relaxed.

"So what sort of work did you think we could do together?"

Siegfried turned, smiling easily. "No time for small-talk, eh? I like someone who gets to the point. Why don't you tell me a little about yourself?"

"Umm... I imagine Camus has already told you."

"Not in detail. So what was this action you were involved in?"

"Oh, you know. This and that," smirked Owen, "in Cambridge."

Siegfried grinned. "Touché! I can see we're going to work well together."

He turned his body to face Owen square on. "Let's get to the point. I know I can trust you. Camus has told me. But you don't know whether you can trust me, correct?"

Owen hesitated, and then agreed. "Correct."

"OK. Let me tell you about what we do, then you can decide how far you want to trust me. Right?"

"Right."

236

"Excellent. You've done some work with Chapter 12, I gather?"

Owen nodded, ambiguously.

"We take over when Chapter 12 wimp out."

"We?"

Siegfried gazed at him, serious for the first time, deciding.

"Retribution. My little group is called Retribution. We're the ... SAS of Wicca."

"Umm... Isn't that a little inconsistent with Wiccan ethics? Having an SAS I mean?"

A flash of passion darkened Siegfried's face for an instant, and was replaced by his suave, patronising smile. "Well, pacifism didn't help the witches in the middle ages, did it? We're a little more flexible nowadays. We might not like violence but somebody has to do it."

"Do they?" Owen was about to say, but swallowed it. Another question screamed into his mind. And did they kill Sarah? Battening it down, keeping it for later, he adopted a casual, conversational tone.

"OK. I see. And what exactly do you do?"

"Ah. 'Exactly' is such a strong word, don't you think? Let's say we do what has to be done. Whatever it takes."

Owen looked up sharply. "What do you mean?"

"Come on, Owen. You weren't born yesterday. If someone poses a threat to the Wakened, or to Wicca, we take out the garbage."

The stress on the word 'out' was ambiguous, deliberately so.

Owen nodded. He'd already guessed, but had stopped short of thinking through the implications. "And what do you want to discuss with me?"

"What do you think?"

As he pondered the question, a dense flock of starlings wheeled like coffee-grounds in some cosmic current above their heads. "And if I say yes?"

"We give you training. A week's holiday in the country. Where we teach you the tools of the trade."

Owen stared at him, saying nothing. And did that include cutting brake lines?

Siegfried paused, meeting his stare. "Maybe this isn't your cup of tea. Never mind. Camus misinformed me. Well, it's been nice meeting you..."

"Wait. I want to join."

"Are you sure?"

Emphatically. "Yes."

Siegfried frowned at him doubtfully. "Do you have a Nokia?"

"What? Yes..."

"Good. So you don't need the charger."

Siegfried fished a mobile out of his pocket and handed it to him. "Check for messages each evening. My number's on it. I'll phone you later in the week and give you the date."

This was all going too fast.

"OK. But..."

"Excellent. Good to meet you Owen. I'll talk to you in a few days. If you change your mind, just call me and say, no harm done." He shook hands and jumped in the Range Rover, winding down the window.

"Blessed Samhain!" he called cheerily as he threw the car into reverse, and screeched off.

"Er...Blessed Samhain," responded Owen uncertainly to the departing car, now reversing expertly at speed down the hill.

As the noise faded into the distance, he felt the tide of silence rising around him once more. In minutes he was alone, save for the larks still trilling invisibly high, and the hiss of tormented emotions crashing around inside his head.

oooOooo

The next day, he returned home to find a coded message from Aleister to call him back, urgently. He drove out of Cambridge and called Aleister on the secure mobile.

"Hi Aleister? How's things?"

"Owen, dear boy. You absolutely have to come down here this instant. I've found a lady who claims she can read the stones."

"What? You're kidding!"

"I kid you not, dear boy."

"Is she for real?"

"I think we need to find out. People suggest she might be."

"I'm on my way down."

"Well, if you... But I must tell you about her. She lives in Chagford, in Devon. It's just off..."

"Yes I know it," replied Owen, suddenly irritable at the mention of the place.

"Oh," said Aleister, taken aback by the sudden coldness in his voice. "Are you alright?"

"Yeh - I'll explain later. Sorry."

"Good. She's said she'll meet us for lunch tomorrow. Why don't you and I get together first - how about in the Ring O'Bells, just off the market place, at about 12?"

As Owen parked near the Chagford bus stop, he felt isolated, besieged by memories crowding around the car, unnoticed by the shoppers milling back and forth across the market place. Other people, other concerns. This is where it had all started to go wrong. The spot where the policeman had dropped them off. The 'Tinners' Rabbits" where they spent a few precious coins on a cup of tea. 'Good Vibrations'. He heard the rasp of crows, and saw them still sitting on the roof above the shop, their black eyes trained on him like laser gunsights, as he walked up to the pub.

Aleister was sitting at the bar, recounting a longwinded story to a bored barman, who nodded gratefully to Owen as he rescued him. They took their pints to a table and sat down.

"So how did you get to hear about this lady?"

"Friend of a friend told me she sang at their Samhain ceremony the other night. In a strange language, which she says she reads from the stones."

Owen frowned sceptically. "Well I suppose we'll soon find out whether she's for real or not."

They drained their pints and walked up to the Tinners' Rabbits. Aleister asked at the counter if Mrs. Huxtable was there, and was directed to a table in the window where an old lady sat, nursing a cup of tea. Huxtable. Where had he heard that name before?

Despite the warm fug of the café she was dressed in an old brown tweed overcoat, and her thick grey hair was tied in a bun. As they introduced themselves, she nodded cursorily at Aleister, but smiled at Owen, peering at him through thick pebble glasses.

"Come and sit down, m'dear, so I can see you proper. I broke my glasses yesterday and these are old ones. They don't work so well."

He shook hands. "It's good to meet you, Mrs Huxtable."

"Call me Francesca."

It was an unusual name for an old Devon lady, but before he had a chance to ask, Aleister, looking slightly miffed, took control of the conversation and ordered three vegetarian pasties, with cups of tea.

"Make mine a diet Coke," asked Owen.

Over lunch, she told them about her childhood as the daughter of a Devon witch, of ceremonies attended by hundreds of people on the moor, and how the numbers had fallen until only a handful remained.

"There's only me and Alfred left in Chagford. We have a little shop up the top there."

Owen felt a chill penetrate the humid fug of the restaurant.

"You mean Good Vibrations?"

She beamed. "Yes m'dear. So you know about our little shop? But I don't think I've seen you in there have I? I'd remember you." She put an emphasis on the last word like a flirting teenager, adding to his discomfort and disorientation.

"No. No I think your husband served us. It was a very long time ago. He wouldn't remember me," he blurted. They both looked at him oddly.

Light dawned on Aleister's face. "So how long have your family lived in Chagford, Francesca?" he asked quickly. The old lady started rambling about her childhood memories, about her grandfather telling her that they had lived there since the dawn of time. Owen shot Aleister a grateful nod.

The meal finished, Owen paid for all three, and they piled into Aleister's ancient Landrover, Owen scrunched up in the back. Driving past Gidleigh, he was once more buffeted by the memories from that day, which banged on the windows and screamed into his ears, unnoticed by his two companions, isolating him. By the time they parked in that same small car park, the harpies of his memory were screeching around his head, rendering impossible any conversation or even rational thought. Released from the car, he cast around wildly, expecting to see marks on the ground, or even a scrap of charred paper. Nothing. Only the ghost of a memory, clinging indelibly to the place. As if waking from a nightmare, he became aware of the cool wind on his face, the concerned expressions on the faces of his companions.

"Are you alright, Owen?"

"Yes fine - sorry - it was a bit bumpy in the back of the car."

His mounting panic attack faded away, to be replaced by a certainty of a wasted trip, to see a batty old lady with her half-crazed delusions about the stones.

They helped her, fussing and tripping, through the gate, and then plodded slowly up the hill, pausing every few minutes to let her catch up, puffing and wheezing. Aleister took her elbow, helping her up the hill while Owen dawdled ahead, listening to the larks singing high above, watching the grey-green landscape unfold as he neared the broad crest. Reaching it, he stood stunned by the immensity of the panorama. Below stood Scorhill Circle, serene and majestic, and far ahead were the misty crags of Watern Tor and Hangingstone Rock. Between them lay the deceitful viridity of Gidleigh Common, where he could almost make out an Owen and Sarah meandering their way across, one sodden footstep at a time. But it was a much younger, more innocent Owen that tramped across the moor, exchanging meaningless jokes with his bride-to-be. Owen's eyes moistened, his throat constricted, bulging, aching with the sort of ache that comes only from the heart. By the time Aleister and Francesca reached him he was fighting back a sob of grief and loneliness welling uncontrollably within.

He felt a hand on his shoulder. "Owen, what's the matter, what is it?"

"Nothing - I just...er..." Through his welling eyes, he saw the astonishment on Francesca's face. Fighting to regain control, he tore away from Aleister, and walked ahead, staring at the ground. He turned. His voice surprised him as it emerged from his throat, low and hoarse.

"I'm sorry, Francesca. My girlfriend and I used to come here before she died."

Her face softened with concern and understanding, and she started raising her arms to console him. He turned awkwardly and fled down the slope.

Approaching the circle, he felt his grief and loss assuaged by the magic that had always attracted him to this place. The stones stood serene, as they had for four thousand years, bathing the surrounding common in an aura of peace. On the right stood a monolith towering above the others, as if representing the lord of all stones. To its right was a short squat stone, then a tall thin one, and so on, alternating round the circle. Male and female, he'd read somewhere. On the left was a curious row of three stones, which looked as if they formed a gateway to the circle. But all these interpretations were mere supposition. Nobody knew the purpose or meaning of Scorhill circle.

He heard Aleister and Francesca approach from behind. The old lady passed him wordlessly and stood in front of the largest stone, her head bowed as if praying. Moving to her right, she placed her hands on top of the next stone. A strange ethereal sound seemed to come from nowhere, and it took Owen several seconds to realise that she was chanting an unintelligible song in a strange language. She moved slowly from stone to stone as she did so, her arthritic fingers fondling their surfaces. Owen and Aleister stood silent and awed. Unaccountably, whether or not she was faking it, Owen found himself transfixed by the strange rhythm of the chant, the haunting sight of this old woman moving blindly from stone to stone in this tranquil, mystical scene.

After a few minutes, having passed only a dozen stones, she stopped, flung her arms out wide, her back to them, and called strange verses to the sky above. She turned and repeated it, and then called it twice again, each time facing a different direction. Closing her eyes, she became silent, her head bowed and cocked to one side. She nodded, as if acknowledging an instruction, and walked over to where Owen stood motionless.

"The Goddess welcomes you," she said, avoiding his gaze, "and wishes you success in your quest." She looked him in the face, trembling. "Owen, the Goddess is with you, and will help you."

Turning abruptly, she started walking back up the hill, as if her mission were accomplished. The two men exchanged glances, and ran after her.

"Wait!" said Owen, "I'm sorry but could you explain what that was all about?"

"I was reading the stones. Isn't that what you wanted?"

"Yes - it was wonderful, beautiful. But could you tell us a little more about it? What were you singing?"

"It was a song from before men walked this land, a song about how the land was created, how the Goddess first stepped onto it, how she created all living things and breathed her spirit into them."

"That's beautiful. But how did you read it from the stones?"

She smiled. "You have much to learn, Owen. Wisdom is a delicacy which is long in the making."

He continued pumping her with questions, but she would not be drawn, either smiling wordlessly, or replying in odd phrases that seemed to have come from some book of proverbs. Finally, he blurted out, "Do you know about the Book of One?"

She stopped, and turned to face him, smiling, as if he'd said something amusing. "Yes, m'dear. I do."

"What do you know?" he blurted, startled by his own rudeness.

She smiled tolerantly. "Maybe you already know more than you realise. But when the Goddess wants you to understand, m'dear, I'm sure she'll show you."

Turning back to her path, she continued to labour up towards the brow of the hill, while he stood motionless, thinking through the implications of what she had just said. *If she was right... But she's probably making it all up. On the other hand...*

They drove back to Chagford wordlessly. It was unusual for Aleister to remain quiet for very long, but he responded to Owen's comments with monosyllables, his thoughts elsewhere. After dropping Francesca off outside "Good Vibrations", Aleister drove to where Owen's car was parked, and looked at him for the first time since Scorhill. "Isn't she a wonderful old dear? I'd never have guessed..."

"I really don't know," said Owen. "Chances are she's making it all up. But there was something else. I felt that..." He broke off and shrugged.

"Maybe you should trust your feelings, more, dear boy."

"Well, what do you think?"

"I feel that we have just been privileged to witness something very special, something that very few mortals ever see."

As Owen drove back to Cambridge, her strange chant resonated in his mind. *If only he'd had a tape recorder.* She was probably no more than a daft old coot who lived in a fantasy world. *But maybe. No harm in following it up. See what he could find out about this strange woman and her chants.*

The next day he searched the Wakened database for any mention of reading the stones. Nothing, but he was surprised to find a reference to Francesca Huxtable. Apparently some years ago a Wakened member had heard about her, and had accompanied her to a stone circle - it didn't say which. He too had heard her chants, had thoroughly researched it, and concluded that she was just a crazy old bat with her private fantasy. Owen closed the database, disappointed, but not surprised. Wicca had more than its fair share of the lunatic fringe, and for every genuine lead there were a dozen like this. He resolved not to waste any more time on her, and got back to the serious business of researching the Book of One.

oooOooo

His research was brutally interrupted by a text message from Siegfried "Drv Macclesfield 5 Nov. Arrv 1200. Wait 4 txt this fone." Just like that. No "Are you free?" or "Can you make it?" He checked his diary. Nothing that couldn't be moved or missed. He'd have to take some vacation that week - people were starting to notice.

The rest of the week passed with agonising slowness, until at last the morning came. In the villages surrounding Cambridge, Owen saw children helping their dads build bonfires to burn poor old Guy Fawkes for his treasonous act. A man who, from a different angle, had been a martyr, trying to restore Catholicism as the mainstream religion of Britain. Before Guy Fawkes, Owen had read, the Pope had burned, and before him, witches. Ironically, witches had started the tradition by celebrating the end of Samhain with a "bone-fire night" on 5 November, until that joyous ritual had been turned against them. Apparently someone remembered: on a bonfire near Girton sat a papier-maché witch, with black pointed hat and broomstick, leering at the passing traffic, as she waited to be burned at the stake. That evening, she would be surrounded by dozens of children laughing at her slow death, waving their sparklers as the oil in her face crackled and spat. Or was it in sad remembrance, commemorating the thousands of witches who met their destiny in this cruel way? Owen saw the flowers laid around her on the funeral pyre, and understood. How many of the people lighting fireworks for the kids that evening would understand? For those with eyes to see, witchcraft was flourishing in the shires, a simple faith openly celebrated in every village, every town, every festival.

Speeding out towards Huntingdon, he watched the grey November fields slip by. More bonfires. Colourful hand-painted banners draped across school entrances. Fireworks tonight outside the Parish Hall. Soup and hot potatoes to warm frozen hands as feet stomped to restore the circulation, eyes gazing upwards through the sulphurous air to a distant starburst spraying coloured incendiaries over the countryside. If only they knew.

By the time he reached the M6, he was questioning his decision. They'd killed Sarah. Luring him into some corner of a Northern field might be a very clean way of disposing of him. A service area beckoned, and he accepted the invitation gratefully.

Passing the shop in the service area, he saw they had a special on Halloween costumes. Plastic witches' hats and broomsticks. And specially for tonight, a plastic witch to burn on top of the bonfire, made in Korea, guaranteed to please, just the thing for the kids.

He queued for his coffee.

"Yes sir, what can I get you?"

A latte please, double shot, skimmed milk.

"Certainly sir. Going far today? Having a bit of celebration with the family?"

Going to burn anyone interesting to death tonight? Owen grunted non-committally, and the man nodded as if he understood.

Sipping his coffee, he gazed into the car park, ignoring the tattered posters falling into soggy shreds before their time. Today he might meet Sarah's killers, and the thought was greeted by unfocussed emotion rising within him. Myopically, he studied it like an interested bystander. Fear? Of course. Apprehension? Who wouldn't? The expectation that his months of flirting with this group were about to be consummated, as he finally penetrated their inner circle? But how? Even if he stood face to face with her killers, knew for certain who they were, what form would his vengeance take? Once, months ago, it had seemed simple. Find the killers. Report them to the police. Job done. But he needed evidence. And he needed to stay alive. The denouement wouldn't be today, and from now on the danger would increase inexorably.

Was this a stupid, foolish stunt? Who was he trying to impress? Option A: get in the car, turn round, back down the

M6, and get on with your life. Option B; get killed, granting another victory to her killers. Option C: meet them, get evidence, report them to the police. And how likely was that? Molecular biologist versus trained killers. No bookie would offer odds on his life.

Even as he left the restaurant, his direction was still uncertain. North or South? The news-stands showed a headline: "Riot in London: Muslim boy killed." He glanced at the paper: Jewish thugs had beaten up a ten-year old Muslim boy out walking his dog. Beaten him to death. And it was Owen's fault. The decision made, he turned onto the Northbound lane of the M6.

oooOooo

Macclesfield, the butt of Python jokes, once clattered with dark satanic mills. Now a commuter town, it nestles in the foothills of the Peak District, Britain's oldest national park. Watching over the gentrified terraced houses with their espresso machines and wide-screen digital TVs are the moors - beautiful, serene, decorated by the lacework of dry stone walling chipped out of the limestone. Ten minutes out of Macclesfield lies a country that has barely changed in a thousand years. The solid grey farmhouses congregate in the valleys while their livelihood roams the high ground, munching on the succulent grass that springs into life eternal from the well-watered, peaty soil.

He nervously followed the ancient Landrover winding its way through narrow streets. The phone call in Macclesfield had been brief and to the point. "Follow the car in front of you." Click. So they had been watching him, following him, and had inserted their car in front. How did they know they had the right car? Maybe they'd made a mistake and he would end up following some bewildered farmer into his yard.

Climbing out of Macclesfield, they followed a signpost to "Buxton", up towards the beckoning green hills. The right indicator of the Landrover flashed briefly, and they turned on to a narrow lane leading further up the hill. Pulling into a small wind-swept car park, he stopped next to the Landrover.

Its door opened, and a grey-bearded man stepped out, wearing Wellington boots, mud-smeared trousers, and an ancient blue sweater. Had Owen, after all, followed the wrong car? He walked over to make his excuses.

The farmer held out his hand. "Hello Owen. I'm Ted. Merry meet." He spoke in a thick local accent, his vowels long and slow, his face friendly, but watchful, guarded.

"Joomp in, lad."

Owen walked to the passenger side and climbed in. There was no seat belt. Ted produced a black blindfold.

"Sorry. Have t' do it. Else they mither at me summat dreadful."

Owen tried making small talk. Who were "they" ?

"Sorry lad. Not supposed to talk. Not far t'go now."

The car pitched and turned round twisty lanes, down into a valley, alongside the sound of running water, and then up again over the top of the moors. He heard the bleating of sheep being driven by a dog that barked in counterpoint to the whistles of its master.

Descending a steep hill, the car slowed, then turned sharply, the sound of the road being replaced by the scrunch of gravel as it ground to a halt.

"Take off blindfold, lad."

His eyes opened on to a pastoral scene from a gushing tourist guide to rural England. The middle of a farmyard. An ancient rust-streaked tractor. Thick limestone walls, chickens scurrying through the yard. Even a duck pond. And here Owen was to meet Sarah's killers, Wiccan terrorists.

"Give it here. Sorry about that. Can't be too careful. Cum and meet others."

Around a trestle table in the barn were seated four people of his own age, who turned to greet him. At another sat an older man, radiating an air of busy professionalism. He looked up, nodded briefly at Owen and Ted, and then concentrated once more on the papers in front of him, making notes as he did so.

248

"Sit thee down lad, and help thyself to soom tea," said Ted. The two girls on the near side of the trestle table shuffled up nervously to make room for him, and introduced themselves - Gina and Lucy. The two blokes on the other side were Paul and Keith. All seemed apprehensive. All equally in the dark about what was to happen that week.

The crunch of tyres announced the arrival of another car. A thick-set man of about 30 entered, crew cut, wearing a black sweater and tight black jeans. Without a word, no eye contact, but with a cursory nod at Ted, he crossed to the urn and made himself a cup of tea. He was followed by a thin, gawky teenager, nervously shuffling in, casting around apprehensively.

"Coom in lad - don't be shy. Join oothers," said Ted.

The boy took his place opposite Owen, and introduced himself in a whisper as Alan. He seemed agitated, as if nervousness was not his only challenge in life. Owen started to shake hands with him, but was halted by a menacing growl from the end of the barn.

"Enjoying your tea-party, ladies? How the hell am I supposed to turn you bunch of piss-heads into soldiers? You sit there yabbering like little girls - nobody ever tell you about security, about need to know?"

It was not the lilting, musical accent of the Southern Irish, but the argumentative rasp of working-class Belfast. The room was silent, tense. The man looked apoplectic, his mouth contorting itself in rage, building up to the next eruption.

"There's one thing you all need to know. I'm Foyle. And I'm supposed to turn you into bloody soldiers, for chrissake. Lesson one - you don't know each other. You will not get to know each other. You will not swap phone numbers, email addresses, or frigging diseases. If one of you gets caught you will not drop the others in the pooh. Right?"

They stared at him, open mouthed.

"Are you all fucking deaf or am I talking too fucking quietly? I said RIGHT?"

"Yes... right", they mumbled, patchily.

He spun on his heel and walked to the end of the barn, cursing.

Putting down his papers, the other man stood, coughed, and walked wordlessly to the end of their trestle table. "Ladies and gentleman, what Mr. Foyle was trying..."

"Not Mr. Foyle. Just Foyle." screamed a voice from the end of the barn.

"Yes. Quite. What MR. Foyle was trying to say..."

A gargling noise resembling "Christ bloody almighty" came from the end of the barn.

"...was welcome to our training camp. I'm Gareth. Foyle has just introduced himself so eloquently, and some of you have already met Ted. Ted is our host, and we're tremendously grateful to him for allowing us to use his farm. His family have served the cause for generations, and without people like him our faith would be extinct."

Owen wondered about Foyle. Why would a Wiccan camp employ such a social cripple, someone with such violence in his heart? And why did Gareth bait him?

Gareth continued. "During the week, I'll be running the course, Foyle will be teaching you weaponry and combat skills, and Ted will be looking after the living arrangements. This room is your home for the next week - meals will be served here, and your beds are up in the hayloft. Toilet and shower are outside, at the back."

Owen peered round the barn for the first time. It was clean and well-swept, but bare of amenities. He could see camping beds in the hayloft. There was a table on one side of the barn with papers and books, and next to it a whiteboard and fridge. A large electric urn sat on the table, already steaming, together with a jar of instant coffee, and tea-bags. That was it. He returned his attention to Gareth.

"Ladies and gentlemen, we have three golden rules that you must obey this week. First, you will not speak to anyone other than yourselves, Ted, Foyle, or myself. We've put the story around that this is a training camp for officer cadets of some obscure branch of the military, so the locals will generally steer clear of you. Second, no - um - intimacies, and no contacting each other once you leave. It's essential that at the end of this week you retain no ties to anyone here. Third, you do not tell each other where you're from, or what you do in the outside world. Except for Foyle, we only use first names here, and keep our surnames to ourselves."

Having already broken this rule, they exchanged glances. Hardly their fault, if they hadn't been told until too late.

Ted had disappeared while Gareth was speaking, and now awkwardly pushed open the barn door with his shoulder, his arms encumbered by carrier bags. He laid out the food on the table - freshly baked loaves, large chunks of local cheese that had never seen the inside of a supermarket, and a box of fruit. As Gareth outlined their week, the six of them took turns to fetch food from the table. Some took cans of Coke from the fridge, others made tea or coffee. The lesson continued without a break. Even Foyle made an appearance, scowling at them as he cut bread and cheese.

Gareth had brought the whiteboard over, and was explaining crowd-control techniques used by the police, and how to circumvent them when you wanted to spin up a riot. But Owen's attention was focussed on Foyle, who had opened a wooden crate next to the table and was carefully laying out an assortment of guns. Gareth, realising that his talk was no competition for the deadly attraction, gave up. Here endeth the lesson.

Chapter 17

"How many of you have fired a gun?" barked Foyle. None had.

"How many of you have even heard a gun fired, in real life?" A couple uncertainly raised their hands.

"Well this is what it sounds like," he said, as he swiftly raised a large pistol. They were shaken by the force of the explosion, which was mind-numbing. Who'd have thought it could be that loud? Nothing like the movies. As the barn - or was it his ears? - continued to ring, Owen could hear cawing outside, crows disturbed by the shot. A cloying odour of burnt explosive seeped through the barn.

"For God's sake, man," cried Ted, peering upwards, "that's m' roof."

"Relax, old man", said Foyle, showing a hint of a smile for the first time, "it was a blank."

Foyle was at ease with the weapons, as if they were old friends, in whose presence he felt assured and confident. He showed off the different guns - pistols, rifles, two shotguns, one with the barrel sawn off, and an AK47. He explained their advantages and disadvantages, how to load them, fire them, clean them, survive with them. He caressed them lovingly as he spoke, these tools of his trade, that had saved his life, vanquished his enemies, and joined him in mourning as comrades fell around him.

He took the group outside, and they spent the afternoon practising with each gun in turn. They started nervously, afraid to touch them, but by the end of the afternoon they could confidently pick up any of the weapons, select the right ammunition, reload, and at least hit the target, even if they rarely approached the bullseye.

"If you're ever going to use one, you'll need to learn a helluva lot more," growled Foyle, "but if you find yourself in deep shit, at least you'll know to switch the frigging safety catch off."

Dinner that evening was a rich vegetarian stew, steaming with field mushrooms, and washed down with a pitcher of home-brewed ale. Ted had lit large paraffin heaters to keep out the biting November cold. Their stomachs full, their barriers lowered, they moved to the other table while Ted cleared up.

Standing at the door, staring out at the unseen moors, Owen was poised in a discontinuity between the warm comradeship inside and the biting pitch-black outside, illuminated only by the glow-worm light of a distant farmhouse. A solitary firework glittered briefly behind it, too far away to hear, and then died away. Above was black. No stars, no moon, no glow of street lights. Just black.

But it was pure, that biting wind. Honest, simple, inviting. He closed the door and rejoined the warm thrill of deceit.

"Would you be prepared to kill someone who spoke out against Wicca?" asked Gareth.

"Of c-course!" retorted Alan, over-eagerly. Gareth made a note. The others were more circumspect.

"Just for speaking out against Wicca?" asked Owen. "Of course not. Otherwise you'd be waging war on most of the western world. Better keep your powder dry for when it's going to be effective."

"So when would killing someone be justified, Owen?"

He paused. "Umm... When someone poses an immense threat to Wicca, and all other avenues have been exhausted."

"But then you would be prepared to kill?"

All eyes were on Owen. "Yes," he lied, softly, convincingly. Gareth made another note. He asked each of them the same question, scribbling on his pad as they answered. The conversation moved on. Most chose a middle path between psychopathic Alan, and pacifist Lucy, who seemed to be in the wrong place. As the conversation ground to a halt, Gareth packed up his notes and ushered them out into the freezing night air.

Ted was standing next to a roaring log fire in the farmyard, his border collie thumping its tail at his side. The fire dispelled both the cold and the dark, forming an oasis of humanity in the centre of this stark black land. Sparks from the fire rocked gently upwards before being eclipsed by the enveloping darkness.

Ted's song started as no more than a murmur, and developed into a soft croon, although the words remained unintelligible. At his gesture, they joined hands to form a Wiccan ring, slowly encircling the fire. As Ted threw herbs into the flames, his chant became emboldened to a distinct guttural dialect. Owen realised that this ancient language was preserved, in these carefully husbanded songs, by the few initiates in the hill-farms of the Peak, words and people melding into one with this land that bred and nurtured them. Ted's coarse voice and strange chant resonated with the surrounding hills, and though Owen couldn't understand the words, they spoke to him deeply, viscerally. Who was he to betray these people in their fight to preserve their religion, their language, and their culture? The chant ceased, and Ted asked for pledges. As the circle stopped moving, Lucy moved away, weeping. The others ignored her, but Owen saw the firelight reflected in their wet eyes. Except for Lucy, each of them in turn softly called their vows to the Goddess, then stood bowed while the others intoned: "So mote it be". Lucy sat alone by the fire, sobbing quietly, rocking back and forth.

Ted pulled out a package of aluminium foil from the cinders, unwrapping it to reveal a steaming loaf of bread that had cooked as they made their pledges. Closing his eyes, he solemnly broke it, whispering "May your heart be pure," as he handed a piece to each of them. Owen was familiar with the ritual - the colour of your piece reflected the purity of your heart. It was said that, in the olden days, a person whose bread was burnt would become a human sacrifice. So, having got this far, would he finally be betrayed by a piece of bread?

254

None looked at their bread until Ted finished, when they all offered their pieces to the light of the fire, and to the fearful gaze of their peers. Owen's bread was steaming white.

Alan's was burnt. Panicking, he cast it quickly into the fire, as if to destroy the evidence. He saw their accusing stares, and that of Ted, sad and reproachful. "Bastard! You gave me that burnt bit on purpose!" His movements became jerky, as he challenged their gazes wildly. "He's lying! That's not my bread!"

He moved to strike Ted, but they stopped him, turning him away. Shaking off their arms, he stormed into the barn, cursing obscenities. Foyle, who had been lurking outside the circle of light, strode after him.

oooOooo

During breakfast the next morning, Gareth asked Alan and Lucy outside for a quick word. They heard Alan arguing, swearing at Gareth, Lucy sobbing, and then the sound of the Landrover starting.

Only four of them remained for the lessons that day, and for the rest of the week. They learnt how to make a Molotov cocktail, how to pick a lock, how to intercept a phone call. In group discussions they learnt techniques for infiltrating organisations, how to recognise when you were under surveillance. Owen was doubly stressed by the gruelling schedule, and the need to act convincingly, day and night. Evenings were the worst. Exhausted by the day's lessons, relaxed after food and drink, they would be subjected to questions designed to trip them up, reveal their hidden fears and weaknesses.

One night, when the rain prevented their evening ritual outside, they sat round the paraffin heater in the barn, drinking home-brew, while Ted told them his story. Christianity had slowly spread through the lowlands, but the hill-folk had been bypassed, left alone to practice the old religion. The townspeople ignored them, except when they came up for a herbal cure. Each Saturday the hill farmers would go down into Macclesfield to sell their produce in the market, and each evening they drank with the townspeople in the pubs. On Sundays, when they heard the church bells ring in the town below, Ted's family went about their business, and worshipped their own Gods and Goddesses as always. Until six hundred years ago, that was. He said this in the same way that Owen would have said "Until last year".

"What happened then, Ted?"

"Summ interfering bluddy suthern bishop came up mithering and worriting, saying that all bluddy hill farmers had t' go t' 'is bluddy church, or else. Well, they wouldn't 'ave bar of't. and said so." He paused. "And then trubble started."

Hordes of townspeople had streamed up from Macclesfield, demanding that the hill-farmers should become Christians. Else everybody in the shire would be damned and end up in hell. For eternity. The bishop said so.

Not one of the adults in Ted's family was spared. Every one of them - fathers, mothers, uncles, aunts, was tied to a stake and burned. Over the weeks, the same happened to each of the hill farms surrounding Macclesfield. Hundreds of men and women mercilessly burnt for failing to change to the new religion. The farms were distributed to townsfolk and to those few hill-farmers who agreed to convert. The children were spared, on condition they attended church every Sunday, where they were told how their parents were evil broomstick-riding devil-worshipping witches. Many became labourers and tenant farmers on the farms they had expected to inherit.

Each of the children grew up quickly, with a smouldering passion to honour their parents and all they stood for. To keep the old religion alive in the hills while keeping it protected, secret from those god-bothering busybodies in the valley. And one day to avenge the death of the ancestral martyrs. Now, six hundred years later, the time had come.

"Ted, that's terrible! Why don't we read about it in history books?"

"Six hoondred year ago, Clough might just as well ha' bin Outer bluddy Mongolia. Besides, even in them days, weren't sorta thing church would boast about. Whole bluddy affair were 'idden. Do a search on yer bluddy internet - you won't find a single bluddy word about it. Nor in any of yer fancy history books, neither. Just 'ere."

He thumped his chest, and growled "We know. We remember. We'll avenge them."

oooOooo

On the Friday morning, Gareth asked Owen to join him for a walk. They climbed the hill behind the farmhouse. It was one of those crisp November days when Owen felt he could walk for ever over hill and dale. They sat on the trunk of a fallen tree at the crest of the hill, Gareth panting slightly from the exertion, Owen listening to the trill of unseen lark-song around and above. A thin column of blue smoke curled from the farmhouse opposite. On the hillside above the farm, sheep cried to each other, the sounds strangely out of synch with the opening of their mouths.

"Owen, old chap, I have a job for you."

"Mmmm?"

"Ayatollah Sadiq Tastani from Iran is visiting Manchester next week. He will be assassinated, apparently by Zionist extremists."

Owen glanced up sharply but said nothing.

"But your task is less demanding. We need you to crash your car in a street, block off the police for a few seconds, give our man time to escape."

He said nothing but nodded. He had known it would come to this. At least he wasn't being asked to kill someone. Not yet.

Gareth was looking at him quizzically.

"OK. That's why I came here," shrugged Owen, "Tell me what I have to do."

Gareth smiled, relieved. "Excellent. Drive up to Manchester on Wednesday morning. Be in Oxford Street, near the University, by eleven. And await orders. Make sure your phone is charged, and that you have a street directory with you. And," he emphasised, "Have an excuse ready to tell the police why you were in Manchester on that particular day."

As they walked back down the hill, Owen pondered his options. If he wanted to jail Sarah's killers, this might be his opportunity. Tell the police about the assassination plan, let them set a trap, and the members of Retribution would be locked up. But why had he been told so much? They seemed so keen on need-to-know - Gareth could have simply told him to crash his car, without saying why. But then there would be no temptation to go to the police. It had to be a trap, another test of his loyalty. And clearly they had an informant in place within the police who would report back to Retribution.

oooOooo

The course ended awkwardly on Sunday morning. No summing-up, no closing speech, no awards or certificates, simply a brief handshake with Gareth and Gina, then Owen and Keith were bundled, blindfolded, into the Landrover. After a quarter hour of twisting, climbing, and descending, Ted stopped the car.

"Stay there lad, this is Keith's stop." Why had they left their cars at different places? Security, of course. The answer to everything.

Owen fumbled, blindfolded, to shake Keith's hand, and they were off again. Ten minutes later, they stopped, and he removed his blindfold to see the same beautiful valley, his car awaiting him. Numbly, he shook hands with Ted, and watched the ancient Landrover rumble off into the distance.

The drive back to Cambridge felt like returning to earth after a space flight. During his brief escape from the forces of reality, an IRA marksman had taught him how to assemble and load an AK47. He could fire from his hip at a moving target while running. He knew the modus operandi and command structure of the British anti-terrorist forces, their weaknesses and how to evade them. What's more, he was pretty sure his teacher was a senior officer within those forces, someone who, when necessary, might open a door here or shut a door there. His host had been a man whose family were all committed to the cause of Wicca. A man who boasted how his son was rising in local government, his daughter a management consultant in London. How many others of their ilk were in key echelons of British society?

As soon as he reached home he switched on his computer and did a search on Ayatollah Sadiq Tastani. The Ayatollah was in Manchester for the next few days, addressing a host of Muslim groups there. On Wednesday he was due to address the University of Manchester Islamic Society.

Owen's next job was to scan the online biology pages, after which he emailed a contemporary at Manchester University.

"Hi Matthew

I saw your paper in Current Biology and have been thinking along the same lines myself. I was wondering if I could come up to Manchester some time this week and talk to you about it. If so, what's a good day for you?

All the best

Owen."

No matter he didn't understand a word of the paper - the meeting would never happen. But it was sufficient to give him an excuse for being in Manchester. Hopefully Matthew, curious as to why Owen was suddenly interested in oncogenes, would email back with a list of days including Wednesday, and Owen could then arbitrarily pick that day.

The email sent, he scanned his other email in his intray. All the usual boring stuff. An email from Sir Ashley Pusch to all staff and postdocs in the department, asking for expressions of interest for a new appointment: Departmental Strategic Project Coordinator. The successful applicant would work closely with Ashley to set new future directions for the department. Owen wondered briefly about applying, and then dismissed the idea. First, he knew he was not in Ashley's good books. Not so much because of the Satanist allegations, which he suspected Ashley had since seen through, although he'd never admit to having made a mistake. More importantly, Ashley had curtly commented in the tea-room the other day that some of the postdocs didn't seem to be around much these days. He'd briefly glanced in Owen's direction and then continued that he had seen much evidence for work from them either, so they'd better pull their finger out or they'd be out of the department.

oooOooo

Owen was parked on Oxford Street in the southern suburbs of Manchester, waiting for the call. It came at 11am sharp. He was to move to Upper Brook Street, and the moment his phone rang he was to crash his car into another, blocking the road. Warily, he moved into position, picking out the parked car up the road into which he would crash. The ring from his phone startled him. Here goes the rest of the no-claim bonus. Charging up the road, he zigzagged wildly, as if losing control, and crashed awkwardly into the parked car. Although his speedometer read only 20 mph, he was astonished at the force of the jolt and the noise of airbag exploding in his face, stunning him. He climbed out, genuinely dazed, and saw he was a long way from blocking the road, with ample space behind for a police car to mount the pavement and pass him. As, indeed, it did thirty seconds later.

The air was filled with the sound of sirens, and the thought dawned horribly that it hadn't been a test. He had aided an assassination. Car after car passed, lights flashing, sirens wailing. Why this road? Was this part of some emergency plan? Were other roads blocked? The stream of cars abated, and still nobody had taken any interest in his accident. He inspected the front of his car. Apart from a dented wing, a slightly crumpled bonnet, and a smashed headlight, it didn't look too bad. He decided that fleeing the scene of an accident was such a minor crime compared to aiding an assassination that he might as well avoid complications. The car started easily, and he settled back into the traffic for the four-hour drive back to Cambridge.

oooOooo

The Iranian cleric was fighting for his life in Manchester Royal Infirmary. The bullet had missed his heart, but nicked the aorta. Because of the prompt arrival of the emergency services, the flow of blood was stemmed, and his condition was described as critical but improving. The newscaster gave a brief smile, as if this might reassure viewers concerned for the Ayatollah's health. The terrorist had escaped, but those who saw him said that he had been wearing a Jewish kippah. Arab-Jewish relations in Britain had plummeted since the torching of the synagogue in London.

Owen gave a groan, as if those last words twisted a knife in his heart, and switched off the TV. His mobile rang. The Retribution one.

"Hello?"

"Owen, Gareth here. Rather stuffed that up, didn't you? But thanks for trying, old chap - we appreciate the effort. Better luck next time." The phone rang off before there was time to respond.

So they had been watching. He had passed, if not with distinction. Maybe that was the best of all possible outcomes. The Ayatollah would have been shot with or without his help, and his intervention had not materially affected the outcome. If he had tried to warn the police, he knew for certain that his report would have been intercepted, and he would now be lying in hospital with the Ayatollah. Or worse.

But what about "next time" ? Next time it would not be a test, it would be the real thing. His role might be critical. So he'd better start working out how to handle it before the next phone call came.

Chapter 18

He was flying over the Peak District, soaring over hills, swooping into valleys, flocks of sheep scattering and dividing at his approach. He found by adjusting his leg... just so... he could soar upwards. It was not clear what force was keeping him up there, clad only in jeans and T-shirt, with no wings or visible support, but evidently he had found the secret. Beside him, weaving around him, flying away to become a speck in the distance, then sweeping in to embrace him, was Sarah. They were free, unencumbered of their earthly shackles, and together. Death has no meaning.

A bell sounded, insistent, clamouring his attention. Ask not for whom it tolls. Sarah kissed him, smiling, "Next time, my dearest Owen." He fell away from her, unsupported, at the same time wrestling with blankets of fog, impeding his progress towards the sound. Fighting his way back to wakefulness, he dimly perceived a scene, Owen, in bed, in his bedroom. Three mobile phones were lying on the bedside table, and one was calling him.

He woke. It was the phone. The frigging Retribution phone.

"He..hello?"

"Owen. Siegfried here. Remember? We met a few weeks ago. At the Motorway Service Area. Hope I didn't wake you?"

He looked at the alarm clock. Five o'clock. Five bloody o'clock.

"No, of course not. Just getting up."

"Good. Bad luck on the Manchester job, by the way."

Owen's mouth felt dry. "Yes. Sorry about that. Never tried to block a road before."

"Not to worry. I have a job for you which is more up your street. Are you game?"

"What? Oh yes. Umm. What is it?"

"Not on the phone. Can I meet you some place?"

"Uh - yeh. Sure. At the gate at the end of the track? What time?"

"No - the service area will do fine. See you in the coffee shop? Eight am?"

He had drunk too much the night before, and still felt woozy. His head ached, and he had no stomach for breakfast. A shower and two espressos later, he hit the road.

For a service area coffee-shop, it wasn't bad. The coffee tasted freshly ground, strong but not bitter, and they weren't blank-faced when he asked for a double-shot. On his second latte, as he started to come alive, he saw Siegfried striding towards him, espresso in hand, dressed in crisp stockbroker clothes which relegated Owen, in his jeans and trainers, to the position of underling.

He fought back. "Hi Siegfried. Umm, good to see you. Please sit down." Indicating a seat, as if he had asked him in for an interview.

"Actually, Owen, would you mind if we sat over here, away from the window?" Siegfried chose a seat and sat there, brooking no argument.

"No.... but... um... how about over here, where the table isn't littered with the last person's rubbish."

Realising his tactical error, Siegfried's face hardened a moment, before he smiled. "Ok. Let's call it a draw." Owen grinned, and they moved to yet another table. "Ever thought of becoming a stockbroker?" asked Siegfried. "You'd be good at it."

Owen smiled in appreciation. "Not in my wildest dreams. So what's the job you were telling me about?"

"Ever heard of Bishop Pemberton?"

"I think so. Isn't he the ultra-conservative one? Ranting about homosexuals in the clergy, women escaping from the kitchen, things like that?"

"Exactly correct. He also rants about Wiccans. Quote. Witchcraft is evil. Witches are devil-worshippers. The people who burnt witches in the middle ages knew what they were doing. Unquote."

"OK - I see. Not a friend of ours then. So what's the job?"

Siegfried smiled. "You expect the odd loony bishop living in the dark ages, but the problem is, he's been tipped as the next Archbishop of Canterbury."

"Bloody hell!"

"Couldn't agree more. Here's the thing. How do we take him out?"

Owen gaped. "Take him out?"

"Exactly."

"Umm. You mean take him out, discredit him, or take him out, kill him?"

"What do you think? Now you're one of us, Owen. I'd value your opinion."

"Well, I suppose I'd go for the minimum force that would tip him out of the running. And minimum risk of course."

"My thinking exactly. Except if you're going to do a job, you may as well do it properly. Discrediting someone isn't always a permanent solution. People have a habit of bouncing back."

Owen frowned at him doubtfully. "What did you have in mind?"

"Seems the old coot is something of a DIY enthusiast. God knows why - he's got pots of money. Could keep a hundred tradesmen gainfully employed. But instead he chooses to do it himself. Says he finds it relaxing. He's renovating a weekend cottage he's bought on the South Coast. Shame if he got his wires crossed and electrocuted himself."

Owen studied Siegfried, trying to hide the dread coursing through him, like an incoming tide awash with bodies.

"And you want me to do this?"

"You're a scientist aren't you? Shouldn't be beyond you to re-arrange a bit of wiring. Provide a terminal solution, so to speak."

264

Owen was stunned. What the hell was he being asked to do? "OK - let me think about it."

"Think about it all you like, old son. It's your baby now. Here's the address." Owen looked blankly at the writing on the slip of paper that Siegfried handed him. And if he said no? This might be his death sentence.

"He's there every weekend. We'd like the problem solved within six weeks. Work out your plan, let me know what resources you need - surveillance, tradesmen, and so on. Should you prefer it to be a one-man job, that's your call. Play it however you want. But I want him permanently out of the way in six weeks."

He stood up, and extended his hand. "Good to have you on board Owen. Good luck. Call me if you need advice."

Swivelling on his heel, Siegfried was gone, leaving Owen punch-drunk and disoriented. He had been asked to commit murder. It had gone too far, too fast. Must go to the police. But how to do that without being arrested? Or worse?

His mind buzzing, he stood and ambled to the exit, not noticing the cable draped carelessly across the floor by the cleaners. Tripping, he recovered by grabbing a nearby table occupied by two girls. Their coffee slopped into the saucers.

"Watch yourself, mate," complained one, "My coffee's gone everywhere..."

"Sorry. Not looking where I was going. Let me buy you another."

She looked at him, wondering if this was a pick-up line.

"Nah. Doesn't matter. It's OK. Go away before you do any more damage."

Hah. Any more damage. If only she knew.

oooOooo

At his desk in the Department, Owen kept reading the same email again and again, without any information reaching his brain, blocked by the fact that he was now a potential murderer. A hit man. How did a promising young scientist, at the top of his generation, fall in a few months to a thug? Sarah. If she hadn't died, then... He recognised this train of thought. A natural stage of the grieving process, it said on the web. You blame the deceased. Crazy stuff. But it was happening. And he was unable to think rationally. He needed distraction, some mental exercise to stop his brain thrashing around from one wild thought to another. The Book of One. He hadn't done any work on it for weeks. Something still niggled him about that old lady and her chanting. Automatically, he googled "reading the stones". Page after page discussing ways of reading gravestones were interspersed with links to geology, runes, and hieroglyphs. But nothing about stone circles. He ran his hand through his hair, thinking this was a waste of time, no point continuing. Then he found a page which mentioned "reading" the stone circle at Rough Tor on Bodmin Moor. Apparently if you placed your hand on the key stone at the right time of year, you would learn the secret of immortality. He typed "Rough Tor", and found pages describing the area and its walking trails, but nothing about the legend. A few more words in the search box, and up came a page from a local Wiccan coven, lamenting the fact that they didn't know what time of year to perform the ceremony, nor which was the key stone.

That evening, Owen looked up Rough Tor in Thom's book, and found that the circle was one of those with a circumference which was three times the diameter at the widest point. A circle so pure. And so it had an asymmetrical geometry, which might indicate the key stone. At Scorhill Circle he remembered there was one stone which towered above its neighbours, next to the stone where the old lady had started her song. Was that the key stone? Despite the negative report in the Wakened database, he had a hunch that he was on to something. Perhaps even a clue to the location of the Book of One. He tried to ignore his mounting excitement. He needed to think calmly, rationally.

He'd need Aleister's help. Aware that mobiles could be pinpointed to within a few metres, he drove out of Cambridge, and phoned Aleister on his unregistered mobile.

"Owen, My dear boy. How wonderful to hear from you."

"Aleister, I think I've got a lead. Could I come down for the weekend? Visit a couple of stone circles with you?"

"That would be splendid. Why? What have you found?"

"I'll tell you tomorrow. Could we meet in Chagford, for lunch?"

oooOooo

The meals ordered, they settled down with pints of Old Moggie. As Owen explained his ideas, the old man's questions and doubts became irritating. Owen heard himself replying more sharply than intended. Aleister became quiet, and listened without a word.

"Aleister, there's no need to go sulky on me. Just because I disagree with you."

"It's not that, dear boy. You're not yourself. You seem troubled, weighed down. Is something wrong?"

Owen paused. Nothing much. Only that I've been asked to commit murder, and I don't bloody know how to get out of it.

"Well..." No. It would be unfair to burden the old man with this. Besides, there was a good chance that Aleister would blurt something out to the wrong person.

"No. Nothing wrong. I just keep thinking about Sarah. I miss her."

He felt limp inside. Using Sarah's name as an excuse. Defiling her memory. But all in a good cause, wasn't it?

After lunch, waiting outside for Aleister, Owen glanced at Good Vibrations. Inside would be Francesca, and her husband "old Alfred". Maybe she could tell him more about the keystone. On an impulse, he turned and entered. Behind the counter was not Francesca, but her husband, "old Alfred". The surly old man had been furious with Sarah and Owen when they said they were scientists. So different from his potty old wife. But afterwards, their car was burnt. And then Sarah was killed... How much did this man know?

But Alfred didn't recognise him. "Yes young man, wha' can oi do fer yer?"

The two pints of Old Moggie threw caution to the wind, Owen lunged straight to the point.

"Earlier this year my girlfriend and I were here. You got mad at us when we said we were scientists, looking at the stone circles."

The old man screwed up his eyes at Owen. Recognition dawned. He set his face defiantly.

"Oi'll be buggered. It is yer. Well. Yer shouldna bloody poke yer noses into things tha' ain't none of yer bus'ness."

"Someone set fire to our car that evening."

A hint of a smirk appeared at the corner of the man's mouth. "Did they now? That be right ba' luck an' all. Ba' luck happens to they who ge' a bi' too nosy fer their own good."

So he did know about it. But on the other hand, he wasn't behaving like a murderer. Owen sized him up, working it out how best to extract information. The Old Moggie wasn't helping.

"Don' ee stare at me like tha' - it weren't me. Do I look like the sort who'll ge' up at a night and sets fire to cars?"

Owen had to concede the point - even walking across the room made the old man wheeze.

"Nah - jus' heard tha' some of them local lads got a bit out of hand," grinned the old man. So he was sticking to that story. Probably a drinking mate of Sergeant Bradworthy.

"What about the spell?" asked Owen, still watching for a reaction. The old man wasn't fazed.

"Wha' spell would tha' be, then?"

"A few weeks later my girlfriend was killed."

The old man's face paled, and his hand went to his mouth. "No... Yer don't say? Bugger ... Oi mean, Oi... Oi be right sorry. Um... Killed, you say. 'ow?"

"Car accident."

The old man seemed genuinely shaken.

"Sorry to 'ear tha'. Not tha' Oi be 'volved, o' course. 'Eard through the grapevine 'bout yer car. But didna know about yer girlfriend. But nobody 'ere would do a thing like tha', would they now?"

Staring at the old man, Owen's resolve collapsed, and he turned on his heel and left the shop. Aleister was waiting at the car.

"Where did you get to?" he complained, and then noticed Owen's ashen face. "Are you alright, dear boy?"

"Just spoke to Alfred Huxtable."

"Was that wise? I thought you were going to keep clear of them. You don't want to blow your cover."

"I know. Probably a stupid thing to do. I actually went to talk to Francesca, but Alfred was in there instead. He definitely knew about our car being burnt, and the spell, but I'm pretty certain he didn't know about Sarah. So either the killers weren't local, or else they didn't trust him enough to tell him. Anyway, I think we'd better get out of here."

Leaving Aleister's car at Chagford, Owen drove them both up to the fateful car-park near Gidleigh. Automatically, Owen scanned the ground for ash, broken glass, anything. Nothing. Leaving the 21st century, they opened the gate and tramped up over the hill and down to Scorhill circle. A bitter wind blew across the moor, forcing hunched shoulders and pocketed hands. Owen walked towards the tallest stone and then stepped to the right, crouching to examine the stone next to it. The stone on which the old lady had placed her hands as she chanted. He'd seen photos of the runes carved into the stone circles in the Orkneys, and wondered whether there might be something like that at Scorhill. He was disappointed. No sign of carvings. It was covered with bumps and grooves, but then old stones were always weathered into bumps and grooves, weren't they? Nothing resembling writing, and any runes had long since been worn away. Anyway, having come all the way out here, he might as well photograph them. Pulling out his camera, he filled the memory card with images of the tops of the stones.

Disappointed, they trudged back to the car, fetched Aleister's battered Landrover from Chagford, and drove in convoy to Tintagel. They ate in the pub that night, Owen moody and silent, wondering what had driven him down here on this wild goose chase, when he should be focussing on how to escape getting involved in a murder. Murder for Chrissake! And here he was fiddling around with some stupid idea about stone circles. Of course, he knew why. It was something he could cope with, whilst the other stuff was too big, too hard to encompass. Maybe this was the right thing to do, see some stone circles, breathe some fresh air, while he tried to get his brain around the really big problem.

The next morning they were parked at the small car park next to Rough Tor. They tramped up to the top of the Tor, Owen repeatedly having to wait for the old man to catch him up, puffing and wheezing. Then down the far side, following Owen's GPS until they found themselves amongst the welcoming stones of the circle. Welcoming? Owen puzzled over the word that had sprung to mind. Yes, welcoming. In the midst of this bleak moorland, there was something comforting, familiar, embracing, about the stone circle. Owen dismissed the idea. Superstitious nonsense. He pulled out his camera, and started photographing each stone in turn. He had little doubt they would obtain the same result as at Scorhill: no markings other than those of weathering.

oooOooo

Three in the morning and he had been awake all night. It was convenient to blame the quantities of coffee he had drunk on the way back from Tintagel, but the reality had less to do with the caffeine than with the quandary occupying his tortured mind. He had to tell the police. But how could he give a tip-off without it being intercepted by Retribution? There had to be a way to take it higher. Involve as few people as possible. Less chance of interception. But how to reach a senior level in the police without tripping an alarm hard-wired to Retribution?

By six he'd figured out a solution, and promptly fell asleep. Woken at seven by the alarm, fumbling to switch it off, he tried to sleep again. By eight he'd decided it was no good. Damn! One hour's sleep!

He showered, savouring the scalding water on his back. Almost as good as sleep. After an uncounted series of espressos, he felt a pleasant buzz in his fingers once more. Ready to face the day. To face the start of a process that might solve his problems, or lead to his worst nightmares.

An anti-terrorist hotline had been advertised on TV. He drove out of Cambridge, so that the call couldn't be traced, and parked in a layby on the A10. He pulled out his unregistered mobile phone, confident it was not being bugged by the Wakened or Retribution. He took several deep breaths to quench his rising panic. Here goes. The call was answered the moment he finished dialling.

"Good Morning. Anti-terrorist Hotline. How may I help you?" Her voice was strangely relaxed. Probably used to work for an insurance company.

"Hello." He swallowed, then spoke quickly. "I have some information about an al-Qaeda cell being set up in Britain."

"Certainly Sir. Can I have your name please?"

As expected. He'd prepared well. "Of course not. I know you're recording this, so I'll only say it once. I'll phone you back in one hour, on this number, and my code name will be Nigel. I have been involved in a minor way with al-Qaeda. I'll give you information that will save at least one life, in return for immunity from prosecution. OK?"

"Sir, if you can hold the line, I'll see if I can get a senior officer to speak to you." The relaxation had evaporated from her voice, which had risen by half an octave. She'd realised that this might be the real thing, that this call would be analysed and dissected.

"No. I will speak to a senior officer in one hour. Good-bye." He hung up, and slumped in his seat, his fingers shaking, his body quivering. He had time for a brisk walk to calm himself before his next call. Maybe even a run. He jumped out of the car, and was nearly flattened by a giant lorry hurtling past, horns blaring, centimetres from his open car door. He ran. Ran and ran and ran, mindlessly, along the side of the road, overtaken by lorries and cars and vans, the inhabitants staring curiously at this figure fleeing for his life along the side of a main road. Step by step, he felt his body relax and he slowed into a gentle jog, and then a walk. He stood on the grass verge by the side of the road, breathing deeply, and vomited.

Thirty minutes later he drove over to Grantchester and parked on Coton Road. From here he could make a quick getaway after the call. His fingers starting to shake again, he dialled the number, and gave his code name. He was immediately transferred. This time, surprisingly, he found himself calm.

A voice spoke in a Cockney accent. "Morning, sir. DI Conrad here. What's on your mind?"

"Hi. Um... I've got a problem. I stupidly got involved with al-Qaeda. Got mixed up in one of their operations. I want out. If they find out, they'll kill me. I want to tell you everything I know. But I need immunity from prosecution. And protection from al-Qaeda."

"Lot to ask, sir. Not so easy to get immunity. Not like that, y'know. Anyway, can you prove that you're for real, like?"

"How would I do that?"

"Ok, you know, like giving me somefin' we can work on now. Somefin' we can verify."

What could he say that wouldn't trigger the interest of a Retribution mole? Any mention of the synagogue, or the training camp, or a suggestion that the terrorist squad had been infiltrated, would raise alarm bells. He needed to talk to one person, off the record. See if it was someone he could trust.

"Sorry but I can't do that over the phone. I'll explain why when we meet face to face."

"How about you go down to yer local police station, sir? 'Ave a little chat to 'em face to face?"

He tried to sound confident and assertive. "I understand your problem, DI Conrad, but I can't do that. Please believe me when I say I've got some enormously valuable information. All I ask is one face-to-face meeting with someone senior, like yourself. Alone."

Something in Owen's voice must have persuaded him.

"Alright, sir. 'ow about I get one of me mates in Cambridge to meet yer right now? Place of yer choosing?"

So they knew he was in Cambridge. Not surprising. That would have come up on their screen as soon as he called.

They would also know he was close to Grantchester. In a couple of minutes, they'd pinpoint his location to a hundred metres. A police car would already be on its way towards him.

"Actually, I'd prefer to come down to London to meet you, if possible - you are in London?"

"Guessed correctly, sir. Scotland Yard. 'ere's me mobile number." - he read out a string of digits, "Gimme a call when you get into London and I'll meet you - later today?"

"OK - around twelve?"

"Good. Seeya later sir."

Owen hung up, and quickly drove off. Half way to the anonymity of the M11 he encountered a police car speeding the other way. Coincidence? But the co-driver was looking at his number plate as they passed, speaking into a microphone. Bugger. Now he was probably on a list of potential suspects. Would the Retribution informer have access to that list?

oooOooo

Owen was too nervous to eat, but had ordered a meat pie and chips so as not to look conspicuous. As he picked at it, his phone gave two rings, signifying that DI Conrad had arrived in the pub. Owen hesitantly put up his hand, as arranged, and a burly man in his forties ambled over, holding a pint. He was dressed in jeans and sweater, with working boots and a grey crew-cut. More like a docker than a policeman. Somehow Owen had expected a man in a raincoat with police boots, and even in his apprehension was amused at his own naivety.

The policeman held out his hand. "Morning. Dr. Owen Davies, right? DI Conrad. Call me Jim. Luv'ly pub, innit?"

Damn! How did they find his name so quickly? All his precautions.

"Umm... How many other people know who I am?"

The policeman ignored his question as he sat down. "So what's up, Dr. Davies?"

Owen was shaken, unsure of his ground. But he was in too deep to back out. The more forthcoming he was, the fewer people would need to be involved. Better take the plunge. Here goes.

"Call me Owen. The thing is, I've just spent a week at a terrorist training camp in Northern England. In the Peak District. But it's not al-Qaeda."

He waited for a reaction. For all he knew, Jim was the Retribution informant. Not much he could do about it now.

"Not al-Qaeda? So you've already told me a porkie? Not a good start, is it? So who are these so-called terrorist chums of yours?"

"Look. Before I go any further, I need to tell you that your unit has been infiltrated by this group. I'm pretty certain that someone in the antiterrorist squad is feeding information back to them. For all I know, you could be that person. In which case I'm dead meat. Or maybe it's your boss, or his boss. And if they are that person, and you report back to them, then I'm also dead meat. You see my problem?"

"Yeh. Maybe. But why don't yer back up a bit? What's yer terrorist organisation called, then?"

"You won't have heard of them. Retribution. They're an extreme offshoot of the Wiccan religion."

Jim seemed amused. "Oh yeh. I've 'eard of 'em right. Bunch of amateurs, wannabe terrorists who don't know their tits from their arses."

"OK - you heard about the shooting of the Ayatollah in Manchester?"

"Yeh. What about it?"

Owen replied slowly, deliberately. "That was them."

"You got any evidence?"

"Yes, but my evidence is going to incriminate me. That's why I'm asking for immunity from prosecution."

As he said this, he knew he was now incriminated. Whatever else happened, they would want to know his whereabouts on that day. He was beyond the point of no return.

The policeman shuffled, clasping his hands on the table in a lets-get-down-to-business manner. "Owen me ol' son, listen up. It's not that easy to get immunity from prosecution.

Only in extremis, yer might say. So what do you want to tell me?"

"How many people are going to be party to this?"

"If yer telling me our unit's leaky? I'll keep it nice 'n tight. Only my boss, and his boss."

Owen thought about it. Probably the best deal he was going to get. "You know the synagogue arson last month? I was there. I can also lead you to the people responsible for the shooting of Ayatollah...."

" How do you know they're responsible?'

"They told me about it before it happened. I was asked to crash my car to slow down the police, so the marksman could make a clean getaway."

Owen awaited a gasp of astonishment, but the policeman looked at him levelly and said, "Anyfin' else?"

Owen swallowed. "I've been told to murder Bishop Pemberton."

The detective regarded Owen over the rim of his beer-glass as he took a swig, and continued staring at him as he wiped his mouth. " 'ow do I know yer kosher?"

Owen spoke without irony. "I can give you some details about the synagogue arson."

"Go on then."

Realising that he was being pushed into a defensive role, Owen decided that he had to regain the initiative, take control of the conversation.

"I'd prefer to discuss what's going to happen if I tell you everything."

Jim stared at him for a moment, and pulled out his mobile phone. Changing his mind, he laid the phone on the table. "Lemme tell you somefin', Owen. If I call me boss now, tell 'im what you've just told me, you'll be in handcuffs in minutes. Arrested on suspicion of. You don't get immunity for pouring yer 'eart out."

Owen had already thought this through. "True. And if you arrested me I'm sure you'd find ways of making me spill the beans. Some of them, anyway. But that isn't very much yet. Probably not enough for you to catch the masterminds behind it. You'd get a few people, and then the trail would go cold, and the organisation would continue. On the other hand, I could work as a mole for you. Lead you straight to them. You could shut down the whole operation."

Jim smiled. "You took the words right out of me mouth. Gimme a chance to talk it over with me boss. Then I'll get back to yer."

"You mean that's it? You don't need more details?"

"For now. We need to play this carefully. This ain't the time or place to spill yer guts. My biggest worry is yer claim that there's a mole in our group. I'll phone yer tomorrow after I've set up a couple of things."

"But the Ayatollah's shooting... Don't you have people working their butts off to unearth who did it? Isn't this vital information for them?"

"Prob'ly. Not that I don't believe you, Owen. But nobody died, did they? And in the long run we're talking about somefin' much bigger. So let's play this carefully. One step at a time, like."

Owen was unconvinced. Even a little disappointed that the whole of the Metropolitan Police Force hadn't swung into action, made him promises on the spot, for the invaluable information he had at his finger tips. And what were the couple of things to be "set up" ? A Retribution hit-squad, for example?

oooOooo

The call came the next morning. There was no point in caution now. He knew he was under close surveillance from people much more expert, with far more resources, than the Wakened mob. As he left for London, no car pulled out behind him, no man in a raincoat sat on a park bench reading a newspaper. More likely a satellite was relaying an image of his car complete with coordinates, while his followers sat in warm offices watching him drive through the map on their computer screens.

He had been given an address in Brentwood. It was a small office block, the sort that advertises offices and a receptionist by the hour. After giving his name, he was shown into a small but airy meeting room, furnished in light blue. Iced water and a bowl of mints were set out on the table, coffee brewing on the side. Standing next to the coffee were Jim Conrad, in jeans and T-shirt, and his boss, Superintendent Bob Gallagher, in suit and tie. Bob was friendly and welcoming, as if greeting a new member of their team. But beneath his avuncular persona slinked a hard-nosed detective, examining him closely, watching for a flicker of the eye, a hesitation in the voice, that might reveal duplicity.

The room was obviously geared to business meetings rather than police interrogations. A projection screen at the end of the room blankly awaited revenue forecasts, while a whiteboard stood to attention to receive flow charts. But the only equipment of interest to the police was an old-fashioned tape recorder in the centre of the table, which Owen saw was already switched on and running. Bob explained that he would not switch it off until they all left. As they introduced themselves, a tentative knock on the door announced the arrival of the third member of their team, a pale unsmiling man, who introduced himself as Detective-Sergeant Dave Lockyer, from the Anti-Corruption Group.

Owen looked around the strange surroundings for his interrogation as he poured himself a coffee, willing his hands to stop shaking, breathing deeply to quell the surge of anxiety storming within. It was an unlikely setting for a lion's den, but he began to feel he'd walked right into it. He saw his pale face reflected in the window, his striped rugby shirt like prison bars across his chest, the three other men behind his back sizing him up, exchanging nods and glances, unaware he was watching them. How had he got into this mess?

In for a penny, in for a pound. He was way out of his depth, and only these people could extricate him. He turned to join them, clumsily setting the coffee on the table. If one of them was a Retribution informant, he was as good as dead.

The relief as he poured out his heart was overwhelming. He hadn't appreciated the size of his burden until he heard his voice quivering with emotion as he told them everything. Everything. The burning of the car, Sarah's death, his infiltration of the Wakened, the Synagogue arson, the training camp. Bob seemed familiar with the activities of the Wakened. They questioned him closely, repeatedly, on his role in the synagogue, trying to catch him out, trying to find something at odds with their forensic information. By lunchtime, Bob announced that he was satisfied. For now. He phoned the receptionist and ordered sandwiches and juice to be delivered, and then asked to be excused for fifteen minutes. To call headquarters on the phone? Or to give Jim a chance to interrogate Owen in a relaxed, unofficial, capacity as they ate their sandwiches. Probably both. The tape recorder was still running.

oooOooo

Bob returned. "Right, young Owen. The powers that be have agreed to immunity for you, on two conditions."

"Yes?"

"First, you have immunity only for what is on this tape recording. If you have anything else to tell us, now is the moment. Afterwards, it will be too late." He waited, expectantly, and Owen shook his head.

"Sorry, can you say that out loud, for the benefit of our audience?"

Owen cleared his throat. "No, there isn't anything else. I only want immunity for the things I've told you about."

"Good. Second condition is that you work with us for a few months to help catch the ringleaders in the Wakened and Retribution, and the informer in our group. If indeed there is one. Agreed?"

"Yes. Certainly."

"Good. That's it then."

Owen rose uncertainly to shake the hand that Bob proffered. It seemed an anticlimactic ending to the emotionally charged confessions that preceded it, until he realised that it wasn't an ending, but a beginning, which might still turn out good or ill.

Bob was speaking again. "Our highest priority is to find out if there really is a leak in our group, as you claim. So we'll sow some seeds and see where they go."

"Just a minute. Don't I get a piece of paper about the immunity?"

"Sorry. Afraid not. Suppose someone searched your house and found it? You'd be dead. So you're going to have to trust us. Just like we're trusting you."

Owen pondered these words for a moment. Seemed a bit one-sided. But did he have any choice? "OK but if it's down to trust, I'd like to get everything on the table. Bob, you're not really Jim's boss, are you?"

Bob's eyes twinkled in amusement. "Why do you say that?"

"The body language between you is wrong. Jim doesn't seem the slightest bit deferential to you. And you seem to know a lot about the Wakened and Retribution for someone who was only briefed yesterday."

"Not bad. You should join the force," grinned Bob, and then his face became serious. "Let me be open with you. I really am a Superintendent and Jim really is a DI, but I'm not in Jim's line management. I run a different unit within the Anti-Terrorist Branch. We specialise in home-grown terrorist organisations like Retribution, while Jim is from the Special Branch. Which is mainly preoccupied with groups like Al Qaeda. Dave, as you know, is from the Anti-Corruption Group. He's been seconded to this project until we catch our mole. Since you claim that our group has been infiltrated, and your story so far checks out, I've had permission from high up to keep this operation very tight. Very tight indeed. The only people who know the details are the four of us here."

"Good. But you're still not Jim's boss."

"The three of us are working together on this, and I'm the senior officer. So in a sense I am."

Owen grudgingly acquiesced. "You say only the four of us know the details. But how many people are aware of the existence of this operation?"

"My boss, the Commander of SO13..."

"Sorry? SO13?"

"The internal name of the Anti-Terrorist Branch. He knows I'm running a covert operation with Jim and Dave which may involve corruption, but is prepared to trust me beyond that. Nobody else knows anything about it whatsoever."

Owen interrupted. "If you run a unit specifically investigating the Wakened and Retribution, isn't it likely that the mole is within your group? Umm. Even..." He hesitated, uncertain how to continue his question.

Bob interrupted. "Tell him about the NTIT, Dave."

Dave, who had left the talking to Jim and Bob, spoke slowly and unwillingly. "We run a program called 'Non-Targeted Integrity Testing'. Which means we routinely set up sting operations on officers in sensitive areas, to see if they can be corrupted. Superintendent Gallagher was tested a month ago, and came out with flying colours. After Jim spoke to you, he contacted the anti-corruption group - or me to be precise - and I told him that it was OK to talk to the Super. I agree that if there is a mole, then it's in the Super's unit, but there's no way he's that mole."

Bob smiled benignly. "Thankyou Dave. The Non-Targeted Integrity Testing is very secret, and very thorough. Of course the Police Unions hate it - but you can see its value."

Owen nodded. He hadn't seriously suspected Bob - he seemed too open and forthright - but it was good to be reassured.

Bob continued. "You have to understand that when we suspect a mole, we take it very seriously. So our first priority in this operation is to identify him. Then take him out as quickly as possible. In the meantime, we'll rent a secure office here, with a safe. The only people who know about it are the four of us here."

Chapter 19

After returning to his office at the Department, Owen was unable to concentrate. He opened his email, but his mind kept wandering back to the meeting that morning. What were they doing now? What was the process? How long would it take? Days? Months? When would they call? The uncertainty, let alone the danger that he'd be "taken out" before they found the mole, left him with a numbing tenseness that made him feel physically sick.

Unable to focus on email, he opened up the file of photos from Scorhill and Rough Tor Circles, a soothing reminder of calmer times. Scrolling through the images of the tops of the standing stones, he saw nothing but random lumps and bumps. He scrolled faster, hypnotised, idly watching them, letting his mind wander and relax. The grooves formed patterns, like the shapes that you see through closed eyes as you fall asleep. Strange tricks the mind can play. Making patterns out of random shapes... Or were they? What the hell...? He scrolled more slowly, moving back and forth between the images, now alert. The grooves weren't random. Instead he saw patterns. Patterns that seemed to repeat from stone to stone. His mind whirred as the implications hit him. If he were right... But he had to stay calm. Stay analytical.

Opening up Photoshop, he tried merging, subtracting, and superimposing the images. The pattern varied in detail from one stone to another, but he could see a common thread running through them. He became absorbed in the task. Was this writing? Or some sort of natural weathering? His gut feeling told him the former, but how to prove it? And, if so, how to decode it?

Working systematically through the pictures, he found a distinct central groove on the stone to the right of the tall one at Scorhill - where the old lady had started chanting. It didn't appear on any of the others at Scorhill. He went through the images from Rough Tor, and immediately spotted a groove on the stone to the right of the gap. He compared the indentations on corresponding stones in the two circles. While not identical, they were similar. Perhaps they were encoded with directions for finding the Book of One.

The immensity of his discovery dawned on him. The marks were clearly ancient, as they were covered with lichens that took hundreds of years to grow. But how ancient? Carved by the Druids a mere two thousand years ago? Or by the Bronze-age builders two thousand years before that? He resolved not to breathe a word to anybody until he had studied them properly. Regardless of whether this led to the Book of One, these markings had been missed by the generations of archaeologists who had studied and probed the stones. They might even be a primitive form of writing. His head spun with the implications. Standing, he started pacing the room, deep in thought. It could revolutionise British prehistory. Everything else paled into insignificance. The police, Retribution... Everything. Whatever happened, however this finished, in a year's time all his worries would be dwarfed by this discovery. He stopped pacing. Would they? Or was this simply a flight from reality, mere delusion, escapism?

oooOooo

DI Jim Conrad met him in the pub at Grantchester the next day. After getting their drinks, he presented Owen with a watch sporting large LCD figures and a plastic wrist-band. "Right, me ol' son. Make sure you wear this all the time. Then we can track you and listen to whatever yer saying, 24/7. If you find yerself in trouble, just press this 'ere button, an' we'll come running. This is a special, by the way, borrowed from Army Intelligence. Can't use a standard police one 'cos your mole would recognise it."

Owen stared at the watch. It symbolised his descent into the netherworld. He'd expected to be wired for his meetings with Retribution, but hadn't realised that the tentacles would be so omnipresent. Just a few months ago, his future had seemed so assured. He'd charted a course in which he would become a successful biologist, with Sarah at his side. Now, no longer in control of his life, he had become a remote-controlled pawn in a struggle between police and Retribution. Perhaps to be sacrificed for the greater good? But now it was out of his hands. He had no choice but to play along and accept whatever was dished out by fate. For better or for worse. Perhaps far worse. "OK. I'll do that. What else?"

"Number one priority is to catch the mole. We've sprinkled bits of information around. With a bit o' luck, you'll 'ear one of these coming back to you. Tell us anyfin' you 'ear or see, straight away, using the watch."

"What if I need to talk to you directly, get your advice?"

"Say so into the watch, and I'll get into contact with yer. We'll need to meet every couple of days in any case, to compare notes an' check on progress. I also need to swap watches every week. Batteries only last a week."

Owen nodded, and then asked the question he had been avoiding. "What about killing the Bishop?"

"Start planning as if you were really going to go through with it. We've talked to the Bishop, and he's going to play along. But we need this to look as real as possible, so I'm not going to tell you anyfin' else. Go down to 'is cottage, start asking around, put together yer murder plan, whatever. And make sure you do it realistically, like yer life depends on it. Cos maybe it will. If yer Retribution mates tumble to yer little game, fings could get nasty."

"But if I join the witness protection program..."

"You've been watching too many TV cop shows. Do you fink we can afford to whisk you off to Australia, give yer a new job an' 'ome, support you for the rest of yer life? Ain't gonna happen."

Owen's face drained of blood, an abyss yawning in front of him. "But I thought we had a deal..."

"Relax. We do. But not like that. You'll get arrested along with the others, so they don' know you shopped 'em. You'll need to keep up the game all the way right to the end.

When you go to court, we'll fix things so you get off. Or maybe get a suspended sentence. Then you won't 'ave to live the rest of yer life looking over yer shoulder fer some Wiccan death squad."

oooOooo

The Bishop's cottage stood lonely, surrounded by woodland, overlooking the cliffs. Agatha Christie would have loved it. Its crumbling brick walls supported a sagging roof, and at the back languished a old-fashioned walled vegetable garden. Outside was a skip filled with rusted cast-iron guttering, and the remains of lime-green melamine kitchen units, which had delighted some avant-garde renovator thirty years ago. No car was parked outside, and no recent tyre tracks or footprints disturbed the mud. But Owen rang the doorbell in case. No answer.

The ancient leaded panes were firmly locked, as were both outside doors. No sign of a burglar alarm. A ladder was propped against the wall, alongside lengths of vinyl guttering. Owen used the ladder to climb onto the roof. In one section, modern tiles had replaced the ancient slates, and not all were nailed down. Lifting four of them, he slipped into the loft, which instead of the expected pitch black, was penetrated by shafts of daylight from gaps between the slates, creating a ghostly half-light. He trod carefully on the rafters, avoiding the ancient lathe-and-plaster ceiling that would collapse if he rested as much as a foot upon it. Finding the hatch leading down into the house, he swung down into a bedroom.

He had just broken into a house. For the first time in his life, he had committed a felony. Apart from the arson of course. And the accessory to attempted murder. And this wasn't really housebreaking, because he was doing it with the encouragement of the police. But as he crept from room to room he felt a vicarious guilt, the fear of being caught, the thrill of covert intrusion into someone else's life, someone else's privacy.

All the rooms were in the middle of renovation, littered by pots of paint, tools, and sheets of plasterboard. How does one electrocute a bishop? Connect the Earth wire to the live wire? Bypass the main isolator switch? But none of these could be guaranteed to kill. If the bishop had any sense, he'd check for mains before he started work. On the other hand Owen didn't actually have to kill the bishop - but appear to do so, giving him a little latitude. But on the other other hand it had to look credible. A half-baked plan with no sure outcome would seem suspicious.

He continued walking round the house, drawing a map as he went, taking photos with his mobile phone, searching for inspiration. None came. After an hour, he decided to leave. Perhaps an idea would come to him over the course of the next few days. Besides he wanted to get back to studying the carvings on the stones. Not to mention getting out before he was caught.

He exited through the front door, locking it as he left. As he climbed the ladder to replace the roof tiles, a car drove off, no more than a hundred yards away. Was he being watched? If so, by whom?

oooOooo

He spent the next few days going through the motions of making plans to murder the bishop. He phoned Siegfried, told him about his break-in, and asked for any further leads or contacts. Siegfried didn't have any, but seemed pleased that Owen was actively working on the assignment.

Woken on Monday morning by one of the mobiles next to his bed, Owen cursed. It was the Retribution phone. Damn! What now? As if he needed something else to worry about.

"Morning, Owen. Something's come up. We need to meet."

He sighed. No point in asking what had "come up". Not on the phone. He scratched his head irritably, trying to coax his brain into life. "Uh - yes - I suppose so. Where?"

"I'm coming up to Cambridge. There'll be four of us. The restaurant next to Magdalene Bridge. I've booked a table outside. 11 sharp this morning."

The phone clicked off. He rolled back into bed, annoyed. No "Can you make it?" or "What's a good time for you?" Siegfried simply assumed that he would re-arrange his life around him. All part of the power play. Still, if only he knew. The watch was taking all this down ... to be used in evidence against him. There was enough grim satisfaction in that. And precious little else to feel smug about. When the unstoppable force meets the immovable object, and Owen was caught between them ...

At eleven o'clock he was standing on Magdalene bridge, watching the tourists wrapped in sweaters and coats. Some were bravely determined to punt on the Cam, defying the Siberian wind blasting across the fens. Turning to watch the students swarming back and forth across the bridge, he saw Siegfried striding towards him. "Hi Owen. Sorry I'm late." He shrugged. "Car parking in Cambridge. Gets worse each time. Let's get some coffee. I'm frozen."

He looked past Owen's shoulder. "Hi Suzy."

Owen turned to see a tall brown-haired girl dressed in black, with Wiccan pentacles dangling from her ears. Siegfried introduced them, and they moved to a table at the restaurant. Suzy was a graduate student studying viral epidemiology. Owen thought he'd seen her in the Department, but they'd never met. She was glancing at him curiously, and he wondered if she knew who he was.

The mid-morning sun gallantly tried to filter through the hazy cloud, but did little to relieve the biting chill of the wind. "Would you mind if we sat inside?" asked Suzy, "It's freezing out here."

"Sorry," answered Siegfried, "less chance of eavesdropping out here." Owen became acutely aware of his watch, that their conversation was being recorded and monitored by some anonymous policeman.

A girl bustled up, her round face red as if from running. Her pebble glasses and multicoloured woolly hat clashed oddly with her long black hair and oriental face. She seemed excited, as if on speed. "Sorry I'm late. Had trouble parking."

They all grinned. Siegfried introduced them. Her name was Xiu-Mei and she worked at an agricultural research institute on the outskirts of Cambridge, working on avian disease control. Why had he assembled three biologists, wondered Owen.

After ordering coffee, Siegfried started talking in a low voice. "Right. An opportunity has unexpectedly arisen." Xiu-Mei giggled, as if this was their private joke, and Owen found himself disliking her intensely. Siegfried glared at her.

"Xiu-Mei here has just returned from China, where she was doing an exchange visit, to a research lab in Guang-Zhou. Where they are researching H5N1."

"Bird flu virus!" squeaked Xiu-Mei in explanation, and Owen saw Suzy roll her eyes at him. Xiu-Mei seemed to be working herself up, as if about to pull a rabbit out of a hat.

Siegfried nodded. "Their security is abysmal. Xiu-Mei brought us a present. Xiu-Mei?"

Almost squealing with excitement, she placed a small wooden box on the table. Inside were ten small glass vials in a foam cut-out, each half-full with a clear fluid. Owen and Suzy gasped. Siegfried sat smugly, enjoying the moment. Xiu-Mei was visibly trembling with anticipation.

"As you know, these are deadly. More than that, everybody's paranoid about bird flu reaching Britain. There's a meeting of the General Synod next week. Several of them will die of bird flu, apparently administered by Muslim extremists."

Owen was shaken. For Chrissake! Aren't things bad enough already? "Why us?"

"Because you seem to be good at this sort of thing, and Suzy knows about transmission of viruses."

"But so does Xiu-Mei. Why do you need me?" objected Suzy.

He gave an almost imperceptible nod of his head towards Xiu-Mei. "Because her strengths lie elsewhere. We need someone cool-headed like you, Suzy."

Xiu-Mei, who had become ominously still, now turned on Siegfried angrily. "What do you mean - are you saying that I'm not going to give those bastards their dose?"

"Xiu-Mei, you've done a wonderful job in getting us these samples. But we need different skills for the next phase of the operation."

Staring at him, her face reddened, anger and disappointment building up within. Her face started twitching with emotion. Suddenly she snatched one of the vials, pulled off the plastic stopper, and drained the contents into her mouth. The three sat watching her, stunned, wordless.

"Now I am a suicide bomber. I will be the first Wiccan martyr of the millennium," she announced.

oooOooo

The H5N1 virus shows no symptoms for about a week, after which the victim typically falls ill, develops pneumonia, deepens into a fever, and usually dies. In its current form, it is not particularly infectious to other humans, and so those around Xiu-Mei were not at grave risk. The meeting of the synod would take place while her symptoms were developing. With nothing to lose, she had become the ideal delivery agent. Except it was difficult to turn her into a stereotypical Muslim.

They met next day to rehearse their plans. Because all four wore surgical masks to minimise the risk of infection, they met in private, in Suzy's house. Xiu-Mei no longer appeared excited, but instead seemed to be drifting helplessly to her destiny in the awful knowledge that her fantasy had become reality, that she had only days to live.

Siegfried had bribed a driver of the catering firm, who was to phone in sick one day. Owen would replace him. As he made the deliveries, Suzy and Xiu-Mei, dressed in hijabs, would sneak into the kitchen, and Suzy would divert the attention of the kitchen staff while Xiu-Mei tipped the contents of the vials into the food. A letter would be posted a few days later claiming responsibility on behalf of Sunni Muslims, saying that more such attacks would take place if Britain didn't pull out of Iraq. By the time the victims were tested, and anti-viral drugs administered, it would be too late. Most of the attendees were elderly, many in poor health, and

288

the effect of the virus would be devastating. Britain would lose most of its senior Anglican churchmen in a few days. The backlash would be swift, immense, and predictable.

"You realise there's no possibility of getting medical help, Xiu-Mei?" asked Siegfried softly. "It would give the game away completely. They'd realise you weren't Muslim. They'd probably find out you were with Retribution, and your efforts, and perhaps your death, will be wasted. But we'll be with you throughout, and the Goddess will give you strength to pull through."

Xiu-Mei nodded, her ebullience forgotten, her face downcast. Her voice was muffled by the mask. "I know that." she said. "I will be a martyr."

"If the worst should happen, just keep thinking of how the Goddess will love you for your noble sacrifice."

Her eyes were moist as she nodded. "My mum won't know," was all she said.

oooOooo

At midnight, the mobile beside Owen's bed rang. "Jim here. This has gone far enough. We're pulling you out, old son. We need to get Xiu-Mei into isolation."

The words shook Owen to an extent that he couldn't have forecast, with an overwhelming wave of relief that he was now to escape this hell-hole of guilt and stress. It was immediately followed by an aftershock of anxiety that if the operation went off half-cocked...

"But you haven't got the mole yet..."

"We've got a lot more than you realise, thanks to you. Anyway, I'm phoning to warn you. You're gonna be woken by a dawn raid tomorrow. They'll know about the H5N1 and Retribution, but won't know you're on our side. Do whatever you're told, don't say anyfin'. Just wait to be charged. Later, I'll interview you and get you out of there. Remember, don't give our game away, and don't recognise me. I'll look after everyfin'."

Owen hung up, and tried to get to sleep. The wave of relief had ebbed, its place taken by a hollow anxiety. He was to be arrested on criminal charges in a few hours. Could he really trust Jim? What if Jim was the informant? What if he didn't get bail? What did 'later' mean? What if he spent the next few nights, weeks, years in prison? He'd kill himself first. And then he'd be with Sarah...

For chrissake. Where on Earth had that thought come from, totally alien to all that he lived by? Who believed in that nonsense anyway? Sarah was dead. Gone. He'd spent too much time mixing with these religious nuts.

Pausing the cacophony of manic thoughts, he listened for that quiet sad voice which could calm him at times like this. Silence. He was alone with his thoughts. Should he get his "affairs in order" ? Pay his bills? His credit card payment was due tomorrow. Would they take his laptop? His backups? Bloody hell! Must save the contents of his laptop somewhere safe, somewhere where the police couldn't seize them. Going downstairs, he logged in, and after paying the credit card bill, set a backup going to the departmental server. Thank God for broadband. Did they have internet access in prison? No doubt that would be the least of his worries if he found himself in that vile place. He poured a scotch, his hand shaking now, and took it to his lonely bed.

It was nowhere near dawn when the doorbell rang. He looked at the clock behind the empty scotch bottle. Six frigging o'clock. He staggered down, in his T-shirt and underpants, and opened the front door.

"Doctor Owen Davies?"

He nodded dumbly at the policeman, taking in the dogs straining on their leashes just behind him, the line of police cars parked in the road, the neighbours' curtains opening curiously. But what shocked him most was that the police were dressed in white biohazard suits with the word "Police" emblazoned across them.

The muffled voice continued from behind the respirator. "Doctor Davies, I am arresting you for conspiracy to murder. You do not have to say anything but anything you do say will be ..."

He gazed in amazement at the expressionless biohazard mask, not hearing the words. Conspiracy to murder? His befuddled brain was having trouble coping. This wasn't a speeding ticket. This was for real. The suit was staring at him expectantly.

Owen hadn't heard the question. "I'm sorry?" he asked.

"Sorry, for what, Dr. Davies?" asked the suit.

"No you don't understand. I meant... Come in and I'll put my clothes on."

Owen drew back but the policeman grabbed him. Another man appeared beside him and handcuffs were clicked on to Owen's wrists.

"Can't I put some clothes on?"

"Get in the car."

He had seen it happen to criminals on TV. But this was no ordinary car - it was like an ambulance with bars on the windows. He was bundled roughly in, and strapped to the bed, men in biohazard suits either side of him, both carrying guns. Immediately his arm was swabbed, a sample was taken, and the van screeched off, siren blaring. Was this necessary? He wished he hadn't drunk so much scotch.

They pulled up at a drab, low, white building, somewhere on the outskirts of Cambridge. He was hustled into a room empty except for two chairs and a table.

"I need to go to the toilet," was the most he could manage.

He stood at the urinal, one hand cuffed to the gowned and masked figure standing next to him, watching. Somehow he just couldn't pee. He strained but nothing would come. He knew as soon as he got back to the room he'd be bursting. At last a dribble appeared.

"Is that it then?" asked the policeman, sniggering. Owen wanted to lash out at the stupid yokel in his sci-fi suit. Thankfully, the dribble turned to a trickle, and then to a stream. His shoulders straightened. How quickly are our aspirations lowered.

He was led back into the room. The policeman removed the cuffs, and handed him a blanket, which he draped over his shoulders. Owen sat in silence, the policeman refusing to answer his questions about what was happening.

It must have been an hour later when an overweight man in a crumpled check suit came in, carrying a file, and sat down opposite without a word. The policeman in the biohazard suit left the room, to be replaced by a uniformed constable, who stood poised as if expecting Owen to jump up and escape at any moment. The overweight man flicked through the file without speaking, and lit a cigarette. He pulled a small tape recorder out of his pocket and placed it on the table, switching it on. At last, he looked up at Owen and blew smoke in his face.

"So what have you got to say for yourself, Sonny Jim?"

"I take it the blood test was negative? Otherwise you'd be wearing one of those suits."

The man peered at him. "Don't try to be Mr. Clever with me, sunshine. You're in deep shit. How about you start telling us what you've been up to?"

"I'm not saying anything until I've seen a lawyer."

The detective looked at him wordlessly, pulled a mobile out of his pocket, and handed it to him. "Fair enough. Call him."

"But I don't have a lawyer."

"Well that's a shame, innit? Going to be a long day then."

As the detective continued looking at him wordlessly, Owen tried unsuccessfully to out-stare him, and then slumped, head in his arms. "Aren't you supposed to find me a duty lawyer or something?"

"Are we? Haven't heard of that one. You an expert then?"

"Of course not." Owen decided to try appeasing this stupid man. "Please, can you help me get a lawyer?"

"Of course. Why didn't you say? We're only here to help, you know."

He turned to the uniformed policeman. "Get him the yellow pages, Alf."

Alf did so, and threw the book on the table in front of Owen.

Humiliated, trying not to play their game, he said "I want to get this over and done with as much as you do. Just help me find a lawyer, please."

"Oh I'm not in any hurry," smiled the policeman, "and I'm not allowed to recommend any particular lawyer. Wouldn't want to influence your decision, would we?" He smiled pleasantly at Owen, who started leafing through the book.

"You can read, can't you?" asked the detective.

Owen ignored him and thumbed through the index. Did he need a barrister or a solicitor? Weren't solicitors people who did conveyancing? But aren't barristers the people who stand up in court?

He found a full-page advertisement with a Cambridge number. "Bryant & Watson - Specialising in Criminal Defence." It had a 24-hour number. Triumphantly, he phoned it. A prim female voice assured him that his call was important to them, but their offices were closed. Please call back in working hours... He tried two more numbers, but failed to find a human. The policemen were watching him, enjoying their game. He closed the yellow pages. "I guess we'll be sitting here for a while then," he announced.

"Looks like it." The policeman folded his arms and gazed at the ceiling. "Pity really."

Owen stared at him for a full minute. Then decided to play the game. "What's a pity?"

"Well you're due in front of the magistrate at ten. If you were helping us, then you could be out on bail in a few hours. But if you don't give us anything, then we have to ask the beak if we can keep you here until you've told us your story. But of course I don't want to influence you. You should wait until you've talked to your lawyer. Don't you agree, Alf?" he asked, turning to the constable.

"Yeh. Really ought to talk to his lawyer before he says anything. Shame, innit? Mind you, there are some blokes in the lock-up who'll be pleased to see him in there tonight. Nice lad like him. Should be a lot of fun."

Owen lowered his eyes, appalled, the horrific reality of his situation rolling in. But they hadn't even asked him any questions. This was no more than a softening up process. On the other hand he wasn't stupid, and he was sure he could out-smart these oafs. Even if he was drunk and disoriented.

"Look. I'm happy to start telling you what I know, and then I'll have to leave the rest till I've talked to my lawyer."

"That's the ticket," replied the policeman. "I'm Detective Lockhart, by the way. Call me Harry." So he had decided to play the good cop. "So why do you want to kill these people?"

Owen smiled. Was that the best they could do? "I didn't want to kill anyone. Why don't we start at the beginning?"

"Fair enough. Tell us about 'Retribution'."

This was safe ground. It would all come out eventually, anyway. He told them about how Siegfried had called him and arranged to meet in Cambridge, how Xiu-Mei had produced the vials and swallowed one. He paused. Had he gone too far? The defence might be that Retribution was just another religious sect, and didn't intend to hurt anyone. But Jim had told him that they already knew about the H5N1, so hopefully he hadn't told them anything they didn't already know. Better to stick to the truth as far as possible. But how to tell the truth without revealing that he was working for the police. If he told these grunt policemen, it might be all over the newspapers by tomorrow, and then he'd be in hiding for the rest of his life. He needed to stop, plan out his strategy, and his whisky-soaked brain wasn't helping.

"I'm sorry. That's all I can say for now."

"That's alright. I'm sure your friends tonight will jog your memory."

"Whatever. I'm not saying another word till I've seen a lawyer."

"OK fine. Just one other thing. Can you describe this "Siegfried" ?" Shaking his head almost imperceptibly, he sat mutely, staring at the table. They kept going for another ten minutes, trying to provoke him, but eventually gave up. He was ushered by a fresh-faced young constable to a small whitewashed room with a single bed and a toilet, and was told this was to be his room for the rest of his detention in the police station. There were no shared rooms, and the intimidating suggestions had been so much bullshit.

At last he had time to think. He decided on his story. For the moment, he'd stick to talking about H5N1 and Retribution. He would say, truthfully, that he had been an accessory to the shooting of the Ayatollah, but hadn't been closely involved and didn't really know what it was about. He wouldn't mention the plan to murder the bishop - no point in complicating matters if they didn't know about that.

The door opened without warning, and he was led back into the interview room. Sitting at the table was DI Jim Conrad, with papers in front of him and a tape recorder at his elbow. Owen tried not to show any sign of recognition, nor the profound sense of relief at seeing a friendly, or at least not a hostile, face. Jim introduced himself and started to interview Owen methodically and professionally. They went over the same ground as they had in Brentwood, but Jim let slip during the interview that they had rounded up other members of Retribution, although he didn't say who. But it was clear that, as well as corroborating his story, Jim now knew a lot more than Owen had told him, and asked him about things that even Owen didn't know about.

"Did you know that Ben was a member of Retribution, Owen?"

Owen shook his head glumly. Not a surprise.

Jim continued. "He told me he set fire to the synagogue. But other members of yer group say that you did it. Who's lying?"

"Nobody's lying. Ben did it, but for some reason blamed me. The others didn't see what happened, so naturally they believed Ben."

"One of yer mates said that you didn't deny it. Maybe even said yer'd dunnit."

"I was confused and shocked; I don't know what I said. Everybody was telling me that I'd done it, and I think I started to believe them. But I can tell you the exact sequence of events. I jumped onto the table, and accidentally knocked over the ..."

Another knock on the door. A man in a suit carrying a briefcase entered. He introduced himself as Alan Wainwright, from legal aid. After explaining to Owen that he would be his lawyer, he greeted Jim cordially, as if they were colleagues, and asked to be filled in on what was happening.

He seemed disappointed that Owen had decided to be co-operative, and mildly admonished him for starting the interview without a lawyer, but on the other hand didn't seem to have an adversarial attitude to the police. Like Jim, he seemed competent and professional, and was there to do his job.

The interviews continued throughout the day, an hour at a time, with breaks in which Owen was returned to his cell. Jim told him he would have to stay there the night, but that they had arranged a magistrate's hearing the next day.

The next morning, he was allowed to shower, and was given fresh clothes. Jim and Alan were waiting in the interview room with a written statement that they went though together, corrected, and Owen signed. The lawyer said they'd request bail, and raised an eyebrow when Jim told him that the police wouldn't oppose it. It had been too easy, and evidently Alan had guessed that there was more to it. Owen wondered whether any of his foes might come to the same conclusion.

Alan had arranged for a suit to be brought from Owen's house. It was his only suit, the one he'd worn to Sarah's funeral. Alan carefully placed a collection of pens in his top pocket, and a paper protruding from his side pocket, turning him into a nerdy academic unwittingly dragged out of his depth by bad company.

He was driven to court in a van with bars on the windows, and eventually stood in front of the magistrate, explaining how he was at the University. He gave the impression he was a student rather than a postdoc. The magistrate either didn't know the difference or didn't care. Owen recounted how he had got into bad company, and hadn't known how to extricate himself. He described, truthfully, his relief at being arrested, his relief that this horrible misadventure was finally coming to an end. He had helped the police to the best of his ability, and now he was ready to face the consequences for his stupidity. He apologised for his naivety, for not realising until last week just how bad these people were.

The magistrate watched him sceptically through this performance. She had seen it all before. But she was impressed by the way his eyes moistened when he spoke of how everything had gone wrong since his girlfriend died, the way his voice faltered. Owen humbly awaited her verdict, his head hanging sadly, remorsefully.

Jim Conrad was called to the front, and confirmed that Owen had indeed been most helpful, they didn't think there was any risk of him fleeing, and the police wouldn't oppose bail.

The magistrate stared at the policeman, and then at Owen. He saw an expression flash across her face. She knew she was being duped, but didn't know why or how. But if the prosecution and the defence were unanimous in recommending bail, she really had no choice. Besides, she went out of her way to stop first offenders spending time in prison, however serious the charges. But usually she had to fight tooth and nail with the police to achieve it. Curious.

Minutes later, Owen caught a taxi back to his house. He fought his way through news reporters surrounding it, refusing to comment, trying not to look guilty. Shutting the door behind him, he breathed out. The nightmare had ended. For a while.

Chapter 20

Sitting in his kitchen, cappuccino in hand, curtains drawn against marauding reporters, he tried to find out what had happened. Since the police had taken his laptop, cutting him off from the web and the world, he was reduced to scant morsels of information from radio and TV. The BBC reported how a modern-day witchcraft cult had tried to kill our revered church leaders. Sky News carried rumours of biological weapons, interviewing self-proclaimed experts who speculated how such a weapon might wipe out innocent people across Britain. Nervous academics, first time on TV, were manipulated by reporters, reluctantly agreeing that this doomsday scenario was, um, perhaps, possible... So our brave policemen had saved thousands of innocent men, women, and children from a gruesome death? Well, yes, I suppose so...

He needed real information, not this sensationalised twaddle. He'd have to escape and buy a new laptop as soon as possible - the police would probably hang on to his for months while they extracted and decrypted every last byte off the disk.

He was suddenly confronted by a picture of himself on the TV, taken from an out-of-date web page that said he was a student. A younger, more innocent Owen, his face radiating dreams of destiny, dreams of discovering how life itself had started. Now he was a fugitive, cowering behind closed curtains, hoping not to spend the rest of his life in some grim cesspool of a prison. The TV flashed to a shot of the outside of his house, recorded only moments earlier. A taxi drew up, and wannabe terrorist Owen, fending off swarms of reporters, skulked his way to the front door, his visibly trembling hands fiddling with the front door key, retreating into his dark lair, no doubt to think dark thoughts and plot dark deeds.

Damn! Everybody would see this. He had been convicted by the media even before his trial had started. Everybody would see it, would know that he had been mixed up in this unspeakable criminal plot. Would he be dismissed from the University? A mug-shot of Suzy appeared, and Xiu-Mei, who they called "a Chinese student", was in an isolation ward with a mystery illness. Jim Conrad's face appeared. No mention of bird flu, or the synod, or, for that matter, the Wakened or Retribution. Despite the best efforts of Sky News, the police seemed to be playing it down. No mention of Siegfried either, although Jim hinted darkly at other people helping the police with their enquiries.

There was a further report from Derbyshire, where police had raided a "terrorist training camp" in the Peak District. Poor old Ted. He was the one person who Owen felt bad about. Hopefully they wouldn't be too harsh on him - all he'd done was make the farm available to his traditional religion.

The impression given by the news was that a group of social misfits had tried to set up a wannabe terrorist organisation, with no clear aims, and had managed to recruit a few naive students. The real pressure was now on nailing the evil men behind it He flicked channels, and found CNN reporting a cluster of arrests in Cambridge and London, but no names or clues to identity. So who did they have? Definitely Ben, since Owen had been told of his boasting in the police station. Siegfried, certainly, since they would be able to track him after the four of them met in Suzy's house. Camus? George? Jenny? He had given their names to the police, but he wasn't sure whether George and Jenny had actually committed any crime. Probably not. And if not, then would George and others in the Wakened see Owen as a betrayer, or as a colleague who had got caught by the police? And what about his comrades in the synagogue attack, or at the training camp in Derbyshire? How many others were there that he didn't know about?

Numbly staring into space, he pondered the question. He had to find out. Without betraying himself. He picked up the phone and dialled. He hadn't heard from her since the night he'd rejected her overture to join her coven. She had been bitter, spiteful, a woman scorned. Would she even talk to him?

"Owen, my poor darling, how wonderful to hear from you. And how lovely you called me. I've read all about you in the paper. Did they give you a hard time? Did they..."

"Jane...JANE!"

"Sorry Owen. Yes what is it my sweetheart?"

"Jane, who else did they catch?"

"I think poor Camus is still at the police station. They came and talked to me, and to George, but then they left us alone, and haven't talked to anybody else that I know. Absolutely rotten bastards, aren't they? Just like in the old days, burning witches for their beliefs!"

Evidently she had no idea what this was about. Making his excuses, declining her offer of dinner, he thanked her, and hung up. He practised his opening line until it sounded relaxed, and then, breathing deeply, masking the tension coiled within, he dialled again. "Hello George. Owen here."

"Owen! I hadn't expected to hear from you so soon. So they let you go?"

Relief flooded through him. He breathed out. His cover was intact. "On bail, yes. I have to face charges of conspiracy to murder. I might get a jail sentence."

"Bloody hell. I'm sorry Owen. We'll do what we can to help you. You'd be surprised how far our influence reaches. Anyway, are you alright? Didn't get beaten up or anything?"

"No, no, I'm fine. A bit shaken, I suppose. And, George. I'm so sorry. I said some things I shouldn't."

George's tone became guarded. "Like?"

"Um... I'm terribly sorry. They're clever bastards. Interrogated me night and day. I'm afraid I told them about the Wakened. About the Book of One."

"Owen, you took a vow..." His voice was firm, reproachful, but beneath it was an unmistakeable softening.

"I know. That's why I phoned. I need to make amends. I'm so very sorry." He acted the part, breaking down, head in hands. Even though George couldn't see him, it would sound authentic on the phone. "God I'm sorry," he moaned.

"Pull yourself together, Owen. It happens. We'll think of a penance in due course, but don't you worry about it now. It's not so bad. You're over-wrought. I suggest you take it easy, and tomorrow we'll get together and see what we can do to help."

"Thankyou George. I really appreciate that."

"You're welcome, Owen. Blessed be."

"Blessed be, George."

He hung up. Yes! One problem solved. How many more to go?

Pacing back and forth, his mind whirred. He couldn't probe any further without appearing suspicious. He needed to distract himself.

Thank God it was the weekend tomorrow. But it would be a while before he had to face the questions, suspicions, insinuations at work. Worst of all, sympathetic looks. Poor Owen. Such a promising young man. All wasted. He couldn't go back to work. Not yet...

For chrissake... What was he thinking? Who was he kidding? Go back to work on Monday? His much-vaunted intelligence didn't make it any easier to grasp the reality, the incomprehensible enormity, of the charge of conspiracy to murder. Instead it assumed the proportions of a speeding ticket, an embarrassment to be weathered. Perhaps, in time, he would come to terms with the towering magnitude of the charges levelled against him.

But right now he needed to know what was happening. He needed a laptop. And bread and milk. And newspapers. The papers would be full of it. Pulling a curtain aside, he saw only two reporters. Excellent. He walked round the house and found his car keys, which fortunately the police hadn't taken. Everything else was in disarray, thoroughly searched and examined. But no actual damage.

He prepared to run the gauntlet outside. He mustn't look like a criminal. He needed to look like a student unwittingly caught up in a plot beyond his control. Which, come to think of it, wasn't so far from the truth. Looking in the mirror, he practised a bewildered expression on his face, until he felt confident of reproducing it in front of a camera.

And he would say nothing. Or maybe... He could use this, say something that would make him seem naive, cooperative.

Opening the front door, he found two microphones jammed in his face. But no TV cameras, thank God.

"I'm sorry, the police have told me not to say anything. It might compromise their enquiries."

"But Mr. Davies..."

Mr Davies, not Dr. Davies. Good - made him a bit less newsworthy.

He reversed out of the drive, leaving the reporters standing in pools of disappointment. Yes - his line seemed to have gone down well. Far better than a curt "No comment".

An hour later he returned to find the reporters gone. Hopefully his 15 minutes of fame were over.

After making coffee, he opened the laptop, spent half an hour installing software, and finally connected to the internet. He flicked through Guardian Online. Nothing more about him and the string of arrests than a paraphrasing of the police press release.

He checked his email. The usual spam, conference announcements, a colloquium on Monday on gene silencing. It all seemed so trivial now, so irrelevant. But after his ordeal at the hands of the police he needed to regain his balance, restore normality, occupy himself.

He decided to start working once more on his quest for the Book of One. If he could focus on that, perhaps he could get some respite from the looming disaster that was threatening to engulf him. He downloaded his backup from the departmental server onto the new laptop.

Flicking through his notes on the Book of One, he discovered his feelings about it had changed. The events of the last few days had somehow cleansed his quest of its baggage, reduced it to bare essentials. No longer was it a means to an end, a ploy to catch Sarah's killers. Instead, it had acquired a purity, a wholesomeness, reminding him of the untroubled passion he'd once had for uncovering the secrets of life. The Book of One didn't belong to the Wakened, or Retribution - it belonged to the thousands of ordinary

302

Wiccans and witches, people who had a simple faith in nature, who didn't involve themselves in power-struggles.

He paused, seeing himself from outside. He had found his distraction. As arrests continued, as the news emerged, he would distance himself from it, immerse himself in the quest for the Book of One. The idea was strangely comforting. The raw horror of prison, fears of interrogations, court appearances, reprisals, were exiled to dim outposts of his mind as his search for the Book laid claim to his entire conscious mind, despatching it to a familiar, comfortable labyrinth of puzzles.

He focussed. Obviously the stone circles held the directions to the Book of One, encoded in some way in the stones, in the songs that people "read" from their lumps and bumps. To find the Book, he needed to decode those songs. But they were so complicated - it would take years.

But why so complicated? If their sole purpose was to give directions to a hiding place? He stood and walked to the window. It didn't make any sense. He watched a squirrel scurrying across the lawn and into the bird feeder. The feeder was supposed to be squirrel-proof, but the squirrel effortlessly hopped over its defences, conquering complexity with simplicity. It emerged and sat cockily on the feeder, nibbling a nut. Was Owen missing something obvious?

A dimly perceived thought appeared at the edge of his consciousness and made its way to centre stage. The thought was this: these songs were not instructions to find the Book of One. They were the Book of One. The Book wasn't written on paper, but was carved into the Stone Circles.

He reeled at the immensity of the idea. Could the answer be so simple? Give it ten seconds, and he'd see its fatal flaw. OK, a minute then. No, it all worked. He stood, and gazed out of the window. Was this it? Do great discoveries happen like this, not with a bang but with a whimper? Was this a discovery? Or a theory? How did it fit the other pieces of evidence?

He remembered the old lady singing - it seemed like a line of verse for each stone. So, something like 500 words per circle, or about 20000 words on Dartmoor alone - enough to fill a small book. Why would it take a lifetime to read, but only a day to sing? Because to read it meant travelling around all the stone circles, an enormous job that few would manage in a lifetime. And yet, once memorised, it could be sung in a day.

And even the story of the novice priest now made sense:

"Each night during his stay, he spent all night walking the circle, caressing the stones, learning their song. After many days, when he could recite our song as well as the elders, he would move on to the next village."

Rushing to his computer, he scrolled through the clues. It all added up. He walked to the window, unable to comprehend the scale of the discovery he had made. His appearance at the window disturbed a group - a murder? - of crows pecking at the remains of some dead animal on the lawn. He watched them rise uncertainly and fly off into the distance. Shouldn't he be leaping for joy, punching high-fives into the air? His hands were trembling. Why had he not seen it before? Why had no-one else seen it before? The answer was only too obvious - the shock of the arrest, the interrogation, had been the trigger he had needed to leap out of the ordinary, to make connections between unconnected facts.

He spent the rest of the day combing his notes, his clues, the Wakened web pages, making sure he understood the implications, ensuring all the facts fitted, before announcing the discovery.

Finally, he wrote a note describing the steps to the discovery, explaining how the idea fitted all the available information.

He clicked 'Save' and leaned back from the screen, exhausted, noticing it was dark outside. Ten o'clock in the evening? Suddenly deadbeat, he stood, and stumbled as his cramped legs refused to carry him. He creaked to the kitchen and poured a scotch. Must eat food. He opened tins, microwaved the contents, and poured the slurry onto a plate. He should phone people, tell them, but was physically incapable. Maybe in a minute, after resting. He slumped in front of the television, waiting for the late news to see who else had been arrested, eating his tinned spag bol, drinking whisky.

Hours later, he woke to a drunken stupor, the cold mixture still in front of him, an ancient movie playing on the TV. Three am. He staggered up to bed and crawled gratefully under the sheets.

oooOooo

The sun was high in the sky when he awoke, refreshed and excited. He needed to tell someone about his discovery. George? Aleister? But first a shower and breakfast. Contain your excitement. Savour the feeling like a fine wine.

Draining his coffee, he picked up the phone. No need for secrecy now.

"Aleister, Owen here."

"My dear boy! Is it really you? How are you, you poor thing? I've been worried about you. I saw your name in the papers. Is it true what they say? Why didn't you tell me? The police have been questioning me all morning. Are you ..."

"I'm fine, Aleister. Don't bother about that now. I've something to tell you. Much more important."

He heard a pause the other end. He could hear the frown on Aleister's face, wondering what on Earth could be more important than being charged for conspiracy to murder. Had the poor boy finally flipped under the strain of it all?

Owen didn't wait for a response. "Aleister. I've found the Book of One!"

There was a crash at the other end, then scrapings, fumblings.

"Are you alright, Aleister?"

"Sorry, dear boy, I dropped the phone. I think I misheard you. What was that again?"

"I've found the Book of One."

No shouts of joy, no yells of congratulations. Instead, a pause. Then "I see. Owen, there's someone with you, isn't there. Can they hear me?"

"No you silly old fool. This isn't a trick or a set-up. This really is me, there is no-one else here, and I really have found the Book of One."

Aleister's voice was still guarded, sceptical.

"Owen, I'm worried for you. If you have truly found it, then I don't think you should be telling me on an ordinary phone."

God this was frustrating. He was close to hanging up on Aleister and phoning George instead. "Aleister, all that secrecy is in the past. There's no need for it any more."

"But if you know where the Book is - someone might steal it before you get to it - or have you got it there?"

"Aleister, the Book of One cannot be stolen. It isn't a paper book. It's written in stone. In the Stone Circles of Dartmoor and Bodmin. Maybe others too."

There was a pause at the other end, after which Aleister's voice had risen in pitch.

"But Owen... Really? Are you sure? That's amazing - incredible! But how did you... I mean - how is it..."

"It's written in the grooves on top of the stones. When Francesca was reading the stones, she was singing the words of the Book of One!"

"But... but I don't understand. When the Druids wrote the Book, the stone circles were already two thousand years old."

"I don't understand it myself, Aleister. Perhaps the Druids carved it onto the existing stones. Or maybe the book existed before that. I mean..."

"Yes?"

"Maybe the Book was already two thousand years old. Maybe Francesca sang in the language of the Bronze Age. Aleister - this could be the oldest written language known to humanity! Older than the Egyptian hieroglyphs, the Dead Sea Scrolls, the Rosetta Stone!"

"And if we can decode it, it might also save Wicca." Amongst the rising excitement in Aleister's voice was a faint note of rebuke.

"Of course. And that's the most important thing of all, isn't it. Aleister, we've done it!"

oooOooo

The weekend was spent flipping between news of the arrests and loose ends of his theory, punctuated by phone calls from the police, wanting to check on names, dates, times.

Monday came, and he wasn't in prison. Not even "helping the police with their enquiries". He could go to work. But how could he face people in the department? Another day or two would let the news die down a bit. He phoned in, said he was suffering from stress. The departmental secretary sounded concerned, and Owen explained that he knew how stupid he'd been. It was all because of the stress of Sarah's death. He'd got caught up in the wrong crowd. Now he was doing everything he could to help the police. He'd start getting counselling to manage his grief.

He hung up, satisfied. That would go round the department within a couple of hours, and hopefully would be old news by the time he turned up for work again. Meanwhile, on the table were his notes on the Book. He found himself being drawn to them.

As he picked them up, the phone rang. "Owen? Jim Conrad 'ere. I'm at Cambridge police station. Could we meet this morning?"

He sighed. Jim had warned him that they would want to interview him regularly as investigations continued. Clarification of something he'd said, confirmation of someone else's story. But surely not now, not while he was on the point of telling the world about his discovery.

"Actually, this morning is a bit difficult for me. Could we make it later? I've..."

"Owen, listen. You're on a criminal charge, for 'eavens sake. I'm asking you politely, but it's not like you actually have a choice."

Owen felt foolish. Of course.

Jim continued, "Besides, it's about Sarah."

"What? What have you...? OK. Where and when?"

307

"Best if we don't meet at the Station. We're surrounded by the flamin' press. How about the coffee shop at the back of Heffers? Trinity Street?"

"OK. Fifteen minutes."

Jim was already sitting with a half-empty cup of tea in front of him. Owen ordered a latte, and sat opposite, churning at what Jim might be about to tell him. Who had killed Sarah?

"When yer told the police that somebody'd fiddled with yer brakes, they didn't believe you, right?"

"Right. Like they'd been told not to."

"Yeh. Bit of a worry, that. So we checked it out."

He paused, but Owen said nothing, staring into his latte as he slowly stirred it.

"Found yer car in a scrap-yard in Luton. Still in one piece. Someone'd nicked the engine. The front left hand corner was gone, destroyed in the accident. Front right-hand wheel still there, though. The flexible line to the brake calipers was split right open. Funny fin' is, you can see where brake fluid has squirted all over the shock absorber. You were right. It was cut."

Owen stared at him, a latent wave of relief submerged beneath a flood of questions. Seeing an elderly couple moving towards their table, Jim started talking about the football results. Despite barely recognising the names of the teams, Owen impatiently feigned interest. The couple hovered nearby, waiting to order coffee, and then moved on. Owen's questions burst out.

"But why didn't the police see that at the time? Why did they refuse to believe me when I said the brakes failed?"

"Good question. Did we have another mole in the force? Far as I can tell, don't fink so. No conspiracy. Just good-old fashioned incompetence. Easier to blame a drunk driver than some long-winded story about sabotage by pagan cults."

"So who did it?"

"Dunno yet. But we have some leads. Let me ask you somethin'. What was Sarah working on at Uni when she died?"

"Stone circles. I already told you that."

"Yeh, but what exactly?"

"Oh - her supervisor - Phil something - had this idea that the measurements of the stones might tell you something about their construction, about..." he paused, staring at Phil, open mouthed. "You think it might be to do with her PhD project? "

"Don't fink anyfin' yet. Just following leads. Know anyone who didn't like her research?"

"No - it was just a PhD project. Although the professor in her department wanted her to do pollen analysis instead, but..."

"Yeh?" coaxed Jim

"Professors don't usually kill students for working on the wrong project!"

"Nah - not very likely," agreed Jim.

"Have you found out any more about our car being burnt? The local police seemed to wash their hands of it."

"Yeh. Interesting. I talked to Sergeant Bradworthy, who filed the report. Told me it was local hooligans."

"It wasn't." asserted Owen.

"I know. Hooligans wouldn't have put a dead rabbit inside. I put that to him. Suggested to him that it might be a Wiccan spell. Poor ol' sod seemed a bit shaken that I even knew about it. Sometimes I despair of our uniformed bruvvers. What the hell do they think detectives get paid for?"

Owen looked up, curious.

"So then he changed his story. Said he thought it was prob'ly local witches wanted to scare you off. If you ask me, he was a bit scared off himself."

"That's what Alfred Huxtable said - about the local witches, I mean. But why are you telling me this? Did you find out who did it?"

Jim turned his empty palms upwards. "Sorry. Nuffin'. Drawn blanks everywhere on that one so far. But the main fing is the brakes. Far as we can tell, it wasn't anyone in the Wakened who sabotaged yer car. It was someone else. Still working on it. But at least now you know it wasn't your fault."

Head in hands, Owen nodded glumly. He already knew that. "But this whole escapade...infiltrating the Wakened... everything... I probably didn't need to do it. I was barking up the wrong tree." Owen slumped, head in hands, the unbearable truth yawning open to him. He'd spent the last year chasing a chimera. He'd wrecked his career, become a criminal, all for nothing.

Sympathetically, Jim nodded. "Well, we don't know that yet. I'll let you know how we get on." He started to rise and then sat again. "Oh. And one bit of bad news, I'm 'fraid. Xiu-Mei has died. Luckily nobody else caught it. Did you know her well?"

He shook his head sadly. Poor, stupid, excitable Xiu-Mei. Now he felt guilty for disliking her. But compared to other momentous events in the last few days, it rated no more than the obligatory murmurs of shock and sympathy to no-one in particular. Poor Xiu-Mei. Her poor Mum.

And yet... the Book of One was real. And he was about to tell the world about it.

Chapter 21

Back home, Owen tried to distract himself by thinking about the Book of One. But Jim Conrad's news had shaken him, making it impossible to revive his excitement. Curiously, he felt angry. But at whom? Obviously at the person who'd killed her. But without knowing who that person was, his anger was strangely unfocussed, an emotion with nowhere to go. It left him disoriented, wanting a fight with some fictitious person or persons unknown. And the search for the Book of One hadn't helped him one iota.

For months he had doggedly pursued his quest, had been caught in the thrill of the chase, until avenging Sarah seemed like a thin veneer of justification. Tracking down Retribution had been fortuitous. True, he had rid the Wiccan world of a cancer growing within it, but why should he care about that? Uncomfortably, he recognised that he did.

He picked up the phone. "Hi George. Owen here. Any news on the arrests?"

George sounded unusually subdued. "Nothing. But they keep returning with more questions. Someone has really spilt the beans to them, told them every last secret. I think this might be the end of the Wakened. All our hard work, all our searching, destroyed by some blasted traitor."

Owen wondered if George thought he was the traitor. "I'm so sorry George. Um... It isn't me you know. I only told them as much as they needed to know."

"No Owen. I know it isn't you, because they've asked me about things that even you don't know about. I have a good idea who it is. But we'll see eventually. The three-fold rule will get him. Or her."

Owen was jolted by George's mention of the three-fold rule: any good or harm done to another person will be returned threefold. The shock of being reminded that he had just figured where this rule came from, had just solved a two-thousand year old puzzle, triggered a surge of inspiration.

"George - I have some good news that might cheer you up."

He started explaining his ideas, how it all tied together. George was sceptical, then tried to pick holes in it, and then his voice gradually lifted as the magnitude of Owen's theory dawned on him. He became enthusiastic, but warned him that they needed to meet immediately, not to talk about it any more on the phone, the need to keep it under wraps, to release the information "in a controlled way." Owen explained to him, painfully, that there was no need for that now. No-one could steal the book, or burn it, and their best protection of the Book now was to make it as public as possible. George tried to bully him, then withdrew as he realised his tactical error. Then cajoling, pleading. Owen heard a lost old man clinging to the remnants of his empire, and said firmly, but kindly.

"Thank you so much for all your help and guidance, George. I'd love to get together with you in the next day or two to discuss this, but I think I owe it to Wicca to make this public now. Blessed be."

He hung up, elevated. Needing distraction, he turned to the paper he had started writing on his discovery, still unsure where it should be published. "Nature" was the obvious place, but would it be a bit too weird, a bit too adventurous, for them? That, of course, was a characteristic of great discoveries, but it was also a characteristic of half-crazed ideas from cranks, and no doubt Nature received their share of those. Maybe his affiliation to Cambridge would tell them that this was a serious paper. Moving to his laptop, he began to write, furiously, passionately, writing and re-writing, re-editing and polishing, so that it read like a serious paper rather than the rants of some True Believer. Carefully, he expunged any mention of Wicca or sacred significance, simply presenting it as an account of evidence that an ancient religious book was encoded in the stone circles. By evening, the paper was finished. He carried the laptop to an armchair, and read through the manuscript on the screen. Sighing, he pressed the delete key. Nature would never publish it. Maybe George was right after all.

He stared at the glass of whisky in his hand, the half-empty bottle beside him. Had that been full earlier? He was exhausted by the revelation that morning, and by his wasted work throughout the afternoon. He hadn't eaten. Staggering into the kitchen, he ate a cheese sandwich, then tottered into bed, his head spinning.

oooOooo

The next morning, as the espresso machine heated up, he started up his computer, clicked on the recycle bin, and retrieved the paper he had so carefully deleted the previous evening. He'd woken knowing exactly what to do.

He reformatted the paper for "Archaeoastronomy Journal" and wrote a new abstract and conclusion stressing the connection to the lunar standstill. The paper needed to contain more than ideas: it needed to make a clear prediction that could be tested. And only by surviving such tests would his theory gain respectability. So the conclusion of his paper now included a testable prediction: that the bumps on stones in circles would show a clear cross-correlation, that they would be regularly spaced rather than random. This marked it as science rather than as a crank's proof of a pet theory.

After reading it through, he made one final change. He put Sarah's name as first author. His final gift to her, his memorial to her, and their first and last paper together. For ever more, the paper would be known as "Ashworth & Davies".

Before he could have second thoughts, he submitted it to the journal by email, and immediately uploaded a copy to the "arXiv" preprint server. For better or worse, his theory was now in the open literature, establishing his claim as its discoverer, and open to the world to test or dispute.

Phoning George, he explained what he had done, and why. He apologised, explaining how he felt he had to follow his conscience, and the guidance of the Goddess. George sounded doubtful but conciliatory, and asked him to dinner so they could discuss it. Owen explained he'd love to, but couldn't really make it today. Perhaps tomorrow. A date was set, and Owen could hear the bitterness and humiliation in George's voice as he realised he was no longer an authority in Owen's eyes, but an old man to be humoured and placated, bypassed by the force of the discovery. Owen felt sorry for him as he put down the phone.

The entire afternoon and evening were spent emailing each person with whom he had corresponded during his search, giving the web address of his paper, and inviting their comments.

He stood up from his work. Despite the prosecution looming over him, he felt satisfied, complete. Free. Ready to celebrate. But not yet ready to face the world. He phoned for a pizza to be delivered, opened a bottle of Cotes du Rhone, and started watching the latest Hollywood blockbuster on cable TV. Happily numb and befuddled by the wine, he munched his way through the pizza, drank the entire bottle, clambered into bed, and had the first night's sound sleep for many weeks.

oooOooo

The next few days were spent answering emails from people who'd seen his paper: some scornful, some gushing, some bearing thoughtful congratulations. He met with George and other Wiccans, furtively huddled in a corner of a pub, discussing the latest round of arrests and ill-informed news reports. The newspapers had linked the arrests to Wicca, and as a result the tabloids were full of conjured-up allegations of black magic and dark satanic rites. The Guardian bravely countered these with a commissioned series of articles about Wicca and the Wakened. Quotes from Aleister and George were prominent. Owen too had been contacted, but had declined to comment. His paper on arXiv had been enough, shooting to prominence, or notoriety, and was widely being misquoted.

The following week, three days before the full Moon, Owen was woken by his alarm radio to hear that the town of Hemel Hempstead had been rocked at dawn by an enormous explosion which destroyed a fuel depot and damaged nearby houses. Police and firemen were at the scene, and it was not yet clear what had caused it.

The phone rang. "Owen. Jim Conrad 'ere. Know anyfink about this bloody explosion?"

"No, sorry. Just heard it on the radio."

"OK. Didn't fink you would. Look, keep this to yerself, but someone calling themselves "Wiccan Action" has claimed responsibility. Can you phone round yer Wiccan mates and see what the goss is? We don't know if this group is for real. Could be a set-up."

"OK. I'll see what I can do."

Owen called Aleister and George, both of whom had also been phoned by the police. Neither had heard anything about the explosion, and George had never heard of a group called "Wiccan Action".

"My guess is that it's one of these right-wing Christian groups trying to set us up, trying to provoke anti-Wiccan sentiment," explained George, glad to be an authority again. "I'm going to phone round my contacts, and if nobody's heard anything then I'll issue a press release."

By lunchtime, no mention had been made on the news of any Wiccan connection, but Owen's email was buzzing with speculation about who might have done it. He phoned George again.

"Hi Owen. No you won't have heard anything about our press release. The police have put a DA-notice on it. And on the claim by the so called Wiccan Action."

"DA-notice?"

"A security thing," explained George. "Stops the media from even mentioning it. Probably a good thing. The police are terrified that this could blow up into factional rioting."

Throughout the day, rumours flew through the Wiccan email network. Owen and his colleagues were called in for questioning, and by the next day the police were claiming that they were following several leads. Wiccan leaders, including Aleister and George, were now working hand-in-hand with the police and the anti-terrorist squad to prevent further violence, or further damage to the Wiccan cause. George and Aleister sent a jointly-signed email to Wiccan groups around the country, reminding them of the fundamental objection of Wicca to any form of violence or terrorism. Any retribution should be left to the Goddess. The blame for starting all this violence was laid squarely at the feet of Siegfried. The "students" like Owen were portrayed as naive innocents who had unwittingly got caught up in evil forces outside their control. Owen's paper was widely received in Wiccan circles as evidence of his commitment to the cause, a true Wiccan who was sadly led astray by dark forces, and had now returned to the fold.

The following day Owen was woken by the phone. Eight in the morning. More questions about the explosion? Someone congratulating him on his discovery? No, Jim asking him in for questioning yet again. This time to the police station.

He arrived with a heavy heart and was ushered into an interview room.

Jim shook his hand and motioned him to a table. "Owen. Got some news fer you."

It sounded important. "Yes?"

"We've got a full confession from yer mate Siegfried."

Owen looked at him blankly, unable to react.

"He knew exactly who yer were, Owen, when he recruited you. Knew about Sarah. Knew about yer suspicions. But he wasn't as smart as he thought, and fell for yer line about joining Wicca."

Owen nodded numbly, unsurprised.

Jim continued. "But Siegfried's real name is Detective-Sergeant Simon Barber, of the anti-terrorist squad. Fanks to you, we've captured a murderer and a schemer. Not to mention a mole in our ranks. 'e'll be going down for life. Well, if the prisoners don't tear 'im to pieces first. They don't like bent cops any more than we do. Bloody shook me, I 'ave to tell you. Known 'im for years." He shook his head sadly, and

316

shrugged. The room became quiet apart from the clattering of keyboards in the room next door, and someone shouting distantly at the front desk. A siren sounded outside.

Jim looked up from his thoughts, focussing on the present. "And there's more."

"More?" murmured Owen.

"Barber spilt every bean in 'is body to minimise 'is sentence - 'e knows the system. Turns out he 'ad an accomplice in Cambridge. Professor Lightfoot, head of the Archaeology Department. She's confessed an' all. Did you know she's Wiccan?"

Owen shook his head numbly, wondering where this was going.

"You said to me she'd told Sarah she'd made a bad choice about her PhD project. Turns out she meant a <u>really</u> bad choice. Lightfoot was searching for this Book of One yer keep goin' on about, and she reckoned it was somefin' to do with the measurements of the stones in the circles. So she was terrified that Sarah would stumble across the secret before she could. You remember she tried to get Sarah to change her project? When that failed she tried to scare you both off wiv the car burning, an' tried to get Sarah thrown out of the Department. And when that failed she killed her."

"Professor Lightfoot murdered Sarah?" asked Owen in a strangled voice, his face ashen.

"Yeh. Well, she got one of her followers to do it, obviously. We've got 'im an' all. And we've got the bloke who set fire to yer car."

Owen stared back, lost for words. A solitary tear trickled slowly down his cheek. So this was it. The quest was over. Sarah's killer had been found and brought to justice. And it was her professor. The answer had been right under his nose. So his satisfaction that Sarah's murderer had been caught was counterbalanced by anger at himself for not recognising the professor as a killer right at the start. Even worse, none of this brought back Sarah.

oooOooo

That night, having finished a bottle of whisky and rolled into bed, he fell into a half-dream. Sarah was standing in front of him, smiling. She came to him, kissed him tenderly on the lips, and whispered "Goodbye, my love". He tried to grab her, but she slipped, ethereal and insubstantial, through his fingers. A few paces away, she turned, smiled and said,

"Goodbye".

The voice was real. It wasn't in the dream, it was next to him. He jumped up in alarm, his hair erect on the back of his neck, switched the light on, and ran from room to room. He stood in the kitchen, naked, searching the shadows. Slowly, his panic subsided. Had he dreamt it? But it had seemed so real. To the empty space, he said "Goodbye, my love". There was a rustle of leaves on the window as a swirl of wind surrounded the house and then departed. A calm silence enveloped Owen as he made his way back to bed, alone.

oooOooo

His head was surprisingly clear when he awoke the next morning, refreshed and invigorated for a reason he could not fathom or remember. Something to do with a dream. A great weight had been lifted from his shoulders.

The sky outside was icy blue, streaks of cloud showing the trails of early-morning planes.

The phone rang. Some constable from Cambridgeshire police. Could Owen please come back down to the police station for more talks. Sigh. OK.

When Owen arrived, he was ushered into Jim's office. Informal then. No tape recorder running.

"Owen. Some news for yer. Lightfoot and Barber and their cronies have told us everyfin'. So 'ardly any of the information that yer gave us will be needed in court. So yer don't need to worry about Wiccan reprisals."

Owen nodded dumbly.

"But now for the really good news." You could hear the drum roll in his voice. "If you want, we'll drop the charges against you."

Owen looked up, astonished. "I'm sorry? I don't..."

318

Jim smiled. "Makes life easier for us, means we can concentrate on the real crims. We'll say that yer got caught up in a bad crowd. The only fin' we could charge yer with would be the graffiti, and the real criminals have owned up to everyfink else."

"Have they?"

"Not yet. But they will."

"What do you mean - if I want?"

"The only evidence we'll say we got from yer is the sorta stuff expected under heavy interrogation. Prob'ly nobody'll blame yer fer that. But, if yer want a cast-iron guarantee against reprisals, we'll press charges and take yer to trial, where yer'll get a suspended sentence. Very safe, but in my 'umble opinion, totally unnecessary. Not to say expensive and time-wasting fer us. But it's yer call. What ya wanna do?"

"Dunno. It depends, I suppose. Who else is being charged?"

"You seem to fink Retribution's some bloody great underground terrorist organisation. It ain't. It was Barber and Lightfoot, and a bunch of their henchmen. They prob'ly had grandiose plans fer it, until you killed it off. They'd only recruited a handful of people. Barber and Lightfoot are the two we're really going after - the alpha thug and the mastermind. They'll both get life. And the bloke who cut yer brake lines, obviously. Not just fer murder, but they'll also be charged under the anti-terrorism laws."

Owen nodded. "Who else?"

" 'aven't been able to catch Foyle. 'e's already on our wanted list of IRA terrorists. Garef Morton, who ran yer terrorist camp, is being charged with a string of offences. 'e'll be behind bars for years."

"What about Ted?"

"Still trying to work out 'ow deeply 'e's involved. Seems like a nice ol' bloke way out of 'is depth. But the law's the law, and 'e's been an accessory to terrorist activities. Prob'ly get a stretch. Maybe the judge will go soft on him, given his age. Maybe even a suspended sentence."

Owen was shocked. Such a harmless old man, simply trying to do the right thing for his religion and for the memory of his ancestors. He wouldn't survive prison. On the other hand, he'd probably see himself as a martyr against religious oppression. No doubt he'd get some perverse satisfaction out of that.

He became aware that Jim was still speaking. "...about a dozen other people that we've interviewed, but haven't been directly involved in criminal activities."

"And Camus?"

"Dunno. Slippery bugger, ain't he? Meself, I reckon 'e oughtta be charged, but we're having trouble finding anyfin' to pin on him, and our lawyers are saying we can't charge 'im. Bloody shame really. But we don't want to build this up bigger than it is. A few real nasties, who need to be locked up fer life, and an 'andful of people like you who've been led astray."

He paused and lowered his voice. "Between you an' me and the gatepost, I just got a phone call from above. Told to play it down a bit. Which is good fer you - makes yer less conspicuous."

Owen was suspicious. "But isn't it in the interests of the government to play up terrorism?"

"Sorry, not mine to reason. Ever since the London tube bombings, the Opposition's been saying that the Government's screwed up on the way they 'andle terrorism. Course, the Government don't want this to look like a major terrorist operation that's been going on under their noses. That's my guess anyway."

"And the Hemel Hempstead explosion?"

"An accident, of course."

"Of course."

In the lobby of the police station, Owen found himself face-to-face with Kim, leaving from another interview room. They both stood stunned, wordless. He hadn't seen her since the night of the synagogue attack. She looked pale, tired. He noticed her lip-stud was missing, her clothing more muted than normal. They stood facing each other silently, neither knowing how to react. Owen broke the impasse.

"Hi Kim. I'm... I'm so sorry. For everything." He started nervously. A torrent of thoughts flashed through his mind as he stood silent, awaiting her reaction. How much did she know? Was it possible that she had been working with the police too? Unlikely - what are the chances? In which case he would have to be very, very, careful, not give her any cause for suspicion. He saw her watching him watching her, and saw that she too was trying to understand what was going through his mind. So what did she have to hide? What was her skeleton?

She shrugged, as if the few seconds of mental confrontation had never taken place. "Guess I was as much to blame as you. Bloody stupid to get involved with that crowd. Anyway, police just told me I won't be charged, thank God."

So maybe after all...

"Fancy a coffee?" he asked, casually.

She shrugged and followed him to the tables on the pavement, under umbrellas advertising Cinzano. After ordering, he looked at her tense face, her tired eyes, her straggly hair.

"So how are you? You're looking well."

She burst out laughing, her Australian accent more noticeable than ever, "No I'm not, and you bloody well know it!"

It broke the ice, and he grinned back, shrugging. "It seemed the right thing to say."

"Always trying to say the right thing, aren't you, Owen." She fumbled in her handbag and pulled out cigarettes, offering him one.

"No thanks. Don't smoke. You didn't used to, did you?"

"On and off. Recently, on. A lot." She looked at him while she lit up.

"Did they give you a grilling? Like, totally?" she continued.

He was immediately on guard. "Yes. Short of being beaten up. And you?"

She nodded. "Same."

"So how come you got mixed up in the Wakened? Attacking synagogues? Didn't seem like you."

She became serious. "I think it was Sarah's death. I went to pieces after she died. The Wakened gave me a new meaning, a reason to live."

Puzzled, he frowned. "So you were that close..."

Wordlessly, she returned his stare, and his guess was confirmed.

"Sarah and I were lovers since high school," she said, quietly. "We were close, really close. Even came to Uni together. I thought we were together for life. Then she met you. She tried to be nice about it, let me down gradually, but I was totally gutted. Even tried to kill myself. I hated you. Could've murdered you. Then I saw how you and Sarah were made for each other. I wanted her to be happy. But never really got over losing her. But you have to move on, don't you?"

He nodded. He'd already guessed, when Kim had spoken after the funeral about their "relationship". Such a loaded word. And the way Sarah's Dad had looked at Kim, with daggers. A lesbian daughter would be even worse than a drug-addict daughter. Wouldn't look good at the golf club. But Sarah had never mentioned it. He could understand why - it didn't fit in with her image. But then there were whole sections of Sarah's life she'd never shared with him. How well had he really known her? He felt as if he should feel angry, or betrayed, but he was numbed beyond such feelings.

Another twist to a chapter that was now closed.

"How's Natalie?" he asked.

"Cute. As ever. You know, sometimes she stares at me and I feel that it's Sarah watching me. I mean, y'know?"

He did, but didn't want to.

They'd both finished their coffees, and Owen placed a five-pound note under his cup.

"Fancy a meal to celebrate not being charged?" he suggested.

Kim looked at him furtively. "Sorry Owen, I'd love to celebrate with you, but I really need to put all that behind me. Start afresh. It's been good talking to you, but. Catch yer later."

Reluctantly, he agreed, watching her get into her car parked at the meter, and drive off without a backward glance.

oooOooo

Waking the next morning with a glow from his previous day's achievements, he found his clarity of purpose had alighted on Sarah's ashes. The answer had come to him in the night. Sarah didn't belong in any container. She could not, ought not, be contained. After breakfast, he carried her out to the car. Five hours later, he pulled off the M5 onto the Moretonhampstead turning, and shortly afterwards parked his car as the base of the track winding up to Mardon Down, where he and Sarah had exchanged their vows of love so very long ago.

Just as on that day, a clear blue sky was filled with lark-song, although on this day a chill wind gusted across the moor. At the top of the track was a ruined cairn, surrounded by the broken remains of its small stone circle. He sat on one of the stones, looking at the box containing Sarah. Opening it, he lifted out the cloth bag and pulled open the draw-string. He stared at the ash, all that remained of his Sarah. He found his tears streaming once again, and yet this time it was the pure sorrow of loss, of grief, free from trappings of anger and revenge. He realised he had come unprepared - shouldn't he say some words, recite a poem? For whom? He and Sarah didn't need that. Carefully avoiding the kistvaen and stone circle, he shook the bag into the air, letting the wind carry the ashes across the moor to settle where they would.

"Goodbye my love" he said quietly, as he watched the cloud disperse. In his hand was the empty box, and on an impulse he flung that too into the all-enveloping gorse and bracken. He sat on the ground, watching a small bird hopping between the bright yellow gorse-flowers, and listening to the lark-song above. Motionless, silent, he stayed for an hour, and then walked back down to his waiting car, for the long drive back to Cambridge.

oooOooo

London - Friday 25 May 2006: The President of the Royal Society today announced the prestigious Royal Society Fellowships...

Dr. Owen Davies, of the Dept. of Anthropology, University of Oxford. Dr. Davies, previously a biologist at Cambridge, is well-known for his discovery of a prehistoric British written language, and the 'Book of One', perhaps one of the earliest examples of a religious text. During the tenure of his fellowship, he will seek to decode the language, thus uncovering the roots of one of our oldest religions and cultures. Many adherents to the new-age religion of Wicca also regard him as a religious prophet, although Dr. Davies has so far declined invitations to occupy a leadership position in the Wiccan movement.

Blessed be.

Acknowledgements

I would like to thank my wife, Cilla, for her help and encouragement at all stages of this book, for being my proof-reider and sounding-board, and for her many suggestions which have improved this book. I am indebted to Natalie Scott-Moyes, my mentor, who patiently helped me turn my first purple and over-blown draft into something approaching a novel. And of course I am also grateful to my fellow-students at Natalie's evenings: Jane, Jonathan, Celia, Jill, Judd, Kath, Kerry, Lisa, and our co-host Andy. And enormous thanks to Penny Nelson who gave me incredibly valuable comments and advice in the penultimate incarnation of this book. I thank my son Barnaby for his help with the cover design, and to the rest of my family and friends for their comments and suggestions on the various drafts of this novel. I especially thank Graham King of Boscastle Museum of Witchcraft for opening up the museum for us on a winter's day, and for his helpful explanations of all things Wiccan. Needless to say, Graham bears no resemblance in any way to the fictional character of Aleister, and any resemblance of Graham's Museum to the one portrayed in this book is entirely coincidental. I thank Sydney Witches for letting me sit in on one of their evenings, and the officers and Rabbis of the Ilford Synagogue, which will hopefully never be attacked by a Wiccan terrorist organisation. Finally, I would like to emphasise that all the Wiccans, witches, and pagans that I've encountered during the course of researching this novel have been the most helpful and charming people you could wish to meet. And of course, to the best of my knowledge, no organisation exists that even faintly resembles the Wakened or Retribution (George told me to say that).